Greville Texidor was born Margaret  in 1902. She was one of the Bright Y Twenties, working as an artist's mod appearing in early silent films, and pa.\..ying with famous painters, musicians and writers. Her adventures led her to Spain, where she met both her second husband, Manolo Texidor, and her third husband, Werner Droescher. She and Werner fought with the anarchist militia and ran camps for refugee children during the Spanish Civil War, before escaping to New Zealand at the start of World War II. In Auckland, Texidor met Frank Sargeson and Maurice Duggan, and began to write. Her short stories appeared in John Lehmann's *Penguin New Writing* and the anthologies *Speaking for Ourselves* (1945) and *New Zealand Short Stories* (1953). Her novella *These Dark Glasses*, which drew upon her experiences during the Spanish Civil War, was published in 1949. She also wrote several radio plays and some well-regarded translations of Lorca's poetry. Always restless, she left New Zealand in 1948, and from then on her writing suffered. Her collected fiction, *In Fifteen Minutes You Can Say a Lot*, was first published in 1987, twenty-three years after her death. Her biography, *All the Juicy Pastures*, by Margot Schwass, was published in 2019.

[I] had been impressed and quietly depressed by [Texidor's stories'] assurance and sophistication.
—Janet Frame

These Dark Glasses is a tale of disillusionment set in the French Riviera, and from its pathological overtones it reads like the product of a sick mind. Yet it is written with such skill, and is so artfully contrived, that its literary merit cannot be ignored.
—Philip Wilson, *New Zealand Listener*

Greville Texidor has a style which, if not exactly her own, she uses with considerable skill; she has also a genuine novelist's eye for significant detail.
—J.C. Reid, *Landfall*

The VUP Classics collection
celebrates more than half a century of stellar publishing
at Victoria University of Wellington

IN FIFTEEN MINUTES YOU CAN SAY A LOT

Selected Fiction

Greville Texidor

Edited and with an Introduction by
Kendrick Smithyman

VICTORIA UNIVERSITY PRESS

TE WHARE WĀNANGA O TE ŪPOKO O TE IKA A MĀUI

VICTORIA
UNIVERSITY OF WELLINGTON

Victoria University Press
Victoria University of Wellington
PO Box 600 Wellington
vup.victoria.ac.nz

A catalogue record for this book is available from
the National Library of New Zealand

ISBN 9781776562268

Printed by Printlink, Wellington

Contents

Preface to the second edition

'The dust-jacket is really wizard', Frank Sargeson wrote enthusiastically to Greville Texidor in April of 1949 – 'three sub-human creatures with their sunburn raw round the edges from excessive copulation'. Sargeson was describing the cover illustration for Texidor's novella *These Dark Glasses*, which, after much delay, Sargeson was finally coaxing into print. Advance copies were about to be dispatched to Texidor, now living in rural New South Wales after abruptly quitting New Zealand the year before. Sargeson reassured her that Caxton Press had made 'a beautiful job', and her book was 'quite up to the standard of the best English [novels]'.[1]

The copulating trio was the work of a young Kendrick Smithyman, one of the many aspiring young writers drawn into Sargeson's orbit on Auckland's North Shore. Smithyman wrote poetry and prose, he drew and painted, and Sargeson liked him – hence the illustration commission. Sargeson greatly liked 'La Texibubble' too, admiring and assiduously promoting the small body of fiction she wrote in New Zealand during the 1940s. Indeed, he later claimed a pivotal role in turning this one-time English chorus-girl and anarchist militiawoman into a writer, a claim Texidor did not dispute. For Sargeson – serving here, not for the first time, as 'god father–midwife'[2] to the work of others – there was a pleasing symmetry in yoking his two apprentices

1 Unpublished letter, Sargeson to Texidor, 27 April 1949. University of Auckland, MSS & Archives A-198, Box 1, Folder 2.
2 Sargeson to Alec Pickard, 29 May 1945, in Sarah Shieff ed., *Letters of Frank Sargeson*, Auckland: Vintage, 2012, p. 79.

to the same literary project, even if their personal connection was tenuous. Smithyman writes of having admired from afar the older and infinitely more cosmopolitan Texidor, a 'strikingly spirited woman whom one met in friends' homes or at the coffee shop in Queen Street'.

Some thirty-five years later, Smithyman and Texidor were again brought together when Victoria University Press approached Smithyman to write an introduction to *In Fifteen Minutes You Can Say a Lot*. This collection of Texidor's short fiction, only some of which had been published in her lifetime, would re-introduce an all-but-forgotten writer to the reading public. By 1987, when the collection appeared, Greville Texidor (her writing name, and just one of many identities adopted over the course of an irregular, nomadic and often transgressive lifetime) had been dead for more than twenty years. After leaving New Zealand, she had continued to write, in a variety of genres. But apart from *These Dark Glasses*, she published little more beyond the handful of short stories that had already appeared in journals in New Zealand, Australia and England. She began and abandoned novels, drafted stories, wrote radio plays, tried non-fiction, translated Lorca and accumulated a pile of publishers' rejection letters she said were unsurpassed in their variety and originality. She moved between homes and hemispheres, burning manuscripts and personal papers as her output and confidence dwindled. After her death in Australia in 1964, nearly all that remained was a blue suitcase containing fragments, workbooks and drafts, much of the work undated, incomplete or unfinished.

Such was the raw material presented to Smithyman. In putting together this collection, he winnowed publishable prose from experimental jottings, the fully realised from the experimental. He determined the probable sequence of drafts – seeking what corroboration he could from Texidor's family – and followed his instincts. They have largely been vindicated. In the thirty-odd years since *In Fifteen Minutes* appeared, little more publishable Texidor material has been identified, although the archives certainly contain much of interest: multiple drafts of a Spanish Civil War novel, some sharp reportage, a longer version of her biting story 'Goodbye Forever' and her Lorca translations – described by the Spanish poet's literary executor Arturo Barea as 'by far the best ever made into English'.[3] One unpublished Texidor story, which Smithyman presumably read but rejected for this collection, appeared in an online journal in 2006.[4]

This reissue of *In Fifteen Minutes* is thus unaugmented by new material, and Smithyman's original introduction – which reflected what was known and thought about Texidor's work at the time – remains unchanged. My own research has amplified but not significantly altered his account: Augustus John's portrait of Texidor, which had not been located when Smithyman was writing, has almost certainly been identified, while another portrait (by the artist Sydney Carline) was recently found under a spare bed in Barcelona. More details about Texidor's peripatetic early life have emerged, and the drafts of her sprawling, unfinished Spanish Civil War novel have suggested more about the artistic and psychological aftermath of Texidor's involvement. But this collection remains a definitive record of the astonishing literary capabilities Texidor, against all odds, began to unlock in New Zealand – and a potent reminder of all that remained unrealised.

Margot Schwass
February, 2019

3   Barrett Reid told radio producer Ron Blair this in 1987. ABC, 'Radio Drama and Features Preview', July 1988. SLNSW, ML-MSS 5235, Box 5, Folder 12.
4   'San Toni', probably written in 1944, according to Evelyn M. Hulse, who wrote the introduction that accompanied the story when it appeared in *Brief*, 34, 2006, pp. 85–119.

Introduction

We boarded the launch, and as we moved on to the expanse of harbour, Miss Lincoln trailed her hand over the side, touching the water. 'Liquid lumps of light.'

'That's how Greville described it,' she said. 'Has Frank talked about Greville Texidor? Have you read her stories?'

I said I had seen *These Dark Glasses*, Greville's stories. I had been impressed and quietly depressed by their assurance and sophistication. Frank had talked, too, of Greville and her life, giving the condensed biography that accompanied talk of each of his friends and acquaintances, and stressing the personal marvel of nature, talent or experience that each held like a dazzling lure: Greville's was the fact that she had once been married to a contortionist and had toured the world with him. 'Very early in her life.' Frank admired her writing, too, but it was her 'experience of life' that captured him: where she had been, what she had seen, and what she had done—with her contortionist husband![1]

Janet Frame's recollection does not quite agree with what Frank Sargeson put into print in 1965:

Long before she reached New Zealand Greville Texidor had been much about the world. As a surpassingly beautiful young woman she had appeared in variety shows in Europe and America. She had been painted by Augustus John, and married to a Spaniard whom she accompanied to Buenos Aires. Then came the Spanish

1   Janet Frame, *An Angel at my Table: An Autobiography*, Vol. 2. Auckland: Hutchinson, 1984, p. 173.

War, and from that she emerged with a German husband. The
pair were assisted to New Zealand . . .[2]

Sargeson in this obituary piece (another version appears in
Never Enough, 1977, pp. 60–6) wanted to draw attention to a
'short novel which is one of the most beautiful prose pieces ever
achieved in this country', *These Dark Glasses* (1949), as well as to
the few but distinctive short stories published (in New Zealand,
Australia and England) between 1942 and 1945.

Greville Texidor came to New Zealand in 1940 and left in
1948, not to return. Effectively, insofar as Texidor is a writer,
she is a New Zealand writer, but the New Zealand connection
is stronger than the few years residence suggests.

Firm facts about Texidor's background are few. Her mother,
Editha Greville Prideaux (1866–1953) arrived in New Zealand
as a child. She began exhibiting her paintings in oils with the
Auckland Society of Arts in 1887 and went on to 1894. She then
went to London and (reportedly) enrolled at the Slade about
1895. She would have been one of few women at the Slade in
those days and a year or so junior in status to Augustus John,
an up-and-coming student some ten years younger than her.

Editha married a barrister, William Arthur Foster, whose
practice was in Wolverhampton. She bore two daughters, Greville
(who might also identify herself as Margaret or be identified as
Margarita) in 1902 and Kate in 1904.

Greville was sent off to school at Cheltenham Ladies' College
from which she is said to have both run away and been expelled.
Towards the end of the First World War Foster took his life, because
of some 'political scandal'. Greville was sixteen or seventeen.

Una Platts understood that after Foster's death Mrs Foster
'went back to painting'.[3] Wolverhampton at that period, one may

2   Frank Sargeson, 'Greville Texidor 1902-1964', *Landfall* No. 74, Vol. 19,
     No. 2, June 1965, p. 135.
3   Una Platts, *Nineteenth Century New Zealand Artists: A Guide and
     Handbook*. Christchurch: Avon Fine Prints, 1980, p. 199.

imagine, was not the most congenial environment for someone lately widowed and trying to re-establish herself. Mrs Foster moved before long to Hampstead. She picked up with, if she had ever lost touch with, painters who were young when she was a student, and with those of the next generation, which meant that Kate and Greville would have got to know those painters—Sargeson mentions Mark Gertler and Stanley Spencer particularly, both of whom were Hampstead painters in the early Twenties.

Verifiable facts are scarce, but Alan Wald, memorialist of Kate's first husband Sherry Mangan,[4] remarks that Kate had been an art student, 'on the younger fringe of the Bloomsbury set'. Una Platts recalls Greville talking to her ('Not trying to impress, she was talking seriously') about being drawn by John ('when she was a girl, or a child') and how she was in love with Augustus's eldest son, David, who was a musician, and how she made up her mind to tell him, went around, walked up and down in the street getting her nerve up, then went to the door to knock, 'But he was practising on his oboe, so she went away'.[5] Michael Holroyd, most eminent of experts on John, has kindly looked into the question of a John portrait of whatever sort of Greville Foster, but to date is unable to identify let alone locate any such work.[6]

So Greville went away, dancing, in a chorus line in variety, into Europe where probably she worked mainly in or from Paris, where Kate later joined her. She also worked at the New York Winter Garden and toured for two years or so, for at least part of this time in an act with a German contortionist

4   Alan Wald, 'The Pilgrimage of Sherry Mangan: from Aesthete to Revolutionary Socialist', *Pembroke Magazine* No. 8. Pembroke State University, Pembroke, South Carolina, 1977, p. 92. Reprinted, *Labour History*, 1978.
5   Personal communication.
6   Personal communication.

(a Skeleton Dance), and for some if not all the time was accompanied by her mother. She went south to Buenos Aires. Somewhere, some time, she had married and soon parted from an Englishman. 'What was his name?' an informant wondered. 'Mr Wilson? Greville used to say he wasn't a very memorable person.' She married again in 1929, Manuel/Manolo Texidor, a Catalan who was setting up as an industrialist in Buenos Aires, a sometime international long distance bicycle rider. Their daughter Cristina was born, they moved to Spain about 1933, and separated in a year or so. A fragment of writing about Buenos Aires survives, a something of South America in one of the stories, and something of life on the dancers' circuit in another.

From Buenos Aires, where Manolo had sought to establish a cork factory, the family returned to Catalonia and to his family's base in Barcelona. Soon they were living in Tossa de Mar on the Costa Brava, a village northeast from Barcelona, a place these days of two or three thousand people except in the tourist season. Tossa de Mar (which figures as Turissa in Greville's stories) was where Werner Droescher, who was to become Greville's next husband, arrived when he quit Germany in the summer of 1933. Tossa was already a refuge point for those in opposition to Nazism, a society of intellectuals, writers and painters. Among the painters who picked on Tossa at one time or another were Chagall, Masson, Brignoni, Frances Hodgkins and Kars, whose house was later important in Greville's life.

Things between Manolo and Greville were not going well. In 1934 Manolo was living in Palma de Mallorca and Greville with Cristina in Tossa. Werner and Greville met and an affair developed. According to Werner: 'We met in romantic places in the Pyrénées, in Valdemosa on Mallorca, in the mountainous region north of Barcelona. As the situation was rather delicate, we hoped that we could meet more easily in the anonymous surroundings of a big city, as in Tossa everyone knew what one was up to . . .'[7]

Things continued so through 1934, into 1935. Werner, who had been working with children, began coaching older students in Barcelona in the autumn of the year. With Greville, he heard Lorca reading; they were both lastingly impressed, and in later years enthusiasm repeatedly took Greville especially back to Lorca and she translated his poems and plays. When the Civil War began in the summer of 1936 Werner was in Tossa, but left for Barcelona to join up with the POUM militia.

Greville and Werner decided to marry, anarchist-style as compañero and compañera. Greville joined Werner as a militia-woman on the Aragon front. After the other members of the original POUM group departed, they became part of one of the Anarchist Centurias in La Zaida, where they are said to have first met Emma Goldman, whom they later encountered in Barcelona and London.

Whatever optimism they had faded. The chances for immediate military success dwindled as the inadequacy of their equipment was borne in on them and the uncertainty of Communist cooperation with the Anarchists became apparent. Greville and Werner concluded that they could probably be more useful doing propaganda work in England and helping to organise relief services. As English-born Greville's fiancé, Werner's entry to England was facilitated, but their subsequent return to Spain around August 1937 was not so easy. They went back to do liaison work for the English Aid Committee, which had some association with Quaker relief schemes and was predominantly concerned with providing help for refugee children from Madrid being relocated in the province of Girona. Later they were to discover that as well as involving themselves

---

7   Werner Droescher, *Odysee eines Lehrers*. Munich: F. Hirsthammer Verlag GmbH, 1976.

with Quakers they had inadvertently involved themselves with a Communist front organisation which, when the time suited, axed them.

They did some further work with Quakers in Barcelona, then Greville returned to England where Cristina was being cared for by Mrs Foster. Werner was to follow, but as 1938 wore on he was prevented from entering England, was sent back to Germany, found teaching for a while in Hamburg, did some military service, and finally was allowed to leave Germany and proceed to London.

Werner had, but lost, an opportunity to migrate to the United States. They thought instead of Mexico, but Mexico looked dangerously unstable. Greville had relations in New Zealand . . . they turned their thoughts that way. Migrating to New Zealand required that they be married in an orthodox fashion which while it solved one problem created another. By marrying Werner, Greville became a German national. Making arrangements dragged on. English Quakers found more work for them meanwhile, caring for children again, this time children from Germany. They were still with the children when the War began. As a German who had fought with the Republicans in Spain and associated with a Communist front organisation but thereafter served with a Wehrmacht Intelligence and Communications unit for a strangely short time and had then been permitted an exit from Germany, Werner was a prime target. He was swiftly put behind the wire in a camp in Devon. Greville passed rapidly into Holloway.

It pays to have friends. Greville had them. Friend spoke to friend among the right people. Greville and Werner were released with a strong suggestion that they, Werner particularly, quit England smartly. Quakers again helped, and they sailed for New Zealand. On the day the Germans struck the Low Countries, May 10th 1940, Greville, Werner and Cristina arrived in Auckland. Mrs Foster preceded them, to Auckland again after more than forty years away, and Kate came as well with her daughter. Werner did some labouring, Greville some modelling for the Art School as well as a stint in a factory making shirts until (the Quaker connection once more) Werner was found work on a farm near Paparoa in North Auckland, housed in what struck them as rather primitive conditions. 'When I visited Greville and Werner the first time, Greville hid. She later said she thought someone had come to feel sorry for her.' Mrs Foster, who was living with them, was remembered on the scene 'doing her watercolours'.[8]

Frank Sargeson, travelling south from staying with Dr G.M. Smith at Rawene, impulsively left the train at Paparoa to call on the Droeschers, 'to take first a bus-ride and then a long walk to the top of a hill from which on that fine spring day there was a superb view of some harbour and much countryside.' At the house was 'the remarkable (not to say remarkably beautiful) woman' who 'surprisingly' was also an excellent cook, the person of an extraordinary life but not as yet any sort of writer. 'No doubt it would be rash on my part to say that without my encouragement, my suggestions and proddings, not to say occasional scornings, and even downright condemnings, Greville Texidor would never have become a name to add to the list of distinguished literary people who have visited our country.' Werner went off to work, Cristina went off to school, Greville was by herself for much of the day. There was a local society of not altogether usual people, in which respect Paparoa was not singular, but, as Sargeson discreetly puts it, Greville was 'unable to establish with this country relations which could be in any degree thought of as a serious love-affair, she substituted literary endeavour for the many-sided involvement of day-to-day living which had been her habit in environments that appealed to her as more congenial.'

8   Gladys Salter, interviewed by Rosamund Droescher. Texidor papers, University of Auckland Library, archive holding A-198, Box 1, Folder 1.

Texidor did not feel at home. If she felt alien she had good reason. She was an alien, an enemy alien, and wartime authority preferred such people out of sight and sound of troop movements. However, towards the end of 1941 the authorities who had kept the Droeschers under observation out in the sticks agreed to let them move to Auckland, to the North Shore of Frank Sargeson and Ron Mason, shortly of Maurice Duggan, and of Ian Hamilton who was on his way to the Conscientious Objectors' camps. Supervision remained and reporting to the police was a requirement, but Werner had work, and in 1942 he enrolled at the Auckland University College for the B.A. degree which he completed in 1944, taking his Masters in German in 1945. He was helped towards this by Professor Arthur Sewell whom they probably first met when Sewell lectured at Paparoa for the W.E.A., of which there is a glimpse in 'You Have to Stand Up to Them'. As the War ended Texidor had a secure home base, her daughter, her husband, and a pleasant enough location.

As well as being the North Shore of Sargeson who was Greville's age and of Duggan who was twenty years younger, the Shore was the place briefly, but for Greville importantly, of her contemporary expatriate Anna Kavan. Like Texidor, Kavan had travelled. She had married more than once, and had a child. But Kavan, displaced and alien, had a reputation as a writer, first as Helen Ferguson, then as Anna Kavan, whose collection of sketches *Asylum Piece* (1940) was very well regarded. Kavan came to Auckland with Ian Hamilton, from Europe, England, and America. When Ian went off indefinitely into the Conscientious Objectors' camps and intermittently to prison the local scene grew even less attractive to Kavan. She left at first opportunity for Britain where she became an editorial assistant to Cyril Connolly at *Horizon*. For a couple of years or so Anna Kavan and Greville Texidor were close, and if Greville learned from Sargeson she learned also from Kavan. And, it might be said, she learned with Duggan.

Greville began publishing in New Zealand in 1942, in England in 1943, and Australia in 1944, where *Angry Penguins* carried along with the story 'At Home and Alone' twelve of her translations of Lorca poems. In that same issue Reed and Harris (who published *Angry Penguins*) advertised as a forthcoming book *These Dark Glasses*.

Werner was to say in his *Odyssey* that Greville 'had always written a bit' but New Zealand gave her the time (and the incentive) to produce stories. This seems to be borne out by the papers deposited at the University of Auckland library and by her record of publication, as well as by Sargeson's view. When in Spain Werner had ambitions to be a writer, producing a novel which he left behind but retrieved in 1954. In New Zealand the ambition remained, but the achievement passed to Greville.

These Dark Glasses was accepted by Reed and Harris in Melbourne by late 1944. However, it was not until April 1949, with the financial help of the Department of Internal Affairs, that it was published, and then by the Caxton Press of Christchurch. It was designed and produced by Robert Lowry at the Pelorus Press in Auckland. Sargeson read the proofs.

When John Reid reviewed the book[9] he opened by remarking that

> this short novel suggests at almost every point the manner of *Horizon*. In subject and emphasis it has, too, a close similarity to Cyril Connolly's *The Rock Pool*, although it does not give so comprehensive a picture of the Bohemian pseudo-intellectual set as the latter book does, and it lacks Connolly's feline malice.

Reid observed 'a main difference' between the two books in what he regarded as a Sartrean existentialist mood in *These Dark Glasses*, something anachronistic to the time and place of the novella.

9   *Landfall* No. 12, Vol. 3, No. 4, December 1949, pp. 376-8.

To be reminded of Connolly in 1949 was not at all extraordinary, since *The Rock Pool*, another short work about the South of France, was reissued in 1947. (It first appeared in 1936.) Whether Texidor read *The Rock Pool* in the Thirties is unknown. That she could have read it before she was at work on *These Dark Glasses* but while her Spanish stories were in progress is possible, especially as Sargeson, if I remember rightly, owned a copy before it was republished. Another possible connecting factor was Kavan's return to London and her employment with Connolly at Horizon.

That Texidor did read *The Rock Pool*, and have it in mind, seems pretty sure. From the beginnings of the two books, where both Connolly's Naylor and Texidor's Ruth Brown arrive alone on holiday, there are close, incidental parallels. It is not that Connolly provided an outright model for Texidor's imitation. The parts of *These Dark Glasses* most reminiscent of *The Rock Pool* come early in the book, and they must be taken as reminders, first, and then as pointers to Texidor, about how to find her own stance (as she does) in writing about a milieu which had been dealt with by others besides Connolly. *These Dark Glasses* starts off, then takes off, from *The Rock Pool*. Texidor's story is set firmly in a place which is not Connolly's Trou-sur-Mer; its people (although they might have wandered in and out of Trou) maintain their own lives.

If some of Connolly's people were not entirely fictitious, so too some of Texidor's. More than once it has been said that '*These Dark Glasses* is about Mark Gertler', which is and is not correct. It is also about Ruth Brown, and about Greville herself if we attend to what Werner said: 'How very exhausted she was by the Spanish debacle only later [than 1938] became apparent when she wrote down her past feelings in a little very melancholy novel about her condition in the period after the Civil War.'[10]

10   *Odysee*, p. 75.

That Ruth is Greville is both true and not true. Greville herself may not have been fictionalised before this, but Gertler had been, back in 1916 in Gilbert Cannan's *Mendel*. Various memoirs and studies testify to the Fosters' involvement with the Gertlers, the Spencers, the Carlines and members of the Bloomsbury circles.

In the early 1920s Mrs Foster and her daughters lived in Hampstead. There they knew Mark Gertler, who was London Jewish of Polish background, Stanley Spencer, and Richard Carline, who was probably the first they got to know. Inferentially, Greville was modelling, Kate a student, who also modelled. The Slade is invoked: 'Word used to go round the Slade' (*These Dark Glasses*, 1949, p. 15) and 'A shade of the Slade was written all over her' (pp. 29–30). Richard Carline records from a diary of Kate's[11] that she first met the Spencers in July 1922 and modelled for Carline in December of that year. An entry for July 1923[12] about a party mentions David John in company with Henry Lamb and Dorothy Brett, and Marjorie Hodgkinson, 'who met Mark Gertler there'; they later married. Kate repeatedly figures in company with Carline whose sister Hilda became Stanley Spencer's wife. In 1924 Carline painted a set piece with Spencer, Lamb, Hilda and Kate. Carline reveals that a 1926 drawing by Spencer customarily said to be of Hilda and Spencer himself is actually of Carline and Kate Foster.[13] A final observation: in the years 1923–6 Spencer was at work on his notable canvas 'The Resurrection', to which the Fosters contributed materially. Mrs Foster (so Greville told Una Platts) lent Spencer the three fancy nightgowns worn by the Virgin in the porch and the two women flanking her which are so distinct from the otherwise plain wear of the rising dead.

Greville's association with these painters was presumably

11 Richard Carline, *Stanley Spencer at War*. London: Faber and Faber, 1978, pp. 141–2.
12 Ibid, p. 142.
13 Ibid, p. 107.

governed by the jobs she took. Her friendship seems to have been more with Marjorie Gertler than with Mark Gertler, who nevertheless painted an oil of Greville in 1929 which is in the Glasgow Art Gallery.[14] In the first half of 1939 (and possibly before) 'the Fosters' were renting the ground floor and basement of Gertler's house. The house was shortly to be sold. 'The Fosters' moved out.[15] This apparently refers to Mrs Foster, Greville and Cristina.

Gertler committed suicide in June 1939. Greville's friendship with Marjorie Gertler continued, and they were together at various times after Greville returned to Europe from Australia.

In the summer of 1938 Gertler, his wife and son Luke, went to Cassis, a place known to Katherine Mansfield. Cassis is not far from Marseilles, on the way to Toulon. Gertler was not at ease. He wrote to Koteliansky about his 'continuous headaches', about how tiresome and irritating his small son was, how tedious the local society 'always at the cafés and restaurants . . . How very futile the lives of Bohemian intellectuals and "artists" are!'[16] And again, August 11th 1938:[17]

> The place itself is charming and *could* make an excellent holiday resort, but it is *filled* with the 'Bohemia' of London—absolutely packed—futile men and prostitute-like women, mostly semi-acquaintances of a sort one tries to avoid like poison in London, and now Greville has turned up! Kate and her 'boy' are coming— Dick [Carline] and his latest girl etc. etc. Even a niece of mine suddenly appeared! So that the whole place seems like a lunatic asylum. The only *human* being is Braque, a tall handsome man, but he keeps well out of the way and one only gets a glimpse of him occasionally.

14   John Woodeson, *Mark Gertler*. London: Sidgwick and Jackson, 1972, p. 136.
15   Ibid, p. 325.
16   Ed. Noel Carrington, *Mark Gertler: Selected Letters*. London: Hart-Davis, 1965, p. 245. Letter to S.S. Koteliansky, July 20th, 1938.
17   Ibid, pp. 245–6. Letter to Thomas Balston.

Gertler found a lonely spot where he could bathe, he worked in the afternoons, but 'I have had some bad fits of depression'. If Greville was not expected, neither was Ruth Brown. If Greville was not altogether welcome, neither was Ruth Brown: 'I wish you could stay here,' says the wife in *These Dark Glasses*, 'but you know what Julian is.'

Cassis has three beaches, steep limestone cliffs, vineyards, olive groves and the village which sits doggedly below a beak-like headland. It is very old, and it is very much of the day. Maps do not show any place called Calanques for Ruth Brown or anyone else to holiday in. What they do show are *les calanques* beside Cassis, a stretch of indented coastline of narrow twists, broad lagoons or lakes, deep gullies and wind-battered cliffs.

In August 1938 Greville went off to Cassis. She needed a vacation, according to Werner, after their experiences in Spain and the dreary dogwork in London. In that summer Werner was in Germany, his future uncertain. In *These Dark Glasses* Ruth Brown arrives alone in Calanques played out after writing propaganda in London, weighed down with 'the debris of our Spanish dream'. Ruth's Victor (the name is perhaps over-ironic) is dead, Greville's Werner has no guarantees. There is a significant difference between Ruth Brown and Greville, not in respect of family (Greville had family whereas Ruth Brown appears to be pretty much a loner) but in political affiliation, since Ruth is a Communist although a somewhat disillusioned one. Nonetheless, wittingly or unwittingly, both have been used by the Party.

Whatever Ruth owes to Greville's experience, she is not so much a projection as a target. Greville is not sorry for Ruth. She will finally send her off with 'no suspicion of alcohol on her last breath. She had not been interfered with (not very much). There was no love lost, nothing whatever was lost. The Party came first and last and was last seen. Lives in our memory. May linger on for years. Tell the proletariat not to grieve. This be my requiem. You have nothing to lose . . .'

The others sail off, Otto making his political gesture, the clenched fist. 'The boat shrinks and stands stationary in space, with its cargo of seated dolls that shine like chocolate papers. Soon it is only the rim of a white nest enclosing coloured bonbons. Now there is no boat but a dark dot, seaweed, seabird, or a trick of the light . . .' This boat and its load is something cinematic, we've all seen that fade and close, something moralistic and parable-like. Yes, we've all seen its like, another version of a Ship of Fools setting off into and under that condition where (this is said just beforehand) *Si le ciel est désert nous n'offensons personne.*

If *These Dark Glasses* has some connection with *The Rock Pool* it connects also with Texidor's own 'Maaree'. Who came first, Maaree or Moira? I am inclined to Maaree, and to think that Turissa, of which traces remain, preceded Calanques. Cassis was merged with Tossa; fictionalising, distancing, and typifying, was in process? Yes, and no. In that process Cassis was at one stage Calanque, only later Calanques which directs one back to rather than away from the literal example. On the other hand Julian (the one surviving worksheet shows) was earlier Julius, so by the change Texidor diminished the likelihood of him being identified as Jewish, as Gertler was. And what about Kate? 'Kate and her "boy" are coming', Gertler wrote, and Kate and her boy arrive, Kate's Otto who is 'a dream of an Aryan'. How distanced is this? Properly, the question is, how controlled is this? as Texidor dances out of experience and into fantasy, where dance is a fitting word, another traditional theme: 'I was glad Otto was with us. All the evening we'd been saying between dances that we were dancing on the edge of destruction, and if this should be true I would still be glad to be having a dance with Otto. Only one. He wasn't a person you could expect to meet again.'

At the end of one of her unsuccessful pieces Texidor wrote an enquiry, 'Have I too much of a mess of metaphors? Ledger?

Gulf, Rock, I think I have.' Not so with *These Dark Glasses*. The metaphors work, the people work, and the poise of the disenchanted Ruth Brown's storytelling works, most admirably.

*

The War over, Werner had a teaching job and New Zealand citizenship. He applied for work in Europe with a United Nations relief organisation, unsuccessfully. Whatever his motives in this, the prospect of returning to Europe was undoubtedly in Greville's mind. Auckland was too provincial for her, and too distant when she tried to publish more. Moreover, domesticity was closing in. In 1947, when she was about forty-five, Greville had another daughter, Rosamund. Caring for a baby takes time and energy, and there cannot have been too much of either then available for writing, however one may remember the strikingly spirited woman whom one met in friends' homes or at the coffee shop in Queen Street where people gathered.

Spirited? One night at a party at Irene and Bob Lowry's home Denis Glover, visiting town, was at his most unlovably provoking. Some of us were in the kitchen getting supper ready. Denis across the kitchen table from Greville offered some opinions on the conduct of the war in Spain, 'Too many on the Republican side fought with their fountain pens and not enough with rifles . . .' A carving knife on the table came up off the table, across the table, and Glover, astonishingly adroit, went back out of its way most advisedly. But as well as spirited Texidor was depressive.

During this period she was at work on a new novel or novella, the sheets of which come from no sooner than 1946 and probably not later than 1947. It seems that she began with a story tentatively called 'When You Hit the Bottom', about Lili having a breakdown, and decided to enlarge on it to produce a longer work with Lili as the central figure. This was to have two aspects of time: a continuing present which runs from about 1940 to post-1945; a past which deals with Lili's life in Europe from childhood to when she migrates. Some of this is indicated in notes or sketches or small episodes, while some exists as complete chapters. The novella has a title: *Goodbye Forever.*

The narration of the foreground is given to a man who is an Aucklander and supposedly a writer. The past is dominantly Lili, though to some extent impersonal narration enters. The present is sequential; the past usually but not always.

The snapshots of Lili's European past bear on her foreground. Lili's family shape a good deal of what she is, and in this respect Texidor is working in orthodox psychological terms. Other indications, however, are that she was working mythically. Lili, who is said to be a witch, marries Hanserl, and a note exists which refers to *Goodbye Forever* as 'the "Gretel" novel'. Texidor was playing with archetypes? Or had she been reading Philip Toynbee's *Tea with Mrs Goodman*?

Lili, like Maaree, as a character is pathetic and comic, bleakly comic. Texidor may excite a feeling of pathos for her, but Lili is a figure of satire as well, of one kind of refugee—Texidor herself being a refugee of another kind, give or take some shared experiences.

The satire is more obvious in the people of Lili's milieu, especially the North Shore intelligentsia. It is not difficult to see whom Texidor has levied for contributions, or to gauge the extent of her disenchantment as the end of her time in Auckland came near and she said her own goodbye forever to the Shore.

She made a break with Auckland, leaving for Brisbane where she had friends. Werner did not follow until August 1948. Auckland may have been, was, provincial. Australia turned out only doubtfully better. In the five years following the household moved from place to place and job to job, spending longest in Hazelbrook in the Blue Mountains. In 1953 Mrs Foster, who had followed them to Australia, died and in 1954 they returned to Tossa, where in 1956 Greville was able to buy Can Kars off Kars' widow. Greville and Werner were increasingly estranged.

In January 1961 Werner flew back to Auckland. The marriage was definitely over.

In these years Greville was not bound hand and foot to Tossa. Part of 1955 she spent in London. At least four of the winters the household passed in Barcelona. Greville had close, very satisfying friendships with Spanish people. She visited, as to London, and had visitors, Marjorie Gertler for one. In 1962 she set off again to Sydney. In 1964, in Hazelbrook, she ended her life.

Texidor wrote only a little before she came to New Zealand. We have Werner Droescher's word for that, and it was also Frank Sargeson's understanding. It is my impression that they were correct. Only a fragment suggests that she tried her hand at any sort of sustained piece of writing before her time at Paparoa. Possibly she destroyed her prentice pieces. Indeed, one informant says that she had 'a big burn up' of papers before she left for Brisbane, but as working sheets in longhand are missing from the Auckland archive, and as evidently she wrote her drafts in longhand (which may be gathered from what remains) I guess that they were drafts of things post-1940 which went into the flames, along with some rejected typed sheets (indicated by lacunae). Along with them, I suspect, went some notebooks or journals, since I doubt that keeping notebooks–workbooks was a habit which began in Australia, from which the earliest surviving derive.

Of the work I have seen which is positively Australian or later, not a great amount of worked up material at that, all that can be said is that I could not convince myself that it merited recovering. Some passages of the notebooks, perhaps. A draft novel, *Diary of a Militia Woman* (which I have not seen, only heard about), I can't say.

The impulse to write did not die when she left New Zealand, but results were meagre. Texidor partially accounts for this in a letter from New South Wales to Frank Sargeson: 'The sad truth is that since you have given up being responsible for it I have never written another thing. Rather I have but I'm never satisfied with them—write several drafts and then chuck in the sponge. This might no doubt be due to other causes. I don't know.' We contemplate an unlikely prospect: a rather remarkable woman came first to a place unlikely to be conducive to an art, and there was impelled to learn how to practise at that art, and practise she did. She removed to a place more congenial . . . and she cared for neither place. She moved away, and as far as I can see the art which she commanded effectively died.

Had she not been so sceptical she might have become her own subject? Her own ironist? To an extent of course, she is. But what is, was, beyond that extent?

Beyond that is the technician. She was travelling fairly fast, learning as she went. She was learning about questions as she set herself problems, for instance, of (crudely) direct and indirect narration and (no way so crudely) of registers in dialogue and tonality. That she could not always solve her problems is for us to regret, but the problems of Texidor as writer were not limitedly those of the page before her. When are they ever so? Was it that she was a perfectionist? I doubt it. As I read her finished pieces, not so many of them, and the unfinished pieces along with them, I am reminded at once of her strong diverse personality and of what a French psychoanalyst René Laforgue propounded; a view of the neurosis of failure, where succeeding is the dangerous thing. But Laforgue also discussed others, whom he described as the Carmelites of neurosis.

Publishing History

Unless otherwise stated, typescripts are deposited in the University of Auckland library.

'These Dark Glasses'
Christchurch: The Caxton Press, 1949.

'Jesús Jiménez'
Previously unpublished; from a corrected typescript.

'Santa Cristina'
Penguin New Writing No. 22, Harmondsworth, 1944.

'Maaree'
Previously unpublished; from the more advanced of two surviving typescripts.

'Time of Departure'
Angry Penguins, Melbourne: Reed and Harris, 1944.

'At Home and Alone'
Angry Penguins, Melbourne: Reed and Harris, 1944.

'Reconstruction'
Previously unpublished; from the most advanced of several surviving typescripts.

'In Fifteen Minutes You Can Say a Lot'
Previously unpublished; from the most advanced of three surviving typescripts.

'You Have to Stand Up to Them'
Previously unpublished; from a corrected typescript.

'An Annual Affair'
New Zealand New Writing No.3, Wellington, 1944.

'Anyone Home'
Ed. Frank Sargeson, *Speaking for Ourselves*, Christchurch: The Caxton Press, 1945.

'Home Front'
New Zealand New Writing No. 1, Wellington, 1942; and as 'Epilogue', *Penguin New Writing* No. 17, Harmondsworth, 1943.

'Elegy'
Anvil, Auckland: Anvil Club, September 1945.

'Goodbye Forever'
Previously unpublished; from a typescript in the possession of
Ms Rosamund Droescher.

Acknowledgements

For their assistance I have to thank the Librarian of the
University of Auckland; Cathie Hutchinson and Kay Stead, of
Reference and Inquiries; and Theresa Graham, Elspeth Orwin
and Vanessa Seymour at the New Zealand and Pacific Room.
Barbara Duggan, Ian and Eileen Hamilton, Una Platts and
Val Purdue kindly answered questions. Margaret Edgcumbe
generously translated much of Werner Droescher's *Odysee eines
Lehrers*.

Use has been made of notes on Greville Texidor's life
compiled by Rosamund Droescher, another set of notes recorded
by Bert Roth from Ms Droescher, and reminiscences by Gladys
Salter, all located with the Texidor papers in the University
archive A-198.

Sir Keith Sinclair located references to correspondence
concerning Texidor. I have to thank him for this, and the Chief
Archivist for making available the relevant passage from the file
I.A. 158/206/ 87. And, the Chief Librarian of the Alexander
Turnbull Library for letters from the Turnbull MS Papers
432:39 series.

Finally, I must thank Rosamund Droescher for her assistance
at all stages of this project.

Kendrick Smithyman
April, 1987

IN FIFTEEN MINUTES YOU CAN SAY A LOT

These Dark Glasses

SUNDAY—Calanques: I am used to not being met. Comrade Ruth Brown is not the clinging type. But it is Sunday, and suddenly the station is empty and the porter says, as though I should have known, It's five miles to Calanques. Jane might have thought of this, but she's scared of her near friends. And I still carry an atmosphere of embarrassment. An awkward silence rises round Victor's name. Even Malcolm, after the first few words that later went into the obituary in the *Worker*. And Jane never did meet anyone at the station. We always considered it bourgeois; though in those dead days before we were socially conscious, bourgeois was not the crime it is now. In those days it was something a little bit common.

The bus is here, is waiting, the porter says. Ah, the bus, the good bus is waiting. Ruth Brown has a right to a holiday in the sun, the good sun that puts everything right.

I enquired for the rue Victoire in a bar on the Place. At last the sea with its smell; not a postcard seen through the train window. But I crossed the promenade quickly. I was the sole spectator wandered in from the dark to this brightly lighted cabaret, where the artists sitting at tables packed against a setting of sea and sunset were making the planned picture.

One forgets the clearness of colours in the south. In London one looked as nice as one could; one looked about the same as everyone else. One got a little coating of fog and forgot.

An off-white Bugatti with a fair girl at the wheel urged me to disappear with its querulous klaxon. The girl gazed over my head; it was only the car it seemed that objected to me.

The rue Victoire was a long dusty road uphill. Jane's house was locked but Paul in pink pyjamas was hanging over the top floor balcony. He scuttled out of sight when I rattled the door but after frantic endearments shouted up from the street he agreed to let me in. I heard his quick feet on the stairs and his struggle with the stiff yale lock.

I can't do it, he said.

Try, old dear, you must. (I will not return to the lighted cabaret.)

He was thrilled and a bit scared when the door opened. I did it, he said. Come in! They put me to bed and go out to dinner all the evenings.

He took me upstairs to his room under the roof. It was hot as fever; a flood of *New Yorkers* and the bedclothes covered the floor.

I never go to sleep for ages, he said. He was flushed and excited. There's a horrible wind all day, he said, that makes everyone feel rotten. You're not really my Auntie?

I read him a couple of stories from the *New Yorker* and said he must try to sleep.

You'll be here, won't you? he said. You won't go out to dinner? Have a banana and some jelly, will you?

There was nothing in the larder but some sour milk and a few grey potatoes. In the salon there were piles of the *New Statesman* and a shelf of Left Book Club books. Really not for someone in my line away for a holiday on the Riviera. I picked up a copy of Lady Chatterley. But being only a day from the class struggle and having missed dinner, Lady Chatterley was just as little the thing as the grey potatoes.

Julian and Jane came in with the Bugatti blonde. They looked interrupted somehow, as if they hadn't expected me just then, but they often look like that, even when they've invited someone to dinner. Soskia, the blonde, did those delightful sets for the Sea Gull. Soskia had a crown of curls round her head that trembled

when she breathed. Soskia radiated sensibility. She made you
wonder whether sitting on committees really did any good.

What a beautiful dress you have, I said.

I picked up the stuff for a song in the market place. You like
it? she said, smiling delicately at Julian. It was seen she was not
a Paris mannequin, nor yet a luxury girl.

Whatever made you come here? Julian asked me. It's like a
hangover from an old Slade party. But still there is plenty to
read, he said, indicating the bookshelves. It goes with the house.
If you can't face up to Calanques there's plenty of proletarian
escapist literature here.

Jane frowned at him and got me out of the room. You'll
have to sleep in the studio tonight, she said. It's too late now to
look for a room. I doubt if there is one. Calanques is ghastlily
crowded. People like us who used to go to Spain. There won't be
anywhere left to go soon will there? I wish you could stay here
but you know what Julian is.

I did not remind her of her invitation. I knew how it was.
When you get close up to things the difficulties appear in
horrifying detail. Jane was up in a corner.

The studio was, like Paul's room, under the roof. There was
not a hint of night freshness in it. The smell of turps and sweat
was asphyxiating. Julian would be painting a scene from the
window, his usual standby on his holidays. He painted more in
these attics than in his fairly comfortable London studio which
was only cold in the winter. Here, he would be shut up all day
and sweat and suffer and grumble because he couldn't paint out
of doors. His friends too would be made to suffer the intense
heat of the attic.

No one was allowed to enter Julian's studio. The canvasses all
had their faces turned to the wall. I would never have dreamed
of laying a finger on them.

MONDAY—Calanques: I choose the smartest *coiffeur* near the café. As Kate and Jane are forever saying, It's false economy not to go to the best. In there the buzz of dryers and curtained conversation and the smell of burnt perfume sum up the heat of the day. A young assistant, Emile, attends to my hair. While he smears on the henna he asks, Do I like Calanques? He is sweating and pale with the violence of the heat and hurry. I doze pleasantly under the hands of the watchful Emile. Then I wake with a jerk. Heaven forgive a class conscious sinner. Here is a French worker wasting away in the heat like the wax bust in the window. He knows his *metier* too, but his hands are very hard, he is over determined. His attentions develop into a contest with my hair which he finally dominates, holding up the mirror. But perhaps because I don't require a friction he takes leave of me coldly.

I pay the cruel-eyed *patron* at the counter. A printed card says *10% pour la service.* I pay the bill adding the 10%. Emile comes out of the booth, follows me to the door, and says quietly, hurriedly. And the *pourboire, ma'moiselle?* So though I have paid I give him another franc.

Across the street the party ghost of the lovely Lawless is naturally unaware of its wine-coloured face and baldness. The girl that walks beside it has stepped out of a show window at Printemps. I fail to believe in this girl. I fail to believe in this continuation of Lawless still bringing out a new book and a new girl.

We exchange sickly smiles of unbelief in passing.

Jane's kitchen is smelly and there is no milk with the tea. She is having a trying time. Julian is in one of his suicidal states. Holidays always seem to bring them on. Having to see all these bogus artists and having to work in this infernal heat because of course he can't paint out of doors. You'll never know how awful it is being married to a genius, Jane says.

The first week when she'd come to Calanques to pave the way for Julian, she'd had an affair with a sort of fisherman she thought he was, from Marseilles. They had had it behind a rock, rather Lawrencian, and afterwards eaten sea urchins roasted. But she hadn't met him again and afterwards she was terrified she felt so ill. There were all those posters everywhere in Marseilles, but then she thought it might be the sea urchins. But now she felt so ill. It might be the mistral. She was sorry she couldn't have me to stay in the house but Julian couldn't work with anyone there. I must have a meal with them. But Julian didn't want much to see old faces. Lawless and people like that.

I would have looked after Paul. We would have entered together the mercilessly lighted cabaret of the beach thinly disguised with books and dark glasses. But a girl had been engaged to look after Paul. Good for his French. Jane thought perhaps I'd be busy. I was always busy with my political things.

I returned to the room I had taken. A nice big room on a street corner with a double bed in an alcove, a gilt framed mirror over the mantelpiece and in another alcove a basin with running water and a *bidet*. The family live across the landing. A woman and a little girl and a husband. They will not disturb me, she says, they are very quiet. They are quiet. They are clean. I see there will be nothing between us. I must pay a month in advance for this quietness and cleanness, on that the woman insists. The room is too good for me, too expensive, but Jane says I'd better take it. Then I can hand it on to Howard and his American when they come.

The room had been scrubbed and the shutters were half closed. It was warm in the pink light from the brick floor. Children played noisily just outside in the street. There was not a sound from the house. I locked the door and opened my note book. There was the debris of our Spanish dream, the words withered with waiting too long. It should only have taken two months, they said at the office. I could easily do it in my spare time. It might be based on Victor's letters to me. Letters from Spain were meant for publication. Never mind about the style though. I was pretty slick with pamphlets and manifestos. And Malcolm was there to see that the outlook was right. The world must know the truth about Spain. But already the truth is disappearing round the corner.

The words are to hand, Solidarity, Revolution. Cannibal words that eat their own meaning. There must have been new words in Spain to catch the new hope that was real there. A Thousand Spanish Words lay on each desk at the office but we were only expected to catch the words through the press translations. Experts were over there to catch the real words and the sound of thoughts, but they did not succeed. Victor did not succeed. He walked into a private dream and was swallowed.

I write a few words then look at myself in the mirror. I am trying to write about a starving peasant, but am haunted by the thought that I shall have to emerge from this room and have dinner alone.

I wait until nearly dark then set out for the Marine at the end of the village. It is cheap and you eat in the open, Jane said. I am too late. The tables are all taken. People are eating soup and mullet and veal stew under the chilly electric lights and the dark vines. Under the lights are vaguely familiar faces. They look up at me as I stand on the edge of the light. I sit down on a wall to wait. From below a smell of decay rises from the rotting edge of the sea.

Julian and Jane have come. People look up and smile and a fat-faced young girl takes out her mirror and lipstick. Please take this table, somebody says, we are leaving.

There's a chair there, why don't you bring it over? Jane calls. So through no fault of my own I am dining with them.

The waitresses are running and shouting in coarse voices. We're coming! *Patience messieurs-dames!* Julian is talkative. He has two aperitifs just before dinner and a cognac afterwards.

That is the only way he can bring himself to face these vaguely familiar faces that haunt his holidays. The only person he wanted to meet was Picasso, but it seems Picasso might not come to Calanques this year.

We drink wine, eat bread and wait for the first course, Jane and I with stretched conversation, in a petty agony of wondering how Julian will take this waiting. At last he springs up and goes away to the kitchen. We exchange anxious understanding looks till he comes back with the waitress and the fish. Now he is simply delighted with himself. The rest of his short evening is assured.

We walk back to the café Glacier. In the full blare of Blanche Neige some Englishmen in French fisherman suits and bare feet are dancing and clowning rather formally with the village boys. One of the Englishmen, older than the others with the face of a statesman, is shaking off his shyness in a *danse du ventre*. The inappropriate impropriety of the creaking dance, the grave face, and the innocent little tune, are making his partners laugh. None of them have noticed that he is insane.

I walk away and along a stone pier that ends with a lighthouse and a red light. Halfway along it Emile overtakes me. Good evening, he says, quietly, hurriedly, it is very pleasant to walk on the pier at night. I feel sure he has never been on the pier before. Madame is alone? That doesn't require an answer. He says, Would Madame care to dance a little? In a place that is very picturesque and secluded?

We have reached the end of the pier and the black sea. I agree to dance a little.

We cross the village and walk up a steep white road. Expensive cars come roaring round the bends. The drivers shout, the headlights flash and flatten us against the rocks. We climb on through clouds of dust and pass the hotel de luxe.

The dancing place is a cement platform under an awning with a shed and a bar on one side. On the sea side there is a drop into darkness. The platform is big and bare under the naked lights. I do not see any English about. That is nice. It is charming, I say. Emile orders a vermouth. I order an anis de loso. Emile says the anis is very strong. Sickly and chilly and strong, the anis releases a flood of French phrases. Little poignantly familiar words, *épatant, copain, chic,* rise to the surface. Good fishing. I happily catch a banality and throw it to Emile. I am very content to juggle with these little words that are in currency at the other tables.

These are French workers certainly, at the iron tables, girls with light dresses and dark brown legs, boys with slick hair and short-sleeved shirts and one or two older men in tight town suits. Undoubtedly Emile is a French worker. I tell him I work for Spain on the side of the workers. That is excellent, he says. He wants to dance. He adores the dance and is anxious to do his stuff.

The American rhythms translated by French orchestras are childish and destructive. It seems a giant child is banging with one finger, a dogmatic *diseur* of immensely simple and sinister *double entendre.* The dances are very long and when they are finished we stand and dance on through the next. Our athletics never cease for a moment. But though the dance is full of vitality the principle remains undiscovered. The only certainty is the bumping of bodies.

I must beg to sit down and order another anis.

You really want another?

But you must allow me to pay for this one myself.

But no, *ma petite.* One mustn't misunderstand. It was only the *patron,* that dirty old *type—enfin* the employees never saw the ten per cent.

Ah, the English, he said. *Ils s'amusent c'est cela que j'aime des Anglais.* He didn't order anything for himself but watched with some surprise the English putting down another anis. He was anxious to show again what he could do. After the second anis the principle of the dance was discovered. It was a sex marathon. It was love on the go.

People were leaving. The place looked bare and grey under the lights.

Fatigued? But no. He was a little suspicious. Still if you like we would return *chez toi*.

There were frequent stops on the road. He was really most anxious to show what he could do now that the evening was unexpectedly shortened. His embraces were on the same lines as the dance. It was hardly fair, but the sterile argument about coming in for a minute had now been short circuited. We were nearly run down by a car with blazing lights. The driver shouted and laughed.

The street door is locked at ten, the landlady had said, with a peculiar lowering of the voice for this mystery. *Voici la clef.*

Emile wished to come in. Why not? echoed from the frowning fronts of the houses. Quiet, I said. We disturb. His protests shamed the silent hostile stairs. But why not? He had paid three drinks and also shown so well what he could do there on the dangerous road. What did people expect? What had one to do to establish oneself? They get what they want then close the door in your face.

The *boîte* has opened up. It is next door in a house that lies across the end of the street. A blues record is playing; a perfectly square tune with four corners. Then an acid sweet anisy French tune, then Blanche Neige and now the blues record. There are no sounds of revelry from the *boîte*. One imagines a lonely gramophone gone mad.

TUESDAY—Calanques: To wake slowly is pleasant. It is very pleasant to be on a holiday. Because there is nothing in the world to get up for. But that is not all. Children are playing just outside in the street. Only the shutters between me and the street. There might be reasons for waking slowly. The hard sunshine outside and the cold eyes in the café.

It takes so long to get up. Just the things you needed are not to be found. Little shirts that denote self respect are crumpled and mauled by the heat. While washing you stop again and face yourself in the mirror. The mirror is in a frightfully good light. With your hands in the basin you stop and start at your sunburned and seared face.

I would like to take refuge in Jane's smelly kitchen. I would bring some milk, but something else would be wrong. Look here, Ruth, she'd say, as if it had been wrung out of her on the rack. The mistral. The primus. Not blaming me, just being overwhelmed.

I walk down the street meeting cleverly dressed people. I meet myself in the mirror outside the *coiffeur*, a female figure in gaunt blue overalls. The henna has blessed the final banality and now I am very nearly invisible.

It is early still for Calanques, and not many people are at the café. An imaginary zone of silence insulates the table conversations. Eyes look up and are lowered. I sit against a partition of potted palms that shelters one side from the street. Though nearly invisible I cannot risk eyes on my back. An old waiter comes and I order coffee and *croissant*. There are hard boiled eggs, he says, not unkindly, but I refuse because I must have one for lunch.

The young men are there. The knowing *habitués* of the *plage* are shoeless this summer; you see them hopping across petrol pools on the burning asphalt or avoiding tins on the beach. The young men are whistling the Internationale. That we should have come to this! I drink my coffee, putting in sugar though I don't take sugar.

A young girl sits down near me and puts a huge sea urchin shell on the table in front of her. She is waiting for someone to come along and admire it. She is certainly silly and not socially conscious but still there is something between us. It seems to me she has come to the wrong place. But before I have praised the shell her friend joins her. The friend is called April. Her hair is done in some forgotten fashion with one peroxided lock. She is clearly an English tart accustomed to sitting in bars and being picked up. April has come, very much, to the wrong place.

The other girl says in a sweet and pure cockney, Isn't it lovely? I was out with Pierre fishing. She has a soft face, false teeth, and terrified eyes.

Jane admired the shell as she passed between the tables. Yes I think I will have a coffee, she said. It's so refreshing to be out of that house. I'm worn out with Julian. It's such a work to get him to do anything. He can't bathe from the beach and we have to go to his own special rock and it's miles away. Then he complains so of the heat. It's unbelievable there in that studio and of course he can only paint in the afternoon just when it's worst. Paul isn't well either. It must be the mistral.

Oh, Moira you mean, she said. She collects shells. (Don't look up so hopefully Moira, remember we're surrounded by an imaginary line of silence.) She held an exhibition here but I don't think anyone went. I suppose by the way of being Bohemian she's fallen in love with one of the fishermen. Pathetic isn't it with her teeth and all.

Paul fidgeted with his fizzy drink and begged to go shopping.

Inside the shady shop, where the little green parrot solemnly hopped on the greens, and eggs were fresh, very fresh and of today, the most cynical visitors felt more healthy and normal. Paul would have liked to stay in the shady shop but they had to start on the long trek to Julian on his rock. And hoping to find another possible rock I avoided the beach.

The only one flat on top and free of sea urchins was occupied by a handsome Jewish couple, but they beckoned, moved up, spread towels, were frank and friendly. They were staying *chez Borodin*, they said. He's painting in Ripolin now.

Borodin from the past. Someone had lent him a house and he'd stayed on and become the king of Calanques simply because he was there and owned an old boat and everyone knew him. Word used to go round the Slade. She's gone away with Borodin in his yacht. But always they came back at the end of the season.

The Germans explained that the lodgings at the Pension Borodin were cellars and tents and chicken runs in the garden. You never knew who you'd be sleeping with. For themselves they found it uncomfortable but enjoyed to observe. He is charming, they said. But he doesn't like the art students copying his suits of sail cloth. He has the stuff faded and patched before it's made up. And Moira? Yes, but think. She intended to stay throughout the winter here. We come in search of the primitive life do we not all? they said. We all love nature but in winter you know the wind blows right through these papery houses. The fisher has a wife who understands in the season but in winter no one at all will speak with Moira. The English do not speak with her as it is, because she is too naive she does not know.

The Germans knew everything but they were nice about it.

In the tepid shade of the café Julian is wedged against a palm with only Jane and Paul between him and the crowd of familiar faces. He looks at me reproachfully. It is certainly hard on him that this is the only café where you can eat hard boiled eggs.

Beer has drawn a warm curtain over the buzz of the café. People are going away slowly to coma in curtained rooms. At last poor Julian, destined to sweat in the attic, rises suddenly and strides off up the hill. Emile sits down nearby with a *copain*. The *copain*'s skin is so pitted with blackheads it seems like something under a microscope. Beside him Emile is almost acceptable. He drops inane endearments on the frizzy café child, looking over its head at the English dame. He grins at the *copain*. She really is not bad *dans le genre anglais*. She is suitably attired for swimming or sport. Now that the others have gone he moves his glass on to her table and asks, not so discreetly today: What would she say to a *promenade en bateau*?

Here it is, the boat and the healthy sea, the primitive life and the French worker. What we are all here for. Just what we need. Just what the doctor—no. I refuse the primitive life.

But Emile is in the right after all. He has a nice feeling for the *comme il faut*. The *promenade en bateau* is the correct adventure for a *sportive anglaise*.

Emile rowed clumsily with a show of strength. He was not familiar with boats. And when the sportive anglaise dived from the stern Emile looked on with anxious disapproval. I thought to go to the Grande Calanque, he said. It's from these Calanques that the town takes its name. He frowned at the water and the swimmer, letting the boat drift.

The water was warm and heavy. She tried to free herself from its dense folds with arms and legs that were heavy. I am sinking, she said to herself without surprise. The heat and the breakfast, the French and the hard boiled eggs. She clutched at the explanation and closed her eyes. The salt was bitter as whips. She called. But the boat, Emile and her voice were far away. An empty voice like the chatter of pebbles on stone was calling Emile, Emile.

He had brought the boat nearer. She could see the name Mirette in gold letters and Emile grieved and annoyed. Why should I notice these things that do not concern me? She said to herself, Mad'moiselle you are drowning. How near it is how very easy it is.

Emile had come up with the boat. Hold on Mad'moiselle, hold. I can't swim.

Her hands obeyed, and moored to the side of the boat, her arms were stretched or loosened like ropes by the pull of the current. After she had been hauled over the side, she flopped like an ungainly stranded fish at the boat's bottom, too tired even to laugh.

Emile said nothing. There was nothing apropos to say about this so out of the picture indisposition. He took off his cotton jersey and rowed sternly.

His eyes, timid and hard, laired in thick brows and bushy low-growing hair. He looked like a crafty little animal. But remember my dear, animals are not crafty. That day at the zoo when poor Paul had said the alligator was ugly. Howard was tender even about the hyenas.

Emile rowed on stubbornly, into the wind now. The surface of the sea rose and fell in liquid lumps against the face of rock. With the stealthy movement of a lift the sea slid up and down the smooth rock. The waves lifted grey voluminous heads, sliding away sideways below the boat.

Ça va? Ça va toujours! Loose ends of a person swaying below in the swell. Emile was trying to bring the boat round a cruel point that guarded the Calanque. You could see, where the Calanque carved its way narrowly inland and ended with a tiny triangle of beach, that the water was smooth as silk. Behind the Calanque rose the jagged rock that was visible from the town. At its summit someone had written in giant letters, *Vive le Parti Communiste.* A picnic party was occupying the beach.

No need to land, Emile.

One must land, Emile said. He brought the boat in nearer to the rock. Now its ugliness could be seen in microscopic horrifying detail. The little boat passed very slowly under the wall. We were passing along the wall of a picture gallery. A black niche, a scarred triangular plaque, sharp edges of clustering mussels, torsos with hard hair.

Do not land Emile. We intrude there. *Prenez garde.* Take

care of the rocks Emile. He had a name, he was human. Under the rock that stared like a curse there were human beings who could still go back.

We could go back Emile.

We shall find a place nearer the town, he said. To him it seemed like defeat.

Towards the town there were villas, twisted pines, stone steps and tea tables standing on bare rock. The backs of the villas were very private and furtive; not gracious because of the rock. At one of these landing places, a concrete square, we stopped and Emile held off the bumping boat. Over a stone wall people peered from their garden.

At the end of the jetty the *copain* was shouting and waving. Emile ignored him. We shall go now in the other direction, to the Cap Rouge, the highest point on the coast.

Across the broken sea, through the almost visible wind that passed in a stream of heat, the Cap bulged red in the sun.

Let us go back now. There's plenty to see on the beach.

The *copain* ran to meet us. Did you not land? he said. For a moment, I said. He seemed very disappointed. Emile threw him a word as we walked away.

He seemed concerned about us, I said.

Oh him. It's his father's boat. He thought his father might be returning soon. We shall sit on the beach? *On est bien* on the beach in the *plein air. Il y a du monde.*

It was a half holiday in Marseilles. The black families were ranged in the plain air. In the stale light of four o'clock they stretched stiffly down the steep sloping beach to the water's edge. Stiffly I pillowed my head on a grey stone. Emile rested his animal head on my knee.

You like the beach? You are not from the coast then?

No, from the Pyrénées. My village is there.

From the Pyrénées? The postmark *Pyrénées Orientales* sweetened the musty smell in the post office.

Before the last month of my military service I shall return there for a while. A pretty little house up in the mountains. You might come and stay there after your holidays here. We should make promenades together. Gather wild flowers. It is charming.

Then pale coffee in the crowded beach café with palms and pillars, that none of the visitors went to. The continental hour that should have been tea time was very long. Emile said no more about his village. That was all of it that was ever presented. We had finished the coffee. There was nothing to say.

The house was quiet, the room very clean, the mirror shone in the gloom of half-closed shutters. Emile undressed in the alcove. You don't undress. He didn't know at all what the answer would be. English dames who make themselves sick by swimming . . . We extinguish the light?

Why not? The room closes in, the bed in the alcove opens its hungry arms.

It is very hot?

So what? It is certainly very hot under the airless night of the canopy shot with sick lightnings of ill-timed endearments. *Il faut profiter* with endearments and loud sighs. Loud sighs and whispers that would burst the lid off a tomb.

Children are playing just outside in the street. *Un, deux, trois.* The house is silent. The walls are deceptively private. Outside the children still pretending to play. Inside the heat, hurry and violence. Splashing in the alcove, the tap running, the drain gulping and groaning. Splashing with assurance because he has gotten or given the full value which ever way things turn out.

One opens the shutters *cherie?*

Not yet. And by the way. One sees a lot of those *affiches* up in Marseilles.

Political ones? Oh *that*. Naturally. Nearly everyone has it. But me no. I am lucky. I wash so well. We dine together yes?

No. (The self-respecting little shirts are all lost. Everything is mauled and crumpled by the heat.)

In a little *auberge*. It is picturesque you will see. The *cuisine* is good enough. Simple it is but very rustic and charming.

I have a date with my friends. (These vaguely familiar faces watching from cafés.)

Au revoir then. In short this is not the way to finish an evening. A little dinner for two . . . *Au revoir* then. I shall leave my shoes here? These shoes I take to change to wear in the café. *Au revoir, tes amis t'attendent.*

When it was dark outside I opened the shutters. The alcove was aflood, the ritual wash, and a pair of confident white and tan shoes made themselves at home on a chair in the corner. I tidied the room with very special care.

I opened my door. The landlady's door opened. A clean smell of ironing came from the quiet kitchen. The silent child, in a white frock and patent leather shoes, was testing an iron with her finger. The landlady wished to give me some clean dresses. I was something she had to keep clean, a foreigner fouling the nest. She only saw the dirty side of me.

She looked at me keenly. Do you find the key turns easily?

(What does she mean?) Yes, I said cautiously. It goes very well.

My husband has oiled it but sometimes it grates a little. Sometimes it sticks a little, the landlady said.

Her smile was too clean.

At the Marine I shared a table with the lonely lady who, being an unfashionable refugee, White Russian, was nearly invisible. She had once been loved by Borodin though, and came every year to Calanques for her holiday. She passed it alone in the sight of Borodin, and her batty and broken heart was handed on year after year to new arrivals.

She didn't talk much, she knew she was only a myth, but was quite polite and over the dessert she chatted a little about the sixteen bullet holes the Reds had left in her body.

Jane called to me as I crossed the lights of the café. We haven't seen you all day.

I was out fishing.

Were you? I see. I'd found a job for you if you had the time. Laurence Prescott. Pressy.

One of the young men with the bare feet but wearing shoes now and a school blazer. He wanted some typing done. What I really need is a secretary, he said. But never mind. Let us seal the agreement.

We sealed the agreement with the cheapest brandy. It was for him rather a cheap agreement. You won't be late in the morning will you? he said. The publisher's waiting for it as a matter of fact.

Fairies are generally clever or amusing aren't they? Jane said, when Pressy had left with elaborate goodnights. I hadn't seen him in that blazer before. It's rather bizarre like the labels on French whisky. But he might be all right. I mustn't keep you now. I know you want to get back to the fisherman.

The room is terribly neat; deceptively cool and tidy. Something has been done to it since I went away. It has settled down again to its prim reserve but still holds a stale animal odour. I have thrown open the shutters and hidden away the confident shoes in a cupboard.

WEDNESDAY—Calanques: I'm afraid I shall have to dictate, Pressy said. My notes are confused and completely illegible, he said with a little laugh. While he dictated he walked up and down. He wore shoes for the house. He did not walk very far for the garret was quite small. It was stifling too but Pressy sacrificed the life of the beach to the pleasure of hearing his own words and having a secretary to hear them too. I was his secretary it appeared. After a good sentence he paused in his walk to say, Have you got that? The secretary nodded brightly. The lunch hour came and passed. Pressy, reminded, pulled up suddenly, startled.

Artists are very naughty about the time. In any case we could hardly stop in the middle of a paragraph, Miss Er. So we finished the paragraph about the two young men, Tresmond and Hanadune.

Back at the café Emile was drinking a vermouth, he and the *copain* talking with violence, uncouthly strong on vermouth, heat and adventure. I turned aside to avoid greetings and smiles.

Pressy paced up and down. At four his friends came, Hanadunes of the café. The secretary was instructed to make tea on an alcohol stove. Delicious *pâtisserie,* Pressy said with a little laugh. His hands hovered awkwardly over the cakes. I haven't introduced my secretary, Mabel. You don't mind my calling you Mabel, do you Mabel? Mabel is such a suitable name for a secretary. The Hanadunes smiled. They put on a Walton record. A little bit bogus some of them thought it was.

Then back to work; the sweetest work in the world. Tresmond and Hanadune. Even when it was dark and people were passing on their way to the café, Pressy wouldn't give in. The mercenary Mabel must remind and the author pause in his walk again, pained. One can hardly break off in the middle of a sentence Mabel.

The deceptive room was friendly and decent, but a chill came through the walls from the landlady, the little girl and the invisible husband. I am alone, furtive and sinister, eating a *foie gras* sandwich in the mirror. I am re-reading a letter with a scented postmark—*Pyrénées Orientales.*

Comrade Brown was much missed at the office. Hoped she would benefit by a well-earned rest. Somebody else had agreed to do the book, but it wasn't a very good time for anything now. Afraid they might have to close down for lack of support. Between themselves things were going very badly in Spain.

The letter breathed the bus-laden air of the Strand, where in the fetid dingy office the staff hammered out a dream of the golden proletariat into persuasive pamphlets. Above the antagonistic Strand they proclaimed. Whoever believes shall be saved. But one of them didn't believe any more. And the dingy proletariat passed by in the Strand.

The French workers were wonderful, Malcolm said. He was coming over to cover the rally at St Cloud. We might meet.

We might meet carrying a haversack. Principles relax a little in Paris.

The light snapped on. Emile was there standing beside the bed. *Me voici.* He was there like the shoes. I thought you might be out with your friends, he said.

Does he suspect? My friends, my good friends.

Emile had brought a present, a bracelet of silvery metal with a heavy design of arab letters and scrolls. You like it? It's only a cheap thing, a matter of twenty francs. The arabs sell them on the beach but I know the English like them. You like it? It fastens like this.

Wonderful to be worth twenty francs. But no doubt the bracelet was an investment in a future of English chic. He probably got it for ten francs from the arab. There was nothing wrong with that. Twenty francs was still the current price. And apart from its price the bracelet carried an aromatic value like the *Pyrénées Orientales.*

The present brings an immediate profit too.

We have amused ourselves very well, Emile said. With some doubt because he added, And you?

An empty voice that would never reach anywhere, like the chatter of pebbles on stone, said, I am not quite myself—the mistral—a touch of nerves.

Emile laughed very loud. But not on account of me. Not of a boy like me.

I don't know of what. But listen Emile. It was nice that he had a name. It seems I am very lonely.

Quelle blague. Hidden, chilling, ridiculous. Laugh over love with the *copain* in the café but with the *amie*—even the English must know these things. To laugh at each other, no. It seemed like defeat.

But he stifled the *arrière pensée.* He was pretty sure of amour. So he looked at the little partner, ready to laugh, while he twisted the words to something fitting and proper. Just like a little girl.

He embraced her. Poor little girl. Still, strangeness was draining the profit from the occasion.

And how could anyone be nervous, he said, with all the *machins* a modern woman carries for safety? My poor sister, now, a *gosse* every year. You can't imagine how backward they are in the village.

Take these my friend. I shall not be needing them myself any more (I am going on a journey).

I will give you the whole phial. It is nothing *mon vieux.* I shall not be needing them. I am leaving soon. (*Je vais faire un voyage. Adieu.*)

Emile's black eyes shone. How many would it contain? One would say he was fond of his sister.

You are going away? You must permit to come and arrange your hair then. It needs doing again, it keeps in badly with the life of the *plage.* Don't come to the shop. The ten per cent he takes but they all do that. It's the hours and other things. It's quite illegal what he does there. You have the running water. Only the cold. A pity. But we shall manage. Till tomorrow then.

Ill-timed *attendrissements* on the quiet stairs. *Au revoir ma petite*, he shouts at the open door.

I shrink back out of range of the landlady.

The opposite door opens and I hear the landlady say, very smoothly, It's you, monsieur. And Emile answering quietly and pleasantly, *Bon soir Madame.*

Bon soir Monsieur. Cool and polite. The password. But between respectable people there is really no need to conspire. About the lodger it is quite understood.

THURSDAY—Calanques: I was dreaming last night about the terrible shoes. I had hidden them in the cupboard but somebody found them. Or perhaps they came out by themselves. And now it is only eight o'clock. I have faced up to breakfast in time to be alone with the old waiter the weak coffee and the Midi in the peculiar peace of the café. Breakfast is the pivot on which day and night turn. Miss breakfast and you might as well give up altogether.

Jane, in a long, flowered gown, was crossing the speckled sunlight of the Place. She was turning the corner. I raced to overtake her. Has anything happened to Julian? It was early for Jane to be out. We had always thought that Julian would commit suicide before breakfast. We talked and joked about it quite freely and yet it was bound to happen.

He's asleep, Jane said. Isn't it fresh and pleasant? One really ought to get out earlier. I thought I would slip out before breakfast and find a few flowers to paint. You know Julian can't paint if anyone else paints in the same house. But he'd never think of the cellar. It has a door into the yard with a beautiful light. You can buy flowers from the garden of the *seigneurie*. Soskia told me about it.

Yes, now I think of it I haven't seen one flower here. All the same it seems funny to have to buy them.

Everything has to be paid for, Jane said. Very little of course but everything costs something. You couldn't just pay an inclusive charge and have the sea and everything thrown in. They won't do it like that.

And that being so and no gas ovens in Calanques, do you know what I am thinking of doing Jane? I am going to climb to the top of the rock that has *Vive le Parti Communiste* written around it, and a frightfully sheer drop on the sea side.

It would be symbolical, Jane said rather wearily.

Or the Cap Rouge, the highest point on the coast. At a place in North Wales where we went for holidays when I was a child there was a thing called the Orme that bulged like that. Only it was green; smooth green grass. One day everyone saw a girl slipping very slowly down the slope. She slipped about halfway and just sat there. People called but she didn't seem to hear. While the coastguard was coming with ropes and tackle she just sat there. She was there for about twenty minutes. Then she started slipping again, faster. Then she went over the edge.

But what about your fisherman? And your writing. Those political things you do are extremely good. I mean the one I read—they aren't written for people like us, are they? But they must do a tremendous amount of good. And there's still Spain going on.

It always seems too late to do any good. It's like slipping down a hill. Everything goes so fast.

But really, Jane said with a touch of dismay, the Left Movement isn't going to be *démodé*—why Auden and everyone—of course Julian is rather down on Auden and everyone so I wouldn't tell him for the world, but I secretly like that boy scout atmosphere.

A year or two ago it seemed all right. Things looked bright in a rather wintry light. But wasn't it naive to trust intellectuals. *Toujours plus haut, toujours plus avant sur les cimes.* It was only a clearing that they led us across. Now they are disappearing into the fog.

Oh dear, Jane said, I do sometimes wish we had lived in the days when one didn't have to bother so much about the masses; having a genius hanging round one's neck is really more than enough for one person. You ought to think of yourself more, Ruth. You should write. You know the doctor actually ordered Lawless to write, and apart from the cure he is doing quite well.

I would still be thinking it might be some use for something.

Well that's perfectly natural, Jane said. I keep all my sketches even the bad ones. I can never show them because of Julian but I go on making notes. One day, I tell myself, I shall know perhaps why I've been doing these things. I do understand though. I wanted a holiday alone so much. I needed it so. It was a mistake having this house even if we did get it for nothing. I wish we could see more of you but you can't imagine.

Oh but I could. Jane was so drained. It was only her snobbishness that carried her through. Through Julian she knew she belonged to the few and that was the best you could do. And however much she hated the bogus ones she would go to Borodin's too if Julian was in the mood, or even to see the colonel who made peach brandy because in Calanques that was the best you could do.

I do understand, she said. It's ghastly being bottled up with these phoney people. We must go for a walk in the pines. We must escape before Kate gets here and begins to insist that we all have a good time. She always has a good time however hopeless things look. What upsets me most is these mannequins. Every girl is a mannequin from Paris. Lawless has one. They simply terrify me.

I looked again at Jane. She was charmingly dressed. She wore a sarong to the beach, but whatever she wore it always carried a shade of her student days. A shade of the Slade was written all over her. I wondered what might be written all over me? Something written in invisible ink that made me very nearly invisible.

We opened a gate in the wall of the arid street. A path under plane trees led to the great empty house with shuttered windows and steep slate roofs. We pulled a bell beside the door and an old lady opened it. Her dark eyes searched us.

We heard that one might gather some of your beautiful flowers, Jane said.

That's true, the old lady said, Two francs fifty.

Jane paid her. You would like some scissors, the old lady said, now smiling and full of interest. She hurried away and returned with some rusty scissors. That will make it easier for you, she said.

The garden had an unexpected depth. It was wild with shrubs and large trees shaded it, and behind the trees stood the sea like a wall of mirror glass. There were flowers but they had to be looked for.

Isn't it quiet, Jane said. I wish we could get away somewhere. Go for a walk in the pines or out in a boat. Don't take the morning glories they droop too soon. The bougainvillea is really useless too.

Under a pool of blossoms a crooked finger moved. Round the Cap Rouge the wind sickled the shallows. The sea was a bitten mirror. The mistral again. I must fly, Jane said. I'm afraid it's getting late.

Pressy looked at his watch. A writer must keep regular hours, he said. But he was happy today. He was wearing a beautifully faded and patched suit equal to Borodin's. The sound of his words made him happy. He frequently stopped to say. It's Tchehovian don't you feel? I feel that this familiarity will shorten my dinner hour.

But perhaps you don't read Tchehov? You should you know, and he took up a book that was lying conveniently near. Pressy fingered the book till a card fell out. Not a view of the Lido nor an invitation to sherry in a mews, but the blue membership card of the Communist Party. Oh, there's my card, he said.

The class struggle! That we should have come to this.

Mabel banged out a line with black crosses.

Take another sheet, Pressy said, like Hanadune, with mock severity. Tresmond and Hanadune had reached the Cote d'Azur. Tresmond was Pressy. The public of course would miss the point of it all but he hoped the story would be a best-seller. Then he and his friends would have the thrill of exhibiting themselves to the public that missed the point.

Lunch time was late. Emile was there already in the alcove, smoking a cigarette. He had laid out the net and the black combs and the pins on a clean towel over the *bidet*. He bade Madame sit down in front of the basin, threw a white cape over her shoulders and pinned it under the chin. *Voilà,* he said. Now we are all set. He lifted her hair with a comb and peered at it, frowning. Madame has neglected her hair, he said.

It may be the perm, he said. There are times when the hair will not resist a perm. Like the blonde I did yesterday. They would walk out of the shop if one questioned them, yet afterwards one gets all the blame. But even the best perm has to be looked after. The sea air is bad and the bathing is very bad.

His competence was catching. I arranged the hairpins in bunches of three to be ready the very moment he whistled for one. His fingers' quick movements made his talk confident. There will be the war, he said. He pressed down a curl that didn't belong in the pattern. I shall not be sorry, he said. It has to come. He snipped off the curl.

He'd been patient till now. *Hein voilà des bêtises,* he said. We belonged to the union and inside three months we were all *foutus.* All except the leaders up at the top. What can you do? The life is like that. One has to make a way in the world somehow. *Il n'y a que ca.* Now I should like to speak English. In Marseilles I should run a private service to the big liners that stay in port for the day. I should attend the ladies in their cabins for hairdressing and cosmetics. These on the liners are the *dames chiques.*

Emile might even speak English. He might steam his life away in curtained *cabinets* following his cosmopolitan dream, but he would never be a first-class *coiffeur.* His hands were too hard and his pale round face under the bushy hair was a peasant's face. A pity he couldn't know. He had such a feeling for doing the right thing.

Tout à fait chic they are. *Les femmes du monde.*

A *petite fille* might do to pass the time but the *femme du monde* was his illusion.

A pity that we have such different illusions. I was looking for the proletarian and realism, needed it so, as Jane would say. Emile, so business-like, is not realistic *au fond.* I am material for his stupid illusion. Everything has been under false pretences.

You won't come here any more will you?

But why? We amuse ourselves.

It's immoral.

Emile, more tolerant now, develops the joke. *Tiens,* perhaps you are thinking of your husband? That's funny under the circumstances, he said. Why do people come to Calanques then?

The pins were all in place. He arranged the net. He was satisfied with his work. And now a little patience while it dries. I could see in the mirror that he was very tired, standing leaning against the wall, smoking.

But when will you lunch? I don't like this at all. Listen Emile, I want to be honest with you. I am not a rich *anglaise* amusing herself.

Not amusing yourself? He laughed very loud.

Indeed no. I work, I swear I do. And because I am poor and want to be honest, let me pay for your lunch or something as a comrade, a friend.

Eh bien, you don't amuse yourself.

Talking into the mirror I looked like a governess in the net. Talking into the mirror I noticed Emile was angry.

He threw his cigarette out of the window. I must be going, he said. You may keep the net and the pins, that's a small matter. Be sure not to take them out before it's dry.

Au revoir, then Emile. Goodbye. Very much luck.

It was clean and fresh, the shampoo and being so honest, and being asleep in the cool draught from the window.

I wake. I am Mabel. I tie a handkerchief over my damp hair and run through the blinding sun to Pressy's house. He's been working himself up.

You've come, Miss Er, he said.

One must have just a little time to oneself. For a swim or anything. It isn't quite a business arrangement is it, so it should be a friendly one.

And have not relations been friendly? Haven't I introduced you to my friends? You've been treated absolutely as an equal. I should have thought my book would come before your bathing, he said, sadly. He was acidly sad. I've been looking over your typescript Miss Er. The punctuation is not my punctuation nor is it an improvement on mine. Editors won't stand for that sort of thing and I'm afraid I can't either. I'm awfully sorry to have to tell you this—

So goodbye sweetie pie, Mabel said. (Better than being paid.)

The lifeless wind passed down the empty street, sucking at Persian blinds, sucking your life away. At three o'clock only an outcast is out in the empty town. Another one sits in the café staring out over a green drink and not even pretending to write a letter. A student staying at Borodin's love pension. Just the handsome healthy young person who should be socially conscious. But now she is shapeless, her face streaming with tears; she is quite dissolved in anis and amour.

But being alone in the café is something between us. I accept an anis de loso. I accept. I understand. Life was not quite right and this led to being informal in a basement in Bloomsbury. The *grand soleil* gilded Carlitos and Emile. Then the mistral picked at the raw romance. Something was wrong and anis gave it a name.

She told me at once that Carlitos had thrown her over. It wasn't that he'd thrown her very far. She'd only been about a week in Calanques. Carlitos, a diluted Andaluz with a plucked moustache, lived at Borodin's too. He really ought to be fighting in Spain, I said.

But Jocelyn, that was the poor girl's name, said, Carlitos could never be on any side. He's an artist through and through.

Nobody went to the café where Carlitos had done a magenta and yellow bullfight. But in return for the second drink I said, You'll get over it in time.

As if I had used a whip the tears sprang out again. But all these days I shall have to stay here. To see him every day with somebody else. She couldn't leave because she had come to look after a friend, a little art student known as the pudding-faced virgin who had never before been abroad.

Don't leave me, have another, stay, she pleaded. But having

another drink meant waking the old waiter who dozed uncomfortably on a straight chair. No nice and normal person needed another drink. Let her drip alone in the café. She had never even heard of the working classes.

I strode off down the street. The tall creature who met me in the mirror looked purposeful and rather *distinguée* today. She was perfectly visible—at least to me.

At the door of the *coiffeur* Emile was standing, pale as wax, taking a breath of air. He made a move to go in but approaching with sure steps, the purposeful person grasped him by the arm. Listen Emile, you may take me to dinner tonight to that nice little place you spoke of. We shall talk, we shall understand.

A voice sounded loud and harsh in the empty street. The *patron* peered round the wax bust of a lady.

I regret. It's impossible, Emile said quietly, hurriedly. That, no Madame. I regret. He lowered his voice, he feared a scene in the street. I regret. I could speak to you at another time if you wish.

No, not at all. It has no importance at all.

So what? So nothing. Another few drinks with Jocelyn. These opportunities seldom come when you need them. Jocelyn is strong, good for the whole evening. A pity one can't drink more than a certain amount.

Something is being dredged up from the bottom. Take care of the rocks. The knocking, the rocks. On my skull knocking and knocking. The whole street is awake. They are waiting to take me. Whistles under the window. Blanche Neige has started up. It is late, very late.

Emile is standing under the street light. The door is closed. Go away. You can't come up.

Very well. And my shoes Madame?

I threw the horrible shoes down into the street. One of them fell in the gutter and Emile dusted it on the sleeve of his jacket.

I closed the shutters tightly and locked the door.

FRIDAY—Calanques: The old waiter has retired and left me alone with the Midi. Today there is nothing about Spain in the news. In the bustle of the office we did not notice this stinking silence. Yes. Spain has been buried even before it was dead.

Duke, the American, sat down beside me. You're out early, he said. This was just a concession to my mode of living, for day and night were about the same to him. He was asking Moira to marry him yesterday, but nobody minded Duke. You accepted his invitations, then when you'd finished the drink you got up and walked away.

I'm going to town for a little business, he said. I mean we're going. Would you care to come along?

A little business. He was dressed very nicely for the excursion but his bleached and ruined face contradicted the silk shirt and pale blue tie. One day soon it would happen. The pale blue tie would be covered with blood and dust.

Let's you and me go to town, it's pretty dead in this little dump.

Duke is rather a grim joke. It is rather tough that everyone accepts his invitations. But in Marseilles are cheerful trams and the shops, and the white cathedral opening sea routes. To go on a journey does it matter with whom? *En voyage.*

I change into a linen suit and a shady hat. Going to town with a ghost. But I am rather tough. You see, I am going away, I say to the room.

Duke had had a few picons at the bus stop café. Was he more drunk? He was exactly the same; a chatty spectre.

We had the best seat on the bus, next to the driver. Crossing an arid plain with rocks on the horizon Duke tried to explain to him that it looked like the Rocky Mountains. The sour-faced driver smiled tolerantly. Even he knew that Duke was a spectre.

Then Duke told his new girl he was looking for someone to love. Some loving baby to care for and marry.

But at the American Express in Marseilles he plummeted into an ugly row with the clerk. The polished frightened clerk, not sure if Duke was drunk or a millionaire, sent for the manager. But while they waited Duke never let up, his insults tore at the clerk who stood at his post behind the counter, trembling. He was not afraid so much of physical violence as of the devil that tore this tourist corpse.

I waited outside in the street out of the way of the corrosive flow. Pressy's more diluted unpleasantness had the same effect, like acid poured on a wound. Everyone had a wound and people were waiting to pour out acid. They actually searched for occasions.

In the street a crowd had collected. A wine cask had rolled off a van and burst open, and the wine ran in the gutter and stained the stones red. The passers-by stopped and looked, and said something droll about it. They were made happy and excited by the waste of wine.

Presently Duke came out. Christ, he said. And then like an echo, Christ. Almost apologising. So after all nothing had happened. One could not remember how the storm had arisen. Perhaps the Express was wrong. There was this affront to human dignity, but technically he may have been right. He hadn't had another drink since Calanques.

Innocent bright shops glowed in the green shade of the Canebière. Beautiful shoes. Oh stop a minute Duke. *Merde alors,* I left my money at home.

But the loving baby had suffered a sinister change. Say, that certainly is a coincidence. The dame I had along the last time, this April had all her money in the bank too.

The note was there in the lining with the lipstick. Now don't be mean. See it's all right. I found it.

Well and so you have. Now isn't that real funny. The other

dame too. It's this way. I can be real mean when I want to. He told me about how mean he could be.

But now the storm had blown over. Well what are we waiting for? Let's go eat. He took my arm. There was no getting away.

Along the port the white tables were spread, and the shining sea and the ships. There was *bouillabaisse* and a cool *sauternes*. No doubt Emile, wearing for town his white and tan shoes, had often been refreshed, passing by this heaven, where the white cloths and the salads and the *femmes fatales* were spread ethereal in the shadow of the awning.

The *garçon* placed the dish before us in triumph. But already the sunshine was darkening and the wine turning sour. Duke was fidgeting with the knives and napkins. The *garçon* was taking his time, Duke's time. The manager came and all the civilisation of the benign white cloths and careful crockery was shattered.

I had to go. Where on earth had one to go in Marseilles? I looked up the address of an American dentist.

The office of Dr Schwartz was in a quiet solid street. I figured the incubus would get tired of waiting outside. But it rang the bell and came along in the lift. The lift man was from Brooklyn he said. And for this or some other reason, before we were half way up, he and Duke appeared to be old friends. At every crack Duke looked at me over his shoulder. (You see I'm quite normal and a good mixer.)

Madame could have an appointment for next week. Wednesday at two? That would be quite convenient. Wednesday is central, far away in the middle of next week. Not an outstanding day. Wednesday embedded in the unlikely future.

Duke was kidding with the next appointment, an immaculate girl who said she was from Wisconsin. She was smiling across to me. (We know your boy friend has had a few drinks.) Duke suggested a party for the evening. The girl said that certainly would be swell. Duke looked at me. (You see you got me wrong. I am the good sport and the old-timer.)

But any minute now he'd be over the edge. The husband of the girl entered the room and was formally introduced. In a moment or two in this formal and friendly room there would be a miniature hell of feelings in chaos. I ran down five flights out to the street.

It was pleasant out in the decorous street in the respectable drone of afternoon traffic. The long afternoon spread out under the plane trees. Nothing could be safer and saner for a quietly dressed and *sérieuse anglaise* than to do a little shopping and then to sit down in a big noisy café, and make up her mind what to do while she drank her coffee slowly. Whatever made me buy those shoes though. How silly the open toes will look on a suicide.

She paid for the coffee and walked briskly away. But on such a fine day to go into the dark, the enclosed place. But here you see it is always a fine day. I might miss the bus back. Yes, bus. I hate a close shave for a bus or a train. A sign of old age they say.

I returned to the same table and ordered another coffee. The waiter there might never have seen me before. He was too old for surprise. People are passing along the sidewalk, that is it. I might get interested in the picture and miss the black sailors, brown sailors, widows, all kinds of people. I drink my coffee. Nearly an hour has gone by.

I find myself in the *ciné.* The lights are down. The air is thick and oppressive. I am sitting beside the dentist. You've neglected that tooth, he says, in a quiet conversational way, but I can still save it.

The film is beginning, an old unpopular film. It is called, *Pour Aller Jusqu'aux Cieux Il Vous Faudrait Les Ailes.*

It will take many hours of work, the dentist is saying. You shall see how frail the shell is, filled with gold.

A middle-aged lady leans across me. After this comes the feature I understand. Of course the little boy wants to see that.

But I've seen the feature. Must I see it again?

And then being a holiday one may expect an extra.

Yes—if we know what we want and speak together our request—

The lady takes the little boy on her knee. *A qui m'adresse-je?* she asks coldly.

Excuse me, the dentist says, nothing should be neglected, the teeth, the hair, the bust. You might have cracked that tooth. Think, you are quietly eating a little spinach then comes the jar, the crack, the smash—

It is not the thing for English ladies to sleep in the open street. I look at my watch. Nearly an hour has passed. I am unobserved, sitting up straight in the café, in the sunlight and the superficial noises of the street. I do not wish to leave. There is no future. Suicide plans are meaningless. If it were Julian I would be telling him to join the party or go to the dentist's and get at the root of the trouble. But Julian is a fool. He is not distraught. He searches for a biting sorrow in vain. The dull stress of politics is oppressive, but he will never get to the point of departure.

There are *ennuis* but no immediate reason. I am invaded by a malaise that is like the toothache before it has settled into its proper tooth. The feet of the passers beat out sentences. The sentences pass. They do not have any connection with what is the matter.

There are no facilities in Calanques. The Cap Rouge bulges, smooth to the sea. No one would wish to roll down a bulging slope. No one would wish to be ridiculous. A hot and tiresome walk to the communist rock. I always turn back when we reach the edge of the village. A maze of burning paths ends in rocky fields and dusty enclosures. Suspicious faces look over stone walls. They say there are wonderful walks once you get out of the town. We must go to the pines. One day we will escape and go to the pines.

An hour and a half has gone by. A family of Spaniards sit down at the next table. I drink in the words of the Spaniards. They do not smudge grief like anis and picon. Their words, Ahora, Lástima, give form and some decency to despair.

I turn to the Spaniards. I smile at the little Spanish girl and her mother.

We are refugees, the mother says, Señora. Yes Señora, we are refugees from the Reds.

They were Fascists then. I left the café at once and walked quickly to the square where the bus waited. The afternoon was over. Nothing could be more sane than to sit in the bus until it was ready to start. Something unspeakable surely had happened to Duke. He had it coming to him.

But just as the hour struck I saw him stepping across the long shadows of the square with his curious tightrope walk.

The reliable bus took the hills bravely. Market women were going home to their children. We are going towards the sentimental sunset. Duke talked of this girl. His greatest mistake thinking that dreams come true. She was all the girls this girl. She was Ruth. Now he was asking Ruth to marry him. To please forgive him and to marry him. Tears ran down his face, dark yellow in the sunset. He had come round the circle again.

Howard and his American met the bus. They'd arrived at midday and were waiting for the room. Of course. I was really thinking of leaving tomorrow. But Howard simply couldn't hear of that. We'll find you something, he said. Who's here in Calanques? Nobody, Jane says. Oh nonsense. They get like that from being married. Marriage is a mistake isn't it Glory? The American, Gloria, exhibited perfect teeth and generous dimples. Well now, sit down with Glory and have a drink. She's just off her lecture tour. She came to Europe with a message of peace and goodwill. I must say they do these things well in the States.

Howard soon came back. He liked for Glory to see he was competent. Everything is arranged. There's a great big cellar and a camp bed at Jane's. I know about Julian and his complexes, it's absurd. Jane encourages him. It's a sin to waste the cellar. I'll carry your suitcases over after dark.

I packed your grips, Gloria said. The owner wanted to come and fix the room. —The suitcases stood open everything tumbled inside. —Howard will fix you a drink. I must take a shower.

I'm afraid there might not be one, Howard said. And in these parts we usually drink in the café.

She splashed in the alcove. The drain gulped and groaned. That was swell, she said. She paraded about the room, nude, hard as pink marble.

She loves the room, Howard said to me at the door. She says it's full of atmosphere. The landlady put up the price a bit though, and all because I arranged for a shakedown in the passage. Really fantastic. Still it's worth it I suppose.

Oh yes, it is worth it. The sheets have been changed, the room has been cleaned, and everything is ready to start again.

SATURDAY—Calanques: It is pleasant to wake in this cool cellar, that has no features, that is not secretive, that will let you live. Subaqueous light comes through a glass door that opens into a deep walled yard. This forgotten yard, strewn with tins and papers, is like the bottom of a dried-up well. On a table near the door, pale in a blue jug, our big bouquet presides.

The tap was running listlessly in the kitchen. Jane was leaning on the sink. Oh Ruth! This Freudian-looking fish has been delivered. Aren't the French devilish! Imagine delivering a fish at this hour. And now I shall have to do something about it before it goes bad. What have we done to them? Why can't they leave us alone?

I helpfully offered to go for the rolls and milk. When I got back Howard and Gloria were there. They had brought rolls and milk. They would come every day, Howard said. It would be much jollier to have breakfast together. Glory would take a turn at it of course. She could do some wonderful stunts with popcorn and things.

Jane looked as if she were going to cry, but then Paul came running into the kitchen. Under his tan he was blue about the lips. Jane said he suffered from the mistral. All day he seemed happy enough, but in the morning he appeared with the face of an old man.

We carried our breakfast to the untidy salon. It was getting warm. Already the butter was melting. Julian was in bed so we had to be quiet. After we'd finished eating we sat on round the table, knocking ash into empty eggshells and getting on each other's nerves. This simply can't happen again, Jane whispered.

A loud tooting outside uprooted us and we threw open the shutters, letting in the sun on the dusty room. I'm particularly proud of this horn, Kate said. We stood round the car, outside the house she had taken, next to Jane's. We admired the enormous old-fashioned Renault Kate had bought for the trip and would leave in France for future holidays, and Kate herself, brown and business-like in dark glasses, her hair all covered with a red spotted handkerchief. Darlings isn't it absurd! she said. She was glad we enjoyed the monster. She dexterously edged it into a side road.

We slept in a barn, she said. She had brought two young men with her, though she hardly trusted Julian's view of Calanques. Both the young men were blond. Otto was a dream of an Aryan. Ivan had large eyes, ethereal freckles and dishevelled hair. His mother was a Russian, Kate said. Otto and I picked him up on the road. He was walking somewhere.

Otto opened the house and carried the luggage inside. He opened the windows on to the balcony.

We'll lunch out at one of the Calanques, Kate said. The village is named after these Calanques you know. Otto'll arrange it.

Jane began to explain about Julian but Kate knew. He wants to get back to the womb. We must go for some walks.

How will that help? Jane asked, but Kate waved the unworthy joke aside. Till twelve then, in the square. The door closed on Kate and her young men.

What a breath of fresh air she is, Jane said. Still she might do Julian good. She does sometimes. She's overdone it though with the refugee Otto. He looks like the things they have on the fronts of cars. But I must fly. I forgot to get Julian up. The wind is rising again. It's going to be ghastly.

Under the wind the beach seemed a battlefield strewn with brown bodies. I stepped my way across them, looking for Paul. He was sitting beside the French girl and her knitting. She was a paragon of silence and industry. Let's have a talk, he said, she won't understand a thing.

Let's play something. Don't you want to play something Paul? We built a house of rough stones for three small and innocent-looking pebbles. We looked through a chink in the roof. There wasn't a sound inside, the floor was spotted with sunlight and three little pigs were huddled there in the shadow.

Paul was entranced. He didn't notice that people had moved away and stood in a knot at the other end of the beach. And when we got there to see what it was it was a tall man lying out on the sand stretched to the sun with a handkerchief over his face. And everyone was saying, What is it? What is the matter? All sorts of answers circulated slowly. A cramp, a heart failure.

Then why don't they do something for God's sake?

All sorts of answers circulated slowly. Perhaps they might if a doctor had been here.

Why don't they do something for him?

At last the answer circulated slowly. The doctor had been. He was dead.

In the centre of the circle the man lay, quiet and confident, and very brown in Jansen swimming trunks.

Why don't they do something?

Who is in charge of this?

An English voice said, They ought to do something. It's disgusting leaving it here on the beach. Here where people are bathing, the voice said.

The man who'd come with the ambulance shrugged his shoulders. Can't be removed without a permit, he said.

People were gathering up their gear and leaving. In a minute or two the beach was entirely empty. The sun shone down, the wind flicked over the sand. The solitary sun bather, very brown, with a handkerchief over his face, had the beach to himself.

The clock struck twelve. Will he stay there all through lunch time? Paul asked.

Jane and Glory were in the back of the car with Lydia, the lonely Borodin woman. How had it occurred to Kate to invite her? She didn't look crazy at all today. Perhaps she is not crazy. Perhaps we are none of us crazy.

Across the square Soskia sits in her off-white Bugatti. Kate's queer car is really much more chic. As she lets in the clutch Kate says, Poor old Soskia. That millionaire man she was going to marry failed at the last moment.

Just another of these Paris models but peddling art and culture. As the car moved off I waved condescendingly to Soskia.

We stopped to pick up a boxer and a musician. I hoped they'd still be here, Kate said. She had given Julian the lie already by producing without any effort a boxer and a musician. Where had they been all the time? They'd been living in a tent on one of the Calanques.

Kate left the car before a dry crumbling house on a rocky plateau where the side road ended. Unpack and carry the things, Otto said. The boxer stretched out his huge arms. I'll carry Kate. This is the Grande Calanque, the best of the lot for swimming. Just look down there.

We could see the roots of the rocks lying in bottle-green water. Below the path the land fell away in an avalanche of sharp stones. The plateau and path were strewn with raw stones as if building operations had been abandoned there. The rocks had a blighted, excavated look. Behind the road the communist crag rose bleak on the blue. It did not drop to the sea, it was not impressive. It would have been no great adventure to climb it.

The skimpy beach was empty today. The sun beat to and fro between the dazzling rocks. The waves of the open sea were smoking under the wind, but inside the Calanque it was still as stained glass.

Only at long intervals the edge of the water raised itself slightly and coiled again round the bearded amphibious boulders that anciently guarded the shore.

The boxer and Otto dived from a high rock.

They seem eagles flying, Lydia said timidly.

You really have to hand it to Kate, Jane said. Doesn't it make you feel grand to be sharing a real boxer. Unfortunately his physique is too startling for anything but curiosity appeal, but from the top of the rock he's superb.

The boxer and Otto dived again and swam away out to the open sea. The rest of us breast-stroked in the placid water. Howard accompanied me. He accompanies you. He carries your bag or your gloves like a good retriever. To Howard all activities are only an excuse for conversation. But perhaps we wrong him. Of course he is thinking of marrying Gloria and he finds it easier to unbosom himself in the water. He is often thinking of marrying somebody but he does want to make sure. Kate hasn't taken to her, and Kate is always so nice about other women. Gloria's vitality frightens her, he said. We're all so over-civilised—all of us. And then you know what Kate is.

Kate had been rather unfaithful to the Party, and Howard implied that she was a social climber. But honest Kate is not a climber, she spreads. She is always benefitting unlikely people. It's true she occasionally acquires a brilliant bargain in refugee professors for her parties, but most of her finds are obscure but interesting and political younger men. She always has enough girls at her parties. They are political too but do not turn out to be interesting to the men. Kate can hardly be blamed for that.

Gloria is still a virgin you know, Howard said, as though that might explain Kate's antipathy. Oh hell, I'm on one of those prickly rocks again. This is a horribly dangerous place to swim. American ideas are strange to us, he said. You all find it amusing that they should send over someone rather glamorous for putting over Peace. (Howard is pleased with his Americanism.) But you needn't think she's merely a glamour girl. For one thing she's much more socially conscious since I had her in hand. She agrees with me now that Pacifism is only a blind alley. You must not think that just because she's so lovely—and she's very young, well, hardly awakened yet. Howard, one gathered, would stage a general awakening.

The glorious gawk, sumptuous in satin lastex, was spread on a lilo, just too lazy, she said. But after Otto and the boxer were back, she rose and took an angry run at the water. She threshed up the Calanque like a paddle boat. Like a beautiful white leviathan, Kate said.

She used to swim a lot in Florida, Howard said.

How awfully tiring for you, Kate said. Gloria, rather blown, couldn't reply. Jane, Lydia and Ruth smiled. We were putting out little feelers, but we knew we were only for show. Improved wax models that could sit in the sun without melting. Lilos would have been better space value. Gloria had usurped Kate's and turned her pink haunches to the sun and was ordering Howard or Otto or someone to oil her.

What say we all go exploring, the boxer said. But just behind the beach the Calanque ended in a curious grotto that looked like a navel.

I think I'd rather stay here, Kate said. I don't feel comfortable under overhanging rocks. Something Freudian. But aren't we awfully hungry? So we straggled back to the house to buy red wine for our lunch at a trestle table under a pine.

This is great, the boxer says. The boxer looms across the table, his face a bronze full moon over balloons of muscle. He has a cauliflower ear, wide wondering eyes and an Irish voice. Without any preamble he falls into earnest conversation with Otto. My girl Milly, he is telling Otto, lives at Stepney a hell of a long way out and then in addition to that she lives with her aunt. Of course I have to be ever so nice to the aunt and so I never seem to get on to Milly. You can see how it is.

Otto was weighing up the boxer the aunt and Milly. Otto's hair and flesh are dark burnished blonde and in this setting his eyes are strangely bright and hard like water under a bright light, almost white. Jane knew he'd had himself lacquered. She was perfectly sure that he was a film actor.

Otto ponders. You'd better come to Paris, he says. You'd like it.

I doubt if I would, you have to know the ropes.

Come to Paris. What ropes?

I wouldn't know how to go about it. What about if you get landed with something?

Otto shrugs, deprecating the boxer's dullness. Not that kind of women. Why should it ever occur to be in a hopeless situation like that?

But how would you meet them? the boxer wants to know.

Anywhere, Otto says, spreading his hands. You meet them, exchange ideas—there may be a sympathy—

Just like that, the boxer says doubtfully.

And anyway, Otto says, with a glance round our party from his sea-white eyes, does one exist only for women?

But Paris is rather different, I said. For one thing you always do meet someone you know. I might have been one of the buzzing flies on the table. Otto's golden profile was for the boxer. They returned to the beach together.

Your refugee is terrific, I told Kate.

Not mine, Kate said modestly. He just came down with me for a few days. He runs that political nightclub in Paris you know.

How should I know. Everything goes so fast. I've been busy hammering out propaganda. And then I haven't been away since . . .

Kate dispelled the silence. It's a *boîte de nuit* with political satires, extremely lively and chic. A refugee artist does the *décor*—Trotskyist.

Gloria who had refused to settle down and was passing across us, announced in her amplified voice: Everyone's going Trotskyite this season.

Isn't she unbelievable, Kate said. You'd almost think she'd had her lines written for her, she's so like that daffy girl you see on the films.

Howard says she has the American innocence—a kind of purity, Howard thinks.

Pathologically pure, Kate said. But that remark was painful to poor Howard. He never errs or strays from the Party Line. The other day I phoned him to come to a party. What party? he said. You know how he bleats on the phone. Which party? What is it for? But perhaps I shouldn't be talking like this—to you.

It doesn't much matter, I said.

Aren't we going on anywhere? Gloria boomed. It's real hot sitting around in the sun. Say Kate—

Yes, you'll have to be careful. It isn't like Florida. And one of Kate's quizzical looks sent her away. She threshed up and down between our basking bodies. This was not Florida decidedly and it looked as if she'd be stuck for the day with Howard. But no, she had raised the boxer up from the sand. They are off for a walk, she announces.

But at this time of day—Howard said. Already they were off tackling the rocks. Howard turned on his stomach resignedly.

He's an awfully nice creature, Kate said. A pacifist too.

Howard turned on his back and covered his face with a towel. We were taking off swim suits. Do stay here with me, Kate said. Try some of this—non-greasy—I used it for ski-ing. She had turned down her suit to the waist and arranged herself to the best advantage. Her legs were perfect, but she had to be very careful about brassieres.

We stretched ourselves to the sun. The musician had left the beach and lay under a pine tree, reading, and Ivan was sleeping with his mouth a little open and his small *retroussé* almost transparent nose, pale in the shade. Like something in an aquarium, I said.

But Kate was not very interested in the Russian. She was rather worried though about the musician. Frustrated, she feared.

Kate is a great believer in proper sex life and had it of course as well as everything else. No one would grudge it her, she works very hard. She supports Abyssinia and China and Spain. And her husband who works very hard and supports Kate doesn't mind if it's on holidays and she spares him the details.

The musician appears to be perfectly happy camping at the beach with his friend the boxer, but Kate has a wonderful flair for frustration. One day she will take the musician for a walk and then she will get her teeth into his neuroses.

Otto, who's been trying to chat with Howard through the towel, gets up and kicks him on what Howard calls his tum. Howard uncovers his face and smiles feebly. Otto stands over him poking the tum with his foot. You swallow your football? he says.

Howard says, with a certain dignity, I work in the city. And then I have my political work too. I only get down to my cottage very rarely. It isn't as bad as all that either, it's only the size of a small water melon.

You should stay home and cultivate your garden, Otto says, like all good Englishmen. You permit I borrow your suntan mixture Kate?

Massaging his glistening shoulders he looks down upon Kate with critical interest. Her breast is escaping a little on either side. You are really somewhat deformed, Kate darling, he says.

Kate smilingly raises her head. It's funny, one can't hear well in these dark glasses.

You're a little deformed. But very nice, he says.

A stinging insult only stimulates Kate. *Tiens*! she says. They continue to talk in French, Otto's almost too cool and colloquial, impersonal as the headlines in the news, as the sound of the waves on stones. He knows that visitors love to speak French, and feel terribly cheated when even the barman won't. That people will go to great lengths to speak French on their holidays, even to swallowing the garlicky breath of a fisherman.

I hear Otto's story. Like all refugees he carries a story instead of a passport. His has the open-your-eyes-about-Russia stamp. It is neatly told. The usual escape from a Nazi concentration camp and a further escape with someone he refers to first as his wife, and later on as his friend. She gets a job in Russia, writes to him criticising the regime, and is never heard of again. I was so fond of her, he ends simply.

Perhaps he was. But I think now he is more fond of his story. The wife or the dear friend is only a peg for Otto's sacred hate of established stupidity.

It's really risky, Kate says in her motherly way. *L'Incendie* is so anti-everything. The last editor was found in the Seine. And no honour and glory. Otto lives at the top of a terrifying hive of workers' flats in the smallest and neatest room you ever saw. Everything is clean and shining, and the cooking pots hang behind a blue curtain. I was most *intriguée* to be admitted there.

Yes, it is thrilling. A life riddled with danger. But picture this brilliant creature alone now, coming back from the night club in the cold light, bringing in the milk bottles off the step, with a cheery word to the *concierge* who watches from his hole in the passage.

The little cell is neatness and perfection. One isn't very often alone there. Just at this hour it would be good to have someone, but not many men or women would care to share this kind of solitude. It is different in the daytime and when there are many.

He takes the folded copy of the new *Incendie* out of his pocket. With the latest news in his hand he looks out from his concrete eyrie at the cold light rising over Paris and Europe. He looks out over Europe and laughs. When the knock comes no wreaths from the Party. Only a wry smile for minority martyrs.

He lights the gas ring and takes down one of the aluminium pots that shine like mirrors behind the blue curtain. Behind the other curtain he hangs up his perfect suit. Before he lies down he examines the room. The *flics* have not been there. When they come, they will not find anything of importance. Otto's private life is of no importance. But more distinguished personages from the *Deuxième Bureau* have visited the cabaret with their mistresses. Sitting in the shadows they enjoyed the show, and the crazy creature who can laugh and dance while they hold the thread of his life in a dossier. It's something that's beyond any understanding.

Kate quivers over the cooking pots and the blue curtain. Tears rise to her eyes. But I fancy our pity is inappropriate. I think if pity had visited him in his neat room he would set to work to clean up after it.

And it's so true, Kate is saying. They pretend it's only temporary, but one can't afford to take a false step on the edge of a precipice.

Otto explains. He's immensely well-informed. Everything is so clever in French. But you don't hear very well in these dark glasses. You hear *bien entendu*, but it's like the French headlines, the French proletariat, the sun on the waves of the stones. It's like the masses . . . the great heart of the masses . . . the great simple rubbery form of the boxer. . . .

But I was putting on the record for the visitors. All our chattels were spread out on the lawn. The gramophone—two gramophones luckily. For the special record there was a needle that branched out at the end like a small comb. This was to reproduce the sound of waves. I was just putting it on when Otto said, Things are beginning to slip.

I looked down the slope to where the old house was and the usual trees behind it. I couldn't see anything. We began to collect the paraphernalia. The rackets, cushions, lilos, tea-things, the gramophones and records scattered all over the grass, in little groups where people had been sitting. Fortunately there was an old tin bath in the shrubbery. Each holding one end we carried it, stopping to fill it with all the odds and ends. There was a suitcase too, but no handles at the ends to grip it by. But we found another and went from spot to spot collecting the paraphernalia of the party.

Oh stop a minute Otto. I am slipping, I'm going to fall. Otto is threatening, stretching above us, crying that we are deformed. . . .

I didn't mean to wake you, Kate said. I was only covering you. A towel is enough. It might be the beach patrol. There's a fifty franc fine for nudism on the beach and twenty-five for immorality.

The higher fine for us, Howard said. To catch the stupid English— they can always pay.

A boat was crossing the mouth of the Calanque. The men on her waved their caps and called a greeting. Otto sprang up and waved a white towel.

Bloody fool, said Howard. But nothing happened. The boat passed out of sight. Now though, we were all awake, our bodies parched and tea suggesting itself. We began to collect our wits and our scattered possessions, and Jane remembered a date with the colonel so we dragged ourselves dizzily over the blazing rocks. Howard carried the lilo. It wriggled and flopped coquettishly on his shoulder. Why are Englishmen always ridiculous? Jane wanted to know. What could be sillier than that measly polygot Ivan, yet he somehow is so sweet and pathetic—like Paul.

The boxer and Gloria waited beside the car. Gloria looked like a spent peony. The boxer had thought she wanted to go for a walk and dragged her up to the top of the communist crag. We had a jolly good laugh too, the boxer said, when she tried to sit down on one of them red-hot rocks.

We settled back in the warm hum of the car, passing bands of bathers along the road. Our lazy talk was carried away and trailed behind us with the dust of the road. Phrases flicked in and out of patches of sun and shadow.

Why did they want to do that? Gloria said. The boxer, his friend and Otto were walking back. Didn't they want to come with us in the car?

Apparently not. They prefer to stride along in a cloud of dust with that Trotskyite wrecker. Oh really, Jane said, don't be so childish Howard. Can't the Party think up some new term of abuse?

And Lydia opened her mouth at last to say, Is it this beautiful man has something wrong?

Oh no, Jane said, lowering her voice and looking at Kate's back. People are so puerile on holidays. Not wrong—only rather extreme. Though of course, as Kate says, with Russia behaving so queerly lately it *is* quite understandable isn't it? With everything being in such a hell of a mess the more extreme the better I should imagine. I'm sorry Ruth.

It doesn't matter, I said.

It does matter, said Howard. As for that chap he's a sort of political pimp.

Oh Howard, Gloria said. She'd been having some talk with Ivan sitting in front. Oh honey I made a kind of date with Otto. Maybe I should tell Kate. Will she be mad?

Be mad? My dear child what a fantastic idea! Oh hell! Why do people *never* bring cigarettes? I always take two packets for an excursion—that's reasonable I think.

It was only when Lydia was disappearing across the square that we remembered no one had looked at her bullet holes. How shockingly rude you all of you are, Kate said, I can't be expected to remember everything.

Jane is invited to tea with the colonel who has an estate and makes his own peach brandy. The colonel's wife descends to Calanques to shop. Her raffia-hatted children, mostly boys, sit in the back of the car while she enters the shops. She is dressed in white and carries a parasol, and she stares vaguely at the crowd as if it might still be an oriental bazaar. Her husband is occasionally seen at the café having a drink with Army and Navy friends. The invitation is an honour Jane says that she simply cannot face without my support.

We sit on a wide verandah and have tea and later the peach brandy. Handing the tea and curry sandwiches are two young men, Anglo-Indians with Edwardian moustaches like a *New Yorker* cartoon. Two of them make it stranger.

After the colonel has pointed out his peach trees and Paul has been rescued from under two of the colonel's boys, we take our leave with hollow promises and walk down the dusty road. We are soggy with peach brandy. The evening sky is a thick sticky grey.

At the top of the steep hill leading into the town we overlook preparations for Borodin's party. The trees are wired for lights; near the gate is a Bali mask in a pram and irrelevant objects peep through a hole in the hedge. Up on the roof the *pensionnaires* are wildly attempting to fix a festoon of frying pans, stuffed owls and cardboard constructions against the irrelevant wind which is rising again.

The café chairs are welcome. We describe the appalling comfort of those wide wicker chairs on the verandah. Kate, very cool in her corner says, That's him!

He doesn't come much to the café the real writer. Not a person like Lawless but a real writer. Julian says he's most disappointing to meet, but he introduces us all in his off-hand way, as though he can't recommend us much to each other, and the writer asks us what we are going to drink.

He is wearing a long-sleeved shirt and even a tie. He looks like a business man but that doesn't help. What makes him write? How does he work? That's what I have to know. Like a child who pulls the insides out of clocks because his questions haven't been truthfully answered, I greedily gaze on the white dial of the writer's face. What is it set for? What is the combination? When will the bell ring?

He has actually been writing on a pad. How absurd for an author! What can I make of that? We scribble on the marble tops of tables, even Julian scribbles on the tables, that is one of the things we have come to Calanques for. But the writer has brought with him this little pad that looks like an order book. I lean across Julian, read the word Calanques.

I recognise the word. Calanques. Calanques is on our lips all day. Calanques, the key word and we passed it by. It had crossed my mind: Calanques; a stone in a bottle. I may have thought, Calanques are calcareous and closed, scenes of excursions ending in narrow niches of hot rock. I have seen black ants suddenly multiply, trapped in a dry spot when the water rises. We teem on a barren land. Yes it is so. We crystallise round Calanques. Now I remember.

The writer is putting on his record for us. A very good record—he has made it himself. It is kind of him but I fear we are wasting time. Already the explanation is on its way. I have only to be there to receive it.

I hurry back to the cellar. Even Julian will be going to Borodin's. He'll be thoroughly drunk as he has to be at a party and very bitter about it the next day. But I shall have the cellar the whole night. Plenty of time, no need to worry at all.

But I can't help noticing the other camp bed pitched at a discreet distance from mine. On it a haversack and Ivan's guitar. Kate doesn't want him perhaps. Or she might think this a nice way of bringing us together.

But the whole evening at least. Plenty of time, no need to worry at all.

I sit down at the table, a little discouraged by the wan withered bouquet, find a sheet of paper and write in crayon, Calanques. That covers it. I am sure it is all there. It has only now to unfold like a Japanese water flower.

It does not unfold. Only a few phrases, none of them mine, float by. I have used other people's words so long. But the real words are near. Set a word to catch a word, Calanques. But the words sit on the fence, or like swallows fly in flocks to Spain, mocking from white walls. Behind them the Revolution, flattened and grey on a receding horizon.

At last I wrote: *Rien n'est vivant ici, rien n'est triste ou joyeux,* and crossed it out. Closed my eyes and the two young men with bland smiles and curious moustaches surged forward. What do they want? Why are they in my story? Will Victor appear? No, he is only dead. Otto is in the story. Julian and some women are on the edge of the story. The rock. Gloria floats past like a pale-fleshed water plant.

The wind is whining and clapping the shutters upstairs. How nasty for Borodin's party.

SUNDAY—Calanques: I awake to a wide pink vista, crossed by a strap, part of the *tenue de plage*, and a thin velvety arm.

But I can't help it honey, Ivan is saying.

But you must baby, Gloria says firmly, for both our sakes. Howard's your friend, sweetheart.

I cough and cover up my head with the sheet. The talk goes on. When I look out again they are still in the same position on the bed. I dress without attracting the slightest attention, wondering whether they or the bed will give way before they are discovered. I fly from the house to escape the horrors of breakfast.

Otto, fresh and bright as a new brass tack, is shaking a mat from Kate's front balcony. *Bonjour*, stop one minute will you? he says. A letter spirals down to me from the balcony. It must catch the first mail, and I have to arrange the house before Kate awakes.

Out of his sight I read the bold address. A baroness—a bogus baroness surely. But a liberal baroness is possible, old and broadminded, fond of young people. The political cabaret must try the police but it's chic and there's the baroness, what's to be done? But then perhaps—I picture her with a twinge, young and almost as beautiful as Otto. He dresses her up as a revolutionist, for the cabaret, in peasant prints, for a song.

But in case the letter is only to fool Calanques I drop it directly into the post office letter box before I take my usual place in the café.

My usual place. I have found a place on the edge of the lighted circle. Kate has made them move up a little for me. Poor Ruth! Losing poor Victor like that. And the way she throws herself into that party work. I know it does make a person rather dreary. . . .

My friends, my good friends. Howard and Gloria have asked me to go fishing. More exactly to go out with the fishermen in their boat. I can't see what fun the tourists get, Howard said, being so out of touch with the life of the village. Not Moira, I said. But both of them sniffed at Moira.

Today there is no news for me in the Midi except the eyes of a young girl condemned to life imprisonment by the Nazis. Her eyes look out from the muddy photograph, clear, with no doubt in them. I remember a German comrade who came to the office. He had nearly been thrown out of the Party even before the Nazis cracked down on him. He had almost taken his life because of his doubts. But being in prison he said, was a relief, because in prison he felt he was justified and so the punishment brought a strange reward.

Presently Gloria sits down with her baby typewriter prepared to be the lonely girl this morning. They all had rather a lot to drink last night and Howard thinks big drinking before lunch is bad taste, Gloria says.

To Howard's stomach it would be.

Gloria taps away disconsolately, sipping a double bock. She will drink anything at any time, even a litre or two of Howard's mother's blackberry wine to tide over a blind spot on a weekend.

But wasn't it a tough break, she said, for that poor guy, Duke, passing away like that right on the beach. From Baltimore too.

She tapped away very unhappily. She was thinking of Howard. He needs me so, she said.

Well marry him. You can always get a divorce.

But there's Ivan, there's the two of them, she said. She hasn't even invited me to a drink.

Well marry them both, you can always get a divorce.

But she thinks that marriage is something rather sacred.

Do you write? I ask. How do you find the time?

I promised a certain somebody I would when he gave me this machine back in Baltimore. Just any old ideas that come into my head. It's no good getting lazy on holidays.

After the necessary tea with Howard we stood a long time in the shop while a heap of crusty rolls and cheese and sausages rose on the counter, Howard pricing things in meticulous French, wondering how many kilos there were to a pound. He liked to have Gloria hear him speaking French. Next we bought beer. Always a handy thing in a boat, he said. They had made it up.

The battered black boat was manned by a worn young man, an old man with whiskers and a boy with a squint. With much cursing and spitting the engine was started and we plodded out through the swell. Howard and I found cleanish places to sit. Gloria perched adventurously at the prow. The coast spread out, the sun set, the puny villas along the parade lit up. The men threw over the anchor and silently doled out the long brown net. But aren't we going anywheres? Gloria cried. Say what a stupid little trip.

The moon rose. Howard, responsive to the moon, leaned over Gloria. Her lips were ready but he passed her by. His face crossed hers with a despairing look as he leaned a bit further; over the side of the boat. To have such mistaken feelings right on the brink of a kiss! But not only Howard is out of touch with himself. Remember the sad story of the *sportive anglaise* who nearly drowned on a sunny afternoon?

Howard, recovered a little, could laugh, and ask, almost with *sang froid,* How long do we stay? The fishermen, Italians, were indifferent to Howard's French, but after a miserable minute the old man held up two fingers.

Two hours, said Howard, sighing, that's what he means. *No poco poco presso?* Howard said.

The young man joined us holding up three fingers. Then the boy held up four and playfully squinted through them.

We were far from all help. We heaved and fell. Gloria sank to the bottom of the boat and lay there with her head on our luckless provisions. The young man grinned and pointed to the roof of the tiny cabin. It seemed natural and safe to lie there flat and abandoned to the sea. My stomach was beginning to stir softly, the feeling of setting out on a long journey. I was *en voyage.* I dozed.

The men sat in the stern silently smoking. Now that I had mastered the boat's rhythm I was once more in the right. I felt as much in the right as the fishermen the boat and the night, and I would have liked them to know.

But they were silent, their faces weathered by the moon-light to the smoothness of old stones on the shore. They seemed to be only a part of the boat and the night. A French sentence fell on them like a stone. I might as well have been throwing stones at the night. But I tried. I remembered a few of A Thousand Spanish Words that had never been of much use at the office.

Cielo? Cielo yes. We point to the sky.

La mar, yes *la mar.* The sea under the sky.

La luna, luna, luna. Aïe la luna.

The moon is beautiful, the young man said.

The earth too, I said.

Yes, yes, he said. The moon is beautiful.

They all waited and when I fished up a word they all pounced on it like hungry dogs. I fished up a word I knew for sure they would like. *Calamares.* Tough aliment of Mediterannean fishers. We chorused *Calamares.* Rich *Calamares.* And the old man added a blessing. Fried baked or stewed, I think he must have said.

Their faces lived now, dark in the white light.

Italia, beautiful, the young man said.

Emigrés, you, *emigrados,* yes? I said.

Emigrados yes.

La politica?

And this. The old man opened his mouth and pointed down inside with a hungry hand.

Fascismo not beautiful, I said.

The moon is beautiful, the boy said.

We fell easily into the swaying silence of the boat. We knew about each other all that we needed. But a bit later the young man fished a paper out of his pocket. The light was not strong enough to read it by. *Anarchismo* he said, while we all looked on and waited, *Anarchismo,* yes. The triumph of man.

Then they pulled in the net, cursing the poor catch and throwing offending fishes back into the water. Gloria, her hands folded, white and pure as Elaine in the moonlight, shuddered and moaned at the cold commotion of fishes. Howard still sat in the same place where calamity had overtaken him. It had overtaken him again and again.

But at touch of land they put on aplomb and Gloria snatched a water plant from the sea debris in the boat, a pale fleshy thing with a blind face. After the young man had handed us carefully to shore, Howard thanked him with a pat on the back. He called goodnight as we turned our backs on the boat. But the boy yelled out. He was standing on the edge of the quay, grinning, holding up our ambitious unfortunate parcel.

But the food is for you and your mates—for your kindness you know, Howard called, and we walked on a little faster.

In the first café he ordered double cognacs. We might have had them for a drink, he said. Were they politically conscious at all?

Not very, I said. A touch of *Anarchismo.*

You'd think they would be, wouldn't you, Howard said, a gulp of brandy chasing a reminiscence, the hellish lives they lead. It's strange too how these antiquated ideas live on in southern countries after they've been discredited everywhere else. Surely Anarchism is quite—

Washed up, Gloria said.

Sometimes I almost despair of the toiling masses, but—after another sip—we musn't despair. Just keep slogging away. I suppose you'll be wanting to make yourselves more beautiful for the dance. I suggest we dine decently at the Superbe. I don't feel we could face the Marine tonight.

The waiter ran after us to the door of the café, a superior smile on his face, dangling the sea plant.

Better leave it, Howard said. That sort of thing goes bad. But as we had brought it so far, pity for its stranded fleshy helplessness obliged me to take it.

And so tonight we dine at the Superbe and just as if by invitation, everyone else is dining there too. Our party is the centre piece at the Superbe and Julian of course is the centre of our party. The manager has brought him a basket of fruit. The head waiter is conjuring *crêpes* out of blue flames. All over the room there's a feeling that something is happening though no one has heard of anything but the dance. At present it's enough that Borodin and his gang are loudly misbehaving themselves in the corner, and the writer, alone, and very *distingué* in the wrong clothes, is struggling with his chop. Though there is no one very notable present, for some reason the French painters have none of them come to Calanques this summer, the patrons have settled down to enjoy Julian with his face of a tired young girl, elected by the manager to be the show piece at the dinner.

But the people nearest to him are not so happy. His prestige makes everyone near him feel snobbish. Some of us have heard his stories and seen his imitations of the Russian ballet, and so that our deference shall not be tinged with guilt we have to be always reminding ourselves of his talent. It's easy enough to forget. We go to see his paintings at exhibitions. They haven't painted themselves; Julian did them. Delving alone in his gloomy studios he mines these heart-rending colours and continues to be in public a bore and a pest.

Jane's anxiety spreads a circle round him. His peach is a little brown, he has pushed it aside. He has had one of his headaches all day. Ivan has bored him just before dinner. He is being very malicious about Kate. She is used to it though. She very often says, the more you do for people the more they despise you.

He disposes of Kate's young men. Ivan a fly-by-night. And Otto? One of these up-to-the-minute lefts. A straw in the wind. At the café he'd kept well out of range of Otto. More and more of his friends were political and he dreaded that they'd get him in the end. He always told interviewers he was an anarchist, till on one terrible day a card arrived expecting him to a small meeting at Clapham.

They'll get me yet, he said.

He likes the boxer though. Do come to my studio, he says. You must come to my studio and I'll show you some paintings.

And the boxer says, guying him rather, you come to my studio and I'll show you some boxing.

Jane winces. She is never allowed inside the studio. She is glad to change places with Gloria. Julian likes the big innocent lovely and over the first cognac they arrange for a lecture tour of the States together. But we must have a little song and dance first, to put the message across with, Julian insists.

Jane relaxes and takes out her powder puff. Julian will be going to bed soon. Howard is deeply grateful for his approval of Gloria. He shouldn't set too much store on it though. Julian has these fancies for what he likes to call real people, but he hasn't the stamina to carry them through. We know what happens when they turn up to tea. It may be partly Jane's perplexity that makes us mistrust him, but his genius and the wretched way he takes it have placed him for years in such a false position that none of us could judge him fairly now.

Tapping me on the shoulder, what a dreadful diversion, Pressy. I'd like a word with you later, Miss Brown, he said, rather solemnly. He had learned my name.

I had let everyone know about Pressy's behaviour.

Perhaps your friends and you naturally would join me for coffee later?

Then there was an advertisement in the *New Statesman* attributed to Pressy. Kate had taken the trouble to cut it out. Writer, young man, invites others, unconvent, anx. relax, inform, discuss polit. music, etc., to form circle Calanques. Atmosphere.

I think I've had the pleasure of meeting you? he said to Julian.

Very likely, Julian said, sniffing his second cognac.

Kate and Jane were running their eyes up and down the stripes of Pressy's blazer.

It turns a bit chilly in the evenings, he said.

Do tell us, Kate said, where you got the stuff. But don't tell us, of course, if you'd rather not.

Pressy reddened.

Kate dear, Jane said, can't you see you're treading on sacred memories?

Do forgive me, how stupid, Kate said. I'm only familiar with the ordinary ones, Eton and Harrow and those. Do forgive me. Of course I could see at once it was based on a blazer, but then you know you might have designed it yourself. And I had a very special reason for asking, so it's all Jane's fault really. You see, we're looking for something declamatory to cover a sofa in her studio.

Not in the studio, out in the hall, Jane said. But I'm rather afraid it might kill the carpet. What do you think, Ruth?

It is rather lethal, Kate said.

But I've always had a predilection for stripes.

It might be something Freudian, Kate said.

Pressy excused himself.

The dance in the square was for charity. *Mutilés de la Guerre*, the old war *bien entendu*, not the one we were waiting for. The lights and the band were exceptionally strong and the English caused great confusion by continuously pushing their way in and out of the enclosure for drinks. They were all there but Jocelyn, who had swallowed a bottle of veronal after our talk, and had not been feeling too good the last few days.

Kate was very quietly dressed in red and had her hair up in curls.

When I dropped into the *coiffeur* this morning I fancied he looked at me with disapproval. I regret, Madame, he said, but it's quite impossible. One of my assistants has just left. One of my assistants left without warning.

But Kate has her hair arranged in curls for the dance. Only this morning she said, most casually, I think I'll have it on top, and so it was, combed up from the neck and nesting there in curls. How lovely she looked!

Kate had discovered a little refugee *coiffeur*. Better and cheaper and in any case one should support refugees.

I am quite *bouleversée*. I cannot reply to Kate. Why had I not sought out the refugee *coiffeur* and been saved the henna and the false step?

Jane is shockingly down in the depths, Kate said. And Julian is resenting it so, that some of us are fairly healthy and normal. Poor Howard, just as I thought he was beginning to see reason had to go off and make his herb tea for his hay fever. He's been taking it over a year to my knowledge always just at eleven whatever else is happening before or after. It's something very Freudian I should think. And that false lambkin I picked up on the road is going all out for the pudding-faced virgin. Not that I mind the poor brat having a good time, but the girl was telling me she always went to North Wales till this year. I fancy flirtations at the Craig-y-Don end rather differently. I only want fair play. Do keep an eye on them.

Gloria's beauty blazed in a backless costume she told us was made of something quite new. Something perfectly sheer and uncrushable. She could hardly believe that there wouldn't be jitterbugging, but finally resigned herself to the old cheek-to-cheek with Ivan. He'd been dancing for long spells with the pudding-faced virgin, their bodies it seemed transfixed on the same pin, their eyes tranced, set on a far horizon.

An inspired idea, Julian said, but it doesn't allow for the curves. Not that it matters—like Christianity. Can't be carried out, but there's the ideal.

He found the dance so entertaining that he wanted to try it himself with Gloria, but as she seemed clamped to Ivan forever he amused himself on the edge of the crowd with some imitations of the Russian ballet, till the evening's cognac wore off and he had to go home.

Pressy still hung about. I say, he said, I just couldn't catch your eye. Shall we dance this? But perhaps on second thoughts we'd better not. The café would be more appropriate. I only wanted to offer you an apology.

Almost before we were off the dance floor he was pressing a crumpled fifty franc note on me. He must have been holding it all the time in his hand. Please take it, he said, or I shall feel so rotten. I do feel rotten you know. I know I was rude, I was feeling so awful about various things. And in spite of having a few nice friends here I don't always fit in. Perhaps I'm a bit more sensitive than I appear, and some people are rather heartless and hard. The way those girls set on me! But you're different I'm sure. You see I never fitted in at home either. My father's a butcher as a matter of fact. Not a bit socially conscious or anything. No rather sensitive person could be blamed for wanting to mix with intelligent people could they? And I had a tough time at first before the magazines began taking my things. It's popular stuff I grant you, but I always kidded myself I was above it. And then at last I did very well with—I expect you've read it—my first novel—a rather political one—

So you're another of us living off the state of the world, I said. But Pressy only wanted to finish his story.

I'd always thought how awfully nice it would be to holiday on the Riviera with a friend. It was just a little dream I'd always had. But everything went wrong. And just the other day I heard. My friend died of diphtheria in one of those filthy old towns in Spain. He hadn't even been near the fighting line. You ought to have seen me when I got the news. You can't imagine what it's like unless you've been through it yourself.

Now was the time to say something human.

Well but it does happen in a war, I said.

Oh, but don't you see? I ought to have been there with him. I feel such a fake. I doubt if I shall ever be able to write again. And I could certainly never go back to England. I might even have to exile myself out here. But I shouldn't be bothering you with my affairs when I only wanted to tell you how rotten I feel.

He waited. He expected me to say something human.

Don't mention it, Pressy, I said. I shall give the fifty francs to the Party funds.

Ivan was vacillating in our direction. He took me aside. My arm was wet with his tears. Have you seen Gloria? he said. She'll never forgive me. It's a hell of a mess. You see he's my friend, he said.

Who is your friend? I asked.

Howard. He helped me in Paris. He's the squarest and finest guy I ever met. It would have to be her. I'm in hell.

Well so is nearly everyone, I said. You ought to think of the class struggle and the people fighting in Spain.

But while I helped him to find Gloria he told me politics said nothing to him. He was left of course, but the whole root of the trouble lay in our sex life. Wars and social injustice were due to repressions. There was an international movement, the Sexpol, with headquarters in Switzerland. He'd been on his way there when Kate picked him up. It seems like fate, he said.

We found Gloria having a few words with the boxer. She was trying to persuade him to go for a walk. The boxer smiled and measured me with his eye. Come on, he said. He was more than ready for any move I might make. For all his rubbery bulk he was fast as a feather, light as a flea. He kept me at bay. I love dancing, he said. He was artful and shy as a balloon off its string.

Jane was dancing with Otto. She looked girlish and hopeful now Julian had retired. I could see as she passed how flushed and flattered she was to be dancing with this dubious Prince Charming, though she knew of course that nothing would come of it as he wasn't the sort of person you'd meet again. But his dancing was an end in itself. He danced the Parisian way, a springy lope, riding the rough ground and the broken music. The French foxtrots suited him perfectly. Everything suited him. The harsh lights on his gold hair and skin, his black fishnet singlet, gigoloing with Kate, and being a wrecking refugee by profession.

Howard came up, looking not too well after his tea. I told him Gloria had gone off with Ivan for a drink.

Yes, we had quite a shindy about it after breakfast. Not that I mind paying for them both in the least, but it's simply unheard of to drink the whole day.

He inclined his head and assumed his dancing expression. Not much fun dancing in this. He steered me out from the crowd.

Julian is enchanted with her, he said. He hates anaemic intellectual women. Of course I didn't mean—oh well, we're all over civilised. Gloria is wonderfully simple in a way. But you mustn't think she meekly accepts our values. That's what I admire so about her. I feel she's a tremendous responsibility. Since we've been here quietly together she's been thinking things out. She agrees with me now that Pacifism isn't enough. She said so in fact to that Dutch chap who followed her from her lecture tour to Paris. He was staying at her hotel when I got there. It made us both rather uncomfortable. He might have considered her a little. But as I pointed out to her he was quite a decent chap and tremendously keen, but she only wanted to come with me to Calanques and get away from it all. That speaks for itself I think.

Howard gritted his teeth. He was put out by the floor and the bumpy behaviour of the crowd, so bad for unbosoming, and by the sight of Kate, holding her head with the curls very proudly because she was dancing with Otto. If they come over here you'll have to excuse me, he said. I wouldn't like to have to be actually rude to that syndicalist, or whatever he is, Kate's parading about. I suppose I may as well tell you, you'll be certain to hear it sooner or later, Kate has lost her onyx shoulder clip. But you know how quixotic Kate is. You see he's her guest after all. And then she doesn't want to look a fool I suppose, so there she is dancing with him as if nothing had happened. I advise you to keep an eye on your valuables. The chap is pretty crook you can see that.

But Howard, I said. If he happened to want an onyx shoulder clip Kate would give him one. She would give him anything that he asked for. Otto is not crook. He holds out no false hopes. He's very well organised for his world.

It's not my world thank God, Howard said.

Don't be too awfully sure, I said.

Excuse me, Howard said. They are coming over.

Kate came alone. She came dancing up and clutched my arm with her crimson tipped fingers. Her Schiaparelli perfume vibrated on the air, she trembled and shone with excitement and secrecy. You see that Proustian individual there by the entrance gate?

Not the old gentleman?

Sinister. Holding a hat in his hand. It's someone from the *Sécurité* watching Otto.

Oh come! He's having us all on, Kate. Unless the old bloke might be something hired by Howard to keep track of our valuables as he puts it. It seems they are being stolen.

Oh but how ghastly! I would never believe it of Howard. Isn't it awful though how living in this political atmosphere makes you suspect even your dearest friends?

And when Otto returned, having dismissed the Proustian person with a handshake, Kate kept a glowing silence that almost spoke of her thoroughly revolutionary training.

I was glad Otto was with us. All the evening we'd been saying between dances that here we were dancing on the edge of destruction, and if this should be true I would still be glad to be having a dance with Otto. Only one. He wasn't a person you could expect to meet again.

But the boxer was signalling from the side lines, entangled with Gloria. She had caught him off his guard with her right cheek, and now had him up against the ropes. Otto left me and went to the help of his friend. Leave her to me, he cried to the hypnotised boxer. He had fixed her already with his sea-white eyes. She was enchanted to be seeing some action at last with this cutting in.

She followed him to the centre of the floor, sweetly and sexfully. He frowned and bent her over as if testing the flexibility of a new shoe. *Apache! Collège!* the other dancers screamed. The two seemed firmly glued from cheek to knee. But as Julian said, that was just an ideal. Gloria's posterior was doing a dance of its own, each movement of Otto's magnified to obscenity by her bulk. There were titters and whistles. Gloria smiled and seemed to be trying to speak. But by now she was looking like a sexy sack, and somebody dancing with a sack is always funny. At last with magnified gestures of cold frenzy, Otto pushed her before him through the enclosure gate and danced her away up a dark side street followed by a goodish part of the crowd anxious for the *dénouement.* There was no doubt as to whom the laugh was on.

Good God, said Howard, standing miserably by. One might have known it with a chap like that. Can't even behave reasonably in public. But he didn't go after them. That would have been too good a scoop for Otto. And very soon the dancers tired of the joke were streaming back again for the next dance.

So Howard inclined his head and assumed his dancing expression. Shall we try it again? Being so well off is Kate's undoing, he said.

And what about *your* income?

Oh really. My piddling little income. Howard looked wretched.

I was sorry for him. He wanted so much to be married or settled somehow, but there were always these girls who couldn't be judged by ordinary standards.

Awfully sorry, he said. He would go on talking and attempting to glide as far as was humanly possible over the bumpy track.

I took him for a turn along the beach. Jane often says something ought to be done about Howard. We are fond of him because we have known him so long. But nothing can now be done. He continues to talk and glide.

When we got back the boxer was semaphoring from the

entrance to the dance. Whatever can he want? Howard said.
You talk to him, Ruth. He's a good sort, but so unresponsive.
One might as well be speaking another language.

You have to go to your girl friend at once, the boxer said.

Thanks, Howard said. Nothing the matter I hope?

It was like this, she was all alone in the café. You see what
happened—

I think we might skip that, Howard said.

She didn't fancy going home alone past that dark corner at the
end of the street, and she said the other night there was an ugly
customer right under her balcony, whistling. So I saw her home.

Thanks very much, Howard said. It would never have
occurred—

She was feeling a bit dizzy so I went upstairs with her and then
she got into bed. She said she was feeling so queer she couldn't
be left alone, so I dashed off here to fetch you.

Many thanks old chap, Howard said.

All okay. No thanks by request. I don't put my fingers in
other people's jam.

The dance was dwindling. I left it for my secret bed in the
cellar. At the bottom of the rue Victoire Julian was walking up
and down in the powdery moonlight. He looked small and sad
alone on the road.

Jane is at home, he said. She thinks I'm in bed. But I never
can get to sleep in this place. And now I've lost my holder, the
one that catches all the nicotine. I don't know what I'm going
to do without it.

I'm awfully sorry, Julian, I said.

I've been having one of my fearful headaches, he said. And
he leaned his head on my shoulder like a child. His head felt
light and small under the impatient silvery waves that were grey
in the daylight.

You must try to sleep, I said. I'll take you home and then
you must try to sleep.

I walked up the hill with him towards my secret bed in the cellar.

I hope you have plenty to read, he said. I've just received a presentation copy from Lawless of *Death's Dolls*. I'll give it to you.

He was like Paul offering the bananas and jelly. He felt better now he had done something for me. But don't you write? Now he felt better he could laugh at me. Don't your things have a dreamlike quality?

I hope not. I write for the Save Spain Committee.

Do you really? he said. I gave a picture to it. I gave a picture of mine to some committee. Picasso had given one.

I knew he was thinking how very risky it was to have thrown a picture, one of his pictures, into the welter of world affairs. The consequences might well be unthinkable—but surely Picasso must know what they were doing.

I found a kaleidoscope in Marseilles, he said. Just lying on a stall.

I didn't think they made them now, I said, very cautiously, because Julian, when there are just people or press reporters about, will say, looking at a lamp-post, a dustbin or whatever is there, Isn't it wonderful? Now what do you make of it? What is it all about do you think?

He firmly believes that everyone he doesn't know is half-witted, and so these things get into the papers, his friends blush and the public goes on believing that artists are cracked. Coming home from a party once, he slipped and fell. His friends walked on without even turning round. They could only think he had done it to make a fool of them in some way.

But when you had a kaleidoscope, he said, did you ever try turning it away from the light? Did you notice a silence coming across the colours? A hush comes over the colours. I wish I could paint at night. If only I could paint or sleep at night.

(And in the kaleidoscope it is so still. The pattern has always been there. Then a rustle and a click very far away. The new pattern. Again it has always been there.)

I'm terribly sorry, Julian, I said.

Good night. Sleep well, he said, letting himself carefully in with his latchkey. Why don't you come and see us sometimes? Come about five on Sunday.

I walked slowly on up the hill, still vibrating with Julian's heartrending colours. I knew that except that he liked fat models, his liking for anyone was a matter of pure chance; but still I felt his confidence was sacred. I felt honoured as if I had been admitted to the studio, and the pictures gloriously turned away from the wall.

When the window upstairs was dark I let myself in with my latchkey. I hoped that Ivan would behave with discretion. There was very little reason to expect that he would. Towards morning there were sagging bumps on the street door. Like a giant playing football with Ivan's limp body. But when I opened the door he was alone and crying. After I'd got him down the stairs he continued to snuffle and shuffle about in the dark.

She will never forgive me, he said. He was sobbing drunk. You will never forgive me, he said.

I will try, I said. If only you'll be quiet. How awful if Julian came and found us here. He might be painting tonight.

A virgin, he said.

Who is a virgin? I said. Gloria's been in bed with Howard for hours.

A virgin, he said. God will never forgive me. My camp bed shook with his sobs. In spite of its cold and crazy narrowness he was so much at home in a bed that he curled there quite naturally, like a worm on the edge of a leaf.

Don't throw me out. Oh do forgive me, he sobbed.

I will, I said. Only think of Julian. He matters so much more than any of us. He might be sleeping. He might be painting. Quiet.

MONDAY—Calanques: An expedition to the furthest Calanque. Kate has hired a *vedette* and at last persuaded Julian to go. She is trying to get him to be analysed. In the meanwhile he's livery being shut up there.

It's not a very large boat you know, Kate says, so I understand I am not urgently needed. I'd planned a walk I say. Oh yes I had. By the way, will you lend me your little rucksack, Kate? (*Prêtez-moi vos pistolets. I am going on a journey. Adieu.*)

We could have fitted you in though, Kate says, gratefully. But of course I quite understand. One does like to get away. We shall miss you. But you really must come next time.

In order to miss the *vedette* I dress very slowly. The withered bouquet is still there on the table. The plant from my sea voyage is dead in a basin. The fishermen have died long ago. Far in the past they await the triumph of man.

Out in the tepid emptiness of the street suicide seems superfluous. There is nothing to leave, there is nowhere to go really. The pudding-faced virgin trails past like a bird with a broken wing. She is still looking over somebody's shoulder to a closed future. Ivan or somebody—while she was stupidly looking out to the future.

Round about the jetty the water dazzles. The white and gold *vedette* is impatient. The overalled owner, unconcerned as fate, throws back the rope that moored her to the quay.

Kate stands up and waves me an invitation. The dancing space of water widens between us. I motion the boat on, smilingly shaking my head. The bright buzz of the boat fills the blue. A wave of transparent laughter breaks against the sleeping houses and cliffs.

The owner, his hand lying loosely on the wheel, ignoring the animated cargo, gazes ahead, set for the horizon of this day's job. Kate has thrown a brown challenging arm over Julian's shoulder. He sits humped and contracted under her spell. She's done the wrong thing for once, he hates public endearments. Jane, romantic, trails her arm in the water. One of Gloria's hands is nesting on Howard's knee, the other flies to ruffle Ivan's hair. The boxer, his mouth full of chocolate, holds out the packet to his friend the musician.

Today is waiting. A long walk to the rock. Is it an occasion for hard-boiled eggs and bananas?

The pudding-faced virgin will be there already. I shall be bracketed forever with the pudding-faced virgin. We won't need an introduction. We'll just exchange hankies for luck.

Poor little thing slipped on a misadventure. Poor little thing those naughty boys again. Cut off she was, perfectly prime she was, a fitting end, a perfect fitting dear. The flesh was willing but the spirit was rather weak. Lay down your lives while the vehicle's still in motion. *Si le ciel est désert nous n'offensons personne.* And I lay me down with the willies.

She had slept as usual, left the house as usual. There was no suspicion of alcohol on her last breath. She had not been interfered with (not very much). There was no love lost, nothing whatever was lost. The Party came first and last and was last seen. Lives in our memory. May linger on for years. Tell the proletariat not to grieve. This be my requiem. You have nothing to lose. . . .

Over the rink of the sea, the glittering *vedette* runs along an invisible line to the distance. Otto is a small solid figure of gold in the stern. He flings up his clenched fist and calls something gay that sounds like the golden fling of the waves on the stones of the jetty. He dismisses me with a cheerful wave of the hand, and looks away out to sea.

The boat shrinks and stands stationary in space, with its cargo of seated dolls that shine like chocolate papers. Soon it is only the rim of a white nest enclosing coloured bonbons.

Now there is no boat but a dark dot, seaweed, seabird, or a trick of the light. . . .

Jesús Jiménez

Madrid. Madrid. Albaceté, Sagunto, Barcelona. Now. The hills, the white hills, the frontier and other countries. In the centre the big red flower Madrid; blue and purple roads leading away. Over there are the Fascists; over here are the hills. The Señora's desk is a high green hill painted with garlands. The Señora sits there making propaganda; I play with my little car.

In the house cold winds and sudden shouts; singing and running, windows and doors banging. Outside the sun shines but he tells me a lie; under the wall the shadows are blue with frost. The holy stove has a red door with a still flame behind it. The warm quiet smell ripples the air as it rises out of three round holes at the top. Only if the red door is opened the flame is frightened and trembles.

In the evening the children enter the room in pairs to tell lies about Madrid. They each tell how they put out the incendiary bomb. The Señora listens. Lies. The light went out. My mother was lighting a candle.

They must not come upstairs in the afternoon. I play in the dark of the landing quietly. My car knocks against the Señora's door; I find myself inside on the soft carpet. I play without making a sound. After tea she gives me the jug to drain, she gives me a Marie biscuit, she kisses me. I take the Señora for a ride in my car. You must come to Madrid, Señora.

La Casa Abraham Lincoln. Is a castle up in the high hills. The Señora Inglesa stands on a flight of steps. She is pretty with pale eyes and thin lips. You are hungry and tired, she says. Wait, I must take some pictures, the foreign driver says, the light is going and I have to get back. Where's Jesús, Jesús Jiménez, the driver says, put him in front. All the way from Madrid I was sitting beside the driver; he promised me I should drive the truck next time.

We stand by the truck and cheer and raise our fists as we did in Barcelona, Sagunto, and Albecete. You needn't do that, the driver says, just smile.

We stand in a narrow passage that ends in a washbasin. Why look he's only a baby, somebody cries, he'll be trampled to death underfoot. They don't guess that I'm six. What does it matter? I am carried away and given a bowl of soup. I ask for some bread with it.

Ahora. We are here. We couldn't have come any further. From the windows we see the white Pyrénées, there is the frontier; France, the Americas and the other countries.

I sleep with the girls; their rooms are called after the names of flowers, Lilies and Roses, and the little girls, Mariposas. We lie on the beds, the bell rings for a walk; everyone hides. Only I am there when the bell rings; I'm excused from the walk because of my crooked leg. They will go for firewood, or fetch the meat or the bread. They will not labour uphill only to return to the same place. Nothing new is to be seen on a walk; the white Pyrénées are just the same from the window.

Extranjeros. Foreigners come in cars. The Señora runs through the rooms, pushing things into drawers, begging and scolding. She talks to the strangers in their foreign tongues. I understand all they say. The Señora says the castle was the summer residence of a gentleman who went away. That is why the floors are thin, the windows don't close and the drains choke up. The foreigners give me sweets; they say what a handsome fellow. They ask if I eat enough. I say, *When the meat is all eaten we shall eat the flesh of the Fascists*. The Señora doesn't translate.

They give us a hundred pesetas to buy comforts. The Señora buys us all green bathing suits; now we can save our clothes for the winter cold. The boys call after the girls in the bathing suits.

A lady comes from the Barcelona Committee. We do some drill for her in our bathing suits; she is angry. All the money must go to the Barcelona Committee, she says, there will be scandals with these low boys and girls in bathing suits. She looks into drawers and cupboards. What have you done with the table cloths? she says. We needed sheets, the Señora says; she is angry. The girls unpick the sheets and then we are photographed having our dinner off the table cloths.

A man from England comes. He wears a white helmet like a jungle explorer. He is going to make a vegetable garden. The flowers are all uprooted; the boys stand round him waiting for his commands. War is very wicked and cruel, he says. Then he gets diarrhoea and goes to bed. Brandy is sent from the village.

A black lady comes from North America. She beats all day on a small typewriter. In the evening she asks us to sing. We all sing: *When I was leaving Madrid, even the stones wept.* I say my piece; she cries. Big black tears roll down her face.

El carnicero. Is next to the doctor's house. The house is closed; the doctor was killed in the night. The butcher's shop is swept and scrubbed and darkened. The calf killed on Thursday is ready for visitors now. The head is ready, the scrubbed butcher says. It's quite good eating. Magdalena falls on the head with her fingers. It's not bad eating, she says.

I sit on a high chair beside Roberto. There is head on our plates and salad. What does it taste of, Roberto asks. It tastes of candles, I say. Yes. It's the doctor's head, Roberto says.

El campesino. The farmer is bent and brown. He says to the Señora, You come from a far country. God will reward you for helping these little ones. I can let you have some potatoes but don't tell or I shall have the Army, the Navy, and all the Parties, coming to requisition my potatoes. And you keep out of my fields, he says, shaking his fist at us.

Caracoles. When a boy finds a big one, he shouts and runs with it to the Señora. Good, she says, now that we have only a little meat. Rice with snails is a Spanish national dish. A Spanish national dish, the boys cry. The Roses, Lilies and the Mariposas crowd round the Señora, fighting and biting each other, to hold her hand. I don't like this kind of love, the Señora says.

I lift the lid of the big stone jar. A cool damp air rises. The snails lie quietly on top of each other. One is climbing the side of the jar moving his limp horns. They must stay there for a week, Magdalena says, till the black stuff has all gone out of their bodies. Then they are clean and good. They are good boys.

We eat the rice, snails appear on the plates of the small children. The piles grow; the top snails fall to the floor. What's the matter there? the Señora says. They are not quite done, says Pedro. Mine are delicious, the Señora says. Eat the done ones, she says. Boys with pockets are offering snails room.

El cuarto de baño. Is kept locked all day; only open when Helmuth goes in his pants. Now the door is open; no one is there. The shower and shelves are of silver; the white roll unwinds for ever and ever. The toilet seat is of many coloured white, like fish that stand in the sun in the market place. I must put my frog down there, Roberto says. The frog jumps. That's a wicked frog, he says. From the darkness under the bath the frog is watching. We sit on the floor with our arms on the toilet seat. It smells sweet and sour. Roberto says, Your mother is down there.

Magdalena. Is like a magpie. She hoards her breakfast bread. She hides cheese and cocoa in secret places, then gives it away to the Señora or me. When food arrives she flies at it with her fingers. When boys come to the kitchen she screams like a magpie; they stand in the doorway and shout, Where is your husband? The Malagueñas bang the pots and sing, You shall see that I love you, you shall see the colour of blood. Magdalena screams: You call yourselves Free Women. As far as I'm concerned you're free to leave. One day they walk away down the hill with their bundles.

When Magdalena sits she takes me on her lap against her belly that curves out like the mountains. Little King, little Sun,

she says, little Jesus. She feeds me with bread and bacon. Little
heart, she says, you love Magdalena.

I love the Señora. When the Señora says a thing it is done.
The Señora is too good, Magdalena says, she doesn't know what
goes on. Oh my poor husband, Magdalena says, the first time
I ever left him to see my sister. The Reds are good. I soon got
into the kitchen. Once in the kitchen one can always manage.
Poor man, I'm sure he's not a Fascist, she says. To me he never
said he was anything.

A dormir. When we wake in the night the light has gone.
But in the morning we see the Señora asleep in the distance.
We are put to bed in the alcove inside the tower. The girls kept
us awake. You'll be a good boy tonight, she says to Helmuth.
She puts some stuff on Robertito's spots. Robertito's spots are
round like pesetas. She kisses me goodnight. Have you said your
prayers? I lean on the bars of my cot and say to myself, Long live
the C.N.T. and all the Committees.

Later the light is out. There is waking up. Screams sound
through the house. They dream their mothers are dead or we
are surrounded. They have a toothache or say the cupboard was
groaning. Whatever it is the Señora gives them a cough sweet.
Then she tries to lift Helmuth from his cot; he lies like a stone,
he doesn't want to wake. Once awake he fights and scratches
her, screaming words that nobody understands. Then he falls on
her shoulder; his tears fall. We hear a trickle in the urinal. But
always in the morning his bed is wet.

Golondrinas. Are in the long light attic with broken windows.
The nest sticks in a corner between two walls. How lucky, says the
Señora. High up there and safe. How well they build. She tells
all the children how lucky it is. One day half the nest has gone.
The young birds scream, hanging onto the half. The golondrinas
come and go through the window calling and flapping their
wings on the broken edge of the nest. Next day it is all gone.
The Señora sees it and goes to her room and cries.

Flores. Pick them, she says; such pretty flowers. The flowers are bees with their bellies hanging out. There aren't enough we say. Count them, she says. One two three, why there are more than twelve.

In the night I pick flowers. They grow on a thick stem, thick and warm, feeling of soft down. I have pulled out the neck; they will never grow again. The bird's eyes look at me. Put it in water, she says. If I put it in water it will go on living. Better for it to die.

Escribiendo. The children hope for rain; they plead for paper. If their parents are dead they write to cousins or the committees. Vicente writes a letter to Abraham Lincoln; they tell him Lincoln is dead and he cries like a baby. The Señora allows us to write to the Lincoln Committee. Don't make it too long, she says. Angeles writes the letter in beautiful writing. We thank you very much for your goodness to us. Madrilenos are very proud people. When the war is over and we are older we shall repay it all. This is a promise.

It was I who stood beside Angeles and said: Don't forget we are a proud people. The children sign. They show it to the Señora. Perhaps we might send it, she says.

Invierno. Is cold. One day it is cold. We wear the bathing suits under our clothes. We wear them at night as well. The wind blows dirty papers; the papers stick in the bushes along the drive. Today it has fallen to us to pick up papers. The cold is eating us. Roberto says, Hombre, your father is dead. No, I say, my father is before Teruel. My father is killing a Fascist. He cuts the neck and the blood runs into a bowl where it makes a bright jelly.

Roberto says, Your mother is dead then. The light went off. My mother was lighting a candle. Madrid is there, the red flower in the centre. The kitchen is there in the light. My mother is lighting a candle.

My mother washed me and put on my nice shirt and combed my hair with cologne. We took our lunch and sat on the benches with others. At midday we ate our lunch and later we saw the doctor. My mother cried and said, You are going away to a beautiful place, next Friday. You must always be good. But when the Friday came I didn't go. How do we know what these committees are like? Better to all stay here and die together.

Mañana. The cold is waiting outside the window. The Señora lies in her alcove of blue and gold. She is not dead, only pretending to sleep. She opens her pale eyes and says to Roberto, You must be quiet for just a little longer. Roberto lies on his side, poking Helmuth through the bars of the cot with the stick he has taken to bed. Helmuth groans without opening his eyes. Magdalena comes in with a bowl of malt coffee quietly, as if someone was ill in the bed. She shakes her fist at us and makes a face.

Roberto wriggles and shrieks; washing is cold on his spots. When the nurse came she said, The sins of the fathers. Roberto's father is far away but the spots are still there, round like pesetas.

Helmuth is washed all over. He stands like a stone. He is tall for five and better dressed than we are but nobody plays with him. At night when the fire is lit he plays on the hearthstone pulling out red sticks. The ski-suit his mother sent is full of holes and his white face and hands are covered with burns. We must all be kind to him, the Señora says. He is a worse kind of refugee it seems; he was born one. The Señora would give him a sweet if he'd been good in the night. Instead she has to give sweets to Roberto and me so that Helmuth shall notice he has not been good.

I wash myself quickly and well so that I have time to stand on a chair and comb my hair in the mirror and see again my handsomeness in the mirror. The Señora says, Jiménez is always good.

Ladrones. Away in a far field stealing turnips. It is nearly night; the sky is turnip colour. A bell is ringing and over the cold fields people are calling. The turnips, washed in a muddy pool, taste bitter.

La Capilla. The gold on the altar is green with cold. The Christ looks cold on the cross. The boys were saying, He's not much use any more. The painted blood on the Christ is shiny and dry.

The boys carry the cases into the chapel. The foreigner has driven the truck across France, over the white Pyrénées over the frontier. He slaps the boys on the back, he is very happy. Some of the cases are opened. Now we shall eat rich things out of the tins. We clash the tins together with joy, and cheer. Come outside, the foreign driver says, it's much too dark in there for photographs. Up with your fists, the anti-fascist salute.

Jerseys. Are on the bed and on the chairs. The children enter in pairs. The Señora throws them a jersey, Try it on. Now you'll be warm, she says, you won't get ill. You mustn't get ill; the doctor has gone away.

I get two jerseys, a red one and a green. On the breast of the red one a note is pinned. To our comrade in the anti-fascist fight. From Marie and Heloise.

Señora Pilar comes in. She lives in the other house that is like a castle, with the teacher Don Carlos some of them say is her husband. The children wait on her and wash her hair. Foreigners should stay in their own countries, she says, then the war would be over. They found a monarchist flag rolled up with her stockings. She is a painted *puta*. Her boys who wet the bed have to sleep on the iron springs. That cools their tails and cures them, Pilar says. The Guardias go to Pilar at night to drink. That is good, Magdalena says. It is good to be in with the Guardias, war or peace.

Pilar smells at the jerseys. New, she says. I suppose what remains will be for us, she says. I suppose the gentleman is a friend of yours. Under the jerseys there is a fur cape. I suppose he brought it for you, Pilar says. Without a word the Señora gives her the cape.

Navidad. Although we are refugees there is Christmas and New Year. The little girls are singing outside the doors. Snow has fallen. We have taken Teruel. My father sits in the plaza drinking his coffee; the snow lies all round. He promised to bring me back the ear of a Fascist. I have the box; I need some cotton wool.

No one is ill. We all sit down to dine in the new jerseys. A pine tree is in the house, surrounded by second hand toys of the Fascist children. There is rich stew, real coffee, a fistful of nuts. We are calling the foreign driver, Uncle Comrade. I say my piece, Black Birds over Madrid: Something more cheery now, the comrade says, surely you know the International. We all weep and sing.

Up in the bedroom the surprise is prepared. The boys received the toys from their parents. The toys scream and then explode like a bomb. We let them off in the rooms of the Lilies and Roses. Some of the girls faint.

The Uncle Comrade is in the Señora's room. She is showing him papers; now he does not smile. They are standing close together; my little car runs into the desk: bang. Be quiet, the Señora says. Take us both for a ride in your car to Madrid.

I drive at a furious speed over the mountains. At tea time the comrade gives me a chocolate bar. We arrived? the Señora asks. Yes but the comrade met with an accident. He fell from the car and was eaten by wolves and fascists.

The comrade drives away in the empty truck. We raise our fists and cheer; we are very sad.

The Guardias were in the Señora's room. They came to investigate her, there in the room. I played outside the door; close to the door. How should I know? she said. He came to us bringing gifts for the fiestas. Funny, they said, foreigners coming here for the fiestas.

And later on she said: Go away. Leave me alone now, as she does to the boys when they tease her. The Guardias with their guns stamped down the stairs.

There was only the hump in the clothes; no one was there. Magdalena came in with a bowl of coffee. Where has she gone, Magdalena, we said. Magdalena looked at the bed and the coffee.

She's gone away, she said. And will she bring us things? Roberto said. Yes, many good things, Magdalena answered.

At breakfast Magdalena screams in the doorway. The plates shake and words fall from the ceiling. The Mariposas sit with folded hands waiting for milk and bread.

The children run out of the dining room up the stairs. They run through the rooms calling each other's names, calling Señora. Marie Angeles carries me off to the alcove. Jesús Jiménez, aye, Jesús Jiménez, better to have been killed by a bomb in Madrid.

I play for a while with my car. Madrid, Albacete, Sagunto, Barcelona. The Señora, the frontier, France, and other countries.

Señora Pilar comes in. Her nails are like the painted blood of the Christ. Where's our Señora gone, Roberto asks. She was tired of you, she went to her own country; help the barmy boy to carry his bedding. We heave the mattress on to Helmuth's back. Like snails we move across the room with our bedding. Helmuth sticks in the door with his stinking mattress.

Santa Cristina

Each day sheds its skin like a snake,
But not the days of Fiesta.

Yet the first of the summer, when the lilies of Santa Cristina flowered out of bare sand, though still marked on calendars at Lloret, passed unnoticed. No one had come but the old tramp who lived on the hill. It was later in May that the fishermen set up their heather shelter. The visitors came in June for the bathing season.

The fishermen sat at their table of two planks, eating bread and fish under a lantern. 'Sit down with us, Auntie,' they said, and they gave her some warm red wine. 'Drink up,' they said; 'old age comes to all of us. Tell us that salty story about the priest.'

But old Cristina, who liked to exchange words with strangers, to tell them she had never been a gypsy, but as a child had slept on white sheets, now that the chance had come, remembered nothing. The thick curtain of night hung too close round the lighted circle of sand. There was nothing but the night and the taste of death in each suck of a hollow tooth.

'You must have had many, many sweethearts,' they said.

'I was pure as the nuns of Lloret' (at this they were ready to laugh). 'I was, you might say, like the Virgin up on the hill.'

Their faces grew larger under the swinging light, their mouths ready to laugh. 'We can't believe you in that,' one of them said, 'but now you won't be afraid to go home in the dark.'

Their laughter threatened to bring down the rocks and the night. With laughter after her, she fled to the hill.

The vine house where Juan kept his sprays and sacks was her home for the summer. Juan left his hoes outside, and she took them in and put them out in the morning. No one entered the whitewashed stone hut that smelt inside of stale sunlight and earth. Here after dark, behind the broken door, she kept watch with the frogs that tolled deep, the coastguards whistling from far and near cliffs, and the owls that called and answered from nests of darkness.

But on nights when the moon and the tide of nightingales rose the watchers were silenced, for now the valley was boiling with light and life. Then if a cloud crossed the white life of the valley Cristina would step outside to curse it away, and sit in the doorway keeping an eye on things, till a grey breeze lifted the night and a bird called with a soft human voice.

At sunrise Cristina sat at the door of her hut. Already the black procession of ants was moving along the ditch between dry drifts of snail shells. The ants, dull black of burnt paper like a funeral procession, were strange in daylight. Often Cristina walked with the procession all down the steep road between vines, then under the level shadows of cypresses. But after crossing a corner of the courtyard it disappeared behind the church, where she did not care to follow.

Cristina looked over the valley. On the silent slopes the many vine houses were white and secret in the early sun. The saint's shrine had the more homely air of a brick villa. It stood near the hut, where a turn in the road gave the first sight of the headland lying against the blue, looking small and sheltered between brown slopes of vineyards, and resting there in a nest of pines, like a white egg, the cupola of the church.

Smoke and clear voices rose from the trees. The day beginning. The summer, the season beginning. Plenty of company. Auntie Cristina.

The Alsatian bitch, dusty and decrepit as Auntie, came silently shuffling in the soft dust. She was looking for her puppies, born yesterday, that someone had taken away. She stopped, sniffed sadly, then padded on up the hill.

A stone struck the wall of the hut, chipping the plaster. The son from the hotel was coming up the road, a boy of six with cheeks like purple grapes.

'Don't you remember your old Auntie?'

'You stink,' he said; 'you have lice in your dress.'

'Don't you remember, dearest, we played in the church where the sacred light strung beads of yellow and blue?'

'I must go,' he said. 'I am going to trap birds in the woods.'

On the sun-white dust of the road the priest's black was outside nature. The black drank his sweat. Even his beaver hat was matted and dull.

He had come to make arrangements for the fiesta. The house where priests once lived was now the hotel, and few masses were said in the church, but the bones would have to be rowed over as usual. He himself had come by boat from Lloret, but the boatman was going fishing, so now he must return on foot in the heat unless he could get a lift along the highroad. People with cars weren't very considerate.

He stopped in the shade of the hut to wipe his face and bless Auntie Cristina. 'You must step into the convent when you are passing. The sisters will welcome you and give you a meal. There is always bread in abundance—good white bread. For a few hours' work you'd be suitably rewarded. The church cares for the poor and lowly,' he said. 'The poorest and lowliest are not forgotten. I could envy you, with nothing on earth to do, sitting here all day in the shade,' he said. And he blessed her and walked away.

Nothing moved. Only the sparrows were keeping it up in the heat, chipping and chipping, like a shower of little pieces of broken china.

Rabbit, rice, spices. A procession of smells took shape and passed the door of the hut on the quivering air. Dinner. 'Your dinner, Auntie Cristina.'

Through air of watered silk she moved down the hillside grey in the midday, a gliding dot in the eye, grey on the grey.

Carlotta looked at the heap of rice in the pan. Then, 'You may as well have it all,' she said; 'it would only go to the rabbits.'

'The señores don't eat well?'

'There is only the one señor from Barcelona. Or rather a mechanic, I should say, who comes down on Saturdays. His friend, a foreigner, is here. I suppose he likes to keep her out of the way. She hardly eats anything. She might be an *artista* from one of the vaudeville theatres, but no, she's not pretty enough. She might be a nursemaid. There are plenty of foreign nurses and maids in town that have been thrown out of their own country, they say. But why should we mind as long as they pay their board? Our regular señores are coming next week. I had such a silly dream the other night—something about a snail I put in the rice.'

'That's all right,' Auntie said; 'it only means the rice has stuck to the pan.'

'Well, that's true, certainly; three months gone now, but why should the dream mean that?'

'Sometimes they mean one thing, sometimes another. It just depends on what's coming, you see.'

Auntie carried her dinner across the sunny sandy space of the courtyard. She set her dinner down on the church steps and went to the tap over a basin of tiles where travellers washed their hands. The Santa Cristina water was cold and good.

One of the maids came out and stood in the shadow of the balcony.

'Ola Auntie, you're back again,' she said. 'After such a hard spring. March takes the old and takes the young when he can. I'll be glad when the season begins. Nothing much goes on at Santa Cristina, but then, of course, something will happen when you least expect it. The foreign blonde is there behind the church if you care to see her.'

A narrow path led round the side of the church, past the dry scrape of sparrows in the dusty geranium hedge, and the sick smell from the pit where the rabbits waited, twitching and nibbling under a cloud of flies.

But Auntie Cristina did not care to go there because the back of the church was round and blank with no window to open its smooth whiteness. Here on hot afternoons the children played, playing at moving statues. How quiet they were. When you turned they had not moved at all. But at last a shadow fell on the white wall. How quiet it was on the hot afternoons, the trees and the rocks standing so still in their shadows.

It was not yet time for the afternoon wind that lived behind the hills and panted down the valley and fluttered the shutters with hot, heavy breaths. Nothing was moving except the ant procession, making a detour to its dark crack in the plaster where the foreigner sat on the wall that rounded the rock.

Under her eyes the sea spread solid to the horizon, as if it had hardened for ever, the rocks embedded in blue. To the south the still surface was smudged with smoke. There Barcelona, clanging trams and factories and manifestos. But what does it matter? she thought. I have suffered enough.

To the north, along the slowly curving coast, pale fingers lying stretched on the blue. On a clear day you could count them up to ten, the last one fading into the Gulf of Rosas. Rosas, the frontier and the other countries that he was always asking her about. 'Europe ends with the Pyrénées,' he said, 'and if it weren't for the news-sheet we get through the union we'd have little idea of what's going on in the world.' But nothing can happen, she thought. I have suffered enough.

'She sits there all day doing nothing,' the maid said.

Towards evening she stood near the barred front of the shrine. She carried a straggling spray of the clematis that tangled the bushes and hedges in white webs. She looked down the road, crushed the trailers of flowers, and pushed them inside the bars. She started when Auntie Cristina came through the hedge, rags and bones walking, and a desolate monkey grin. She was angry, too. Nobody should have seen.

'It's all right,' Christina said, 'he will come for sure.'

From the back of the shrine, just out of the sun, but remote, the little image, in shiny painted robes and a filigree crown, stared straight ahead over a litter of brown flower hay. An engine throbbed like a heart on the distant hills. It stopped. The two stood still in the stillness that was coming out of the shrine. Then they caught it again. He had turned off the main road.

He came rushing round the corner and stopped in front of the shrine. 'Anyone would think you were saying your prayers,' he said. He unwound the silk scarf from his throat and brushed the dust from his light town suit.

'And why not? Dearest, you're looking so well today. The spring here is curative. Apart from all the superstition there is, a doctor in town told me, it's wonderful water.'

He propped his motor-bike against the shrine. 'See what I've brought you,' he said. '*Film Fun* and peanut candy, American cigarettes and a manifesto.' Then he found a silver *peseta* for Auntie. 'Now tell the pretty young lady her fortune.'

'Give me your hand, little one. Don't be afraid. My hands are black, but my heart is white as snow. I see a tall, handsome man—and a priest—'

'A marriage, no doubt. And don't you see a baby? A baby or two? That's the best fortune she can do. If she were only a little cleverer she'd be a saint like my aunt in Badalona. She may be alive still for all I know, bedridden, and lying on the bare bed-springs. One day she bought an old Virgin they were throwing out from the church. Took pity on it perhaps. The carrier delivered it in the afternoon, and the next day it broke out with a miracle. So it went on. Miracles every day. The priests were wild. Of course they tried to buy it back from my aunt, but no. She had come to an understanding with the thing.'

But the girl, though she laughed lovingly, was not listening. The vine houses, in slanting sun, seemed white shrines, inhabited by a white and simple secret, almost transparent. Finding the church so empty they have tried to cage it here in this pretty villa. The clematis is dying behind the bars. This is the priest's province. The black, busy priest should know. If I thought so I'd go to church, buy candles and other junk. But no, he doesn't know.

'Still, they don't care to move,' Cristina was saying, 'our Virgin now. Her head is down there in the glass box—'

'Well, hurry up and finish the lady's fortune.'

'I think I'll last longer than she will,' Cristina said.

They are angry, Cristina, they are going away.

Dusk comes up from the sea. The saint fades and retreats to the end of a tunnel of silence. An old woman sits alone on the hill.

The days between fiestas are all alike, but the day of Santa Cristina is blue and gold. Cristina's procession of golden boats crosses the blue sea. The delicate skeleton, pure as a white flower, wrapped in white shawls, is being carried to Rome.

The wind rises, waves crash on the rocks. The ship is lost, but the skull, frail as an eggshell, finds its way to the beach under the pines. Here she wishes to rest and the church is built. Later her ribs appear on the beach at Lloret and are joyfully installed in the church of Our Lady. Though people think more of the head, there is never ill-feeling, and on her name day there is a sea procession bringing the bones for a visit.

From the edge of the cliff Cristina watched a black fishing boat beached. Then she hurried down to join the procession. The ribs, resting on velvet, were carried by a priest up the rocky path. A boy walked behind, swinging a censer.

'There won't be much doing today,' she grumbled to the

procession; 'the priest, two serving boys and two fishermen and a stranger from town with a cigar in his mouth.'

The church was swept, there was clematis on the altar. Light poured like wine over the rough stones, wax arms and hearts materialised in corners, a model schooner waited a breeze from heaven.

They made good time with the mass and in half an hour the skull, a desolate monkey grin under its wreath of paper orange blossoms, was reverently hurried back to the glass case. Then they all sat down to lunch in the shade. Carlotta, who had not appeared at the mass, now came out to ask if the rice was good.

The mechanic walked by with his arm round the foreign blonde. He was saying in Spanish, and loud enough for everyone to hear, 'What a charade! Education is needed in this country. We shall soon see what the Popular Front can do. And if the politicians won't act—then we shall see—'

One of the maids came out and sat down on the church steps beside Cristina. 'Listen to this. A dream ripped through my head. I only caught the tail end of it. You know how the buses whizz down the hill in August? Well, I dreamt the Blue Line bus drove right through the church, shattering it like an eggshell, and then right on over the cliff, with all the holiday-makers still in their seats. I looked in the book. There's brooms and blood and brambles, but nothing whatever about a bus there. What do you make of it?'

But Cristina was out of sorts. All day she'd been whining and worrying the Father for candle ends, though she knew there were only the few Carlotta gave.

'What do you need candles for, old lady? You can say your prayers in the dark.'

The stranger from town wandered out of the church, lighted the cigar that was in his mouth, and seeing Carlotta, gave her ten *pesetas*. 'When do you think they'll be returning the cutlets?' he asked. 'You see, I have to get back to the city tonight.'

He sat down again and gave the priest a cigar. One fisherman was smoking, one was asleep. The acolytes were making obscene shapes with bread. 'Yes, we might as well be starting,' the priest said.

There was no ceremony for the walk back to the beach. A fisherman handed in the bones and shoved the boat off the shingle. Then they rowed away and Carlotta released the rabbits tied by the legs, ready to kill if more people had come to the fête.

The days between fiestas are all alike, but Our Lady of Mercies is a rich day. People leave things behind under the pines. Small and large copper coins fall into outstretched hand. A letter, a visit, some trouble, a dark stranger. Ten *centimos* for Santa Cristina's sake.

'These are bad times, old gypsy, terrible times.'

'Yes, sir, I know. I know. He played with his son on the sand at the mouth of a cave. How did the story continue? With spinning and suffering. Always the man said Death. There were journeys to make. We lived on the edge of the sea, a phosphorescent thread drawn between us. The end did not kill me. Only a pricking when the King died. It was on the next day that I saw my son. "How do you feel?" I asked him. "I feel all right, thank you, mother," he said. And all the time a grey snail was peeping through a hole in his head.'

'She's like Rosita that runs about on the Ramblas. Coming home from a night out you'll see her all dolled up, on her way to meet the Majorca boat. Her son or lover it was that never came back.'

'No, no, not like that shameless one with bows and paper fans stuck in her hair. As a child I knew the feel of white cambric and the feel of velvet, too.'

The days between fiestas are all alike, but at night the sky is red. To the south the sky is red, and the moon is weak in the dark half of the sky. The old dog whines and circles about the hut. Cristina screams her away and stays at the door, keeping watch with the weak moon. At the hotel they were just sitting down to supper. 'Something is passing along the road,' they said.

He stood in the doorway, darkening the night. He stood above the hut like a dark tree. 'Let me come in,' he said in a voice that was hardly heard.

Cristina said, in a voice that was hardly heard, 'You can't come in. You have come to the wrong house.'

'Let me come in,' he said. 'I have to lie down here for a while, old mother.'

'I haven't a bed to offer you,' she said.

'I was thinking of white sheets, but never mind. I was on my way when I got this little wound. A little one, you can fix it up for me. Don't be afraid now, give me your hand.' And he pushed her fingers under the folds of his scarf and inside the folds of his scarf it was warm and wet.

She gathered her voice to shake off the weight of his presence. She screamed. 'Take your death out of here.'

'Quiet. This is between ourselves. You know me,' he said. 'I gave you a *peseta* only last week.'

'Take it again!' she cried. And fumbling in her bundle she scattered *pesetas* and pennies over the floor, screaming to drown the voice that was saying, 'You know me.' She screamed and cursed till the doorway was light again. He had gone and she was alone, keeping watch on the empty vineyards.

Down at the hotel they were all awake, listening for late news. 'Oh, hear old Auntie! She's bad tonight with the moon.'

A big black ant was crawling on the white slope of the vineyards. Cristina ran to the hut and hurriedly closed the door on the priest's blessing. 'What do you want this time?' (But the latch of the door had gone.) 'Surely you haven't come so far and so late to take me away to the convent. I know what you have come for, you green old man.'

'You've nothing to fear,' he said, 'now that the devils are loosed. But I'm on my way to the north. Give me a shawl and some rags to cover me, else it's all up with Father Josep.'

He strangled her screams and held her against the wall, dragging at the rags of her petticoats. The skirts gave way without a sound, like cobwebs, and she lay quiet, a heap of pale bones on the ground until a finger of moonlight entered the hut. Then she gathered her bones together and covered herself with a sack.

Down at the hotel they were all awake, listening for shots in the trees. 'How quiet it is,' they said. 'Well, everyone has to sleep sometime.'

Three cicadas were keeping the day going. Aunt Cristina was resting under a fig tree. The midday meal was over, the shutters closed, and the house and the fields were silent. The sea was only a whisper far away. The sky was soft as bloom on grapes, hundreds of soft blue shawls and always another behind. Juan moved along the rows of vines that waited like good children. And when he came up to where Cristina lay and called, 'How goes it, old lady?' because she loved the sound of a human voice, she threw off the blue and answered, 'All is well.'

At least one can say there's nothing wrong with the vines. We know the days of miracles are past, but what luck, all the same. For I don't think the season will open for us this year. No one will come with this unhappy war. When the foreigner heard her young man was dead she lay down on her bed without a cry, and still she's lying there. What could we do? The doctor has gone, they say. No one could do any more.

Let her lie. No one could do any more. The sky sank and covered Cristina with soft blue shawls. Slowly as the afternoon, Juan stooping and stopping, moved on between the vines, over the hill.

Like a ladder the white road stood on end in the heat. The Virgin's villa quivered in the sky. Cicadas screamed. The wind came suddenly up and tapped the shutter of the sick girl's room. The fig tree stretched in its shadow and advanced with all its branches. A wave crashed on the shore.

Cristina slept. She was so tired of keeping an eye on things.

Maaree

When I asked for Maaree they said, But she's not with the Girls any more. She dresses with the Spaniards.

Just call me Maaree, she said. That was what she called herself. She was crying over some black cotton tights. My legs are my great drawback, she always said, and Cortez always picks on me. It was bad enough in the Carnations with my legs but he's gone too far putting me in the bloody Black Cats. The management seems to forget I'm not one of the Spanish girls.

The Spanish girls squeezing their round behinds into black cotton tights were silent. The Inglesa was going off the deep end again. Being what they called 'a legitimate blonde' and being too thin for their taste and having a blank blue eye, in short being English, set her above the easygoing black cats who worked all day in offices and factories. Then, she had a squirrel coat and a radiant set of removable teeth, relics of a bygone love in Buenos Aires, and she still had Enrique. Nevertheless her life was precarious because, as she said, They always go after the new girls.

The new girls were from the Jackson troupes and others of unknown origin, Sunshine, Coktel, or merely Les Girls. They kept arriving in batches from Paris. The agents said it was difficult to get nice girls from abroad, but after they had been in Paris it was easier to get them to go to places like Java or Barcelona. When the troupe moved on they always lost some of the girls in Barcelona. Those who stayed on were called the Old Girls.

Some just hung about the Grill and got too bad, and Jack, the waiter there, paid the fares home of those he could persuade to go. The others waited for the weekly visits of their *novios* in furnished flats. They couldn't go to nice places, like the Ritz, because they might meet family girls there. That is to say, girls with a family, like the sisters of the *novio* who would resent meeting a girl without a family. Nor to the Grill where the Old Girls who just didn't care, and the French *poules* and the *novios* themselves went every night, and where old Carlotta, dressed in decent black from top to toe, would throw baleful glances at the Old Girls as she ushered in her prostitutes who were certainly prettier, two by two, like a girls' school.

So, with a *novio*, no Old Girl who cared could go there or to dances, but if he couldn't afford to be so jealous, they could still work in the theatre, but only with the Spanish girls; propping up the scenery for three *pesetas* a night. The managers rated them with the Spaniards, the Consul turned his blind eye, the Old Girls had no status at all.

Now the glass of gin came up from the café and Maaree calmed down a bit. The management will have to learn where it gets off, she said. After all I come here to work, not to make a fool of myself. Then while the Spanish girls were down for the number she showed me her leg pads in pink satin and elastic. They should stick on with the suction you see, she said. But that man let me down over them. He swore pink they wouldn't show under the stocking, *but* my dear, they look a sight on. And last night one of the calves slipped and I nearly lost it in the finale. Twenty *duros* he rushed me and I've had to take them back three times.

A pretty little girl came in, collecting small silver on a tray. She had recently had an illegitimate child and the collection was to buy sweets for its christening party. Later the sweets would be distributed and the child would be given to the nuns.

Maaree lived in a room at the top of a house in the Plaza Universidad. *Sencillo,* she said, to avoid embarrassment, but nice and high and central.

It was plain indeed. Even for a Spanish furnished room. The basin and bidet had wobbly metal legs, and there was no cupboard, only a chintz curtain. But, it's nice, I said. It's like a country attic in the centre of the town.

She showed me her 'squirrel' behind the curtain. It was well preserved, still going strong like Maaree. She showed me Enrique's picture. A middle-aged young man with pince-nez and a haughty, what the girls would call rather a constipated, expression.

Does he often come up here? I asked.

Oh yes. Generally on a Saturday. And on the Sundays we nearly always go somewhere in the car.

Very Señor, I said, returning the photo, and very serious, this meaning in Old Girl jargon, successful in business and sincere in love, a most unlikely combination of virtues.

And you must be pretty clever too, I said. You never seem to be in the usual trouble.

Oh no (knock wood of course) nothing at all all the time I've been with him. Of course I douche afterwards, but I really think it would be the same as a matter of fact, being so run down and my ovaries and my cough and everything, I don't really think I could get that way if I tried. Of course it would be the end with Enrique if anything did happen. On account of his family. He has to build up the business his brother neglected you know.

Maaree had been five years with Enrique. Only five years ago she had worked with a sister act at the smart Eden Café. What they did in the act I can't imagine. The 'sister' who had been awfully popular and had red hair had 'gone back' and Maaree had stayed.

He swept me off my feet, she said. Although it doesn't lead to anything in a way. I was doing better for myself in Buenos Aires if I hadn't left to get married to that American boy who didn't turn up. I'm too romantic I know.

That's the trouble with all the old girls, I said, Look at Milly.

Yes. I said to her only the other day about Francisco, It's no good crying in front of them, it only puts them off. And he won't marry you, I said, no, not if you were the Virgin Mary dear he wouldn't. It's always this family business. But still I can't complain about Enrique. Apart from his family Enrique is one in a thousand. Enrique's been a wonderful friend to me.

Maaree made tea on a wobbly alcohol stove and we sat on the bed to have it. The iron bedstead had thin legs like everything else in the room.

I'm afraid I've crumpled your nice clean bedspread sitting on it, I said when I got up to go.

Oh don't let that worry you, I bought it at Siglo, but the material does crease awfully easily.

I was quite sorry to go. The room had a neat virginal look, like the room of someone who still hopes to get married.

A year or two later at Christmas I asked Maaree to dinner. She was teaching now at the Cosmopolitan School of Languages. Only the Principal knew that her English was worse than her Spanish. The Cosmopolitan flourished, employing at pitiful salaries Old Girls who had stayed too long.

Mother will enjoy it, she said. She had taken a little flat with her mother. Having no relatives it meant me sending her money home, she said, and then I always think when you have your mother with you, you can do no wrong. She *will* enjoy it. She doesn't get out a lot. The stairs, and then the language.

The mother, a Mrs Elliot or Mrs Rodgers I think, seemed to have no real existence apart from her large shiny spectacles and the false teeth too large for her puckered mouth. But she said Thank you very much to everything and ate well. When the pudding came on she said, Do you remember, Maaree, the puddings Auntie Ella used to make? And after a glass of port, looking timidly round the table, Maaree's been a good daughter to me. She's always been a wonderful daughter to me, Maaree has. And now she's had me over here the first time I ever crossed the water.

Dressed all in white, on legs like stilts, Maaree a foreign body, stuck out a mile from the drifting crowd on the Ramblas. What! You still here? we asked each other.

We had tea at the Granja Real, up in the gilded gallery where the Girls always go. The orchestra played Little Grey Mornings in Montmartre below. They're all the same, said Maaree. But it's a bit thick after nearly seven years. I never looked at another man, but that's how I am. Perhaps I imagine things but he doesn't turn up. Oh always a good excuse of course, and then there's this girl his family wants him to marry.

The tea was in a metal pot with a silly strainer. Discarding the strainer and disregarding Maaree's sniffs I poured out the second cups. Well! now you're for it! she said with hysterical resignation. Or perhaps it's me but I should be the one that pours.

They all believed that if two poured one of them got into trouble. Then Milly an Old Girl Jackson 1925 came in.

She had a villa well out in the country and a baby Peugeot and even a baby. Being half-married she couldn't be seen with the other Old Girls so she hardly saw anyone now.

How's his lordship? asked Maaree across the tables. Milly too obviously waiting for someone, turned round, surprised, and said, He's wonderful thanks. She went on studying the swing doors, but then relented and said, He gained a pound in just over three weeks.

He's the sweetest bunch of cuddles you ever saw, said Maaree to me. Such wee little hands. When I go there to mind him he coos and holds out his little hands as if he knew me.

One day in midwinter Maaree rang up. I wouldn't bother you, she said, but mother's had such a bad turn and I'm not feeling too good myself.

They lived in a cheap flat in a fairly respectable quarter. The blocks of flats were new and tall and forbidding, but small shops blossomed at their feet and crowded the pavement with piles of pimentos and greens. The house had five flats on each floor and a fragile lift went up but you had to walk down. Maaree lived at the top. She came to the door in a blue flannel dressing gown.

Come along in, she said. Mother was taken suddenly. She couldn't move her left arm, it went all like dead. But the doctor's been, she said in a louder voice, and he says she's not to worry. Go in and see her. Then she went back to bed for it was icy cold in the flat. The bedrooms opened off the dining room and I went in to see Maaree's mother.

She lay quite still looking up at me, like someone in a street accident caught unaware and disgraced. I'm going to get you a nice cup of tea, I said.

I lighted the gas stove in the kitchen. You boil the water in the aluminium hooja, Maaree called through the wall. The aluminium hooja got hot in the handle and I cursed them for not having a kettle. The thought that they lived on the edge of refinement yet couldn't afford a kettle made me angry. There were six cups and saucers, and a red glass jam dish with a plated handle on the sideboard. I found the teapot of 'ware' with something bucolic scrawled on its yellow belly in glazed letters, and some biscuits in a tin.

Well here's your tea, I said to Maaree's mother. She managed to take the cup, her right hand shaking, her left lying still at her side. I asked if there was anything I could do. My hair net dear, she said. It should be on the dressing table. With her right hand she bundled her false looking frizz into the invisible hair net. Then she straightened up and asked me to close the door. I'm worse than what Maaree thinks, she said.

But the doctor said not to worry.

The worse of it is that while I'm lying here I'm a burden on Maaree. She oughtn't to be on her feet so much and now with this chill on her stomach and everything comes on her. She's not strong Maaree isn't. She's always been delicate from a child.

I managed to persuade her that she was going to get better. She said she thought she could feel a bit of movement coming into her arm. And Maaree has such good friends, some wonderful friends we have, she said. But I was the only one of them she had seen.

When I took in the tea to Maaree she was lying on the bed, she said Close the door please, in an exhausted important whisper. It's this dreadful dragging pain, she said. It was nearly three months, you see. I had to go to the woman in Paseo de Gracia and she put the hook up. But if it doesn't come away in a few days she has to do it the other way. I'm keeping it dark from mother.

Enrique had gone to Valencia on business. Had gone just like that. I thought this might bring things to a crisis, she said. Being so late in the day to do anything about it I thought he'd give way when it came to the point. When he wouldn't hear of it I cried for it must have been two hours in the Granja Real and he had to bring me home in a taxi. And not a word since.

Clasping herself and moaning she opened her saucer blue eyes. You remember the day in the Granja Real? Well there's many a true word spoken in jest.

If she could get even me to take a tiny bit of the blame. She had known that day that she was in for this. For the same reason she had brought her mother from England, believing that he would have to do something about it. But no one had ever done anything about Maaree when it came to the point. And mother was kept in the dark. There was nothing for me to do. She had to be up and about the next day to visit the woman in Paseo de Gracia. So I went.

But once you knew Maaree she stuck. You couldn't swallow her, but you couldn't cough her up. Nothing I have said can give you any idea of her wrongheaded refinement. Of the way she always looked wrong in a crowd. The dignified decisive way she mispronounced in an A for Apple voice. Then, her appetite for calamity and bringing things to a crisis; as if the sour boil of circumstances could be suddenly dissolved when it got bad enough. And then her cordiality and goodwill. The bright and breezy way she ushered you into her chamber of horrors.

One day passing her flat, I saw the squirrel coat and followed her in. Hello stranger, she said, I haven't seen you for donkey's years. Come along up and have a bit of lunch. If there is any I should say; I left it with mother. Mother's a terrible tie, she hissed as the lift went up. She can't get out of course, and she won't raise a finger to do anything knowing that all the work falls on me. She let me into the flat.

It's lucky I have till three. Usually I have them from lunch onwards and three evenings a week as well. But I knock off eight hundred pesetas a month, she said with pride. You can do more but you can't keep it up. But I can never get ahead with mother drag, drag, drag on me. She didn't bother to lower her voice. Perhaps mother had gone deaf. But now the mother appeared at the door of her room.

Well is the lunch ready? asked Maaree as if she didn't expect it. I put the stew all ready. You only had to peel the potatoes and put it on. The mother passed like a somnambulist and went into the kitchen. We heard a crash. That's something gone, said Maaree. It's a wonder we have a plate left in the house.

I followed her into the kitchen. The mother stood in bright sunlight by the window. She held two halves of a plate in her hand and was trying to fit them together. You needn't bother to do that, said Maaree. That won't mend it. I don't know where you think all the money comes from to buy all the things you break with your carelessness. Oh and the stew's half done. I shall have to gollop it down or be late for my lessons. I don't know what she does with herself all day I'm sure, but as for being a help she's more of a hindrance, and as for leaving anything in the oven with her . . . Well, aren't you going to say good morning, mother? This is Margot, mother.

Good morning, said the mother.

We all went into the dining room. Why you haven't even put Dixie back, said Maaree. The canary they had 'to be company for mother' was spattering grain from his cage on a corner of the dining room table. The mother stooped slowly like a weight lifter and carefully gripped the cage. Her glasses fell and shattered on the hard tiles. Maaree was livid with hate. She couldn't keep the satisfaction out of her voice. Well, there's your glasses gone. And you won't get any more I promise you that.

The mother stooped lower, then lifted herself slowly and went into her room. It's no use expecting *her* to pick them up, said Maaree. Someone else can do the clearing up after *her*.

We sat down to lunch. Isn't your mother having any? I asked.

Oh no. She'll have a bit of something later on. While we ate the old lady never stirred in the room behind me. Had she picked up a bit of crochet? Or was she just sitting still? I wondered what she did all day.

When we were parting outside I told Maaree what I thought of the way she treated her mother.

It's no good you talking like that, she said. You don't know what it is to be in the position of having a mother who's a burden on you. And she may linger on for years like this. As a matter of fact it would be a merciful release if she passed away. I saw that Maaree was trying to kill her mother and had partly succeeded.

I didn't see Maaree for months but I hated to pass the street. At last I looked in to see what horrible thing had happened. I rang the bell downstairs and Maaree was waiting for me when the lift got to the top. She was standing under the skylight, under the spring sunshine. Her hair was gorgeously hennaed and she was wearing a new blue tailor-made. She was evidently having one of her new starts. You had to admire her and her face was so round and girlish you could almost imagine somebody liking her.

She took me through the spotless dining room to a strip of roof. We looked out over half the town to the sea. It's nice being high, she said, as well as being cheap. The roof is lovely for drying and Dixie can have his cage in the sun, although I'm always afraid the cats will get him.

She returned to the dining room to bring a tin of biscuits. I'm afraid they've gone a bit crummy, she said. A visiting card appeared between the biscuits inscribed in Spanish, *To my English Doll. Your slave, Ramon.* It's from one of my little pupils. He *will* bring things to the lessons. I told him he really shouldn't but he's so enamoured I had to let him have it his own way. You would laugh my dear, he is such a babe. But awfully sweet with long eyelashes and all that. He's quite presentable too, but I found out he works in a boot shop so of course it's only to pass the time. You have to draw the line somewhere, poor little thing.

What have you done with your mother? I asked at last.

Oh mother? She's with some nice people, but very nice my dear. They don't mind having her. I pay for her keep of course. Two pesetas I pay.

A day?

Oh well, she doesn't eat so very much you see.

Time went on and so did Maaree. She wrote she was coming to spend her holidays in Turissa. She hadn't seen me for ages. Enrique and she had parted as friends but he was standing her the holiday.

So of course I shall be quite independent my dear, and no bother to you, I'm coming for a real rest and build up. Would I book a room at the Fonda?

I knew she would pay the hotel bill for her code was strict. She always embarrassingly paid her share in the café. She would never accept a favour from a girl, she often said. By booking her a room I would be in for something far worse. I should have to do something about her at last. So I wrote saying the Fonda was full, only to find she had previously written to the patron and he had let her the chicken roost. They called it the chicken roost because the chickens roosted there in winter. In rush times they had to make way for visitors.

It's lovely, said Maaree, so high and with a view, and only eight pesetas with washing included.

Leaning on the balustrade of the roof, after the bother of breakfast, you could look down into the cool funnel of the street, which echoed the cries of the visitors on their way to the beach. Painters and writers from Paris came to Turissa. Also the vanguard of the English visitors had appeared, declaring that it was more paintable than Mallorca. The German refugees who really ran the place hadn't made it look as much like the Côte d'Azur as they would have wished, but the prim Spanish pension and the rowdy fonda were living under the shadow of the projected Grand Hotel.

This was the summer of the Supervielles. The elder girl had black ringlets and bathed in Hawaiian costumes. The little Supervielle sister, gathering shells on the beach remarked, *On a ramassé les plus beaux coquillages à Bali.*

Bali, it's finished now, said Supervielle.

I enquired about other places.

Yes, we frequented St Maxim. He meant perhaps himself and the other Parisians of all nationalities who were now in Turissa.

At St Maxim a Grand Hotel arose on the beach. The same thing happened at Cassis. So they had come, leaving a trail of Grand Hotels behind them, to Turissa, the only place where one could live this summer.

I apologised for the English art students.

But a place cannot be chic without a few English. Just a sprinkling you know, said Mme Supervielle politely.

The English art students in Oxford Street cruise-clothes, shepherded by an anxious man with a beard, were the first on the beach. They 'worked' in the afternoon. They were pretty lively in the heat and the man with the beard was naturally anxious that 'The stimulating sights and sounds of the South' promised in his prospectus should be reflected in their 'work' and not in other ways. He was wishing he had taken them to Cornwall even before his betrayal by his own countrymen (and artists too) my friends Dick and Hugh.

Dick and Hugh, having wisely decided that their French was not good enough for Mme Supervielle, who spoke perfect English, had settled down to their usual holiday task: turning the English Colony upside down. They sabotaged the 'Professor's' Sketch Club Talk and before he had time to recover, the slogan was going round the school, 'The business was built on his beard'. They made elaborate plans for seducing most of the girls and improving their minds. The students were far from being socially conscious.

With all this on hand they wouldn't look at Maaree but I thought she might like looking at them if only at meal times. Being socially conscious was beginning to show in their shirts but they were still perhaps presentable. What she didn't like was their idea of a joke. When they were allotting marks to the girl visitors, with minuses here there and everywhere for frigidity, her gay smile simply froze.

I'm sorry I can't join in the laugh, she said, though I do admit those girls are asking for it running about in the nude and even chasing after fishermen. I can't fathom why girls with private incomes should go out of their way to make themselves so cheap.

Every morning Maaree, in last year's sandals pipe-clayed, and long shorts, and a suntop that had nothing to speak of to hide, would grab the dog or the baby because, as she said, With a child or a dog you naturally fall into conversation, and set off to the beach to search for security in the shifting sands of Turissa society.

You must take her out. Just once, I told Richard and Hugh.

After they had gone I walked down to the beach. It was getting dark and the village children, who dozed all day in doorways, had come to play on the sand. The lights of the café went up, showing the visitors sitting and chatting. It was nice to think that even Maaree would be part of the scene for an hour or two.

Then I saw my three friends walking slowly across the square. Richard hurried on ahead to explain.

She isn't at all the type who would murder her mother, he said, and it wasn't as if we could lose her or talk to anyone else. She kept everyone at bay with that basilisk blue eye. We simply couldn't afford to waste a whole evening of our holiday on someone who's only funny without being vulgar. Do forgive us. Take her somewhere yourself.

They took a circuitous route back to the bar leaving me Maaree. She was furious. They had let her pay for one of the rounds of drinks and she was more outraged than if she had been raped outright.

But still something might have turned up. The art students were busy with the fishermen but there was generally a lonely Englishman in despair. There was a chap she met up at the ruins, though everyone said he was homosexual; but then she got a blister on her mouth. That's torn it, she said. We thought at first it might be chicken lice which infested the attic, though they hadn't bothered her up to now. Oh dear, I'm breaking out all over, she said brightly, dabbing away at the blisters. Perhaps it's the food's too rich.

I said I was sure it was and that perhaps she was eating more than she was accustomed to. The hotel people had sized her up and knowing she would eat the last crumb of the six courses and drink the last drop of her litre of wine, they would heartlessly slip

in extras, just to see what she could do. I regretted having said
to the patrona, Maria, Miss Maaree has to fatten. She is looking
for a *novio*. I was flattered at the time to be joining in a laugh
with Maria's family. But in my thoughtlessness I had started one
of their cumulative family jokes which would go resounding
round the house for weeks to come. Señora Maria would yell
from the kitchen when Maaree came in from the beach, Well,
have you landed a *novio* yet, Mees Maaree? Even the six year
old Angeles, when she came to collect the plates, would say, We
have found a *novio* for Mees, pointing to a poor relation, an old
fisherman eating his soup in a corner, and winking wickedly at
the other guests.

Maaree bore up brightly, plastering the scabs with grease
paint, and eating, and eating. But I have to get something on
these legs, she said. I want to get the benefit of my holiday. I tried
taking her for walks in the vineyards where people wouldn't see
us but she slipped about so hopelessly on the sun dried earth,
and seemed so uneasy wasting, as it were, a whole afternoon of
her holiday, that I gave it up.

Still she was having a lovely time, she said, till one afternoon,
when I had asked her to tea with some people who wouldn't
mind, she didn't turn up. As I feared, I found her face down on
her bed in the Chicken Roost, her face all red and swollen with
tears and sores.

It's just that they have their own friends, I said.

It's you, she blubbed, rubbing her bloated face in the pillow,
you having a husband and the baby and boyfriends, and getting
invited everywhere, and all you would have to do would be to
take me along. And thinking I haven't noticed!

It was sizzling hot in the attic but I had to stay for over half
an hour, persuading us both that what she said wasn't true.

I looked forward so to my holidays, she kept saying. I had
a feeling it would be now or never. And you who's supposed to
be my best friend!

I thought after that she would leave, but she stayed on nearly as bright as before. She had to eat the rest of the meals and get her washing back and a bit more tan, all she could save from the wreck.

After that I was hardened to Maaree and did not mind seeing her occasionally. She shared her flat now with a girl who was out a lot, to help with the rent. Enrique had faded away but there was a Dr Schmidt, a dentist. Not much to look at, Maaree referred to him breezily, but very thoughtful in little ways. But when she asked me to come round it was about her mother.

You couldn't really expect them to put up with her when she wets the bed like that, she said. So I just thought, Margot, that knowing such a lot of people you could pull a few strings with the nuns. Her being a Catholic you know (I had no idea of it) the nuns might take her. No one else will keep her you see once they find out.

So I promised to do what I could.

And everything always comes at once, she said, if you only knew what I've been through with Dr Schmidt. I ask you, him having nowhere to take me but a sofa in the surgery, he came here with nothing but his instruments you know, and now when he has his flat, he's got this woman there that is supposed to be a housekeeper. I may seem rather simple perhaps, but thank God I'm not promiscuous.

Of course not, I said. And I'm sure there's some mistake. Look how nicely he fixed up your upper plate for you. Perhaps she really is a housekeeper. Some men expect to have someone to cook for them and clean up the flat and so on. Of course not the men you are accustomed to, I said apologetically, but Germans and people like that.

Don't be funny, she said. He's tired of me. I was good enough for the office but now, having the flat he'd like to make a change. It serves me right for getting, serious with a Jew. But I'm going round there in half an hour. They'll be having their supper then, and I'll have it out with him and his cow of a housekeeper.

The trouble with you is you're much too sensitive, darling. He isn't worth it, you said yourself he wasn't. Now stop crying and fix your face. We're going down to the Ramblas to have a drink on me.

It was probably called the International Bar for faded flags, English and German, Spanish and French, were crossed in a stage embrace between the bottles. There was also the usual lonely Englishman in a mac. Maaree knew him. No man's worth it my dear, he kept saying to her, with slaps on the back that made her rattle. Oh for a jug of wine beneath the bough, he said, Maaree's one of the best, one of the boys, but I want to see that lovely Irish smile again. So Maaree tearfully showed her upper plate and we went on drinking up. Maaree was a real sport, he said, turning his attention to me, a real little pal, but she knew where to draw the line. It was so far and no farther with Maaree.

He was starting up greyhound racing in Barcelona, and said the Spaniards had a great idea of sport; they only wanted educating a bit. He had a lot of time for the Spaniards. He seemed to have a lot of time for me too, and when he turned round to say, The same again? Maaree was gone.

I was not surprised to hear, at noon on the following day, that Maaree was taken ill and asking for me. The distant voice on the phone conjured up nurses and doctors, It might have been Maaree herself speaking.

The door of the flat was open, and in the darkened room Maaree was lying in bed with a basin and two empty aspirin bottles, and a photo of Dr Schmidt alongside.

Oh my dear, she said weakly, I hardly recognised you. I only came round about an hour ago. It didn't work, she added.

It never does, on top of the alcohol. Most of the Girls had tried it at various times. But perhaps she had thought it would, and that being dead would be better than nothing. Dr Schmidt would have to do something about it if only to bury her. I made her some tea but she wouldn't touch it, so I sat beside the bed and stroked her hand and smoked as there was nothing to read in the flat. After an hour or two she was looking much better.

I sent for him, she said. He can't refuse me now. Do you think he will come?

Who? Dr Schmidt you mean?

As soon as she came round, she had settled on a solemn death bed scene with Dr Schmidt but now the poor thing was getting better every minute. It would be too late if he didn't come soon. The girl friend had suddenly gone away for a week, so Maaree would soon have to get up and look after herself, and her illness would go for nothing.

I tried to think of someone who would come to see Maaree in bed. At last I thought of the Englishman, and found his number and phoned.

Oh rather! I'll drop round with pleasure, he said, I'll do what I can.

Which he did, as I afterwards heard from the girl friend who came back the next day and found them in bed together. I was shocked, for knowing Maaree's code I knew how far she had fallen. For this was not a case of being let down, but simple sin, without any hope of return, in her own virginal flat, sacred to hopes of marriage.

Then the war came and the Dr Schmidts joined up. The Enriques, the half-married and the partly-kept, disappeared overnight. Even the prostitutes disappeared from the streets; it was said they had gone to form a women's battalion.

On a day in winter, with a stiff wind blowing, flags flapping, radios roaring, I watched a funeral passing. There were many grand funerals in those days. The procession moved like a black river, bearing banners like boats. Conquer Or Die (Carpenters

Union) was swept along on the flood. They Shall Not Pass (United Hairdressers) faltered and came to a halt before me. Then looking round I saw the squirrel coat cornered by the crowd. I edged my way through weeping women to where she was wedged under a radio.

What, you still here? I bawled.

But only just, she seemed to say.

How's life? How's your work going?

Very slack, she bawled through the strains of the International, everyone's left town you see. Can't we get out of this and have a talk?

We pushed our way through weeping women up the steps of the Communist Headquarters. The guard let us stand beside him in the doorway. You can see everything from here, comrades, he said.

I always said you'd never leave us, I said.

Well it will be a wrench in a way. But still I'm getting a bit homesick with all this upset. Oh to be in England, now that spring is in the air. She was having another of her new starts. It was the Consul this time. He's getting us on a British battleship. Something was going to be done about her by the Consul.

The Consul's been so awfully kind, she said, and as he says, having mother and all, and he's responsible if anything happened.

But have you been in any danger? I asked.

Well, not so as you'd notice it. Except the nasty shock I had the first day, when I was caught crossing the Plaza on my way to school.

Maaree all surprised, hurrying along in a dignified English way, on those long legs, taking cover behind the marble nudes in the Plaza. It might have been better if she had stayed like the young Fascist Assault Guard, who gained fame for a day, by lying dead, with his head in a puddle of blood and being photographed thus. The caption: He Was Misled. It might have been better for her than landing in dead of winter 'at home' with her cough and her mother, and a letter recommending her as a teacher of English.

You'd be better off here, I said. There's plenty of work. You know the Anarchist Culture Centre on the Gracia needs teachers? I'll give you a card. They're crazy on foreign culture. I'm sure you'd find your little boot boy there. You'd be internationalism and culture personified. You'd really be someone there, you'd be the belle of the ball for once in your life. They feed you, clothe you and look after your family when you're in prison. I can get you a card. But this is the last time I try to do anything for you. I might as well have said, The first time.

Of course she took it as a joke, so determined she was to give up what little she had for this free trip on a British battleship.

Some months later I called at the Consulate. I was ushered into the waiting room by a poor girl. There was no one there but the Englishman in the mac, looking as if he sat there every day. He was pleased to see me. Still hanging on? Same here. Damned if the Reds can scare me away. We must all stick together, he said. It won't be long now.

He was very bitter because his greyhounds had died. I'm not scared by the Bolshies' bluff, he said. I know what I've got behind me. The British Flag and the King and Queen, God Bless Them. Some people seem to think they're out of date but I have a lot of time for the King and Queen. His wife had a baby but they couldn't get milk for it. It was in danger of dying like the greyhounds. All the milk went to the Anarchists. But the Consul will look after it, he said. That's his job you see, looking after us British subjects. Unless you're on the black list, but I've never been political thank God.

He stopped when a prim youth came to the door and ignoring him said, Would I please come in? I could see the Acting Vice-Consul. The Consul and the Vice-Consul happened to be away, in a place of greater safety. The Acting Vice-Consul was away too, but the Assistant Acting Vice-Consul received me. I thought

I had seen him before, around the Cosmopolitan School of Languages.

Not registered with us, I see? after I had asked my favour. Oh, I see. Been away. Ah. Better have a smacker on your passport. No time like the present. It was like being vaccinated again.

While my passport was in an inner office, having a smacker put on it, he took me into his confidence. There's trouble brewing, he said.

I said there certainly was trouble enough.

You don't understand me, perhaps you'd better take one of these little things. He opened a drawer in which lay a pile of stickers with a Union Jack and the Consular seal on them. I had seen one on the door of the Consulate. It certainly looked very good.

My front door had been blown from its hinges by the bomb blast from an explosion. No one had bothered with the door since, but I took a sticker. No wonder Maaree had been all up in the air with these attentions. When the School closed it would be embarrassing for the Assistant Acting Vice-Consul to see the teachers starve or go political. Much nicer for them to starve in safety. But of course he was doing his duty. He looked a kind man.

By the way, I said, do you remember Maaree? One of the girls at the Cosmopolitan School.

Maaree? Oh . . . Miss Fitzgerald of course. A teacher of languages. Such a nice girl. So conscientious and such a nice nature. They got off safely. We saw to that of course. But the mother died on the ship.

So you knew them did you? Yes. Very sad. But one might say a merciful release.

Time of Departure

Outside the office I examine the coloured labels given to me by the travel bureau. The labels and the pictures on them are round. Seen from a dark interior, perhaps the round mouth of a porthole, on the travelling waves of jet blue sea, the white liner and the white gull. The advertisement boat and bird of the travel bureau still needlessly invite to the prize that is life itself.

Before returning to my room, the room that does not change with my travels, that does not belong to any climate or country, its wallpaper neutral, and its window giving on to a court, I sit down with some friends in a deserted café.

They are superstitious. They still indulge in dreams and disappointments. I dream only at night and only of a time that has gone. In my dreams is a question and a journey but just as in life, nothing is ever resolved.

A warm breeze blows from the dock where the white dream is tethered. Water carts are sprinkling the dim streets and oleander flowers fall on the café tables. Even to my neutral room, through the window that gives on to a court comes the last scent of a distant summer.

Summer. Unlikely that I shall see another.

Summer in Switzerland and still together, the sanatoriums crowded with patients still, the hotels with visitors, and in the hotel garden, flowers and fountains.

Jan sat beside me on a garden bench. When I spoke he did not raise his clear grey eyes. I turned to my sister on the other side. Did you have a nice summer Cristina?

In my room there was early summer light. Someone was walking up the garden path. A blind man with a straw hat and a stick. I moved aside from the window and stood by the dressing table. As he passed under the wall I could only see his head. But he looked up. His look though blind is piercing. I moved to the back of the room. I was afraid.

I woke from warm depths in the white bed. A fire had recently been lighted in the tiled stove. Kind of them. This fact of the fire settled my wandering fears. I fear they are going to treat me as an invalid. Yet I am momentarily stronger. How hungry I am! Beside the bed is a plate of cheap cakes. The bright pink sugar on one of the cakes is dissolving. Another of the cakes is heavily varnished and has a currant on it. Surely flies too have sat beside the currant. Cannot they give me something better to eat?

I rose from the bed and took my silk dressing gown that hung on a peg. My silk dressing gown (I must be rich) and walked out to the garden.

It was then that we sat on the bench. It was then I walked slowly up and down the paths with Jan. Is this death after all such a mystery? I said to him. Cannot we swallow this event too? Everything that happens is natural even though it should happen very rarely.

I said to Jan, Death is a wrong diagnosis. (How simple after all.) The diagnosis of a country doctor. Jan did not raise his eyes.

I could not remember the details of my illness. It ended in my being found in a filthy pool . . . all the symptoms were those usually associated with death. I had been pronounced dead but it was not so. Now I could walk and move about freely, but because they lowered their eyes or looked at me blindly, I felt at times that they feared or hated me. And I too was afraid of my new strength. I almost suspected the effortlessness of my movements. I felt no strain in the white flesh of my limbs. They moved softly as if on a silk thread. But if it might be only for these few days I wanted still to be loved.

Though Jan had lain beside me in the white invalid bed, he had not looked at me. He was afraid and hated me perhaps. I said to him, Go away if you wish. You must go away if you feel it too strange. But I could not believe or understand that he should. Then as he did not speak I got up quietly and left him.

I walked to the end of the garden where a small ruined pagoda was hidden in vines. I felt no cold; the dusk was light and mild. My limbs moved lightly, without resistance, moved carefully, strung on a silk thread.

I sat down in the pagoda trailing with mad vines and looked out over the lawn in the mild evening light, wondering how long? The silk thread is thin, yet feeling half sadly my strength returning.

People were pacing up and down the lawn. Jan came out to play a last set of tennis with an Irishman, one of the guests at the hotel. I came and stood in the court watching them. I was stronger in spite of having been so long without food.

Jan looked at me kindly now. But I couldn't join in the play. I will go to my room, I said to him. I am content now to go to my room and rest. Still weak, you see, I said to the people who were there watching, sitting on a bench in the pale light. But Oh! I said, stretching out my arms, what is this round my wrists? (Underneath the rich dressing gown I am wearing a strange shirt, thick, coarse, white.) But Oh! I said, I am glad I enjoyed this. The game. This lovely evening. All.

They have been to my room. Beside the bed is a glass of something that is not milk. Why am I treated so? It comes to me in a flash. Not the persecution of the police but poison was the cause of my illness.

I lift the silver speaking tube near the bed and am about to ask them to put me on to my mother's room. But no, that's too risky. I put the receiver down. I shall go to her room myself. I am strong enough after a little rest.

As soon as my mother comes in I tell her my plan. A nurse, a newcomer to the place, and the little maid I trust are to cook my food and sit with me night and day. I tell my mother she must send for the maid.

The maid in her white cap and apron enters the room. Jan comes in too. I tell them my wishes. They do not look at me but begin talking anxiously together. My voice is weak, I have to strain it and shout. Then I am afraid that someone outside the room may have overheard. My voice is weaker now but I have to shout because they are talking together. How can you all talk together like this when I'm just in the middle of telling you my plan? The maid is to say this:

I became interested in cooking when I prepared Fraulein D's food. I bought a small electric stove with my savings and took lessons in cookery.

Thus your cooking for me will be explained. Now for the rest—why are you talking together?

It snapped . . . a voice broke . . . it began to groan and gabble . . .

I return to the room that is always the same, that does not belong to any climate or country, whose wallpaper is neutral and whose window gives on to a court. The bug left in the dry cracked basin to starve, is full of life still. He crawls to a certain point on the shiny side helping himself by the crack. He slips down to the bottom and starts again.

I place the coloured labels out of the breeze from the window.

Seen from the dark mouth of a cave, the white liner and the white bird invite. Their invitation could once be bought for money but now the transaction is more complicated. Money, the ever recurring change of address, submission to time while boats and trains leave and everything passes till the will is dead.

But not yet. Hours of crawling slowly towards the *guichet* only to be thrown back by a blind look and a hard smile. Not yet. Submission is not enough. It is not enough to deny three times. Their attitude suggests there is nothing to deny. Let us agree. No targets for martyrdom are visible through the smoke of burning

Europe. The boundaries of the just cause waver. Comrades and oppressors are swallowed in the smoke. There remain These who exact submission with smiles.

The bug in the basin gives a little jump. He crawls to a certain point on the shiny slope helping himself by the crack. He slips back to the bottom and starts again.

The psychologist sits in the café, happy in the vacuum of his explanation. He tries to unravel the last shred of my personality. This is to cure me of fear. He means me to feel my submission is not final. The final submission shall be to his explanation.

But have I no reason to fear Them? He allows that I have. He allows a good deal. But think back. You've always been afraid of something, he says.

Although the psychologist does not deal in morals his arguments have a moral overtone. He would like me to feel it is I who am to blame in wilfully guarding the last irrational shred. And I take no blame. I take what I get from Them. I talk to him though, because that is what he wishes.

Frankly, I put my misfortune down to a mere slip. A very simple decision to do what was right (or so it seemed at the time). It was not a political act or hardly so, though I have learned since that even a whisper may be politically significant. But we did not expect or hope to change Europe. It was just a slip, a private misadventure.

Been dreaming lately? the psychologist asks while we sit in the café waiting for drinks and waiting. Of my sister. As a matter of fact I have heard from her again.

Tell me about it. Which comes first the fact or the dream?

My friend is pleased. You have never loved your sister Cristina.

I have never loved the circumstances of our lives . . . I dream also of an underground nightclub. And truly it seemed a dream that day of the charity carnival, the dull grey day and the crowds in the streets, stopping and moving on, as though they were searching for something.

I had come from the Ritz. I wanted a room with a bath so I stayed at the Ritz. For that and other reasons. On the ninth floor though I have always been afraid of the elevators.

When I came downstairs my mother was there. I remember her sweet anxious face, her homemade dress a shade too original, and a rough straw hat with a quartz ornament in it. A page girl was bringing a letter on a tray. She caught us at the top of the steps, in the deep carpet, the orchestra playing inside. She stood there waiting while I opened the letter.

It is one of these advertisement letters, I said, that anybody gets when they land from a liner. They obtain the lists of names from the hotels . . . The orchestra played.

The messenger stood still at a little distance—not moving nearer not moving away, while I read the letter again. At last it was clear . . .

Give her a shilling please, I said to my mother.

Then I walked out, into the lonely and puzzled carnival crowd. The folk entertainment was in another part of the town. I took a cab with people going that way. Outside the door the prices were pasted up. 10.—7.30 and 5. For charity! Another proof of the decay of the capitalist system. They won't get me to pay these prices though.

I went downstairs to a big basement room. There were sofas along the walls. It was a comfortable sort of night place. A waitress in peasant costume said the dancers would give another performance later, so I sat down pleased not to have to pay yet. The waitress went away.

The room was empty at present. I was alone with my sister. She was expecting me. We did not speak. We looked at a price list on the wall, a number of things to be had for 2.50.

I will try to get you something, I said to my sister. I went outside and walked up and down in a passage where there was a bar and also a buffet covered with various kinds of food.

At last I returned to the room.

There's a nice little buffet out there, I said to my sister. If you would come with me we could choose and bring it back and eat in comfort here while we wait. It seems there is no one to serve us. No doubt you want to know what was in the letter?

So, I said to my psychologist friend, you see how coldly I recall each detail. You wouldn't say that was a dream, would you? You arrived at the town yourself by the next boat. From what were you fleeing?

I remember, he said. That was when you received the first letter. It preyed on your mind. It was largely due to your subsequent behaviour that your associates fell under suspicion.

I hold no responsibility for that. It had to be, once the small act that then seemed right, was committed. It started long before that childish political gesture. It started long before when I met the schoolboy Kling and opposed him, and ended with my walking into the trap.

The trap that was never laid for you . . . and introducing a feeble minded bureaucrat into your home, and irritating them all with your false confessions. Prophetic confessions.

There was nothing supernatural about the matter. You need never have shown them the letter. How could they know the letter was in your pocket? A harmless letter this time, perfectly harmless.

Exactly what I said to the ticket girl as we stood at the bottom of the escalator. We could have kept the letter in our pocket, I said. But now it seems that we have started something . . .

It is always well to remember the regulations. To outdo them if possible in a strange town. Some means of identification should be presented, if only out of politeness, on entering a station. But by some unfortunate slip, when we passed the barrier, grasping the permits and also the envelope for double assurance, we were each of us holding out a half of the letter, under the eyes of the girl who was clipping the tickets.

Just a moment, she said.

A boy in uniform was standing by, a portentous cheeky child. They puzzled conscientiously over the pages. I explained that it was two halves of a letter my friend and I had been reading as we came down the escalator.

What is in it? they asked.

There was nothing in it. A few vague hints from my sister. I tried to remember some of the longer words—to think of some of the words that would puzzle them.

You ought to have a dictionary, I said, kidding the boy and two young girls who stood by.

We have one in the ticket office, they said. This way please.

We all went into the niche where tickets were sold. The other passengers had disappeared. How long are we going to be held up here? I asked. The train leaves—

Their conscientious faces had a look of deprecating politeness and forbearance. Over their duty some people were irritable. Not they. They were prepared to spend any length of time on the matter.

The solemn cheeky officious boy was despatched to a higher official, I following him. We waited for some time in a wide passageway where people were passing. Is this holdup going on for ever? I asked. The chief's very busy, he said.

But just at this moment by luck the chief came out. He was hurrying somewhere with a pile of papers in his hand, and bundles of tickets of various pale colours. I suppose there are disputes about tickets, I thought, season tickets and so on. I wonder is that what all his business consists of?

Excuse me, I said, stopping him in his flight.

He was what you might call good looking. A pale pink nonentity of a minor official.

Please come inside, he said. It is more comfortable in my office.

I sat down in the office on a padded chair. The boy had been told to return me the letter, which the young ladies had been afraid to let out of their hands.

Bah! What incompetence, the official said.

Preposterous, I said. A letter from my sister that's been through the censor twice. (I doubt though. Do they go through the censor twice?)

Of course, he said, so pleasant and reasonable that I was only sorry I hadn't the letter with me. I even remembered sentiments in the letter that might be interpreted as patriotic.

It was comfortable in the artificially lighted office. I am happy to clear up a misunderstanding, he said. He rose and held out his hand. He touched my hand.

I follow my mother across the wood floor of an attic. It is full of wheels, large wheels, smaller wheels, more wheels. All is still. In the rooms and in the passages leading from room to room, something is missing in the timeless stillness.

. . . in the artificially lighted office, coming comfortably out of a deep warmth.

You may go now. It will be quite all right, the official said.

You are sure? I was deeply relieved.

Certainly. I'll accompany you to the stairs.

By the way, you hypnotised me, you know.

He admitted it with a smile.

People have tried on other occasions but I've never gone off like that. In fact while I was coming round I thought I was at the dentist. Did I talk at all? I asked.

Yes indeed, you jabbered a lot, he said. Some wonderful nonsense. Did you not hear yourself laughing as you came out of it?

I examined his face. It was friendly.

I suppose, I said casually, all the usual symbols, the wheel, and escalators and odds and ends from the poor old unconscious.

No, he said.

The uniformed boy stepped off the escalator, touched his cap, and presented me with the letter we had forgotten.

I insist you read it, I said to the official. I held it out.

He glanced at the envelope. No matter, he said.

So that was what all the fuss was about. Only some long words.

The girls are abysmally ignorant, he said. But now to speak of more agreeable things, the address on your letter tells me I know your people. A happy coincidence. He bowed over my hand.

As soon as I reached home I told my mother. I've never been hypnotised before, I said.

You were once, she said, by a schoolboy called Kling whose father your father knew.

That was all in fun. We were children. I didn't go off at all, I resisted him. This time it was as if I'd been at the dentist's. He had no right to do it. My mother agreed.

I told my father. He listened heavily. He is not interested in my affairs.

But soon the official, Herr Kling, came to call. This time I noticed he looked and spoke like a woman.

A pleasant coincidence. A compatriot far from the homeland. His papa and I used to do business together, but he's changed out of all recognition, my father said.

Herr Kling bowed and smiled like a woman. You had no right, I said. You were taking advantage of my situation. I mean of course, my being alone in the office. But how did you do it? You must have touched me without my being aware.

We'll show you, my father said, with a heavy laugh. Remember, Mother, what fun we had with the table? He was going to allow Herr Kling to demonstrate. Kling touched my father's hand with his mouth. Then he took his bare foot out of the slipper and bent over it as if he would bite it gently. (Dirty ugly old foot. My father should be ashamed.)

Then Kling put his hand on my father's head. He is not a good subject, he said. But as he spoke my father half fell all in one piece against the table, and I saw that his eyes were blind.

Now you've got him I said. But you've no right. This is a terrible way to get hold of a family.

But no he said quietly, it is just a knack. We are all old friends. It is just friendly fun.

To get a hold, I said.

He smiled like a woman. But everyone is tied in some way.

See, mother said, your father is quite himself.

You shall take nothing more, I said. Tied in some way . . . for long hours a wage slave . . . a slave to many other circumstances—

Quiet dear, my mother said. Hush dear you will—But always there's a bit of me that's my own.

As I spoke I felt something snap. It began to groan and gabble . . . a voice broke . . .

The clerk at the shipping office says to me: Be down an hour or two before the time of departure. It's always as well to leave yourself plenty of time. There may be be a few final formalities.

I thank you, clerk. All preparations are made, all precautions are taken against the certainty of the unexpected.

Down at the wharf the liner, immense and white as a dream, enclosed by the dark crowding houses, is tethered. It expects freedom and motion but now it is still and near, a hand's touch away, with the white gull circling overhead as promised.

I shall be there before the time of departure. I shall step past the guards and cross that narrow gangplank. I am not superstitious. Only the suitcases containing my human relics, summer dresses, brooches and silk flowers, are vulnerable. Jan's small suitcase, standing apart from the others, with its little blind eye where his name was ripped out, unopened since we packed the shirts, the ties, the yellow bag containing threads and needles. If it was opened what would be still there?

Take care of it for me, he said as the gates closed. The psychologist sits in the café, looking at things from the back.

How do things look from the back? I ask. Do they look any better?

Had time allowed I might have been able to help you. Been dreaming again?

Of frontiers. The frontiers are still there are they not?

So I believe. You tried to cross one I think?

Yes. We took our tickets. We packed our clothes. We walked about as if anaesthetised. Then at last we were on the Express with our visas to America where my sister and brother in law, respected, living clean lives, would look after us. Jan had found two seats in the second class. We left our haversacks and the luggage on them. Now we were really *en route*. Like children, full of excitement, we explored the train. There were better carriages where we could have lain down for the night but as we passed they were taken possession of.

Why did I say to Jan that we could have done better? Always he is so good, finds seats, attends to details as if our lives would still go on. Often when there was madness in the office he stood in front of a desk, as if he lived still in the sane life. A bit dull, a bit stupid perhaps, but he did not stammer or redden under the blind looks and the hard smiles.

Patience, he would say, while I raged and hoped and feared. Patience. You may as well leave your luggage in the cloakroom. You may as well take a chair. You see this is going to last a long time. It is no use objecting to being photographed. It will all be over in the click of a camera.

He was always so, standing before the desks, carefully dressed in an innocent neat suit, a boy who had been to school, who had been to church. He behaved as if the old life was true. Was it choice or stupidity?

The train was racing over the open country. In a third class coach, men were crowded round a guitar player. He had a lined, Latin face, and wore pince-nez. He was singing a revolutionary song.

Is it all right? Are they not from the Brigade? I asked.

Everyone must know they are from the Brigade, Jan said. Otherwise they would not be on the train.

You are right, I said. Everything is known. Some of us joined in the song. We were all in good spirits.

Returning to our own carriage to eat our rolls and fruit, I spotted another vacant place where one of us might have lain down. I wonder if it's occupied or not, I said to a girl we had made a train friendship with.

What is that?

Above the train noise the roar of aeroplanes. God what a target we are! All lights ablaze, helpless under the planes. A death box lighted up, trundling peaceably on through the night. The planes have come down and are flying beside the train.

What are they doing?

This is a neutral country.

Still there's no certainty. No certainty.

The planes are lighted too. The tail lights dip and dive. This reassures me. But why do they follow us?

At the frontier the empty carriages were coffin-like in the grey morning light. Passing the empty carriages I walked beside the girl we had made friends with. I believe that place was vacant all the time, I said. Do we go on in this train? If so perhaps we can get through quickly and grab it. We try to be first past the authorities. There's a long journey ahead, eh Jan? Jan said nothing.

We lined up before the authorities. There were only a few of us crossing the frontier. The authorities, in grey-green uniforms, sat in a booth before the iron railings that surrounded the station. First came the Brigader of the song. They hardly looked at him. We know you, they said.

His body was transfixed against the railings. There was a quiet click on the soundless picture. In the picture I seemed to see, clothes and organs bursting between the railings.

The picture disappeared. In that click it was over, so quick and quiet that I didn't quite understand. But I said to myself, I have seen a man's death. Like that it happens in the click of a camera.

Now it is my turn to be questioned. I present the papers. The agent looks at me indifferently. He is not interested in my affairs. You didn't really think we'd let you go through?

Now I do understand. How could we have imagined it would be otherwise?

I mention my sister in America.

Yes, he said.

The visa is in order.

He moves it aside to make way for another paper.

You'll be quite willing to return if we should allow you to go?

Yes. Indeed, indeed we will go back. Certainly, yes we will do what you suggest.

He looked over at Jan. You, he said.

I stand aside. He looks at Jan heavily.

Jan stands in his usual patient attitude, in the innocence of his new town suit. He does not raise his clear grey eyes.

We might allow your companion to return.

Jan does not reply. He stands there pale and polite. He has a smudge of soot from the train on his cheek. What are you doing here?

Jan moves his head stupidly as if he has been asleep. I do not know what he is thinking. He does not speak. Only puts down the suitcase he has been holding.

Days run like water through the lonely room that holds no time nor climate, nor shadow of trees nor any trace of friendship. They have been to the room and taken away his suitcase. The patient little case with the blind eye where they had ripped out his name.

The psychologist sits in the café taking life to pieces. Calm and preoccupied he sits there, like a child surrounded by ruins of a clock.

It was I who took the suitcase away, he said. It might have been an embarrassment at the last moment. I will look after it for you.

You are very kind. (I can do without even the case too if it must be. I have sometimes wondered lately what is inside it.)

It is little enough I can do for you, he said, but I ask you to fix your mind on one point.

My mind is fixed, I said, on the time of departure.

Your papers are all in order, but remember, he said, you carry fear in yourself.

I still react in a normal way to danger. You want to kill that too. The last shred of me.

This shred of yourself you speak of, this shred you guard so jealously from me; you confuse it with self respect. Where is this self respect when you face the ship's officials? Unless with my help you can come to certain conclusions you may never pass the Statue of Liberty.

Is this to give me courage for the journey? Does all that is past and the journey depend on me? Have I not told you that my well meant act, that changed the rational world I knew to chaos, that even that was almost an accident?

Your moral problem is only a small link in the chain. Yet when I once did something I knew was right, and that by accident, I was not forgiven. It could never be proved that it was accidental.

I cannot help you. Time does not allow. But listen to me as a friend. There will be further formalities. You will cringe—

There will be many formalities. I pray that cringing will be enough for Them. They smell out hidden resistance in the soul.

They are not interested in your soul. He sighed. Nor in your sufferings, your severe sufferings, not least of them the delusions while you were confined in the sanatorium.

But now I have no delusions. I learnt not to wish or ask for an explanation. This is my last wish—not to wish. This is the last thread and you try to break it.

I try to recall you to yourself, he said.

Strange to wake late on the day of departure. I might have slept until the hour was past. But no, the bug still climbs up the basin. The psychologist will appear on my last shore, he who hopes to unravel the last thread.

On the floor at the foot of the bed, my patient tragic suitcases silently weep. But I am not superstitious. With steady hands I tie on the coloured labels to take us to the new life that is promised. If the suitcase with the blind eye were here I would give it a label too. Because I am not superstitious. It was different when we believed. What did we once believe? What was betrayed?

A siren from the port rends the room. The time has come again. The time of departure . . .

At Home and Alone

So all the morning I stayed there in the room, sleeping and thinking. I will go out, I thought. There is nothing to stop me. I will send a note to the Aizgorris, I thought. But I didn't want to do anything wrong. I was afraid for Santiago and Rosa. If I sent a note the whole village would know. I did not want the whole village to know.

I do not know myself what it really means. Waking up in a strange bed in my own village I closed my eyes again and saw, What does it mean? A great boulder lodged on a hillside. Really? What does it really? And I Pachi with *really*, trying to prise out the boulder with *really*, a weak curled leaf, when what was needed would be dynamite or at least a pick.

After lunch I will see the Aizgorris, I thought. Then I shall know. The war is over now.

I had signed the paper of my own free will, being an orphan and fourteen years of age. Most of the children had signed when the war was over. The hostel people approved, the Hon. Sec. cried, there was an uncertain air about the office, no more was said about the fascist terror. For myself I preferred even very much work in my own place to the dark days of Bloomsbury. Arriving always late in the dirty morning to light the coal fire in the Hon. Sec.'s office, then leaving the gaslighter in too long, until it was discovered by one of the typists. Being called all day like a dog, with strange sounds, in the basement office, crowded with papers and people. Sticking on stamps and making cups of tea. For Spain, they said. But Spain was far away. And back at the hostel was cocoa and cold bed. But bed was still the best place in Bloomsbury. So I was always late for lighting the fire.

High up persons came to the refugee office. What is your name and what is your village like? It was like an old song. I could not remember. Sing us a song then. The twelfth day of October, One thousand nine hundred and thirty-four, is remembered in History. Is remembered. I could never remember more.

After lunch I shall go and see the Aizgorris. If I must meet a friend, What do you do here Pachi? I am going along to see my master and mistress.

No one has come to tell what to do. A gentleman met us at the frontier and checked up our papers. Work will be found for all of you, he said. He bought me a ticket and told me to stay at this place for the night. Provided for in your own district, he said. The other children were going to other places. We didn't speak much on the journey. Everything looked the same but from having been away we were not sure.

At first when the letters came children would say, Everything is just the same in my village. Under the stamp on my letter there's a message. It's in code, of course; only myself can read it. Someone read out, The sky is blue and beautiful sunny weather but there is an illness about and every day people are taken away to the cemetery.

You see? they said. A secret code we arranged. It means they are bumping off the fascists as usual.

In my letter it said: Friend Pachi, After saluting you and your good guardians hoping you all enjoy perfect health; Pachi, we received the favour of your parcel with its contents with which we are pleased, we remain grateful for all, we found in it, one kilo of flour, another of beans, another of something unknown or of which we are ignorant of the name, the parcel pleased us infinitely, but now between good friends one sees that already you have forgotten us for you know my taste for coffee. Well we shall see whether I can ever taste it again. Yes I must tell you the parcel made us happy and Aizgorri says you can send a little tobacco, a little and all shall be repaid, he says.

A pity you are so far. A pity you are not nearer to us. On the twenty- first it snowed. The wind and the sun made the snow disappear but it has left behind it a wave of cold. Everything is frozen as I write. Nothing more for today and at last receive an embrace from your friends who do not forget you.

This letter was addressed in my own hand. That was strange was it not? In the uncertain turmoil of departure I must have left envelopes ready addressed to calm them. Strange too that they were so formal with me and that they said I had forgotten them. It was as if they knew that after my departure all was changed. Everything was changed when we got there. Around the refugee camp everyone lied. Even the radio lied till we smashed it up; but that did not help us. And I knew by the faces there that I had been mistaken in coming away. And the parcel was wrong. Because supposing things were very bad or that their lives were in danger what they would need would be coffee and tobacco. I thought I would write and tell them that other people put the things in the parcel—that I was nobody now. But I did not write.

After lunch I will walk round and see them. Halt there! A Guardia. Where are you going you? I was only going to see my master and mistress.

I dreamed last night of the Hon. Sec. She was fair and her teeth stuck out which gave her a stiffness in talking as if her mouth moved on a little hinge. In the dream I questioned her about my situation and in the dream she spoke to me (which she seldom did at the office). But her answers were nebulous and inconclusive like the climate of Bloomsbury.

After lunch I will go to the Aizgorris. If I see Don Lucio in the grey raincoat? Excuse me my son but where is it you are going? Nowhere Don Lucio. Nowhere, Nowhere at all.

I was treated like a guest in the restaurant. The fat patrona in a pink dress, a woman I heard called Lola, spoke to me in my own language, but it did not sound right because she was not of the village and looked at me strangely. There was nothing wrong with the food. Only it was of the kind they give in restaurants and hotels. The sweet was a lemon sweet. It tasted strikingly of the real lemon. But as I had never tasted a sweet of this kind before it tasted bitter and strange. They did not make sweets of this kind at the Casa Aizgorri.

After lunch I was alone in my village. I went outside and looked at the front of the café. It was in an antique house in a dark corner between two streets. It was famed for its coffee but we never went there. Strangers went there and we did not know the owner. The air and the blue sky above the houses had the sad freshness of spring or autumn. Being away I had forgotten the seasons. What I had forgotten was very much. My own birthplace and who I was in it. So that now the stones of the street, the deep kerbstones, the walls round gardens and tops of lemon trees were like something remembered that has stopped still. Though it was all the same I felt already I had done wrong. Just as I knew as soon as I was away that I was mistaken. That I was nobody now.

The village is very quiet in the afternoon. The streets were quiet. The doors open, empty chairs in the doorways. I did not wish to meet someone I knew. Particularly I did not wish to meet Don Lucio. Though we had always said good morning to him, Don Lucio in a grey raincoat, I did not know how I should greet him now.

I met no one I knew but halfway along the long empty street, the thought came very near of the Casa Aizgorri, the good food and my past life with Rosa and Santiago, and how much liked they were by the whole village, and it struck me as if I had done them a great wrong. No one had told me it was wrong to leave. No one had told me it was wrong to return. The steep kerb of the pavement, the open doors, the walls and the lemons against the sky were the same and yet nothing was sure.

I had met no one I knew. I turned into my street almost opposite the door of the house. The door of the house was open.

I noticed that the blue sign over the door was gone but it seemed natural that it should not be there. As if there had been a slip in my memory. So long away I might have forgotten my own name and address.

I walked inside. I called out an Ave Maria. Nobody answered. I did not call out Rosa or Santiago. Perhaps they had gone away. I could see through the door that opened into the entrance the rather dark room that led to the kitchen. A long table covered with oilcloth and a sewing machine and shelves were in there and always people stopped there to talk. Señora Rosa standing in front of the shelves with a plate in her hand, and Santiago, his leg across a corner of the table, a bit of a cigarette in his lips, ready for arguments. You are sure? Yes. You are sure? Quite. You are sure?

But now there was no one about.

At the back of the stone floored entrance room stood the big wooden chest. I don't think they valued it much, it was shabby and old and always stood there and bills and magazines lay on the top.

I looked through the papers. The house was perfectly quiet. I was looking for something with the date on it. I thought that with the date it would tell me something. From between the dusty church magazines a cutting from a newspaper fell out. It was old and yellow, the paper was very thin, I picked it up off the floor. No writing, just a picture of two cadavers shot down somewhere. I couldn't have identified the bodies. They were not like people, only a furry blur that might be bushes, a twisted boot and darkness dividing a flat white space. The dark shapes of holes on the white. Where blood had run out of the holes the printers' ink lay heavy and thick and black.

I did not know them. No, they were nobody. I did not call out Santiago and Rosa. I did not even call an Ave Maria. I did not do anything yet.

Reconstruction

The tall street lights had been painted over, a thick dark blue. Darkness muffled the crowded sounds of the square. Out of the body of the blackout soundless shapes emerged furtively, without explanation. The phosphorescent frame of a bus hung on the air, then dropped away to an unknown destination.

The trusty little trams stop at the corner. They rattle past on their fixed orbits, complaining against the darkness, the work, the war. I boarded a tram that was going uptown. Should I find the room? I had forgotten the number of the house; the name, if it had one, of the narrow turning; but only because I knew the location so well. Once at the corner of the Via Oscure I should know it again so well, the café with phone box, the shop where they sold chairs, the decent enclosed smell of the alley with its tall, shuttered houses.

The tram shrieked away up the straight street. In the yellow shade of the interior, the faces of the passengers hung like dark lanterns. 'Steady there.' The conductor called the name of the street like a mother calling her child. Enclosed in the yellow darkness of the car, in the sudden silence, we stare at each other and wait.

The old woman opposite stared and smiled. A ragged youth, just to be doing something, moved my suitcase out of the way of feet. 'What a journey,' the old woman said. 'I was down to the port today to visit my daughter but after all the baby hadn't come. The poor bambino does not want to be born.' And as, to be doing something, we all laughed, and I caught the eyes of other passengers, lanterns were lighted in the blackout of my bewilderment.

The familiar is strange due to the war and the blackout and also perhaps to the manner of my return. A curious chance enabled me to return. Call it the fortunes of war. War like a lava flow, crushing out the old rights and wrongs, flattening landmarks, erasing the past. I return to aid in the work of reconstruction. But mine is a private mission. To search for little treasures among the debris.

The rising cry of the car splits open the muffled night.

The sun is overhead and from it the deep blue sky rolls away like the echoes of an explosion. The sunlight breaks on the brilliant white houses and strikes white hot glances from a tram circling the square. A flashing figure swings on to the step, bright shirt, brown lifted arm, speeding in splintered sunlight. I have been walking in the gardens with Vero, talking of Giustizia e Libertà. In the gardens there is a bust of Garibaldi and a fountain shaped like a shell. Trams shriek in the square. They break from the circle and race to the hills, breasting rivers of sunlight at street corners. At the end of the street, of every street, are the hills . . .

The conductor holds out his hand enquiringly. We stare at each other and wait for what I shall say. I cannot remember the stop.

'Near the Via Oscure. Then I shall know.'

'But you're on the wrong car,' he says. 'You should have taken one, any one, of Corso Vittorio Emanuele if you wanted the Via Oscure.' Though the two streets run parallel, this, to him, is a matter for regret.

'I know the way right enough, once I get uptown.' His face smiles now, but he punches the ticket with a general regret for the mistakes of people. 'You should keep your eyes open, pretty stranger.'

The tram groans. The road lifts to the hills.

The hills that were so near on the long last day, across a narrow placid stretch of water. On that day when I came to the port, alone, they said the ship out there in the bay would not be sailing yet. There was plenty of time. Yes plenty of time now. Then the driver of one of a row of dusty cars that stood on the wharf under ragged palmtrees, said he would take me for a ride round the town. Without charge, he said, because you are young and pretty. To see, the town . . . I was a stranger already.

As we were boarding the ship somebody said, 'You never really see it but from the bay.' Across the water, over there in the past, the hills stared over the town, that hummed in the sun, but seemed unaware of them. A man brought a deck chair, wrote my name on a card and made me comfortable—facing the town and the hills. Passengers talked of a journey; still it was there, all the day I had left, just out of touch, in the past. On the hills where there was no whisper of motion, only the light changed, and in the evening their outlines were cruelly clear. I could almost believe we had sailed and that already we were far away, and that these hills, this past, would always be with me, compressed by perspective to a small, clear plan.

As the day lengthened the hills opened like a white scroll on which I could read the signs. The deep blue O, like the eyehole of a skull, that is the pass. That black thread is a stream, the snake is a valley. Under the peaks are the white grottos and columns. Vero was there. But now I cannot read where he is.

We are nearing the end of town where the hills wait in the dark. Soon I shall see the room. Home at last, a stranger as I had foreseen, for as I believed it impossible, whenever I dreamed of returning, it was always thus, as a stranger. It strikes me with surprise that I can read the notices in cafés and trams; it is as if I possessed some unusual secret, the ability to fly or become invisible, which I keep to myself and use to my own advantage.

But though so much is strange, the landlady, hard as wood, her head in a handkerchief, is still the same. 'You are back,' she says. Nothing more. 'All well?' I say. Nothing more. I can hardly speak for you. The landlady is a valuable landmark.

'She never talks' (a hint to me perhaps) the two girls say, now that we sit at the table in my room, with Robert from the Reconstruction Committee.

'You found the place?'

Robert frowned. 'I asked of course.' He's unduly irritated by the suggestion that he might not be just as much at home in a small Sicilian town as he is in his office. Cultured people are at ease on the continent. His French is good—one can always make oneself understood with French. He is not at all the average Britisher, helpless, encased in a cocoon of superiority. He is cultured; believes in freedom of speech and so on. This rock strewn country is the cradle of culture and he feels a certain responsibility towards it. He will assist. He will take the rough with the smooth. He will take what he finds and try to reconstruct it.

At present, sitting a little back from the table, tapping his pipe, he is out of it, and for this I am glad, for his reconstruction has nothing to do with me. But his stylised shyness saves him from any appearance of stupidity. His clear cut features collect information. Later he will enquire about things that no one will know. 'These people! They don't know what's going on in the next village!' And the people he asks will be silent because there are so many things they know that he does not know. But he knows that so many tons of wheat will last so long for European relief; and how many tons were burnt; and how much converted into alcohol. Massive and abstract facts that stand like the mountains and Etna in the distance.

His questions aim at establishing contact. It doesn't do to tread on people's toes if you want to get things done. (He will get things done, he will make himself understood.) And then of course we are all good antifascists. We must all pull together.

'And do you like the room?' I asked him now. Against this dark, muddled and hostile background, how like the others he looks, with their Jaeger pullovers, pipes, and enlightenment, the ones who make England free, that refugees may sell their wretched antifascist rags on the street, or even, if attached to a recognised party, be invited to private parties at Hampstead. In these non-stuffy circles it's quite the thing to marry a refugee if she is youthful and pretty. It gives a cosmopolitan cachet to the parties and like the ravioli and the red wine it is smart and inexpensive. But also it's a matter of principle, as Robert has often stressed, to make her an honest woman on the passport. A jolly and decent gesture. Don't mention it, dear! We are all good antifascists.

And now he is here to relieve and reconstruct for in spite of the war he believes in humanity. You do what you can for it. He is here to make friends with suffering humanity. But his English tweeds carry an air of authority.

'This room? A bit overcrowded,' Robert said.

Room of hot nights and hurried departures, had I ever seen it before? I looked round the room. The big double bed. Had I slept there with Vero? A clumsy chest of drawers blocking the window, a crag of a cupboard, hangings of dust colour taking up the air, the table we sat by crushed to the farthest corner.

'A good enough room,' I said. 'The matting is clean though you might not think so. The landlady is honest. I am glad to find it again. Knowing a place saves trouble. Now if we could find the flat.' (In a sunny situation on the outskirts of the past.) 'It must be still there I suppose. Rather out of the way but a pleasant place. A garden with railings in front. It wasn't ideal. Too many other people in the house. But the sitting room had a grey carpet and mirrors in gilt frames that reflected the hills.'

Why did I talk so? Why did I wish to exhibit the flat to them? Vero was not there. He is not there. His desperate life is not in gilt mirrors, pressed flower recollections, and the pale dramas of dreams. These things that remain have nothing to reveal.

'Don't trouble,' Robert said. 'The authorities will have to find us decent digs. It must be time for the news. Is there such a thing as a radio in the house?'

I translated. 'Some of the boys took it away.'

'Been a lot of looting no doubt,' Robert said.

'It belonged to them. More than likely they had to leave suddenly. You know how it is. We are all good antifascists.'

'But we needn't look for trouble,' Robert said. 'Let's hope there are no more intrigues going on here now. In our position one simply can't be too careful. It isn't as if we had only ourselves to think of. And I trust you are not going to take a romantic, feminine view of the present setup. There's no point in trying to run before you can walk. It simply leads to anarchy and chaos.'

'You think a fascist government would be better?'

'My dear girl! The democracies are standing by to assure that a moderate government is formed representing all shades of political opinion.' His eyes half closed, he enjoyed already the harmonious range of shades. 'Nothing is gained by individuals, or groups for that matter, trying to take the law into their own hands.'

'You needn't tell me,' I said.

I plunged into conversation with the girls. We swam in another element. Robert was stranded. It was fatally easy to talk to the girls. They were pleasant looking still, with their dark hair rolled back from their faces in the prevailing world fashion, with their soft plumpness, a plumpness now too soft, deflated by privation. I looked into their smiling mouths and their dumb, plum coloured eyes. Words spun from our tongues.

'You are glad to be back?'

'I am glad to be back. I have waited for the chance. I thought it would never come but now the Allied occupation has changed everything.'

'Perhaps,' one of them said. 'One doesn't know. The war continues. We are still in the blackout.'

'We have met with nothing but kindness,' I said. 'No difficulties in landing.'

Robert tapped my arm. 'We needn't look for trouble,' Robert said.

Of what was I thinking? It is natural to meet with cordiality. We are here to do the right thing for these poor liberated people provided they pull together in British fashion. We are experts here on a job. My knowledge of the country makes me an expert. *Mentire!* Robert's Harris tweed is my passport. Thanks to the war and the Harris tweed I am here.

'Still it feels strange at first. The tram conductor called me pretty stranger.'

'And why not? You are still young,' they said, 'English ladies never get old.'

'Not English,' I said.

They smiled. 'English now.'

'Not altogether English.'

They laughed politely.

'The others didn't laugh in the days when—'

They lifted their eyebrows for silence.

They are right. Certainly right. I was going to speak of it. It is not even clear to me how much they know. There may be reasons for caution here in the town. In the village, in the hills, one would not have been able to keep up this farce.

Under the peaks are the white grottos and columns. Here in the hot green hollows boulders are scattered like sheep and sheep graze between them. The sheep nibble, and white silence radiates from the rocks, and the asphodels, hardly pink and hardly grey, not coloured, not lovely, not like other flowers and babies' hands, are straight, dry, and secret, will not decay between the rocks and the sun. In this old meeting place of men the decision is made. Here the will lives.

There in the hills everything spoke of him but now nothing can tell me where he is.

'It is good to be back,' I said. 'I wish we had some of the pink wine and could make a party of it. My first night.'

'There is no more wine,' they said, 'only this fake coffee.'

'But everything will be the same in time. The same life as before without the terror. We shall live again, because this is a war for democracy.'

'Who knows?' they said. 'Nothing has changed much. The war continues. We are still in the blackout.'

'There is nothing to fear.' (Nothing to fear, with Robert, Democracy, the conquering Allies.) To an authorised British worker bringing relief, this is only another town where children suffer. Nothing to fear now. Nothing to hope.

Through our dream-fluent talk a phrase floats. *While there is life there is fear.* And then that other. *We needn't look for trouble.* Better not look for it—

'Just a moment, Robert.' Robert knocking out his pipe on a saucer, catching a word here and there, and all attention. A moment, Robert, to share something in the loved language that has nothing to do with the war and reconstruction.

His desperate life is hidden in the hills.

I asked after friends.

His desperate life is hidden in the slogan, Giustizia e Libertà.

I asked for Mario, Colonna, Reccione. We hung on the edge of things better unsaid. The plum coloured eyes of the girls said nothing.

Almost certainly they knew little. And should they know more . . . In that case also better leave it unsaid.

In the simple slogan Giustizia e Libertà. He never learned to decipher the figures and trends of the far away and frowning political parties that change their shape like the hills on nearer approach.

'And Vero?' (A common name. A common enough name. A very common name and no harm done.)

They made no reply but one of them lifted her thick china coffee cup. She held it high, looking at me meanwhile, as if to drink a toast. Then she quickly turned to Robert and said to him in pretty, halting English, 'Only this poor false coffee.'

'About the coffee—' Robert is in charge.

'And the oil is scarcely—' the other girl said. She had a few words of English. Enough words to make it ridiculous for me to refuse to speak it. We should not speak again the loved language. The words were gone. Robert had banished them. I had selfishly guarded the conversation from Robert. Now they were all content. Spectral dimples appeared in the soft hollows of the girl's cheeks.

For them Robert is solid as the two-kilo loaf. He embodies the loaf, and a kind of security they have never known, that emanates from a status quo of the mind. They flatter and flirt with Robert, a pale flirtation, a worn out record of the music of love. Their cringing smiles entreat my kind permission. What have I to refuse? There is no more love. Only this poor false security.

'After the war all will be speak English.' Everyone will be speaking English soon. Without doubt I am on the safe side.

In my safety suit of English cut. Immune, a ghost, in a town without substance.

'Frankly my dear, this room you cracked up so, looks pretty gruesome to me.'

(Yes it is gruesome, Robert.)

'You're certain you really wouldn't prefer the hotel? It's a shambles, but that is where we're supposed to be. It wouldn't do to tread on people's toes before we know who anybody is. And I shall have to be there in any case. Tomorrow we're getting to grips with the local authorities.' (A shade of a smile for the local authorities.)

'Go Robert, naturally, you will have the bath, and it doesn't do to tread on people's toes.'

'You've been so awfully helpful,' he said to the girls. He said goodnight to us all. 'Goodnight my dear. You'll be there at nine-ish to translate those reports. You're sure you won't be lonely or anything.'

'I suppose we may go to bed now,' I said to the girls. 'I suppose no one else will be coming tonight. No friendly visit from the *polizia*, a pure formality, nothing of that, eh?'

'No,' they said.

'No one be dropping in?'

'No, signora.'

'No one I used to know?'

'No,' they said. 'Surely no one else will be coming tonight.'

In Fifteen Minutes You Can Say a Lot

Crossing the railway the road descended between blank walls of windowless warehouses and came to an end before the prison. Seen from the respectable heights of the town the castellated prison resembled the forts supplied with sets of toy soldiers. Under a sky the colour of ashes, the mock mediaeval aspect of the place still suggested a huge plaything, a joke, a fake, the 'folly' of some cracked and tasteless eccentric. It was neither functional nor fearful. Its facade of unnatural black, on which the absurdly large stones might have been painted, the tin toy sentry with his gun walking the ramparts, did not inspire the appropriate feeling of awe; only the uneasy horror of hoax.

The taxi man waited, staring in front of him. His manner suggested that this fare would be too distraught to ask for change. This kind of fare to the prison never did.

Perhaps he knows best, she thought. At all events I can't make the effort necessary to break down that manner and give him a smaller tip. When she got out the driver woke from his trance. He banged the door and the taxi drove away. Overhead, on a jutting platform, the sentry with his gun walked up and down.

The big grey door had knockers and bolts of brass. It was studded with details not seen on other doors. She raised the knocker and knocked. She rang the enormous bell. A shutter slid back. 'To see Mr Seymour,' she said to a face through the bars. 'Kirk Seymour. He's in here. They said I might come.' The shutter closed. A suppliant, she faced the blind door and the theatrical grimness of the dark walls. No detail had been neglected. A veritable caricature of doom. Abandon Hope All Ye Who Enter Here, spoke with Victorian discretion in the grey silence. No wind stirred in the dead end of the street but the stones distilled a bleak, creeping cold. There was no sound but the shunting of trucks on the not so distant railway line, and the heavy steps of the sentry. He took six steps, then turned with meaningless smartness.

'A friend are you?' 'His wife.' A small door opened in the large one and she followed the turnkey across a courtyard. Inside the buildings a youth was scrubbing the floor. She apologised for making it dirty again. The youth didn't look up.

'Step this way please.' The turnkey shuffled along like an old man, all the keys at his waist seeming to weigh him down. His uniform was grey drab. It was colour putrified. He had a mottled face and watery blue eyes. The kind of face that makes a pretty child and later a fine fair meaty man, till the eyes fade and the weak skin becomes permanently reddened with beer.

'In here please.' He switched on the sickly light in the waiting room. He seemed proud of the place. He might have made a good undertaker, she thought, or a shopwalker, but this suits him best of all. False tears oozed from his eyes. As his look glanced off her fur coat, she knew he was thinking, 'With their fur coats!' She knew he was proud of the effect the place had on people who got in. Once inside, fur coats or no, they could see how matters stood.

'You may have a bit to wait.' He smiled, the ghost of joviality. *Treat them polite. That's my little joke.* 'Take a seat please.' He rolled the 'please' with saliva on his tongue, savouring the situation. *Fur coats or no fur coats, lady or gent, they might be here themselves one of these fine days!* Her mind muttered, 'Only an old drunk!' 'What was that?' Her lips had moved. His sagging body tautened. He bared his teeth like an ancient watchdog.

'Nothing,' she said. 'The weather. The weather outside.'

Unnecessary to have said a word. It stood between them clear as a transparency on a slide. *Watch your step. They might even get you certified, fur coat and all.*

Furniture of the waiting room was yellow varnished. The light bulb was of minimum size. Tattered *Digests* neatly stacked on the table reflected the mock civility of the turnkey. A narrow window of frosted glass admitted neither light nor air. The air that seeped through the open door was dead air, cold and thick with the smell of disinfectant. Away in the distance a key ground in a lock, doors slammed, and a clatter of metal filled the building, but the steps that passed in the passage fell with a dead sound. Waiting there, eyeing the tattered *Digests*, she imagined that everything inside this building, enveloped in its artificial air, was dead. The movements inside the prison were not life. What it housed was kept from decay merely for hygienic reasons, preserved there by the cold and the disinfectant.

'This way please.'

Kirk was sitting behind a wooden counter. He made to get up when she entered—a broken gesture. She moved towards the counter. 'You have to sit down,' he said.

The counter was wide and high. When she sat she could see only his face and his neck and shoulders bent forward. He was wearing an old flannel jacket he used to wear for gardening. She had prepared herself for the shock of seeing Kirk, of seeing him changed, terribly changed, but not for the meeting with this old jacket that used to hang on a lilac bush while he dug.

'Well and how are you?' he said.

'How are *you*?' she said. She tried to look him straight in the face and smile as he did, but her eyes slipped surreptitiously to the warder who sat beside him. A great expanse of uniform showed above the counter and over the uniform a fixed and yellow face. She dragged her eyes back to Kirk.

'Oh fine,' he said with his obstinate old smile. Kirk was dwarfed by the warder. That face must have been a foot long, she thought. Must have been? Is. I shall keep my eyes off it. 'You look fine, Kirk,' she said. 'You look just the same.'

It was somehow shocking that Kirk looked still the same, sitting behind that barrier. The same? His face seemed swollen. The clear outline of his cheek was lost. But much the same. His hair the same. His eyes. But his eyes examined her searchingly, suspiciously, as if there were something in her face that he questioned.

'It was nice of you to come,' he said.

Funny of him to say that.

'I wasn't allowed to come till now,' she said, raising her voice against the silence of the warder. 'It wasn't allowed because of your—' the monstrous magnetic silence of the warder distorted the word 'resistance' into '—behaviour. I got your letter though. I brought the enema you asked for, but they told me you were receiving medical attention.'

'I knew they wouldn't let me have it,' Kirk said. 'I might have died. A lot they'd worry.'

That day after the raid. The people hurrying from shattered homes. Trailing from shop to shop among the ruins. The poor discreet distracted druggists. Not without a doctor's certificate, madam. The rubber shortage—the Japs you know. So many demands. The hospitals, the wounded, the dying. We try to do what we can for everyone. Such agony of mind, such effort of will, so many people involved to produce the enema for the hunger striker. And at the end of that day (so many lives lost) being turned away from the prison. Standing outside the gate with the ridiculous parcel. The clumsy can breaking through wet brown paper. A lot they'd worry. The futility of it. And all the time Kirk knew they wouldn't let him have it. It was just another trial. His will against theirs. They would refuse and the case would draw public attention to the hunger strikers.

'When is Levinsky coming again?' Kirk said. 'He isn't much of an advocate for us. Doesn't seem to have his heart in the job.

He ought to try being in here for a bit.'

'The end of the month. There's another man in here he has to see.'

'That will be Green. Green was on the fast the same time as me. A pretty thoroughgoing chap Green. A resister. Not muddled up with any religious beliefs. We might be going on another fast soon. Makes you feel wonderful.'

She listened, thinking, Has he forgotten that he is speaking to me? That telling me about this will hurt me? Has he forgotten altogether that other people can be hurt?

He was still speaking about Green and she noticed how bright red and swollen his face was, as if he'd been too near a hot fire. 'They can't keep you here—' but the phrase broke on the gigantic silence of the warder. 'I mean it can't go on forever.'

'That's what all the chaps are telling each other. Been telling each other for the last year or two.'

'But the war's over,' she said.

'Not with the Japs. The Japs will go on. The Japs will hold out. They're worth ten of us.'

That was what she had always admired about Kirk—his fearlessness in argument—his readiness to take the unpopular side. But now she could see it was only a reaction. He was so conditioned to taking the 'wrong' side that he was feverishly standing up for the Japs.

'They can't,' she said. 'The atomic bomb. We're blowing the whole place into the sea.' How blustering and false her voice sounded. The warder had made her say that. She was taking the warder's side against Kirk.

With thinning patience, 'Much good that will do,' Kirk said, 'blowing everyone into the sea.'

'It will make it end quicker,' she said. Without ever moving her eyes away from Kirk, she could still see the face that seemed of a more rigid substance than flesh, the large mouth closed and fixed, the fixed stare of the large opaque eyes. When the pacifists talked of policemen as Gestapo, 'You're only making them more like it,' she would say. 'Gestapo is fantastic. The job makes them get to look like that. They have families at home—like us.'

In the presence of the warder it was no use. Her mind muttered: Gestapo. Fake Gestapo agent. Hollywood. But too fantastic and crude for Hollywood, the movies are a little more subtle lately.

'We'll be in here for a year at least,' Kirk said.

'Well but think about what we'll do when you come out. John will be home soon. We'll be able to start the cooperative farm.'

'I don't think your brother would be much use for a show like that. Not after six years of war. Jack Green would come in. You see, living under these conditions you get to know on whom you can rely. The ones who don't crack up—who can take it.'

'You used to get along well with John,' she said. 'You always respected each other's opinions.' And she wondered, But can he take it? Can he take ordinary life? Here he has nothing to live for but resistance. How can he take the world outside of here?

'Fasting makes you feel wonderful,' he bragged. 'It's the only break in this kind of boggy existence.'

'I suppose the food is pretty rotten,' she said.

Kirk shook his head and they both looked at the warder. He had not changed his position, but something about him had begun to creak. The large eyes had switched in their sockets and stared at her. A Rider Haggard god, she said to herself, that begins to take notice when you least expect it. I wonder if it understands at all or only responds to certain stimuli.

She started, fearing she might have said the words out loud. They would have amused Kirk.

'We're not allowed to talk about it,' Kirk said. He was smiling the way he used to before the war, at their private and particular jokes.

'Plain English cooking,' she said, turning with an unthinking civilised gesture to include the warder in their laughter. He was staring straight at the wall opposite. No flicker of eyelid betrayed humanity. Their laughter was quenched. It was like being hit in the face with something flat and cold.

'What's new?' Kirk said. As if he were humouring a child.

'I haven't much news for such a long visit. Oh I didn't mean that. I mean the time element. It makes each word so important. You feel you must weigh each word like a telegram. Nothing seems important enough to say.'

'I don't see that.' He was bristling for argument. 'You can say a lot in fifteen minutes.'

So that Kirk wouldn't talk, so that he couldn't hurt her any more, she chattered desperately about mutual friends, wondering then if she should have mentioned names, whether she should have brought them into the prison. The innocent names. Aunt Mary, the Allinghams, seemed somehow soiled as soon as she had pronounced them. But she wanted so to share something with Kirk, something of theirs, that did not belong to this place. She revived a family joke. But they did not laugh again. The names sounded strange, the sense of the words was sucked away by the jailer's presence. But Kirk followed the pointless story and trivial items of family news with concentration, as if he thought he might discover in them a message of real importance.

Seeing his eagerness, 'It all seems so humdrum,' she said. 'Oh yes, and then about what we hoped?'

He shrugged his shoulders. 'What do you mean?' he said. 'Can't you say what you mean?' His blue eyes blazed. 'What are you afraid of?'

'What we hoped. You know. What I expected. Nothing came of it. The doctor said—It doesn't matter,' she said. It would only have mattered if Kirk had wanted to know. Whatever I say will be wrong. It doesn't matter what we say. The warder registers my thoughts. He registers what I am saying, and what I am thinking he registers only wrong. They were silent. Kirk lifted his hand and rubbed his forehead where his hair sprang back in a clean wide sweep. She hadn't seen his hands under the counter. As he lifted one she could see how it shook. He held it hard to his face to keep it still. 'How's the garden?' he asked.

'The garden? The garden is lovely. Everything in the garden is lovely. We grow all the family needs and more and the gardener sells them. Such lovely vegetables—' Kirk had loved the garden. She wanted him to think well of her gardening. But here in this place. The lovely vegetables? She was throwing the lovely vegetables in his face. She felt like a criminal.

'Who works it?'

'I'm doing my bit.' (That sounded too much like Digging for Victory.) 'I do quite a bit, and a man comes in to help, a returned soldier, such a nice chap, invalided out with war neuroses.'

'A lot of them will come out like that,' he said. 'Wrecked. Never be good for anything ever again. Shell shock they call it.'

'Some kind of shock. They treated him in a mental hospital and he came out cured. They call it cured. Like this.' She lifted her hand and wobbled it painfully to show Kirk how unsteady the returned man was. Her hand fell suddenly and she looked at the warder. There was warning in his silence. Something wrong. What have I done now? It was wrong. Then she forgot the warder, remembering Kirk. His hand shakes, too. He topples from reasonable words into a senseless rage. His eyes burn. I did not think. This barrier destroys all human feelings. No more humane than this wooden god of a warder. Everything you do in this place is wrong. We are under a curse. She stared at the gloved hand on her knee. This horrible hand she had shaken for Kirk to see.

'It's all right,' Kirk said. He thought she'd been scared by the warder. She raised her miserable eyes. His cheeks blazed. His whole face was a question. Even in happier days before the war, he had never looked in her eyes with a more eager scrutiny. But after a moment the interest drained from his face and he turned his head away and shook it slightly as though he would say, 'It's no use. I can't guess.'

Mistaking the movement of her hand for a sign, he paid no attention to its obvious meaning. He had thought she would make a sign that he could interpret. But now his face was lifeless. The red light had left his cheeks. He shrank back in his chair.

'I'm sorry,' she said. (What was it? Some private thing? A message from outside to another prisoner? What did he want to know? What could I have told him?)

'You can write, Kirk.'

'Yes you can write. They censor the letters. Mine must give them a headache.' A beacon gleam of pride lit in his smile. The pride of the persecuted.

Without warning the warder rose. Forestalling the order Kirk was standing beside him. 'I have to go now,' he said. He strutted dwarfed and futile beside the tall warder. She had never thought of Kirk as a small man.

'Cheer up, you'll be out soon,' she said. With the warder he moved towards the door behind the counter.

'I don't think so. The war can go on almost indefinitely.'

She knew now. He didn't want the war to be over.

'Yes, you'll be out soon—'

He spoke across his shoulder, propelled by the warder. 'Not under another year at least. I bet you.'

In the time it took her to reach the passage by the other door they had gone. In the empty passage there was no sign of them.

Only the clatter of keys and the clamour of metal on the dead air. She was still holding the books she had brought for him. The spirit of the place had taken her. Kirk is mad. Resistance is madness. Inside this mausoleum madness is directed against madness. She walked slowly back by the way she had come. She knew she would be watched, would be directed.

'In here please.' Another waiting room. With shelves and black leaded grate and a coal fire. It was like the waiting room in a stagnant station where no train would come. The official waited for her to make a request.

'Can I leave these books for him?'

'What are they?'

'Just some books and gardening magazines. Can he have them?' The official was noncommittal. 'Leave them here.' She put them down on the desk and waited for him to say, 'That will be all.'

She walked without hurrying on towards the entrance hall. She was being invisibly watched, she was being directed.

Across the courtyard the turnkey hurried to meet her. 'You'll have to sign the book,' he said. 'Sign here please,' he said with obsequious, watchful jocundity. As on a lantern slide she could see between them simple patterns of hate and fear. The pen spluttered and stuck. 'No hurry,' he said. 'Take it easy, miss.' He was in no hurry. He liked the work. It was his pleasure to watch the visitors sign. They had to give up their names whoever they were. It was just as well they should see how matters stood.

'That's all.' For the present, his voice seemed to add. He touched his cap. The great door banged behind her. The fake facade spilled discreet gloom into the cold blank day. She waited, still looking along the empty road that did not appear to lead anywhere. She counted the steps of the sentry. One, two—and up to six. One, two, three— 'Hello there!' Out of the grey silence the sentry had called. She could see his face now looking down on her. He was quite young, was grinning. 'Did I make you jump?' 'Take the first turn to the left,' he told her. 'That brings you out on the road. You can get the tram from there.'

'Thanks,' she called. 'It's so very kind of you. Thanks so much—' but he'd turned and was walking away.

You Have to Stand Up to Them

To supplying new element. To adjusting and testing. Clapping and static that sounded like lost souls. The drone of the flies.

Ernest called from the shop. 'Why don't you throw out those flowers, Ethel?' The flowers had been on the counter since Mack left, he always arranged them himself. 'And couldn't you rub up the nickel stuff sometime? The shop doesn't look like it ought to today.'

To time and trip. Nothing looked like it ought to what with the war and the weather. Not at all like when she'd started working at Mack's. Then the music that cured poured from the open shop door, like a sunny sweet sauce, over the packing cases and the lines and the Post Office that still had V.R. on the letter box, had made her feel that Electrical Supply and Fitting was really a wonderful business to be in. And then, when she sat down to start entering up on the cards, Mack would ask, 'Now are there any little problems today?'

Mack never nagged. Just got people conscious of this or that. And Ernest was decent too. But she pitied Ernest. Having to remember the meat or the fish and having to yarn with his wife when she gave him a ring. So now she only said, 'The flies are bad, it's the weather.'

They were always bad in summer. They spotted the snowy stoves and the nude hall-nymph that lighted up opalescent. The farmers, too narrow-minded for that sort of thing, looked at her out of the corners of their eyes, but Mack and Ernest took a pride in the nymph which was put out by a very good firm.

Flies gave such a wrong impression, Mack always said. People had thought he was funny. In fact they kidded about the shop at first, the psycho-salesmanship and the reading lamps and the gadgets. But once inside the showroom where a washer, clean to the touch, and pink and blue rangettes, not overcrowded, stood in the pale hygienic light, and Mack with his nice blue eyes and golden teeth and action-back jacket was there to help with all their little problems, they felt it was not plain shopping. More like the doctor without the unpleasantness. Or even a chat with the minister. Only the minister hadn't kept up with the times.

And the cheery chap that tested the radios, and the bright little cosmic hum that came from the workshop all day, and the pretty girl they had keeping the books. . . .

To re-charging fence battery. To time and trip. The flies and the stupid hum from the battery charger. It sounded small and sad today like a kid whining.

'I could do with some tea,' Ernest called from the workshop. You could hardly get inside there these days. All these repairs. Another wreck on the bench. Mack had guaranteed it. He shouldn't have done. Nothing ought to be guaranteed any more. Dead valves . . . elements burnt out . . . having to do with parts that didn't do . . .

Getting snowed under.

And it wasn't only at work Ernest missed Mack. They had their other interests outside the business. Civilisation was on the skids and they did what they could about it—belonged to the Red Book Club, had leaflets sent from town, and ran the Workers' Enlightenment Group. Some of the farmers thought that was going too far and threatened to boycott the business and Ernest was nervous but Mack said, 'Just stand up to them and they'll pipe down. They need us. They have to send for the doctor when they're ill, and you'll see, if the fridge goes crook they'll send for me.'

So the Workers' Enlightenment went ahead, and when the progressive professor came from Auckland (the first group up

north he had visited) all those who didn't want to get in a rut
had attended. The professor enthroned on the Kosyback chair
they had just got re-covered in time had looked very solemn
and very pleased when he said, 'We have our organisers to
thank . . . this active group . . . wonders of science . . . freer
and fuller lives . . .'

'Hear hear. The scientific approach to Christianity, some of us
have it, I think,' the minister chimed, but they hushed him up.
They were all waiting for Mack who leaned on the mantelpiece
in front of discreetly leaping electric flames, ready to thank the
professor. While Ernest, just back from holding out the perfectly
balanced kids who had slept all through it, handed the walnut
sandwiches. Myrtle's idea. She liked to cooperate. And they'd
tried to sing the Internationale (Mack knew the words). And
going out to their cars people were saying, 'Yes, you have to look
ahead.' And for such a scattered district it was a beginning. Had
really been a stimulating evening.

But it was the last. Petrol was getting short and Mack was
called up. He didn't mind so much. Nothing really to mind now
Russia was in it, but the week before he went he was rather quiet
and not so interested in people's problems. 'You'll be getting
leave in three months though,' Ernest said. 'And there's one
thing about the war, it will make people think. Of course it
will set us back but I'll manage somehow . . . keep everything
going . . .'

Ethel came round to the door of the workshop. 'There's an
old chap after a Savetoil,' she said. 'He's after a stove too.'

'Well, don't forget the Savetoils are both sold and the paint's
only coming in in dribs and drabs. In fact if it's a large order at
all, all you can do is take their names and addresses.'

'He's rather persistent,' she said.

'Well, come on with that tea. My head's aching like fun.'
Ernest turned off the radio he'd been testing and turned on his
salesman's smile. It was not very bright today.

'I meant to have come in before this,' the customer said, tapping a stove with his stick. His pale blue eyes lived in grey nests of wrinkles.

'Yes, that's a fine little cooker,' Ernest said. 'Not for sale I'm afraid.'

Though he probably wouldn't be selling him more than a torch unit he looked the customer over. The Sunday-school-looking blazer, dark serge trousers tucked into gumboots, the broad old-style hat with a bound brim, all looked as neat as if they had never been worn. One of these early settler diehards, living without the barest necessities, not even a phone. Not knowing they were alive. Ernest had placed him.

'You never forget a face?' the customer said. And Ernest, a bit embarrassed, shifted his eyes to the counter.

'Wonderful work you do here,' the customer said, staring at the shelf of table lamps. 'Bringing light into the darkness, aren't you? I'll take the stove.'

Ernest began his anti-sales talk. 'Regular customers have to come first you know—'

'I come last then,' the customer said.

'We can only supply regular customers now. People are touring all over the country trying to pick up goods in out of the way stores.'

'But I've come such a long way,' the customer whined, holding his hat in his hand like a blind beggar.

'I'm sorry to disappoint you,' Ernest said. 'Do you happen to need a bulb now while you're here? Or a tin of paint? We still have some black and grey. Is there anything else you'll be needing?'

'I'll just take what I can get,' the customer joked meekly, and Ethel, giving him his tea, thought, Blue eyes the colour of Mack's. Only the eyes. Everything else is gone.

'What a nice electric kettle, Miss,' he said. 'I've always wanted one.'

'We have one more put away,' Ethel said, and brought it out and put it down on the counter. 'Not so reliable but you must blame the war.'

Ernest was mildly surprised. But really it was rather funny, the old joker enjoying himself so much, fascinated now by the sparkle of a radiator reflector. 'For the long dark evenings?' he said. They put that aside for him too. And a pretty Rangeware casserole tempted him.

'Fleshpots of Egypt. Ah, the fleshpots. Fleshpots.' He looked from the Rangeware to Ethel. She began to think he was not so nice after all and ducked back to the office.

Ernest didn't want to begin all over again. 'Well have a look round,' he said. He started to roll himself a cigarette but found he couldn't be bothered. He wondered why he was letting the goods go to a stranger. Mack would have sent him away with a catalogue.

It was very warm and quiet, sleepy weather. The little pottering noises the customer made going round the shop were like the soft fall of coals in the grate when you sat up alone reading, long ago before the heaters came in. Ernest had read a lot. Books on problems. No time for a novel. But he'd read the classics of course when he was young. And now his mind wandered to something he must have read about a stranger who came in one day . . . they got away with a hell of a lot in the classics . . . But a story must have a plot. Real life was different. Things went all right with you, or not so good. As often as not your plans just fizzled out. And even in spite of the Left movement and Progress sometimes you couldn't see the use of it all. It might be different in Russia.

It was very quiet. Only the little singing from the workshop. Wasting, wasting away, it whined. Ethel was putting on her hat to go home. Another day over, Another day . . .

It was too quiet. Ernest tuned in the radio on the counter and the customer hurried over, walking a little sideways, loaded up with lamps he wanted to take. Ernest put aside everything he asked for. He'd quite decided not to deliver the goods. He could say that his partner being in camp there'd been a mistake.

'The daughters of music,' the customer said. 'They have sought out many inventions to while away a long dark evening,' he said.

'Perhaps I should take that too?'

Ernest had been wondering all the time whether the old stick wasn't pulling his leg. It wasn't a feeling he liked. He was all on edge. 'You don't have to take it,' he said. 'As a matter of fact, I don't want to part with it. It belonged to my partner. And if that's all, it's closing time,' he said. And he switched off Sunshine and Love.

The customer took out a large white handkerchief and rattled in his throat. 'Very close,' he said.

Ernest looked through the dim window at yellow-grey clouds, muffling the sun, like phlegm in an old man's throat. His own throat felt strange when he swallowed. Perhaps he was in for something. The flu was going like wildfire throught the camps.

'Believe it,' the customer rattled again, 'or not. I'm quite in love with all these modern things. I try to get hold of everything new I can.'

Ernest forgave him at once. 'That's the spirit,' he said. He looked amongst the piles of bright catalogues that had most of the items crossed out. 'Here's an interesting little pamphlet just come. Change and New Values. Take one along if you like.'

'Change and—? Yes, I'll accept one,' the customer said.

'And New Values,' said Ernest. 'I'm a socialist. My partner's a rationalist too but I've often told him that's just a side issue. Young people today aren't interested one way or the other.'

'A line that isn't selling well at present,' the customer said, just beginning to smile. He brought out a black book and slapped it down on top of the pink leaflet. 'But you know what it says: Behold I come as a thief.'

'Well and if it does? I think you chaps just pick out what suits you,' Ernest said. Ernest knew the look of the black book. They would open it, pretending to search for something, but they had the grisly bits all off by heart. Must be a Plymouth Rock or a local preacher. There were still a few of these old birds in the backblocks. When they went off into a sermon across the counter, Mack would listen to them and smile, and send them away with a few hard facts to chew on.

'It all boils down to economics,' Ernest said. 'Take the war now. With a reasonable economic system there'd be no necessity for wars, because you see, without the vested interests and with a decent standard of living—'

'What then?' the customer said, working round to some point he wanted to make.

'Security of course,' Ernest said. 'Nice homes and kiddies. People just want to live, don't they?'

The customer smiled, clicking his teeth together. The dark porcelain teeth reminded Ernest of something. Was it the rows of fence insulators that were kept in a box on the counter? Or was it those old thick jam pots you used to see? There were some in the cemetery with dead flowers in them. That smile was certainly leading up to something. A small subscription would always get rid of them. Mack never gave though. A matter of principle.

They didn't dare come out with the hellfire now. Not like the minister who used to darken your Sundays. Only a bogey now, dead long ago. The anecdotes and the traps they led up to were so crude that even a boy could see through them. All through the little lambs and poor blind girls you knew what was coming.

'I hear you've done much good in the district,' the customer was saying, working round in the same sly silly way.

'Oh I don't know,' Ernest said. 'I haven't done as much as I'd like to have. Especially since the nippers came. But my partner, a single man, was very active. We did what we could to wake people up a bit.'

'Ever wake up in the dark?' the customer said. 'In the dark. Without any order, and where the light is as darkness.'

'It's known as claustrophobia,' Ernest said. (You have to humour them.) 'There's nyctophobia and cynophobia too, and quite a few more. Our last course, Fear and Its Causes, dealt with them all.'

The customer was opening the black book. Pretending to read out of the black book. 'And I heard the second beast say: Come and see.'

Eleventh hour stuff. All the tricks of the trade.

'Come and see. So simple. Are you prepared?'

'I think so,' Ernest said, standing up very straight behind the counter. 'I haven't led anyone up the garden path. Of course having a wife and the kids to care for I haven't done as much as I ought to have, and under the present system we have to make profits. But we're looking forward to great social changes.'

'So you're ready then?' the customer said.

It always happened like this when you were alone. When you were a little chap. The old man. You played a game with him. Snakes on a board. You always let him win. Because he persisted so—because he was old. There was another game. It ended up with the old man saying, 'Just lie down now and pretend to be dead. It won't hurt you at all.' And you had to play just to get rid of them.

Hemmed in there by the counter, Ernest was sweating. 'The customer is always—' he started to say. (You have to play just to get rid of them.) And the Judge of course. The Judge is always right. The Judge is always old and always right. It was all the same what you said. You were all alone. If only old Mack . . . The night at the party when they all felt so alive their lives had a meaning when they were singing, *And each stood in his place.*

You had to stand up for yourself.

'We believe . . .' he said to the Judge who was looking the other way. 'It all boils down . . .'

The Judge said nothing, baiting the trap with silence.

The silence was long. Ernest was very tired. Even the flies were tired. There was only the little singing from the workshop. Lonely, it droned.

'Yes, a nice little business,' the customer said at last. His eyes roamed the shelves, but halfheartedly now. 'I might as well take the icebox too,' he said. 'Not that I need one much. Don't trouble to wrap the things. I'll take them myself.' He began to carry his purchases out of the shop. Ernest followed him, toting the baby fridge.

Outside the sky was a thick bilious grey, and a dusty wind was rising. Ernest had half expected some queer conveyance with horses, but there was only an old Ford with a trailer attached. Behind it the pinetrees looked like nodding plumes. Those sickly classics—

'You wish to pay cash.' Ernest totted up figures. 'There's the discount off if you pay cash,' he said. 'Quite a bit it will be.'

The customer leaned on a radio cabinet. He dropped a lizard lid over one blue eye. 'I'm not really interested in economics,' he said. And he spat something black onto the clean tiles.

Ernest went to the phone and dialed a number, keeping one eye on the shop. While he waited for the number the customer moved the hall-nymph on the counter, then surreptitiously stuffed her into his pocket.

Ernest let go the receiver.

'Nice for the dark passage,' the customer mumbled, just beginning to smile.

'Put that back,' Ernest yelled. (They heard him right across the road at the Bank.) 'It belongs to my partner, Mack.' The customer held out the opalescent lady, but his hand was shaking so, she fell and broke on the floor.

'Oh dear,' he said, in a broken childish voice, 'look what you've made me do.'

'At least you've stopped smiling,' Ernest said to himself. 'At least we've got that nasty smile off your face.'

It was true the customer didn't smile any more. He only just managed to get out of the shop. He tried to make for the Ford but kept walking sideways and over into the road. Ernest, guiding him, found it hard to get a grip. 'Steady, now steady on,' he was saying, to something that twitched and slid under the spruce little blazer.

'You're feeling queer,' Ernest said, 'I won't be a minute.' But he came back too late with the knobby stick and some water in a teacup. The car was already out of sight round the bend.

Turning back to the shop, Ernest talked to himself. Too easy going, Mack always said. Just stand up to them and they run away. But seeing the glass bits of the nymph he banged his fist on his head. The same when the shop burnt down! Rescuing knick-knacks and leaving the car in the garage! He hadn't even taken the customer's name.

'It's done now,' he said. 'At least I got the ugly smile off his face.' He picked up the glass and tidied the shop before closing. The customer had just about cleaned out the last of the stock. Wouldn't like old Mack to see it like this.

Mack didn't see it. He went straight to the Islands. But there wouldn't have been much point in his coming back now the showroom was closed. What few goods did come in were delivered direct and Ethel had gone to release a chap from the Bank. The cards, *To time and trip*, lay around in the office, and old customers came to the back door, to yarn with Ernest, busy in the little buzz from the battery charger, while he tinkered with their transformers and condensers, more snowed under than ever.

An Annual Affair

It almost seemed to be blowing up for rain. Every minute or two the wind came across the paddocks, like a lorry changing gears, and round the lonely store corner. The store looked lonely because it was closed for Boxing Day. The orange drinks and Weeties in the window and the country scene with stout letters, KEEP FIT cutting across made you feel sad, as if you had eaten too much. The wallops from the wind made you feel tired. Joy sat on the step of the store.

Come on, get up now, her Mum said. You don't want to dirty your dress before we start.

Joy got up. The wind passed again blowing up dust and rain. It was late. It was nearly nine. Mum reckoned Auntie Laurel was holding them up.

Before the lorry came round the corner they could hear the kids screeching. It was like a cage of cockatoos on wheels. Uncle Nick was in front with Dad. Behind, besides the kids, there was Auntie Laurel and a flash lady from town. She had brought something for the children for Boxing Day. It was some crackers, but they couldn't pull them because Mum said it wasn't the proper time. Mum didn't think much of crackers.

The Domain in front of the hotel was packed out with cars and lorries. Dad growled because the place near the fence where they always parked, was taken. Mum only said, I thought we were going to be late.

The cars looked funny all packed round the hotel because there was plenty of room along the beach. The hotel stood by itself away from the baches. It was tall and a dark red colour like the one in Joy's Granny's picture. *The Broad Way*. They didn't have pictures like that in Joy's home. They had one of a bunch of pansies and one of a cathedral. In Granny's picture the hotel had a Union Jack on top and through the windows you could see the people inside, playing cards and dancing. But the real hotel windows were always closed. It looked as if nobody lived there, but round at the side there was a small door and men going in and out.

The old jetty was standing over the mud with only its last two legs in the water. Brian and the boys made a dash for the trolley that was used for loading timber in the old days, and started to push each other up and down, but Mum yelled to them that they'd fall in the water, and Auntie Laurel said the jetty was dangerous and ought to be seen to.

Mum and Dad and Miss Jenkins, the flash lady, sat down on the step of the lorry. Miss Jenkins had several rows of rolls on top of her head, and slacks which were tight behind, and dark red fingernails. She said how pretty everything looked after the rain.

Dad kept looking hard at Miss Jenkins' fingernails, then looking away.

Everyone seems to think it's nice down here in the summer, Mum said, of course we're used to it.

I suppose you always come here, Miss Jenkins said.

We always manage to get down for the picnic, Dad said. It's an annual affair.

Mum said, It looks as if we've been unlucky with the weather though.

Dad said, It's generally like this round about Christmas.

But anyway, Mum said, it does make a change and the kiddies do enjoy it.

Dad took out his cigarette case and offered Miss Jenkins one but she said, No thanks. She did occasionally, but not just now.

Dad said, Excuse me, he had to meet a chap, and went over towards the hotel.

It began to rain a bit and the wind was chilly. Mum said they might as well go for a walk as it wasn't lunch time yet, and Miss Jenkins could see the view from further up. Everyone always said it was rather nice, only of course the tide was wrong now.

Joy had to fetch Terry and Mavis. Mum was nervous about them falling into the mud. They were right at the end of the jetty pretending to fish. Jim was there too, he had rigged up the lines for them.

Jim didn't come round to Joy's place any more. Dad reckoned that scholarship he won hadn't done him much good. He had just picked up a lot of weird ideas and was always slinging off at everything. Dad would say, Where's the Red Flag? And Jim couldn't be bothered with Dad, so he didn't come round any more.

But the first Christmas Joy could remember he was there, and gave her a bell that was meant to be put on a tree and soon got broken. What she remembered about that Christmas was the colour of the bell. Auntie Laurel said it was a nile green, but it wasn't at all like a nile green dress Joy had. She never could get it with her paints either, so after the bell was broken she never saw that particular colour again.

They had the socials at the station hall then, and Mum and Dad still went out together sometimes, and the imaginary man came at night to keep away danger. He wore historical clothes and was called Mr Charles but he looked very like Jim.

And after that nothing much except the picnics. Jim went away to the town and didn't come home very often. He was saving up for a trip to Europe, he said.

The kids didn't want to stop fishing, and Joy had to promise they could come back later on. I'll be seeing you later on, she said to Jim.

With Terry and Mavis dragging behind they walked along past the baches. The baches were mostly empty, and as they hadn't been painted for years, were greyish-white like the sky.

The Dacres were coming. They talked away to each other looking along the ground, not seeing Mum and her friend till they got quite close. Then they stopped and smiled and were introduced to Miss Jenkins. They said the glass had gone up quite a bit this morning.

When the Dacres were out of sight Miss Jenkins said she *would* like a smoke now, so Mum suggested they climb up the bank and sit under the pines where they would be sheltered from the drizzle and not be seen. Mavis slipped down the bank and dirtied herself but Mum was quite calm about it. She had brought another dress and panties for Mavis to change to for afternoon tea.

You keep them so nice, Miss Jenkins said with a smile.

When they got back to the lorry it was lunchtime. Auntie Laurel was there with the rest of the kids, waiting. She said she hadn't seen Uncle Nick all morning. He's always Hail fellow well met, she explained to Miss Jenkins.

They sat on the grass on coats and macs. Mum took off her hat with the felt feather. Whew, isn't it hot, she said. The sun had come out and it was stifling hot between the cars. Mum unpacked the peanut-butter sandwiches, and the date scones she had baked on the Happywork stove Dad gave her for Christmas. Well we might as well start, she said, as Dad hasn't come. She sent Brian off for the hot water from Mrs Withers. Then she passed the scones to Miss Jenkins. I baked them before we started this morning, she said.

Miss Jenkins took one. Oh aren't you clever, she said. I must confess I often pop round to the Cosy Cake Shop for scones and things, you know how it is in the city. She didn't look at all ashamed of it though.

They say our baker bakes a fair fruit cake, Mum said, but I prefer my own. You know what's in it.

I suppose you do, said Miss Jenkins.

Dad came and sat down and started fooling with Terry,

turning him over and pretending to smack him. Terry didn't know what to make of it but he laughed till he turned red and hiccoughed. Dad had red patches on his cheeks and his eyes were swimmy.

Brian came back with the teapot. In his other hand he carried the broken off spout wrapped in a handkerchief. Mum couldn't let fly at him with Miss Jenkins there. Dad took it as a joke.

The tea was terribly strong and Miss Jenkins said, Couldn't we borrow some hot water from the hotel? But Mum said, I don't care about asking favours when we don't know them.

You needn't trouble for me, Dad said. He wouldn't have a scone either. He ate one sandwich quickly, then started telling one of his funny stories to Miss Jenkins. He said he knew some better ones than that, but he didn't think he could tell them. This made Miss Jenkins laugh but Mum was rather quiet. She was handing round some of the Christmas cake. This year it had white water-icing and desiccated coconut, but as Mum said herself it had turned out rather plain. No one took any. Terry was being a bad boy because Dad had been taking notice of him, he was wanting his banana now, but Mum said, No, you know they're for later on. But he howled so loud she had to give him one and then the other kids grabbed bananas too out of Mum's bag, which was bulging with bathing togs and things to change and knitting and Miss Jenkins' *Gone with the Wind,* and other things for later on, and ran off to the shore. Mum called after them not to play in the mud and not to go on the jetty.

Miss Jenkins said she'd had such a lovely lunch and she thought she'd retire to the lorry and have a smoke. Dad offered to go along with her. Only in fun of course.

Pull your skirt down a bit Joy, Mum said. The Reverend Allum was walking over their way. He sat down on the grass beside Joy and smiled all round. He always smiled in a special way as if he were much happier than everyone else. Joy looked away so as not to be hooked with his smile and be asked something. She'd been in his bad books since she let out that she was reading the Bible verses at night. The verses to be read were marked on the card and if you were regular you could get right through the Bible in five years. Only the morning wasn't really a good time, Mum was tired after having done so much before breakfast, and the kids had to be got off to school. But the verses are your armour for the day, the Reverend Allum had said, You wouldn't put on your armour when you lie down to sleep would you now? Whoever heard of such a thing as that?

Do have some tea, Mum said, it's rather thick I'm afraid.

Thanks but I've had a cup with Mrs Withers, people are so hospitable. I only wanted to enquire about your little laddie. The one who wasn't at Sunday School last week.

It was only a cold, Mum said, but they hate to miss. It's nice for the kiddies having the Sunday School so near.

Yes and for Mum and Dad too, Joy was thinking, they can have a lie down on Sunday afternoons.

Miss Jenkins came out of the lorry and was introduced. Dad stretched out his legs on the grass till his foot was touching hers, then said, Oh, beg pardon.

Quite a good crowd down here today. Mum said. But the Reverend Allum's smile was for Miss Jenkins.

I expect you must find it pretty quiet, he said.

Oh no, she said, I love a day in the country.

You're right too, the Reverend Allum said. When she was younger Joy had used to think that when the Reverend Allum said You're right too, she'd hit upon something clever. It always turned out though, when he'd enlarged on it, that it wasn't what she had said after all.

The Reverend Allum took a deep breath in and a long look all round him. Yes, he said, on the out-going breath, when all's said and done nature takes a lot of beating. Jim was walking past, carrying a bottle with a straw stuck in it. They all looked away and pretended they hadn't noticed but Auntie Laurel said quietly to Mum, Fancy bringing it out here, where everyone's having their lunch.

But the Reverend Allum went on as if nothing had happened. We country-dwellers now, I sometimes think we're apt to forget perhaps. He looked all round him again. His all-embracing glance skipped the hotel and threaded its way through the cars to the strip of shore. The tide was nearly out. There was only a grey snake of water in the channel, and the steep mud-slopes were steaming off in the sun.

Yes, it's a pity Muriel and Winnie couldn't get down, Mum said. They've been in hospital with their appendixes, she explained to Miss Jenkins. Doctor thought they might as well have them done together and get it over.

Yes. We only see the sunny side of life over here, the Reverend Allum said. It's difficult to imagine what it must be like over there.

Dad had his eyes closed and a dribble of spit on his chin. Joy gave him a quiet agonised poke and he opened his eyes and smiled, looking like Terry. Mum was getting on with her fancy work. Yes. Quite a good crowd here today, she said, but a lot of them have to leave early for the milking.

I don't know what others' opinions may be, said the Reverend Allum, but personally Miss Jenkins, I like to think of this little affair as a sort of commemoration. The settlers in these parts landed here. Quite near where we are sitting now I believe.

There wasn't anything here then, Mum said, her eyes on the hotel.

The settlers had faith, said the Reverend.

Too right, said Miss Jenkins, putting her hand to a yawn.

Dad had found a pair of pink art silk panties that Mavis had had for Christmas. They had been in Mum's bag for Mavis to change to. Dad kept holding them up and squinting between the legs in a comical way. The Reverend Allum went right on about the settler who had stuck in the mud and they never found the body, but Joy felt hot all over. As if something awful might happen. She got up quietly and walked away to be out of sight of Dad and the lot of them.

She said hello to the Dodds, the Band of Hope Dodds, they always came early and got the best place nearest to the hotel, and went round to the yard. The hotel backed onto the shore and the yard was quiet and secluded, with empty cases to sit on and a nice view over the inlet. Jim was there smoking a cigarette with the cider bottle and the straw beside him.

Hello, she said, what are you doing here?

Oh, nothing, he said.

I thought maybe you had a date.

Who with? he said.

Joy pulled little bits off the straw, wanting to cry. Mum had stuck to it that the navy was just as smart and safer for washing, and the perm she could have next year when she worked at the store. Next year it would all be too late. The other girls had florals, the kind with elastic round the waist that fits almost anyone, and their hair nicely set with steel clips and invisible hairnets. Merle had blossomed out with lipstick too, but really it didn't look so hot with her pimples.

Cheer up, Jim said. How's old stick in the mud?

As usual, Joy said, he's on the settlers again.

And your Dad and the others?

As usual, she said. Dad's had a few of course. You know what he always says, It's a free country.

The curfew shall not wring, but Dad shall turn the wringer tomorrow. He'll have to take his headache to church as well.

Jim was always making fun of Dad and Mum. It wasn't true either, Dad didn't go to church any more. There was only the wringer. It was always like that with Jim. Just as you were settling down for a nice yarn he would start slinging off at Dad, or his Dad, or the capitalist system, so that it never came to anything. Still, of course, there would never be anyone else.

It was sunny and quiet in the yard. The people walking up and down, up and down, between the hotel and the jetty, stopped and turned back where the metalled path ended. Joy moved along closer to Jim on the box. The people seemed far away. It had to happen then that Murrey popped his head over the fence, grinning at them, showing his black stumps. A horrible boy Murrey, with filthy tricks.

It's only Murrey, Joy said. He'll be having his new teeth when he leaves school, his mother says.

The big thrill that only comes once in a lifetime. Well, my big thrill will be getting out of this. I might get my trip to Europe after all.

More likely land up in the desert though, Joy said. Why couldn't you help your Dad milking and get exempted? You don't want to go and get killed do you?

Get killed for these stick in the muds? But you have to think of the future. A lot of chaps are relieved to get into camp. It's a change from mowing the lawn and all that. It's going to be more of a change than they think though. A change is going on all over the world. Before the war governments had to make camps because the prisons couldn't hold the political prisoners. It's never happened like that before. The bosses are hoping it will blow over, the war will give people something else to do. It was only the old red spectre walking again, they think. But the change that is coming is rising like the tide. It will reach even this little place one day. But I'm going to be on the spot when the big things happen. You have to think of the future.

Joy was looking at the hills across the inlet, not thinking of the future, thinking the hills looked empty and strange today. She had always meant to go over there sometime. It looked lonely, but pretty and peaceful, the grass a soft green, not the metal green of the properly fertilised paddocks, the hills split softly into creeks full of scrub and shadows. There were Maori lands over there. Better than on our side, Dad said, they are dirty and carry diseases. There wouldn't be much to see over there, he said, but Joy had always wanted to go sometime.

The sun was bright and a cool wind blew from the coast. It was a lovely day now. Cheer up, Jim said. Joy sat still, for fear of disturbing his hand settled on hers, feeling his cool fingers and the heat inside her hand where the straw was crushed.

A man came out of the hotel back door. He was little and sandy, and walked slowly and sadly. He must have lost his way.

He crossed to a box and sat carefully down. Then he remembered something and got up again with a nervous look round the yard. He saw them but it was just too late by then. He took out his false teeth and was sick on the ground.

Joy got up. Jim said he'd have to be getting along too. Outside the yard they ran into the Young Men's Bible Class and the Reverend Allum in bathing togs. They were larking and making funny remarks like a boys' school story. Come along in and have a good swim, they shouted to Jim as they passed, it would do you good.

I'm afraid I haven't been introduced, Miss Jenkins said to Jim when she overtook them, but I've heard such a lot about you. Joy introduced them and she got confidential at once. Rather a queer idea for all the men to go in swimming together, Bible Class or no Bible Class, she said. And it was pretty hard to keep up a conversation with some people, and she asked him, had he read *Gone with the Wind*?

Jim said, Well, yes, but he had to be going himself now. He started up his motor bike with a bang and rode off up the hill, the bike making scornful explosions.

After that there was nothing much to do. It began to rain again, and Mum sat on a box in the bathing shed with her fancy work, pegging away at the big rose in the middle she had promised herself she was going to finish today. Joy could see there was something wrong but Mum said it was only her legs.

They swelled up, generally in the evening, about the time

Dad came home, and she would say to him, Just look at my legs again, it's from being on them all day.

You must have got up too early, Miss Jenkins said.

Oh no, I always get up at five, Mum said. I like to get things done before breakfast.

It's a puzzle what you find to do all the rest of the day, Miss Jenkins said.

I find plenty to do thank you, Mum said, as if she'd been offered something she didn't like.

You must have a gift for it, Miss Jenkins said. And she laughed.

Like some people have a gift for fooling round with men, Mum said. Joy felt as if something horrid was going to happen. But Mum couldn't have meant Miss Jenkins.

The Bible Class was swimming still in the rain, and the other unmarried men must have been in the pub.

When it cleared up it was time to get Mavis changed and line up for the ice cream. Mrs Dodds, Murrey's mother, and Mrs Chapman were doing the refreshments this year. Mrs Dodds always got first prize at the show with her sponge surprise, or else with her ginger kisses. But when Mum tasted the ice cream she said there was nothing in it but those powders, and Auntie Laurel said, Mrs Dodds and Mrs Chapman might have put in a bit more sugar and a drop of cream for the kiddies. And only those cheap soft drinks.

The soft drinks were mixed in two kerosene tins. One of the drinks was red and the other green. There was plenty of it and some of the boys got as many as ten drinks. To end off with there was an orange, but Mum said that was extravagant at the price they were now.

Then Brian was sent to fetch the hot water again, and Mum and Miss Jenkins and Auntie Laurel had afternoon tea with the rest of the Christmas cake. The kids hung round, pestering to go in swimming and Mum kept saying, No you might get in the current. You know you can't go without Dad.

Mrs Chapman passed with her husband. We're off home, she said.

You've got him well trained, Mum said. That was one of her jokes.

Terry getting sleepy, worrying to be taken notice of, was saying over and over again, Where's Dad?

Now what did you promise me this morning? Mum said. What am I going to tell Dad when he asks if Terry has been a good boy all day?

Daddy's having his tea somewhere, Miss Jenkins said.

But Terry said, I know where he might be. Drinking beer in the hotel.

Mum suddenly gave him such a crack on the side of the head that he couldn't even yell for a minute or two.

The tide's about right in, Joy said. It made noises like smacking kisses under the banks where the kids were sitting looking down at the water. After a while Mum came over and said as the sun was going and Dad hadn't come yet, they could put on their togs. But they mustn't stay in for long, it was getting chilly. The boys rushed off to the shed to change. Joy and Mavis undressed in the lorry.

Terry stood on the bank and cried while the others were in. He hadn't been allowed to paddle because of his cold. The sun was off the water now but he cried so long that Mum undressed him and put on his bathing pants, but when he got down to the water he wouldn't go in.

Joy rubbed down Mavis and dressed herself quickly and walked away along the shore as if she were meeting someone. Passing the Withers she saw the dinghy tied to a post by the bach, and got in and let it drift into the mangroves. The wind had died down. It felt like a warm damp hand across her hair. The ugly old twisted mangrove trunks were all covered up and only the branches with dark green leaves were showing. The water made roads between the tops of the trees. Joy moved along the roads and little lanes till a branch scraped the bottom of the boat. Then it was not a road but only all that water underneath, enough to cover a tree.

She began to row out across the inlet. The sun had set and the valleys and creeks on the other side were smoothed out. The hills were black and flat, like the advertisement letters across the picture, painted across the sky for some reason.

When the boat swung in the current she turned. The kids had stopped shouting on the jetty and everything was quiet, and over towards the sea a crack in the sky opened into a still shiny lake, exactly the colour of the Christmas bell.

When Joy got back Brian and Mavis were sitting in the lorry because it was getting chilly, playing I Spy. Terry was asleep on the floor. He had a blue mark down the side of his face. Mum was walking up and down outside. She said Auntie Laurel and Miss Jenkins had gone home hours ago with somebody else.

It was quite dark when Dad came out at last. He said he had had to stay for Uncle Nick who was not feeling too good. Mum wanted to have it out with him but he only smiled. Might as well be the wind blowing, she said. But perhaps you'll be feeling differently tomorrow.

Mr Chapman, who hadn't gone home after all, sat in front with Dad. Uncle Nick was inside. He was carrying on about his kidneys, how bad they were, they didn't seem to get any better, he was sure he wouldn't pass the medical test, and everyone ought to do their bit, and the loved ones at home. He got so worked up about it he started to cry.

The kids feeling a bit awkward piped up *Roll out the Barrel, We'll have a Jolly Good Time,* just to change the subject. I wish it was next year, Brian said, for the picnic.

Joy said nothing. Brian was such a kid. He never stopped to think that everything might be different next year.

Anyone Home?

Looking at himself in the mirror, at brown flesh of neck and arms, and breadth of chest under the loose shirt with the big red flowers on it, he knew quite well what the old man would do. After the first politeness had worn off Lily's old man would work his annoying laugh that was like a rusty alarm clock. The old man would always do that if your hair was not clipped up the back or you had a new coloured shirt.

Running the comb through his curly wet hair and seeing his brown flesh and the red flowers, Roy smiled at himself in the swaying mirror. He was good and brown. He looked good in that shirt. Lily would like it. A lot of the boys were wearing them for the beach. And what the hell did it matter, anyway? They'd be getting some shocks now the boys were coming back. It wasn't going to be like before the war.

Our innings now, he thought, lifting his new suitcase down from the rack. It might have been only a notice in the *Herald. I'll always remember you, dear, And happy times in the past. Inserted by his loving fiancee Lily. Our dear one sailed away. In a beautiful ship called Rest . . .* and me rotting over there at the Canal.

And as the train entered a tunnel, in the timeless grinding anaesthetic darkness, he thought again, That smack was a near go. He knew again what it was like to die. (It was not what you'd ever thought it was. It was dull. An imposture in a hypodermic, the sweet-frigid Godspeed of a false friend on the journey through ether. While your eyes looked at grey rain through glass and a clock that pointed to three. The rain falling and the hand moving, familiar, unintelligible, an insult. The minutes not moving, nothing moving, only a hoax, malevolent no-reason. The fraud that would take my name. Down in the wicked silence my name is Roy.)

But when the train flashed into open sunlight Roy only remembered how lucky he was. And lying on a beach in the Islands. And buying fruit and a necklace of pink shells. And women, Lily of course, gleaming through deep dreams, like golden tropical fruit. And being strong again and outraged at all the grey waste. Drab duties springing like toadstools in a swamp, and the dull stress of hourly expectation. The war. But when you'd somehow come through all right then you knew. The others knew too. But we're still young, they said. It couldn't have been for nothing all this.

The racing paddocks, scrub-shadowed, slowed and steadied. This was the way he liked to remember it. A hot afternoon, the smell of shadow round the pool, and Lily standing on the log shaking her pale hair, splashing the silence with laughter, cracking the black silence of the pool as she dived in.

As Roy jumped down from the train the jigsaw bits of the picture fell into place. Willows, and the bridge without a rail, the steep green slope, the red roof of the house, and the silver dead tree in the top paddock. No one was on the platform. Trains didn't run to schedule. Mr Withers would be sunk in a Sunday stupor, Mrs Withers scratching and ferreting round the house. Lily would be standing on the verandah, dressed in blue, and wearing the stockings he'd sent that were almost as fine as her skin.

As he climbed the rutted road, he looked up several times to the house. Nothing was moving but the sheep and a cloud slowly unfolding over the ranges. He passed the empty verandah with its closed doors and windows looking blankly on to the near green, and went round to the back. 'Anyone home?' he called.

Mr Withers sat by the oilclothed kitchen table. He was cutting an apple into a very small pieces and putting them one by one into his mouth. His eyes moved rigidly, like doll's eyes threaded on a lead weight, to Roy, to the apple, then slid away guiltily. 'I was just having a sit down,' he said.

(And why not on a hot Sunday afternoon? The money tumbling in. You're free to.) Roy didn't say that. Mr Withers was a little deaf. He never could hear what he didn't want to hear. And there was a muffled shuffling and shutting of doors, that meant Mrs Withers was about. Even on Sunday! Roy thought, remembering the precautions he had to take when he was working for the old man. She was always being caught either with teeth out or with curlers in, or boiling up mutton fat, or the house not done. You'd hear her footsteps coming along the passage, then she'd remember something and go back. And when she came, ready down to her corset, she would apologise, as if to say. It seems all right, but still there is something missing.

'Oh, Roy! I'm sorry,' she said. 'Dad reckoned the train would be late. I'm afraid you'll find us in rather a mess, but you know what it is with the hay all cut, and now Dad thinks the wind's going round, and, being Sunday, there's only the Maori to help. I would gladly have lent them a hand, but my leg has been bothering me, and then there was all the baking for this evening. Lily should be back any time now. The train is usually late, so not to waste the afternoon, and as she was getting a lift with the Massey girls, I don't know how they manage with the benzine, but they manage to save enough for the Bible class, and then we naturally thought the train would be late.'

'I'll hop down to the road and meet her,' Roy said.

Lily was coming up the steep path, wearing a blue dress. He ran down to kiss her, but her face was muffled up in a silk scarf, so he patted her shoulder and asked, 'How's life?' instead.

She was walking ahead of him into the kitchen.

'It's only her teeth,' Mrs Withers said. 'We wanted to get them done with you coming back. She can't expect to be feeling very grand, but we'll have a cup of tea and one of the sponges to try.

It cracked a bit, the mixture was too moist, but the others are for this evening. Dad needs a cup of tea.'

Mr Withers' eyes were burrowing into a red flower on Roy's island shirt as if he expected to find an insect there. 'A party,' Mr Withers said suddenly. 'Lily come home the other day and announced she wanted to have one like Mrs Edmonds had. Little plates handed round. Wasn't it, Lily? And ashtrays and cigarettes lying about beside the chairs so that they could reach out for one.' Mr Withers began to laugh. The aimless, dull laugh Roy remembered so well, that cut across whatever you were saying or doing, and went grinding on until you were sick and tired, and whatever it was seemed not worthwhile going on with.

'Well, really,' Mrs Withers said, with a crippled smile at the mention of ashtrays. 'I'm not much for that sort of thing. Aunt Maud did offer to have it at her place, but we couldn't let her go to all that trouble, she does too much, she never spares herself, so at the finish we decided to have it quietly. Only as many as we can seat round the table. But now the Reverend Rigby can't come.'

Mrs Withers' talk was like something left running. Something seeping colourless from a wound. A warm white flow that eased her irritation. Her talk dripped stealthily. Mr Withers didn't listen. Mr Withers knew very well what was coming out. He could staunch it whenever he liked.

'Well, back to work,' he said. 'Cows have to be milked, Sunday or no.'

'Come on, Lily,' Roy said quickly.

'Don't be late back,' Mrs Withers called after them. 'I don't know what I should do if they all arrived and nobody here.'

Lily stopped at the gate, waiting for Roy to suggest which way they should go.

'Along to the pool?'

'Yes, we could. Yes, if you like.'

'Don't you want to?'

'It's that awful paspalum,' she said doubtfully. 'But it doesn't matter. I'd like to go wherever you like.'

'I'll carry you over the bad spots,' he said, though it never did seem right that she always wanted to do whatever he liked.

Roy carried Lily carefully down the steep sheep track to the pool. Her legs, stockinged in yellow varnish colour, like little wooden legs, stuck out stiffly and caught in the tea-tree and fern. Though she looked so frail she was heavy against his chest. It seemed a long way down. Pushing through the branches, he couldn't help thinking of a mate he had carried back there in the jungle. How light he looked and yet how heavy he was, heavier all the time, and when they got to the base he was quite cold.

What a time to think of a thing like that, he thought. Now that he had her in his arms he wanted to say something funny or something loving, but he was out of breath, breathing in her pale hair, that smelt a little of earth and antiseptics.

He was glad to put her down beside the pool, in the silence of the sombre bowl of the bush. Tall banks gave the trees a tremendous height, thick green edged down to the black water, and a fallen rata lay like a bridge across it. On the marble-hard surface of the pool every leaf of every tree was reflected. Each detail was there without life or sound, and across the colours strangely dark and cold, a bright shuttle was weaving meaningless traceries. A dragonfly was passing and repassing, but in this flat, black world of pictured silence it had no destination.

'Look, Lily,' he said. 'Remember the times we used to catch dragonflies? Remember the day you were standing on the old rata there and I took a snap of you that didn't come out? What a kid you were! Why can't we be like we were then?'

'Oh, I don't know,' she said in a pale little voice. 'We were kids then. We didn't have anything to worry about. I'm sure I've been thinking about you enough and worrying about what to do for the best. I lie awake nights. And lately I've been on the go all the time getting ready to get married. Don't you want to? Or was it only a joke?'

'Yes,' he said. 'No,' he said. 'I'll take a picture of you. Get out to the middle where the sun is.' He helped her up on to the wide trunk, then went back to look. 'I can't get you in all that shadow,' he shouted. 'Further, further out.'

She moved along slowly, timidly, on the trunk, out to the middle where the sun struck it.

He watched her reflection crystallise in the sun. Stretched on golden bird's legs, in its dress of endless blue, it slanted bright-balanced, its delicate head glistening against the sky in a clearing between dark and monstrous shadows. When it moved it did not disturb the surrounding air. The face, small, light and almost transparent, looked up, yet it was not lying, nor standing, but floating stationary, an angel in dark ice. The blue space behind the skull was staring through eyes like crystals—

'Got you!' he called out. 'Now laugh, for God's sake.'

She laughed. 'Aren't you coming to get me down off here?'

Before they left he took a last look at the empty, flat world on the water. (Below were black depths and intricate weeds and measureless, moving eels that only had meaning when they spiked the still surface.) He threw in a dead branch and the black world broke into soft eels of light. But before they turned their backs it had closed again. It was always there like the night or the rubbery darkness of the anaesthetic.

(The numb dullness that was always there, where bodiless problems spun with no meaning and no direction because it had always been there, and time was only a load of rubber darkness. Where there was no Roy, no me, no life, no dying, no rest. Only the suffering speck not-I. And the pointless joke of grey rain through glass and a clock that pointed to three. The hand pointing the fraud, the dream that is no dream and lasts for ever. The fraud that would take my name. My name is Roy.)

'You mustn't mind me,' he said. 'I haven't got the war out of my system. I get these fits. Your old man gives me the willies. But we shan't be cooped up with the old people for long. I'm going to build on the hill. I like the site. I like the trees. When it blows we can think we live by the sea.'

'Dad cut them down for fencing posts,' she said. 'He thought you wouldn't want anything wasted in wartime.'

'Just thinking of me? Well, he won't have to think any more. Everything's going to be different from now on. We're going to please ourselves. We're both young. We'll go away to Auckland or to a beach somewhere.'

'Before we get married?'

'I don't know. It was just an idea. It's about time we started to enjoy life. We're both young. We're both young,' Roy kept saying.

And to everything she said, 'Yes, Roy. Yes, of course, Roy,' in the same pale voice that held a 'no' in reserve.

Roy stopped in front of the house where the silver dead tree clawed at the evening sky. 'I don't even feel like going in,' he said. 'The old buzzard. If he'd nothing better to do, why can't he shift that blasted dead stump? The meddling old devil. Why don't you say something, Lily? Why do you stand there looking as if I'd hit you?' 'You didn't used to talk like that,' she said faintly. 'I never thought you'd come back like this. After all the happy times in the past. I didn't think you'd forget so easily after what happened the last day at the pool—it was you that wanted it.'

'Why harp on the past?' he said. 'As if there was nothing to look forward to. Of course I remembered the day by the pool. Everything. Your reflection in the water. It looked so pretty. Like an angel. Just the way you seemed to me that day. But if you keep on like that I'll begin to think it was something I imagined.'

Have to start over again, he thought, for she had covered her face with the scarf and was running with small steps into the house. Have to explain how it is when you've been through that sort of hell you get queer ideas. Have to kiss and make up . . . He remembered then that they hadn't kissed yet.

'What am I doing,' Mrs Withers said. 'It looks as if everything isn't on the table.'

The sponges, sandwiches and sausage rolls looked clinical under a starched muslin shower on the white cloth, in the cold radius of the naked light bulb, surrounded by swallowing darkness of rust-green walls.

'Doesn't that stain grin out,' Mrs Withers said. 'I had another go at it yesterday. I suppose when you've been away you notice things more.'

'I suppose you do,' Roy said, 'and by the way, did Lily like the stockings?'

'Oh, yes. They were very nice. I told her to put them up in a mason jar, but the silverfish got them. The shells were very pretty. We had them on show for the patriotic tea, and everybody said they were very pretty. But what am I doing? There they are at the door.'

'Just seat yourselves anywhere, take it as it comes,' Mrs Withers said with her crippled smile, and in the polite confusion of the colliding chairs of Uncle Herb, Aunt Maud, the Masseys and the Pritchets, Mr Pritchet said, 'Roy musn't be shy—he must come and sit over here by Lily. By jingo, it didn't seem like two years. You've forgotten all we taught you at school young man?'

'Most of it,' Roy said. 'Most of it, sir.'

'Well, well, we'd hoped you'd be carrying on at 'Varsity.'

'Plenty of time to decide that,' Roy said.

'I see you've donned native costume in honour of the occasion. A tribute to the Islanders. Very fine chappies the Islanders. Done their bit in the war, I understand.'

'Well, anyway, it is nice to see you, Roy,' Mrs Pritchet said. 'We were almost afraid we wouldn't be able to come. I couldn't get anyone to sit with the kiddies but Molly. I didn't really like leaving them with her, and they cried so. But there isn't anyone I would trust with my kiddies, would you, Mrs Withers?'

'I wouldn't,' Mrs Withers said. 'When Lily was little—'

'But then Mr Pritchet said we'll just have to go and give Roy a welcome, and then we've been meaning to come for such a long time.'

'It's rather a headache with the benzine,' Mr Pritchet said. 'We shall have to try and make it up somehow.'

'Have some cream with your plums,' Mrs Withers said.

'You mustn't tempt me,' Mr Pritchet said.

There was a respectful silence.

'We don't care about it,' Mrs Withers said. 'Dad can take it, but he doesn't care about it. Won't you have another plum then, Mr Pritchet?'

'Just one. Only one. They're delicious, thank you. I can always take another bismuth tablet. An extra tablet ought to balance it up.' When the laugh finished there was another silence. The light glared frantically.

Uncle Herb took two sausage rolls on his plate. 'Might as well eat them now,' he said. 'I know what it is when Maud has company. I have to eat them stale for a week. It's all done for show. The ladies trying to outdo each other.'

Because he was over eighty, Uncle Herb's joke drew a watery, dutiful laugh. While they were still in the trough of it, Mr Pritchet handed a plate with a flourish across to Roy. 'Have a bit more of this sponge, old boy. We can't let him get away with that. Feed the brute, eh?'

'Lily's very quiet,' Mrs Pritchet said.

'It's her teeth,' Mrs Withers said, talking loud now that attention was focused on Lily. 'She can't have the new ones till they're all out.'

'Well, it's soon over,' Mrs Pritchet said. 'Mr Evans is so quick. Mr Rigby was pleasantly surprised when he took Lou. She was ready to go into hospital the same day and have her tonsils done, so they could do it all on the same trip. What a pity it was the special service tonight. I always think if Mr Rigby is present you can depend on some real good laughs.'

'But Lily's nervous,' Mrs Withers said. 'She's always been nervous like me—'

'In that case there's nothing like facing up to things and getting them over with,' Mr Pritchet said. 'The wife is wonderful in that respect. Do it today is her motto. And I'm sure Lily has grit.'

As Lily was clearing the plates and didn't speak, 'We'll see,' Roy said. 'We'll be going to Auckland,' he said, very loud for Mr Withers to hear.

Mr Withers had heard. His eyes rested rigidly on his daughter, shifted slowly from the bulge of her breast, up the white neck to the small red gash of her mouth.

'She'll do as Mr Evans says,' he said. 'It's a waste of time and money otherwise. You wouldn't want to have her with an abscess?' This set Mr Withers' laugh going.

Miss Massey turned on Roy her sculptured smile. 'I've never regretted it,' she said. 'So you'll be having the ceremony in town. I daresay Lily will be glad when it's over.'

'I'm sure she will,' Mrs Pritchet said. 'But it's so nice to look back to. Mr Pritchet always remembers our anniversaries.'

'We want to go swimming and dancing,' Roy said. 'I can still dance.'

'That's the idea,' Mr Pritchet said, 'killing the two birds with the one stone. By George, it doesn't seem like ten years since the wife and I were in Auckland on pleasure bent. Mrs Pritchet is so tied.'

'Terribly tied,' Mrs Pritchet said with her brightest smile, 'but I've never regretted it.'

'You really do too much,' Miss Massey said, 'you know you do. You'll be having a return of your old trouble.'

'Doctor says I'm a very obstinate case, but I feel well in myself,' Mrs Pritchet said.

(Lily will smile. The daily smile that covers the old trouble.)

'You'll always be on the go, Lily,' Mrs Pritchet said, with her bright, curdled smile. Mr Withers' laugh ground round. The walls drew closer. The light glared frenziedly, ringed with glazed faces and china-white smiles. A dream that was no dream. Mr Withers, the dentist, the Reverend Rigby, the surgeon with his knife, Mrs Pritchet with her smile, closed the circle.

'I knew this would be of interest,' Mr Pritchet was saying, 'so I brought the jolly thing along with me. Roy will be able to identify the places for us,' he said, bringing out the album from under a chair. 'I hope you'll agree that I can catch an effect. And then they say photography isn't an art!'

Roy remembered the snaps and the slides they had shown at school lectures. He had laughed at the one of women carrying fruit—just at the way the women's breasts stared in the black and white silence, and Mr Pritchet had taken him aside after and told him it was nothing to laugh about, that it was the most natural thing in the world and then he'd been caned, and Mr Pritchet had said, 'Stay in and think it over. If you think it over then you'll see for yourself.'

'You'll remember this.' A strip of grey on white. 'By jingo, that was a trek we had up there with some of the native chappies from the mission. You'll remember this, of course.' A strip of white on grey. 'You'll remember this . . .'

After they had looked at each page, Mr Pritchet looked at his watch and got up. 'About time I think . . . A pleasant task . . . The last war . . . A little incident . . . Met for the purpose . . .' The words left behind in the relentless race of the knitting needles.

What purpose? Roy wanted to ask. For what purpose? What meaningless ordeal? (While the talk goes on, rising and falling, while the light shrieks silently, while the eye strains, while the brain bleeds, to lend a semblance of purpose to the livid patterns on the dark walls, endless combinations of ships or tables or equally of coffins, valueless forms that rise and fall and regroup; bodiless problems holding no solution.)

They were calling on Roy to say a few words.

'I hardly know what to say,' Roy said. (The click of knitting needles was light and fine, like the tiny bat-cry breaking of wires, inside the brain, down there in the darkness.) 'Except to thank you for your kind wishes and to suggest you drink my health and Lily's.'

'Oh, dear,' Mrs Withers said. But after some fussing with the sideboard top shelf, the glasses granpa had brought from the old country were dusted and on the table, and filled with sherry Roy had brought from town.

Mr Pritchet, to set the tone, sniffed his and squinted at the light through it. He looked round the table. 'Has everyone a glass?' In school he would say, 'You all have your pieces of igneous rock formation? Is there anything you notice particularly? Any remarks?' 'I think on such an occasion as this,' he said, 'a tribute to our brave boys, I'm sure we all see it in that light?'

There were no remarks.

'Of course it would never do in this country to let liquor fall into the hands of those who cannot practise self-restraint. The Maoris a sacred trust, and others too I'm afraid. But personally I have always advocated moderate abstention in all things. A little incident to illustrate this. When I was over in France in '15. A glass of wine? Merci. Think nothing of it. Most natural thing in the world.'

The strain was too great. Self-restraint was of no avail. It sounded like the despairing wail of a siren. Miss Alice Massey blushed.

'To the ladies, then,' Mr Pritchet said, 'and to our brave boys.' Roy drank his. Lily fingered her glass. Mr Withers was looking at it. His eyes licked slowly round the little glass, then slid away. 'Lily's never tasted it,' he said. 'It might not agree with her.'

'I'll drink it for her.' Roy gulped it down. The two glasses of wine raised in him a small patch of warmth that seemed to spread round the table. There were flickers of talk. The Miss Masseys choked and giggled. Roy was telling them about the Islands. The nights were beautiful. You could sit outside in a café under the moon.

(Thank you for your kind wishes.) Because there must have been kind wishes, he thought. They must have been interested in the Islands, or why did Pritchet take all those photographs and Miss Massey say so many times, How corker.

While Roy talked he measured the wine in the bottle. It would just do another round, which would get them going nicely. He talked about things that were not in the photographs. The colours. The colours and the dances. And about how lovely-looking the Islanders were, and the Miss Masseys said, 'How corker!' Lovely but false it now began to seem, like something he had invented. But he went on talking about the dancers, trying to make it all seem real—the most natural thing in the world.

The knitting needles were still. He began to notice a waiting silence. Then Mr Pritchet coughed, got up, said, 'I hope we are not breaking up the party, but really it's about time.'

'Yes, I hope we're not,' Mrs Pritchet said, shutting her knitting into a zip bag, 'but some of us have to be up early.'

They were up like a spring released. As if the weight had been lifted that kept them sitting there, counting the minutes over their bedtime.

'All good things have to come to an end,' Mrs Withers said, as she hastened after them into the hall. 'Come along, Lily dear, and let's get through with all this washing up.'

Mr Withers said nothing. His eyes were still where they'd been most of the evening, burrowing into a red flower over Roy's heart, but he hadn't said anything yet. He only stretched out his hand for the wine bottle and put it away inside the cupboard that locked, where medicines were kept.

After the washing up Roy and Lily stood in the open doorway. The light from the house caught the top of the dead tree. Behind it glassy stars made the night darker. The frigid pulsing of the stars ticked unthinkable time. One fell, slipping swiftly across the sky, and something brittle splintered inside the brain, down there in the darkness.

'I knew it was coming,' she said. 'I knew from the first we should have to have it out. You don't care about me.'

'Nobody cares about anything,' he said.

'You haven't even given me a kiss.' She held up her face to be kissed. Her mouth was a closed and cold sea anemone. Her voice was faint and false and far away.

'You know I never regretted it,' she said, 'but now—oh, I wish I was dead.'

'You make me laugh,' he said. 'You don't know what you mean. There's no point in it. No future in it.'

While he tried to laugh she slid over to him in the dark. All her soft weight rested on his chest, a nightmare in the night of his body, the night inside his clothes, inside his skin, in which lay chained the suffering speck not-I, observing the horror of the unfelt.

'You're perfectly free, though. Just think it over. Don't speak now. Don't say anything yet.'

Her voice was soft and bitter and far away, like the voice of an old person. 'You're perfectly free . . . Don't say anything yet . . .' Her pale hair that smelt of earth and antiseptics covered his mouth and nose and stifled him.

The light clicked off. The dead arm collapsed in the night. From the house came the little irrelevant sounds of tidying away and doors closing. Something had amused Mr Withers. His laugh went on and on like an argument, drawing its own conclusions from the darkness.

Home Front

The small sharp hills over-lapping like green waves converged on the train. The sun flashed out and the dead trees littering the hillside shone like white bones. Then it was raining again. The train stopped at a station and the carriages were suddenly empty. The passengers surged into the café, then hurried back with moist white sandwiches and tea. The station where Rex got down was only a long shed with an iron roof, standing alone in the middle of the green.

It was raining again, and there was no one about to tell him the way to Isaiah Chapman's place. He hailed a car that was passing along the road and the man driving said he would take him to Chapman's.

Old Chap as we call him is a cousin of mine, he told Rex. We're pretty near all related around here.

Rex asked about the farm.

Well, it's a pretty place, said the man. The park we call it. He has this hobby of growing fruit and other trees. It was clear the other dairy farmers thought it a crazy hobby. It's behind the hills over there, he said. There's a shorter way through the paddocks.

The mountains in the distance that looked wild and grand under the rain were only hills when they got up to them. Little green calvaries topped with tall dead trees.

I suppose it doesn't pay, said Rex.

It doesn't. But Isaiah's an old man. You can't tell him anything. He's really more of an idealist than a farmer.

Then, remembering he was talking to Rex he looked a bit awkward and said, You'll be the new man, I suppose? Oh well,

I hope you'll like it here. Old Chap's a great Bible reader and all that, but a real good sort when you get to know him.

Rex was put down at the gate and waded through mud the half mile to the house. Mrs Chapman welcomed him at the back door and made him take off his shoes in the kitchen. She asked him if he had had a pleasant journey from Auckland and he said, Yes, very pleasant.

I expect you will find it very wet and muddy, she said, it's our normal winter state. But the spring flowers are coming on apace. Are you a flower lover too?

Mr Chapman would be in soon, she said, and Rex would like a wash in the bathroom after his journey. That means they don't wash there themselves, thought Rex. It was cold in the bathroom. The solitary towel hanging beside the coffin-shaped bath was hard and thin. Round the walls stood bottles of petrified plums and jam, all neatly labelled with the name of the fruit and the date. There were several years of fruit and jam on the shelves.

Mrs Chapman was waiting outside in the passage to show him the way to his room. The room held the cold of a whole winter. The lino was shiny as ice. A framed printed card, hung near the dressing table, looked like the rules they have up in hotel bedrooms. Rex read, To A Pound Of Love Add A Liberal Measure Of Understanding And Mix. On the dressing table was a doily, and a shell with a ship painted on it that no one could ever mistake for an ashtray.

Facing the walnut double bed with its blue-white cover, two dreadfully enlarged Chapman ancestors in thick dark oval frames possessed the room. They had dark flaws in their faces like craters on the moon. Behind the glass a cheek-bone, a button on the man's coat, and a highlight on his hair stared blankly.

Rex began to unpack, looking for dry shoes. His brush and comb looked so uncomfortable beside the shell with the painted ship that he began to feel, not homesick for any particular place, but lonely and stranded. He reminded himself of other rooms he had slept in. This one would be no worse when it had been lived in. Someone must have slept in the bed once, and sat at the dressing table doing their hair, and looked through the window over the fields when it wasn't raining like this.

Rex opened a door which he thought was a cupboard, but it opened into a small sitting room which had the same clean but stale smell. This end of the house was a blind alley. There was a fluted fireplace and a firescreen with birds on it, an upright piano, upholstered chairs and a round walnut table. Rex smiled over the things laid out on the table. The velvet album, the stereoscope, the Family Bible. These objects looked familiar, he had met them so often in books. They were always amusing. He tried to think of a funny formula for the room, but nothing crossed his mind but the Spanish slang-word, *fatal*.

Thinking of Spain Rex saw the sun on the white wall of a house.

Big black ants were busy about the cracks in the plaster. Pots of carnations basked by the wall. A fat red flower burst its sheath with a silent explosion.

The shadow under the fig tree is round like a pool. Dipping your hand in the shadow you feel its edge like water. Jim is sitting waiting under the fig tree where the plates and salads are set in the shade. The midday silence is full of life, and an exuberant smell of flowers and frying.

An old peasant sits down at the table, and cocking his head at Jim hands him a wine skin. Jim takes off his shirt, is standing up and throwing his head right back to catch the crimson trickle that floods his teeth. He raises the wine skin higher and higher. The wine falls in a thin bright arc.

Rex was lucky. He had had two years of living up to the hilt, then slipped out when the game was up. He hadn't said goodbye to his Spanish friends. Jim had been killed at Huesca.

Perhaps, Rex thought, his excitements over committees, his travels, his political work which had led in the end to Spain, were only forms of escape from what he was feeling now in the Sunday smell of the sitting room.

He was young when it first got him. It was after dinner. The rain seemed to have set in and he had settled down with a book, when suddenly the sun came out in the watery way and he was told to go and play in the garden.

There was nothing in the garden but the long watery afternoon with Monday on its horizon. He walked down the path till he came to a jungle of trees and a high brick wall at the end. This was called 'down the garden'. Under the dripping wall was the puppy's grave, and an overturned flowerpot which Rex sat on when he cried about something. He didn't cry now. This wasn't something that had happened. It was there.

You're just a lump of misery, Master Rex, his nurse would say when he had the Sunday feeling. He grew out of it. It only came back in waiting rooms, and long dull dreams. But when it did he knew it was there all the time, and his interesting life was only painted over it.

The door of the sitting room creaked and a child came in. A plain little thing in a gym tunic.

Dinner is nearly ready, Mr Rex.

So you are Lila, said Rex, and the child came over to him.

Were you looking at the pictures? That's St Peter's at Rome on top.

I've seen that one, said Rex. It has a great wide space in front dotted with frozen fountains.

Oh Mr Rex, could you play the piano then? Can you play a hymn? Our Lord Is Ever Present has a pretty tune.

I might have a try sometime.

Oh do have a pop at it, Mr Rex.

But not now. I think they're calling you to lay the table.

Mr Chapman was small and bald, and wore a neat white beard. He shook hands with Rex and they all sat down to the meal. After piling the plates with pumpkin and potato, the old lady abruptly laid her hand on her forehead as a signal. They bent their heads in an attitude of prayer. During the next few minutes' silence Rex looked through his fingers at Lila, searching her dull face for a clue that would lead back to Jim.

Rex sat facing the clear blue eyes of the old man. He talked in a slow, high, gentle voice about the government and the weather. He seemed to be looking at Rex from a long way off. He said something about Spain. That it was through lack of faith that the Republicans had perished. But when Rex began to argue the point he was not listening. Rex thought at first that he was deaf, but he was not deaf. He was only out of focus.

Mrs Chapman kept urging Rex to have some more.

I hope our simple fare agrees with your taste, she said. Our neighbours don't bother to grow veges, but Isaiah has been on a sort of diet for years. You forget to eat while you're talking, she said to her husband.

I have sufficient for my needs, said Mr Chapman. Then turning to Rex, he began to denounce the forces of evil which he said were undermining the churches. Rex didn't know what the forces were. Whether it was the brewers or the Catholics or the Anglicans who were doing all the harm. When he appeared to have finished Rex tried to say a word about Jim. But the old chap had withdrawn again, and was absorbed in scraping the burnt edge off the pudding dish.

In the afternoon they went round the farm. The mud was so deep it oozed over the tops of the good boots Rex had been given in Spain. Rex had to see everything, Mr Chapman pointed out the places where he should have sown lupins to keep down the weeds, and telling him where things were, and where they used to be, and what might have to be done sometime.

Half his words were lost in the sudden gusts of wind that passed with a rattle of rain on the iron roofs like the sound of machine guns, leaving a dead stillness behind, and the rain quietly falling. Then the sun burst out with a startling feverish glare between the black clouds and the shivering green of the pastures.

Rex spoke of a plan that Jim had made for the farm. The old man stood very close to him while he was talking, as though he was waiting for something. Like a child who has run up with a treasure in his hand, and well-trained, waits quiet and expectant, until the people have finished their talk and will look at it. The old man waited, then with a meek insistent smile, he brought out what he had hoarded up to say.

They walked and walked through wet grass. Mr Chapman was amazingly active, and rosy as a child, but from time to time a wave of milky pallor flooded his face, like the first waves of death lapping over him, and receding so gently that he was unaware.

You see yon trees, he said happily. I have seen them all grow.

He started little gardens all over the place. Stopping at one of these forgotten gardens he said, That was Jim's garden. It's Lila's now, but she doesn't take care of it much.

The afternoon seemed endless. When they got back Mrs Chapman and Lila had changed into different dresses and they had tea, stewed apples and scones and home-baked bread. Mr Chapman was quiet now, he had talked himself out. Mrs Chapman was worried because she had made too much tea, and Rex had to have a third cup. The child would go to bed soon, and then they would want to hear about Jim's death.

But when supper was over Mr Chapman began to turn the knob of the radio. There are several services on the air, he said. Managing the radio the old man was pathetic. He got first a waltz, then someone talking fast in a frightening voice, but at last the organ burst bitterly through. The Presbyterians I believe, he said. He smiled like a conjurer. I hope that will be agreeable to you.

Rex longed to smoke to take the edge off it, but it was no good upsetting these left-behind old things the first night.

After the service ended Mr Chapman drew his chair to the

table and began to write very slowly in a large book. Rex, passing behind him to get nearer the fire read, 'August 28. Burnt bullock in three days.'

Mr Chapman read over what he had written and shut the book. Mrs Chapman counted stitches.

Shall I bring in a log or two? asked Mr Chapman.

I hardly think it's worth it, said Mrs Chapman, looking at Rex for assent.

I suppose you heard that Jim died very bravely. I sent back the few things he always carried with him. You got them all right?

Mrs Chapman nodded. Yes thank you, we got the parcel. And then we got your letter saying you would be coming out to New Zealand just the same.

I didn't give the details of his death in my letter. Rex seemed to be saying a lesson to the old things who happened to be Jim's parents. What was left of Jim seemed now to be lost between the three of them.

He had only been ten days up at the front. The front was changing all the time and we never knew where we were, but Jim and I were always together. On this day they asked for volunteers to go to some comrades with a machine gun a bit further up the road that went to Huesca. The road was impassable, but there was some cover beside it. We thought someone could get round with a mule load of stuff. They were out of munitions, you see. Jim passed an open vineyard, but when he was under the trees a stray bullet got him.

Rex got through the story he had told again and again. It was stale even before he had begun to tell it, because so many people had been killed that way.

The old man frowned, seemed to be groping for something. Mrs Chapman flushed and swallowed. Rex thought, They still don't really believe it.

Do I understand you to say that my son met his death as a soldier, a combatant?

Why certainly, said Rex. He was a good soldier. He died like a hero.

They sat in silence while a death ripple passed over the face of the old man.

It must have been a terrible shock to you, Rex said.

It is a terrible shock, said Mr Chapman.

You see we didn't know, said his wife. He went over to do relief work for the Quakers.

Of course. Anyone could have known it. Jim had even told him once about some sect his father belonged to. Why couldn't he have remembered? How easy it would have been to say their son was killed bringing in a wounded comrade. He might have been killed any day bringing children away from Madrid. The idiocy of implying that Jim was a fighter. Even his death of a hero had been an accident. Other people had been over there to the machine gun post and nothing had happened, till in the end it seemed pretty safe to go.

Done now. Couldn't be helped now. He would leave in a day or two and find a job in Auckland, perhaps get back to Europe before the next war started. Thank God he'd hedged when he'd replied to the old man's letter offering him a job on the farm.

Well I suppose it's time to turn in, he said.

You know the way to your room, said Mrs Chapman. There's an extra blanket under the mattress if you should need it.

She said goodnight and went out to the kitchen, where Rex could hear her fussing about preparing for breakfast.

Now that Rex had said goodnight and was standing up he wanted Mr Chapman to understand. It was easy now. The same as when you leave a house and have a last word over the fence, or when you go to bed and come back for something and stay for hours talking to the person you've supposed to have left.

If you had been there yourself I know you would understand, he said. At the front you were spiritually safe, but when you went on leave you'd find you couldn't sit in certain cafés because the 'others' were there. Jim thought it was mostly the fault of the foreigners who were coming and going, raising money and sympathy for Spain, and raising hell too. Political parties couldn't agree about what their adherents were dying for. Jim couldn't have stood any more without losing his faith.

I thought he had stuck to the Quakers because they did the least harm. They were too busy saving children's lives. But as the war went on there was too much relief and advice. Jim said he wouldn't consider the children saved if the war was lost. One day he'd been to the centre with posters they'd asked him to get. Pictures of children playing and studying with underneath, Revolution In Education. They blacked out the R before they would use them. So Jim walked out and joined the Brigade.

If only Mr Chapman would sit still. He was busy again searching methodically among the papers on top of the bookshelf. He brought down a brown paper parcel, and coming quietly round the table while Rex talked laid it in front of him.

Some of Jim's books.

Perhaps some weeks before he had thought about the books and placed the parcel there where he could easily find it, to show Jim's friend. Though he seemed so vague the little plan, independent of anything that might intervene, had firmly stuck in his mind. So now Rex had to sit down at the table again and open the parcel, and turn the leaves of the books. The first page of an exercise book had written on it in curly writing:—

September 4th 1915.   *Padded*
                        Purr
                        whisker
                        curley claws
                        paws hungry
                        rosy

Poetry
This is the weather the cuckoo loves

And so do I
Be careful always look first to right and then to left
People generally travel on camels when crossing
Dead said the frost
Buried and lost
The leaf buds are covered with tough leather flaps called scales
We must not bring razor blades to school because they are dangerous
Do unto others (I know the rest) This is called the Golden Rule . . .

Well, I think I'll turn in now, Rex said. I'll take the books with me if you don't mind.

Certainly, said Mr Chapman. We rise at six-thirty in winter. I hope you will find your room comfortable. We call it the guest room now. I thought you might find it more convenient later to sleep in a smaller room that opens onto the back verandah. It's very handy for the sheds and you wouldn't bring dirt into the house. That's a great consideration with Mrs Chapman you know. But there is time enough to make the change after you have started work and become familiar with our way of life. Mrs Chapman was insistent that you should have Jim's room at first. I suppose you saw his picture over the bed?

Elegy

The dinner would soon be ready, Jim said, and meanwhile I must have a look at this book he had just bought. It would open my eyes, he said. I leaned on the trunk of the *Pinus insignis* that lay beside the house, its dead branches sticking up from the ground, and the roots, too, bare in the air like dead branches. It had been in the way there, and the needles fell into the spouting. It didn't matter; it wasn't a native tree, Jim said.

They had promised me a swim when I came down, and arranged that we all go in together while Jim was free. Jess had begun putting on her rubber bathing cap before we got to the shore, and they'd both splashed in ahead of me. So in spite of the greyness of the sky and the water I'd had my swim and soon we'd be having dinner.

It's always like this when I come to the farm for a nice rest. I am suddenly savagely tired and resent any little thing they may set me to do, even to washing up or having a swim. It's not that they're not good hosts. They don't mind the extra work. They take everything in their stride.

Farming's a great life, they tell you, provided you don't let yourself go to seed. They have not gone to seed. Though they are up so early and on the go all day, and live so far out, they manage to run in to the settlement for the Workers' Enlightenment lectures, leaving their child with neighbours. With their new radio they can get Russia just as clear as if it were in the room. They have overseas magazines and belong to a book club. The friends who come for a nice rest at weekends are all interested in various things. But still these weekends are full of blank spaces.

There was one while I washed up the dishes after dinner. Jess was in the kitchen preparing something. This getting ready for the next lap makes me feel somehow guilty. 'We don't bother much about supper on Sunday,' she said. 'I have things arranged so as to have the afternoon free for my friends. I can always make time somehow to get into a suntop and relax. So we're only going to have stuffed eggs and a caramel cream. I hope it will set in time; it's close today. We can go for our walk in about half an hour.'

In about half an hour I was half asleep, reading *Russia To-day,* in the cream-painted verandah-living room, with no uncertain art in dark frames on its walls, but shelves of bright Penguins, and a photograph of Mt Cook they had taken themselves.

'We'd better go now,' Jess said, 'if we *are* going. It's clouding over. We can walk up with Jim as far as the shed, and he can carry Felicity. Look at her, Jim. She knows her Sunday bonnet. I thought you might like to see our cemetery.'

'Less bourgeois than a rockery,' I said. 'Is it really yours?'

'Oh, yes; it's on our land, over there, up in that bit of bush. I go sometimes for the walk. There's nothing much of it. The railings have fallen down. When are you going to use those railings, Jim? We can't get the fencing wire because of the war.'

'Doesn't it make you feel a bit strange?' I said.

Jim laughed. He laughs when he's angry. He can't abide a vestige of superstition. Superstition and vested interests. 'And think of the waste of land in the big cities. There's a problem that will have to be faced one day. Jess and I will be cremated,' he said, 'if it isn't too darned expensive.'

I agreed, of course. Nowadays, with so much extra death one can't be bothered with graveyards.

'We like the view from up here,' Jess said, 'but, of course, it isn't looking its best today.' She was annoyed that the Kaipara wasn't looking its best; not like Felicity in her Sunday bonnet.

There wasn't much I could say about the view. It was strictly neutral. There were the rich wet paddocks, there was the white water and the grey sky and the tin-roofed house that should have made the centre. It was worse since the tree had gone. Eyes wandered. There wasn't any place they wanted to rest. It might have been this that made these weekends so long. You could sleep, of course; but there wasn't any place you wanted to rest.

Jim, hollering at the cows round the shed, and Jess, hopeful in her suntop, though they lived right off the land, yet didn't seem to belong. Even the child and the few flowers round the house didn't make them belong.

Inside the narrow strip of bush the stillness was more insistent. 'Doesn't it look funny standing there all alone?' Jess said.

The genteel little white gate stood between two tall kahikatea trees. Beyond the gate the bush ended. There was nothing over there but a green space and a square of wooden palings. The palings, with thicker posts and knobs at the four corners, looked like an old-fashioned bed. Tea-tree and briars burst between the bars.

'Because the stock can't get at them.' Jess was cross, seeing me taken aback by the burst of briars, the silent invisible push against the palings.

'There was a nice rose bush on one of them,' she said.

We pried through the small night of a dusty jungle of stems, to the grey face of a headstone. A dirty dove emerged from the stone, bringing a marble twig. It must have been costly to carry this stone up here, so far from the sea and the road.

There were other graves, the plantation opened out. Bertie, aged nine months, son of Albert and Jane. Shall we just put Bertie? God called him away so soon. All had been called in the nineties but Decimus Giles, drowned on the Kaipara in 1906.

I was alive then. I might have known Decimus Giles. I might even have known I'd be standing here one day, thinking, if only there would be somewhere to sit down and have a chat—an inn or a churchyard. Thinking if only there'd be something to do in the evenings, somewhere to rest. Saying stupidly, I was alive then.

Behind the genteel white gate some paths in my life converged. I ought at least to know how Decimus drowned.

Jess didn't know. She had heard that when this cemetery was made, the settlers buried near the landing-place were moved in, except in one case where they couldn't obtain permission from the relatives. That grave was about a mile down the road, on the corner.

'And after that the relatives went away?'

Jess didn't know.

'But wasn't Felicity cute?' The child had taken the palings for a cot and was jigging up and down with wet noises. 'Isn't she clever?' Jess said. 'Shall we look at the view?'

We sat down on the coarse, damp grass with our backs to the quietness of the plantation. The bubbling child and the busy milking machine could not alter the quietness in any way.

It was time to be getting home, though—Felicity's bed time. The child was feverishly at work on her bonnet—like a cat in a bonnet or a lunatic in a bonnet—and I was so quiet. Was anything on my mind?

Nothing. It certainly was quiet up there.

But when we got back to the caramel cream, which had set, after all, in time, and turned on the radio, the shell of the house was filled with world echoes.

Goodbye Forever

And to make it worse Lili had her hair up in curls, on top a perm, a rather bad perm she had got in London just before she sailed. And then she had arrived without any money because it was so awfully crowded in the third and she and Tessie, an Australian girl, a very pretty blonde she had made friends with on the boat, had decided they just couldn't go on sleeping six in a cabin so they went and spoke to the purser Mr Weever you know, and he asked them to tea. Lili had nudged Tessie and then started: Are you married Mr Weever? Mr Weever said, no he was not married, then Tessie (very silly) spoilt it, she said: Oh Mr Weever aren't you really? You look just the type of someone who would be. And then she said: Why are you kicking me Lili? So it was spoilt and Mr Weever said they would have to pay three pound extra each to share a cabin on B. deck, so they talked it over and decided they would. Refugee or no refugee it was terrible six in a cabin round the equator and they wouldn't be spending money on the ship. But they spent a pound on cigarettes and things so when they landed they both had only a pound left.

The ship docked the Thursday before Easter and Mr Groz of the refugee committee had left a message that he had been called away on business (most likely with his girl friend) but Lili was booked in at the Auckland hotel. Then Tessie who couldn't get a room anywhere came back to the hotel and they persuaded them to cram another bed into the awful room and the two girls ate all the meals at the hotel, they couldn't go anywhere else without any money. So they sat round the hotel with all the awful people who stared because Tessie was very pretty and Lili very smart in Viennese style and wearing a bright green hat on top of the curls. It rained all the time and they couldn't go anywhere so on Sunday they enquired where the churches were (Tessie was a Catholic) and went to the mass. But Sunday was the worst day, it was fine on Monday and they went out walking to see the view from Mt Eden. A man was following them all the way in his car but as they never looked at him and walked on proudly he didn't dare. Lili had seen him in the lounge and said to Tessie: He's a refugee I'm sure. I don't like his face.

On Tuesday Mr Groz came back and Lili said: I think it was too bad to go off like that and let me arrive alone in a strange country. Mr Groz said: Well now you can go on to your guarantor in the King Country. Here is the train fare, three pounds ten. Lili said: I think I prefer to stay and find work in town. And Mr Groz said: It is nothing to do with you. Mrs Kinnaird guaranteed you over here and you are going to work for her. Here is the fare, get on the train tomorrow. Mr Groz never spoke to her for years after that.

Tessie said: This is an awful place, you'd better come to Australia. You can come and stay with me any time you like. Tessie left the next day and Lili found out from the man who had followed them, he was a refugee, a business man, that the Goldings were there. She found she had known their cousin in Vienna. Fritz, who went round saying things like: It would take a fortnight to sleep with Lili. After that of course it was finished with him and she didn't like him. Mr Golding was working in a factory and Mrs Golding let rooms to other refugees there and cooked all the meals. They lent her three pounds but couldn't do any more could they, so after a few days she thought she would go to the King Country.

Mrs Kinnaird came to meet her at the station and though Lili had dressed very simply and was wearing no lipstick, hardly any, Mrs Kinnaird just looked and said: You are much younger than I thought you would be. She just looked. From your description on the passport I thought you would be quite different. She could see at once that it was the wrong person. But she just looked and said sadly: Oh dear!

Mrs Kinnaird was a very good woman. She got up at five every morning and never called Lili till the breakfast was on the table. She looked at her with sad mild interest without speaking, as if she had been a new plant in the garden. Mrs Kinnaird loved flowers. She took her to afternoon tea with the farmers' wives. This young lady is from Vienna, she said, and the farmers' wives said: Vienna, fancy. She let Lili sew for her and for the neighbours so that she made a pound a week as well as her keep. But when they went down to the settlement to shop Lili sat in the car she felt so awkward, everybody staring at her though she was so simply dressed in sports clothes and no lipstick, hardly any, and her hair—her hair was up on top in the curls still because she was too unhappy to think about it. And back at the farm there was a boy called George who never said anything and outside the windows there was nothing for miles and miles, there was really nothing and Lili thought all New Zealand was like that.

There was trouble in the family. Mr Kinnaird was never there in the evenings, he was out from seven after the evening tea. But after Lili had been there nearly the three months she had come for on trial Mrs Kinnaird said: Do you really think you'd be happier in town dear? And Lili said she thought she might be. Mrs Kinnaird understood she was very sorry. I'd hoped to get somebody permanently, she said.

Back in town Lili went to the biggest department store and said she was a Viennese dress designer. The manager engaged her on the spot, starting at five pounds (not bad) and put her in the cutting room. The head cutter had been with them twenty years and was jealous of Lili, and that winter nineteen forty was not a good time for refugees. Lili had only made dresses with Vogue patterns and nobody helped her, they wouldn't tell her what they wanted made and then it was always not just what they wanted, they didn't tell her the girls should do the machining and so she tried to make the dresses all herself, there was never a machine free when she wanted it so at the end of the month she knew she would have to leave. The manager said: If you feel that way about it perhaps it is better you do.

She did sewing at home to pay the rent at the Goldings. The Goldings took photographs. Mr Golding's brother asked to take her out, she didn't like him he was just like cousin Fritz in Vienna. She put on her evening dress with the buttons made of antique Austrian coins and they went to the opening of a Dreamland Club, everyone in evening dress it looked like a real cabaret and there were some Englishmen at the next table. They were looking at her. Jock Campbell, nice boy, fair, nothing particular, Scotch type. Franz Golding was dancing with other girls, till Jock Campbell said: Could I take you home later on as I have a car. But Lili said: I'm sorry I came with my partner Mr Golding so I'm afraid he'll have to take me home but we shall be round here again taking photographs. Then she was sorry for after they got in the car Franz Golding said: You don't mind if I drop you home quickly, I have to go on somewhere else to see a girl.

Jock came the next day to the Goldings. They were moving house and trying to clear up all the rubbish and dirt there was with all those people living there and make it a bit clean for the new tenants and staining the floor. All in old clothes they were staining and painting, it was very Bohemian. Jock had a little truck, it was not a car. He asked if he could help and did some painting and he moved everything in his little truck. He was so in love just like a young boy. What are we going to do? Lili said. I shall never get rid of him.

Jock couldn't live with his wife. He slept in bunks and garages all over town so as not to go home. She didn't mind at all. He was sleeping on a bench in a shed behind the funfair. Couldn't

I rent your veranda? he asked Mimi Golding. Why not? This is a boarding house, Mimi said. Ten shillings. It was a glassed in veranda. Whatever have you done? Lili said: Now I am never going to get rid of him.

He was an expert at repairing slot machines so the owners of funfairs liked to keep him around but he wasn't the kind who would ever make much money. He was intelligent but too soft. They would ring him up at ten o'clock of the night to say a slot machine had gone out of order, he would get up, out of his warm bed, dress and drive off in his little van. When he came back to bed Lili would say: How much they pay you?

Oh ten shillings.

They should pay she said in her clear high voice that easily struck a harsh note: They do not consider you. They should pay they should pay!

He could take her out dancing in the evenings. They could go in free where there were slot machines or where the Goldings were taking photographs and he had an evening suit, tails, and he looked all right. His wife didn't mind, she went out with other men. She was a waitress. They'd got engaged in England and he said he'd bring her out and he had and married her and they had three children. He adored the children.

He told Lili all this. He was very serious. And English! When he took her home from a dance he gave her a kiss on the cheek like a boy of seventeen. Englishmen! Imagine. He didn't know anything. He had been three times with his wife and had three children and once on a weekend with another waitress and that made four. A man of twenty-nine! He was so shy.

Why don't you come in my room and talk to me?

Can I really? He would sit far away on the end of the bed and talk.

You can stay here if you like.

Can I really? He didn't know anything but he soon picked it up, a man in perfect physical condition, imagine!

When he was in bed with flu the children came over. His wife didn't mind, she was probably going away with another man. They were marvellous children a boy of eight and twin girls of six. That woman! Lili said, they have only rags on their bodies. They were clean, yes they were clean, but those poor children were ashamed to be undressed, their clothes were full of holes and safety pins. And the things they knew. How Uncle Bob liked his porridge a certain way. They knew all the names of the men who came to the house.

Lili told Jock: What you must do is to put a detective after her and divorce her. Better to put them in a good boarding school than paying money to that woman who doesn't look after them. Jock was scared. But I would look after them, Lili said, we could get married. They were marvellous children. And when they got home they would only talk of Lili. Then the wife got worried when she found it was a foreign woman they'd been with and she said she was never going to divorce Jock, no court would ever allow the children to be looked after by an immoral foreign Jewess. And Jock wouldn't do anything. The children. His wife. Not done. He was too soft.

The last time they met he said he would feel terrible if it was his fault. If Lili had got like this because of him. And Lili said (it was too late by then, she didn't care for anything at all) that he mustn't think he was responsible because it would have happened anyway, she liked him so much and she so loved children but she would have had the depression anyway. To live, what for? And the rain and nothing nice to see anywhere. Unheated cinemas and draughty dance halls. And hardly enough money to pay the rent. To live just to eat and sleep. And no love.

Lili was coming home from work wearing the dirndl dress with the little flowers, old white sandals, a white hat. The Yank was standing outside the door of the Waverley. When he saw her he smiled as if it was somebody he recognised. He didn't say anything, she walked on. When she got to the corner she turned round, she didn't know what made her, something, a feeling. He was walking after her. She went on to the bus stop and waited in the queue, he had come up and was standing right at the end of the queue. But the end of the queue was left when the bus started.

She said to Sophie: Such a nice Yank, we smiled as if we had recognised each other but then I couldn't do anything further because if a man expects that I never have, there is something wrong, I couldn't do it and that is all. But the next evening he was there at the bus stop.

What? she said. What is this?

All right this time. I timed your bus right.

But what happened? What about yesterday?

I'd just landed off the plane. I was very tired and then I could see you were not that sort of girl you could just walk up to and say hello. I couldn't think up anything else. I was tired you see. I guess my brain wasn't working too well. Would you care to have a drink?

I'm sorry but I am on my way to dinner at home. She had the packet of meat in her bag.

I have a date for dinner too with the consul. Maybe tomorrow we could have a drink together, maybe we could have dinner together.

It was very nice, Lili said to Sophie, specially for a Yank officer because they wouldn't be troubled to walk to the end of the street after a girl. Why should they? It was too easy for them.

Charles was tall and brown, he was well mannered and kind, he had brown eyes and a brown moustache. He was goodlooking in the well cut cool pale khaki uniform. The N.Z. uniforms were a laughable fit, they were hot and uncomfortable to dance in. After dinner they sat in the lounge of the hotel only for American officers. They could get as much whiskey and cocktails as they wanted, everyone around them was drinking but they didn't drink much, they sat there talking. Charles was married, he liked his wife, but after all they had been married about ten years, but he was crazy about the children, a boy of nine and another boy of seven. They were marvellous kids, he showed her the photographs. He asked her what there was to see in Auckland. It was Friday and he was flying back on Tuesday. He had come over for some business with the consul because the Yanks were all moving out.

She said if he was going so soon he ought to see the West Coast at Piha, it was lovely scenery, and he said he could borrow a car would they go together? They went on to dance at the Civic. It was very hot. There were no drinks there. No drinks at any cabaret in Auckland but they didn't mind. He liked her and she him. Going home he did not put his arm round her or kiss her, he did not even suggest it.

Saturday was another perfect day. She wore her dirndl dress, they started early. She offered to drive as she knew the road and then he could rest. She would look after him, that would be fine. She missed the turning twice, they went miles out of the way on bad side roads. When they got to the last bit, the sheer turns and the breakers down there below, Lili was happy. It looked worse than it was but she noticed how quiet he was and then she saw he was hanging onto the door. She laughed. He was hanging quietly onto the door. She could do what she liked, they flew down round the bends.

When they got to the beach they were both breathing hard. First they both undressed in the car. They lay on the sand, it was very hot in the sun, beyond the breakers the sea was calm as calm. It was easy to get out and beautiful swimming there beyond the breakers but coming back—the first time she had ever thought she would have to give up. She had never known the sea could be like this. But she wouldn't call to him she wouldn't let him see. He was finding it hard too, he was always further away from her being carried away towards the rocks. Saving all her breath, making her voice sound natural she called out:

Don't swim over there you silly boy, make for the beach. And then another wave and she was sucked down, banged on the sea bottom, and every time she gained she was dragged back. It was the first time she had ever had this sensation that she could do nothing, that she must give up.

When they got to the beach they lay there quite exhausted but they didn't say anything. She wasn't going to and he wasn't going to admit it. After a while they were terribly hungry. She had said they could eat there for there was a boarding house but the boarding house was closed until February. Nobody in the baches would sell them anything. All they got were some apples and stale scones. They didn't mind, they only thought it was funny. Lili said: New Zealand, they will only do anything for you if they know you. We can go back to town.

He was sorry to be going back to town. It's beautiful here, he said.

Then she had a brain wave to stop at another boarding house on the coast, and because she was known there they gave them dinner of fresh fish.

Could we stay here for the night? Charles said. But Lili said it wouldn't be all right because she was known there.

What a country, Charles said, but he wasn't angry, he was very nice. It was only a suggestion because it's so nice here, such a beautiful place.

Going back he drove, he thought it would be safer, and having his arm round her he ran the car off the road into a sandy ditch and there it stuck. Look what's happened. Well now we shall have to stay, he said.

You didn't do it on purpose, Lili said. But a man coming along the road helped them, they put stones under the wheels and all pushed and got the car back on the road.

No, Charles said, but I'll tell you I thought of taking some part out of the auto when we were down there. But I wouldn't do a thing like that with you.

After dinner in town they sat in the lounge and talked and Lili showed him the photographs of herself as a little girl, her father and mother, that was the wedding one—no the fiancés, the wedding one was a group, with my beautiful Auntie Lisa who died of T.B. and my little cousins Fritzerl and Hanserl. Isn't my mother beautiful? Look what a thick plait of hair on top of her head the same way they do the hair now, I do mine like that sometimes, and my father, I get my light eyes from him, here they are on the beach at Paris Plage, that is me and my sister Mitzi, here they are in the funicular, in those funny hats. Up there is the White Horse Inn? You know the play, there is a real White Horse Inn.

When they got back to the house they sat in the car for a long time and talked. And he kissed her goodnight.

Why not kiss me last night?

I don't know. I suppose I thought what would be the use. You know I love you so what would be the use of starting anything when I'm leaving on Tuesday?

I'm sorry we couldn't stay at the beach.

Better most likely and anyway we shall all meet tomorrow.

Sunday was another perfect day. The Goldings had invited Charles to come riding with them, when Lili took him there for coffee, and he said in his shy way, he hadn't ridden for years but he'd like it. The Hoffmans had their own horses, the first thing they did when they had some money saved was to buy horses so they could use their riding things tailored by the best tailor in Vienna, then they had joined the ski club so they could use their skiing outfits, they had bought a V8 because it was good for business, but they all still lived at the Goldings because it was cheaper. The others hired horses at the riding school. They rode along the tracks above the sea, Charles not saying anything, looking at Lili. There were too many people all round and presently they got away and went for a walk to the other end of the beach. They went to a movie and when they got home that night they sat for hours in the car. I wish I could stay over a few more days, he said. But everything is arranged for me to go back. Maybe it's better that way.

She knew he was thinking, because he liked her so much. Because of his wife and the kids he was crazy about.

I like you too, she said, it has been so nice. Not many people are nice to refugees.

What are you trying to tell me? A girl like you with everything.

I don't mean that. Everyone will stare at me in the street. Silly old women will have their frocks made by me because I am a smart Viennese—they hate me really, not many people are nice to refugees.

You must come to the States.

I will soon when I get a quota number.

Neither of them believed that she would.

The next day she was going to have lunch with him but a client made her late. Charles came into the workshop and when she'd got rid of the client as quick as she could he said: Lili could you do me a great favour? Could you possibly take the afternoon off so we can have the afternoon together? He was very pale.

Yes I will. You can manage this afternoon? she said to the girls: Do what you like. Shut the place up. It doesn't matter. The girls had never seen her like that before.

After lunch they sat in the lounge. Then they went up to his room to make some calls. The sky outside the window was grey. It was hot, heavy, clouding over for rain. Charles rang every hotel in Auckland but not a place could take them for one night. He rang through to the rooms of other Yanks, they said if it would be any other place they could but being Auckland they didn't know what to tell him. They'd never hit such a town if it was a town but they said if it would be sly grog or a cat shop—

So there was nowhere they could be together for the night because the Waverley was for officers and she wasn't even supposed to be in the room. So there was nowhere, unless some little place out at Ponsonby a place like that, one of those places—

We couldn't. Not with you Lili. No. It's better not. I guess we'll have to eat and go to a movie. I'm not hungry though. Sick sort of.

I'm not hungry either. Excuse me. While he thought she was in the Ladies' Lili ran to the phone booth. She rang Sophie.

Just for this once Sophie.

You know what I think. You know what happened with Jock. You know how excitable. You know how all your friends tried—

For this once—Lili's voice was very small.

If you come in after nine after Karl and I are in bed and if you don't make a noise—

Lili suggested they should go and eat.

He wasn't hungry and it made it worse to watch Lili eating a beefsteak and then another. He pushed his plate away, put his head in his hands. What's happened to you Lili?

He was annoyed she could eat like that, her cheeks were flushed, she ate ravenously without tasting like several cocktails on an empty stomach.

What's the matter with you Lili? He was tired of it all and sad and sore at her. Shall we go to the movie?

I think it would be nicer to go for a drive round the waterfront, you haven't seen it.

There was a place looking over the harbour where people parked their cars. It was not allowed to drink on the waterfront and the police came round sometimes and looked in a car but in the next car against the street light they could see the silhouette of a lifted bottle. Everyone in the cars round was drinking but they were not. They just sat there without saying anything. He held her by the wrist, she could feel her pulse under his fingers.

What time is it?

Half after eight.

We ought to go home.

You want to go home? he said. You really want to go? You want to leave me?

You come with me. I arranged it with my friend if we get in after nine and don't make any noise. They're in bed. They don't need to know.

She was glad she had made the little room pretty. Though the light was only on for a minute. Before he went to sleep he said goodbye. Please Lili, he said, be sure to wake by five o'clock at the latest, I've got to make the airfield by six. You sure you can do it?

Yes I can do it. She woke him just before five and then it was really goodbye.

She sent him the photo and he wrote once or twice. But when she said she'd applied for a quota number he didn't write again. Lili thought it was that he really liked her and it would make difficulties for him with his wife.

The winter was very long. The last winter of the war. Not over yet. Next we would be in the equinoctial gales. Why mention it? The climate isn't something to kick about when it grows things. My rows of peas and beans were wonderfully advanced. As for myself, I had nothing to kick about either. The mild grey winter was long as life is long, and would end in its own good time.

'Yu huu!'

Ursula coming up the garden path between my healthy rows of peas and beans. As usual she carried a big leather bag. The Yanks carry bottled beer in these bags. Ursula carries books and knitting and fruit and pyjamas in case she decides to stay the night. She is twenty-one and broadminded. She leads a natural healthy life. Our relationship is matey and hygienic. When I see her coming up the path with the bag I think of a visit from the district nurse.

'Look here, were you busy?' she said. 'I only just dropped in on the way home.'

'It's all right,' I said. 'We'll have some tea now you're here.'

'Tea is so bad for you. Let's have coffee with lots of milk. I'll make it. Have you been writing much?'

'Not very much.' On the page in front of me all the lines had been crossed out except the last, 'The winter was nearly over.' I must have been thinking of another country. The word winter is cold crisp and definitive. One of those words we're obliged to use wrongly. At this time of year everyone talks about the end of the winter, though they know that changeable weather continues the year round and after two months of drought it will start again. Words like winter, spring, cathedral, the country—the original meaning has nothing to do with us. Yet it pulls so strongly back to the past, the distance. Disorientated by our vocabulary, no wonder we're rather inarticulate.

Ursula took off her manly macintosh, she's a rather large girl, and unwound the red woollen scarf from her head.

'What a day,' she said. 'I always expect to find the bach has blown over.' She lit the gas. Soon she was going to find out there was no milk. 'You know the doctor told you you should have two pints and you know milk is the cheapest thing in food value.'

I knew. I asked her how she got on with the exam.

'Fair enough. About what I expected for ethics. I think I've scraped through. Next week is logic. I'll just have to swot it all up at the last moment. That's the only way with logic, it's always a bastard.' Ursula was going for a B.A. It was such hard work and she wasn't very quick. 'Do you really need a B.A.?' I asked.

'Oh I don't know. Everyone goes to Varsity or to Training College. I don't really want to teach. I want to go to America after the war. But you have to have a degree to get any sort of decent executive job.'

'Why don't you marry a Yank? There are plenty about.'

'Oh you're being cynical again,' Ursula said. 'You know a person has to have some education. As much as you can get in a place like New Zealand. What are these dirty underpants doing over the stove?'

'They're perfectly clean,' I said. 'They're for drying up.'

'I just don't like the idea of it though,' she said. 'I must make you some tea towels.'

'No. No. Please Ursula.'

'But I have some unbleached calico at home. It was two and eleven. Quite a bargain for now. Is the coffee all right? I can't make it like Lili. What did you think of her? Isn't she perfect?'

'Perfect.'

'Is that all you have to say?' Ursula was anxious about Lili. She was going to be sturdily, stolidly, in her favour. It must be upsetting, even for Ursula, having something like Lili in the house. 'You don't really like refugees, do you?'

'I like them all right. I don't like those masochistic coffee parties with all the intelligentsia squirming with culture, hearing what's wrong with them in a foreign accent.'

'We ought to be grateful to them,' Ursula said. 'Professor Salmonson and all the intellectuals go around with refugees. In a place like Auckland who else is there to go round with? Of course I know they do grumble a bit. Dr Lewenthal is rather trying but then look what he was before Hitler. Lili isn't specially highbrow, just you know—civilised. I won't have any trouble with Lili. I'm sure she appreciated not being in just an ordinary New Zealand home. She's trying to go to America after the war.'

'She'll fall on her feet.'

'Yes. Would you ever think to look at her that she'd be able to cook so well? You know what I mean. The way she looks—I feel quite worried that we haven't someone to clean but she doesn't seem to mind—of course she knows you can't get anyone.'

Ursula moodily fumbled in the big bag and brought out a smaller bag about a foot long, and from it a mirror. She scrubbed at her long face with a square of sheepskin. It was really no use, I often wanted to say. Her face had a shiny skinned freshness that contradicted every shade of cosmetic. 'I know you don't like that kind of girl,' she said, 'the kind who wears black chiffon nighties.'

I had barely ever seen Ursula so put out. She wears men's pyjamas in winter and in the summer nothing. She is genuine. She does not hanker for elegance and romance. She is very nice and modern and practical and can be put to various practical uses.

I was surprised to see a tear was running down her cheek. I am mildly surprised when she cries. Her eyes are like the eyes of a friendly cow so naturally tears seem out of place in them.

'Do you think I'm going to fall for a black nightie?'

'It isn't that,' she said. 'But foreigners always do everything better.'

'Look here, I'm sick of your always slinging off at New Zealand. This is the last time.' (It was too.) 'Who pulls my bach to bits and sprays it for borer? Who cuts their own hair?' (Which is more than I can do.) 'Who can milk cows and sit for B.A.? Who can run up a dress and knock up some scones—is invited to all the parties such as they are?' (Ursula's way of describing a party.)

'Oh I don't know,' she said. 'Nothing seems to come of it somehow.' A new squall was blowing up. The mimosa leaned against the window frantically clasping and unclasping its fronds. A bucketful of rain burst on the glass.

'Does it?' she said.

After she'd gone I sat down again at my desk. Her coffee cup had left a brown ring on my manuscript . . . winter was nearly over . . .

Fred and Eileen also wanted to know what I thought about Ursula's refugee. Fred was taking Eileen home from the pictures. They'd seen my light was on—'What a night!' Eileen said. They wouldn't take off their macs till I'd lighted the gas ring to warm up the bach a bit. Then we made coffee.

Eileen Farnham was a war widow who had come out from England with her husband, who had some job connected with the war, and lived with an aunt when he got himself killed, and was lonely in Auckland. She didn't meet any interesting people. It was hard to find out just in what direction her interests lay. She found the drinking, bridge-playing set vulgar, they were only nobodies with pots of money; she wasn't interested either in exchanging recipes with her suburban neighbours so she tagged along with the 'intellectual set'. This was easy. It just meant drinking coffee instead of tea, eating at the Chinese, and probably sleeping with Professor Salmonson.

She visited the bach from time to time to discuss the barbarity of New Zealanders and I could see that she really meant it, she really was missing some kind of culture, so vague and diffused, that the nature of it escaped me. Whatever I had to offer I'm

sure was not what she was looking for but still it was something.
I would listen. She came and cried to me.

'It's quite a common type you know,' she said. 'There are
thousands of them in London. Refugees like that are two a
penny, nobody pays much attention to them.'

'She struck me all of a heap, at the party,' Fred said, 'she made
the other girls look like farmers' wives.'

'Did you think so?' Eileen said. 'Did I look like one too?'

I fancied Eileen looked like a squire's daughter. I could not
see my way clear to say anything further. Walking about in a
park—further than that I cannot follow her. The fun she misses
so—the interesting people—are lost in the English mist.

'Ursula is rather heavily built. I'm trying to make her dress a
little better. She's a dear. I'm awfully fond of her. She's about the
only person I've met here'—That was how she honoured us, the
few people Eileen went about with—'About the only person I've
met here . . . It's nice to meet someone a bit more broadminded.'

I knew they were thinking how awfully lucky I was that there
are people who are broadminded like that. Whenever anyone
talks about broadminded I always see a terrible broad behind.
Ursula has one like that. I know they think how lucky I am. No
money no prospects, an invalid, a writer . . .

'I think she is one right out of the box,' Fred said. 'A jolly girl
and a very good sport.' Fred came from England fifteen years
ago. I don't know what he's been doing all the time, but now
he is working for the radio. He uses a lot of Olde English Slang
along with such New Zealand expressions as he's got hold of.
He reckons himself a real New Zealander and has a cultivated
colonial accent. He was educated at a public school he says. I've
never heard of the school but still I believe him. He's coming into
money one day, he says. Maybe he is. He's always very easy with
money. He is an idealist. He talks about this rotten civilisation,
we'll never be any good till we get back to the earth. That was
what he came to New Zealand for.

'I suppose you've got your eye on Lili?' I asked him.

'Oh rather!' he said, a pale flush covering his thin face. Though his sandy hair is a little thin in the middle, he looks very young and blushes easily.

'What about this civilisation? She isn't exactly a milkmaid is she? What about the black net nightie?'

'I think she has all the best things of civilisation,' Fred said rather huffily, 'although I don't approve of it really. You can see she has thousands of years of culture behind her. Her cooking and the way she dresses and the way she sits on a horse. By God she'd make a wonderful wife for someone.'

'Well why don't you try?' Eileen said. 'Take her to that island you're always talking about where you can grow things and start a new civilisation. I'm sure she'd love it.' It was not very kind to mention the island. Fred had once bought a little rocky island up North. He meant to farm it. I think he pictured himself as a sort of Gauguin, only beneficent, bringing health and enlightenment to the Maoris. He'd even been meaning to marry a Maori girl and had had her to housekeep as a tryout, but after three weeks she'd run away. It couldn't have been that Fred was unkind to her—he couldn't have been unkind to a living creature. It might have been his food—reform food—raw wheat and grated cabbage and such like.

'You ought to write about her,' Eileen said. 'I'm sure she must have had an awful time.'

'Why ever should I?' I said.

'I thought you seemed to admire her so much. I don't suppose she's awfully clever really but anything she says sounds quite sweet in that Viennese accent.'

'I say, you know that job's still going,' Fred said. 'Mentioning foreign accents made me think of it. I wish you'd come along for a test. All you have to do is read some Shakespeare and then there's a bit you can do in various accents. You don't have to do them all, you pick the two you're best at, say Scotch and Yiddish, or French and Irish.'

'I don't think I want to be a ham actor,' I said.

'Well it's a job,' Fred said. 'Easy as falling off a log. Eight hours a day at five quid a week.'

'I wouldn't have time to write.'

'You'd have plenty of time evenings and weekends,' Fred said. 'You don't write awfully much do you?' Eileen said. I could see they had cooked this up between them. 'I don't think you write at all some days. There's no reason why you should moulder away here. I'm sure it's awfully bad for your writing.' She looked around the bach for signs of mould. Perhaps it wasn't very cheerful at night. The gas gave a morbid light that showed only the dirt on things. The gas stove was very black, the camp beds sagged, my books looked dilapidated, the pictures pinned on the wall curled at the edges. But I'd lived here for ten years, I liked it, and on a fine day it looked all right with all the windows opening on to the garden. It was my place. I didn't want anybody else to like it.

And when they had gone, commiserating with me on the cold and damp, I got into bed to keep warm. I lighted the candle because you couldn't turn off the gas from the bed, and prepared to read. But the candle flame was too restless. I had to wait each time while it righted itself, so I gave it up. I thought of these people—my friends. How extremely important we were to each other, how everything that we said mattered so much, how everything had to be discussed. I began to wonder how long I should stay in the bach. Whether anything would happen to rout me out.

On a night like this, black and the wind raging, you could forget Mrs Jeffries, on the left, who once in a while brought you a home-baked cake, and Mrs Salter, who reported you to the Council for not cutting the hedge, only a stone's throw away on the right. On these nights of hurricane, the little set of friends seemed very small, in the snug little suburb which might blow away into the sea, and no one would ever miss it.

No one would ever miss the intellectuals. I thought of Ursula who read everything and had the sad look of a cow gazing over a fence seeing all the juicy pastures of civilisation. Perhaps when we talked of other countries we all had this look of a cow. All the intelligentsia. Young. It worried them. It was a strain. What good did it do them?

Hypnagogic constructions. A little group of people cast by a gale onto an island. Far away from the world? The rest of the world submerged. A group of people having nothing in common. Yes one thing. A leper colony.

Then a couple sitting at a little table under a striped umbrella drinking champagne. Myself and Lili. Lili wearing a wide shaded hat, waiters in white coats; music somewhere, and lilacs in blossom. A sweet little picture from a Hollywood movie.

Just then the wind gave a long ear-splitting whistle. This was a rare one, among the noises it made round the bach. Most of the others I'd long ceased to hear, but this whistle, on two perfect notes, perfectly inhuman, and still somehow derisive, always caught my attention.

On Saturday everyone was at Ursula's. When I say everyone I mean of course the intelligentsia. Myself and Ursula because she sleeps with me, or rather calls round with the bag. Professor Salmonson with half a dozen bottles of beer, John Priest who had written some very good poetry once and was reckoned a brilliant conversationalist, the refugee doctor Lewenthal with his case of classical records, the painter Peake with his beard, and Fred, and sometimes a reporter from the *Star,* and varying numbers of Varsity students who give one to understand that they write poetry.

The girls are nice looking girls who go to the Art School or to Varsity, or write a bit, or are friendly with the men. They talk of themselves as the intellectuals, but what they really mean is unconventional. They are all so delighted to have got away from their background, which is likely as not a prosperous cow farm. They try very hard to be unconventional. They really put up a tremendous struggle. It doesn't seem an attractive proposition. It might be all right in old Vienna. In Auckland it just means staying part of the night with other students, who are generally drunk and don't appreciate it, taking themselves home on rainy nights, and after all eventually marrying someone.

Ursula was lighting the fire. 'It isn't really cold,' she said. 'It's only the weather. But I thought a fire would brighten us up a bit.' Fred asked if Professor Salmonson was bringing the beer. 'He always does,' she said, 'but if he doesn't we'll have to make coffee that's all. I've starting saving to go to America.'

'Anyone else coming?'

'The usual crowd,' Ursula said.

'Just the jolly old leper colony.'

'Well who else *is* there?' Ursula said, sharply. 'That boy you brought last time, you said was half Maori, never said a word.'

'He didn't get much chance to,' Fred said. 'And I think your Ngatawa accent put the wind up him.'

'I can't help it can I?' Ursula said.

Then Lili came in. She was dressed in black or something dark and a great thick plait of black hair lay across the top of her small head. She smiled and chatted while she set the table.

'You won't like her,' they'd said. I am not supposed to like fashionable women. (All this talk, all these endless discussions, all this worry about who we like and don't like.) But hers was no uncertain elegance, hastily gleaned from six-month-old fashion papers. It was not an imported superimposed style. It was herself. She brought another world with her, another world from ours.

'You know she's a rattling good cook,' Fred said. 'She's frightfully practical.'

Lili put on the soup. It had some red in it, some green, some white, it tasted of spices, it was worth the trouble if it had been any trouble. I was used to Ursula's soup and apologies. Without apologies the meal was very pleasant. In the firelight the room had quite a dashing appearance though I couldn't note that anything in it was changed, except for a cream jar on the window sill with a single branch of fruit blossom in it. I thought this didn't look much like Ursula, and yet the whole room was changed.

'You like flowers?' I asked Lili.

Her thin black eyebrows were raised in what is best described as a question mark.

'?—Oh yes I adore them,' she said. A stupid question. She did not like flowers, not in that way—not for themselves—she didn't think about them in that way.

'New Zealand women are great gardeners,' Ursula said '. . . They are very keen on flowers.'

'Ah yes!' Lili said with her light laugh. 'Here if you like flowers you must grow them yourself.'

'But it's great fun making things grow,' Fred said. 'I mean if you grow them the proper way with compost. We don't really know what life is, here in the city, we're only parasites—'

Lili was laughing at Fred with her clear pale eyes. 'Parasites? You would live on a farm then?'

'Not in this country,' Fred said. 'It's been so bitched with artificial fertilisers and then a cow farm is just a bloody factory, milking morning and night, year in year out.'

Keith was annoyed with Fred putting on his radio manner for Lili.

'That isn't the case,' he said. 'On most cow farms they only milk the house cows in the winter.'

Fred shrugged as much as to say it was of no importance. 'Oh well it goes on pretty near all the year round,' he said. 'I only had six months of it luckily.'

When the others came Lili made coffee. She made wonderful coffee, but soon they were all on to the beer. The students sat on the floor and listened to John Priest, who kept the art of conversation alive in New Zealand. He kept it alive with many quips and puns. If he ever addressed a remark to you, you were pretty sure he was working up for some mot. This was only his lighter repartee. When he got into deeper subjects he was well worth listening to and it was no use trying to interrupt him. Hardly anyone would have had the heart to for he would break off at a question as if he'd been awakened from sleep, clasping his beer glass, looking helplessly round, not knowing where he was, having lost the thread.

But tonight he was going to play ball with Salmonson. A rehearsal for their public appearances. They would sometimes put on a debate at the W.E.A. or the Varsity and one of these, 'Whither New Zealand?', had been made into a pamphlet for the Vanguard Bookshop. The young women were still being rather noisy. They looked round, raised their voices, picked up a chance remark and started.

After the beer was finished and they'd more or less exhausted the subject the conversation became more general. Everyone talked but nobody listened to anybody else. Perhaps from living a little out of things they were very dogmatic. The ideas they'd brought with them several years ago, perfectly good ideas, looked a little dowdy like the clothes in the shops, whatever idea anyone happened to have they worked tremendously hard to put it across—the reformist spirit of the early settlers' forebears was extremely strong.

She told me about it sitting in my bach in a strip of sunshine. The warm good smell came in from the garden. It had been a wonderful spring, the weather warmer than usual, not too rough with light showers. The tomatoes were well ahead, the peas up. The green rows were shining still from the last shower. Lili's face was clear and fresh and shining. Her eyes candid, a bit of rainwashed sky. Persephone returned.

All the dead year, she had haunted me. This beautiful shell filled with the thought of death. Now she was alive again. Alive, tender, sweet smelling, alive as the spring.

She wanted to talk now. She only wanted to talk. 'It won't happen again,' she said. 'It is like this. You can't sleep. Of course you go to the doctor. Ursula went with me to the doctor, I all the time knowing it is no good. The doctor: "Why can't you sleep?"

'"I don't know."

'"Why can't you work?"

'"I don't know."

'"Mrs Lehman don't you think perhaps you are a little bit lazy. Don't you think it's up to you when you live with your friend who gives you every care." She must have told him I couldn't pay the rent.

'Ursula too said I was lazy. She made me get up in the morning. "Now snap out of it Lili get to work." There were materials for three dresses for Mrs Samuel. Green red and blue. I sat down at the table. Sitting in front of my patterns I didn't know what to do.

'It was too much trouble to get up in the morning. It was too much trouble to take a bath. When Ursula made me go to the bathroom I locked the door, turned on the taps and rested awhile. I tried not to look in the mirror because I knew. My hair was so thin I could not arrange it well; it was not worth to try. I was ugly now. What did it matter? I was untidy too. You might not have noticed it but knowing myself I knew that if I was neglected something was wrong—you see?

'Ursula saying, "You shouldn't let a thing like that get you down. Even if you're in love with him, he's treated you very badly, he's not worth it."'

'So I wasn't allowed to see you. Only the time I talked to you through the window. I wanted to take you away. To take a room for you somewhere—away—away from everything you didn't like—'

'It was very kind of you—very,' she swept it away with formal gratitude. 'But a room—sitting there—what for—what can I do? I can't work. Can't pay the rent. What to live for. Only to eat and sleep and I don't do these very well. And so one night I go to the bathroom. There is the bottle of sleeping tablets the damn fool doctor gave me—half of them left. I find a Gillette blade. Go back to bed. Take all the tablets and cut the vein in my wrist. Then I went off. I had arranged myself with my arm hanging over the edge of the bed so that the blood would run out.

'The next thing I knew was looking in a hazy way at the faces of Ursula and a man, the doctor. I could see through a sort of haze that she looked angry. "What did you do that for?" asked the doctor.

'"What? What?" I was half stupid still.

'He bound up my wrist. "Why did you do that?"

'"I was too tired. I don't know."

'They put me in the ambulance. Sent me to the hospital to the causality.'

'Casualty dear.'

'To the causality. There is no room so I stay in a corridor.'

Since Social Security it is always overcrowded.

'I am in a corridor with a screen round. There was another bed beside mine. A woman sat there and watched the two beds all night. I wondered why she was watching me so kindly. In the morning the doctor visited me again. "Are you feeling better? What did you do it for? What have you to say?"

'They had stitched up my wrist and stitched it very badly but I thought I would not say this to the doctor.

'The next day a detective came to see me. He was really a nice detective. I saw him again later on.

'So that was it. I had to make a statement. What should I say? What did they want me to say? But my friend Miss Price had made the statement for me. I was very unhappy over a love affair.'

'Lili!' (How can human beings suffer so much. In this tough age what could I tell them?)

'Then I found out what they were getting at. Didn't I know that it was against the law?

'"I'm sorry," I said. I see what they wanted was an apology. "I'm very sorry," I said to the doctor. "English law is not familiar to me."

'That is strange is it not? At home my husband could commit suicide if he liked. No one would say a word. I had thought that was one thing that is always free. But now it seemed I would have to appear in court. The woman watched all night. Watching the two beds, mine and that of a fair girl, who said to me, "Hello dear? How are you doing?" then slept. I didn't sleep.

'The second day they take me to the police court. There is the doctor, the dick and Salvation Army people. "Now are you sorry?" They all want to know. "Oh yes." I could see it would be no use telling them the truth. That I should never get well. For this they did not want to believe. They made little speeches. I must say I was sorry: All they wanted to know. If I was really sorry . . . "Because," they said, "we should really punish you. But as you're alone here . . . as you don't know the laws . . . as you're a refugee . . . we will let you off lightly." And then a fine of two pounds seven and six. "Give your word of honour you will never do it again." I gave it them. What was my word of honour. And I was brought back. I told them I'd have the money back at the house like paying the taxi. I went in and borrowed the money from Ursula.

'So it began again. At night I walked the streets so that I might be tired enough to sleep. But I couldn't sleep. I couldn't sleep in the day. I had only one idea any more.

'At the bottom of the road was an arm of the bay where covered boats were moored. I sat in the boats. I would sit in a boat all day—anything not to go back to the house and Ursula who wouldn't leave me alone. She was angry still and who can blame her? We get easily angry when our plans are upset and we turn out to be wrong. That was what chiefly made her angry. She must have a way of accounting for everything. Nothing about me fitted with her ideas.

'So I sat all day thinking of one thing. Could I hang myself? Could I hang myself with a rope? Go to the country and hang myself on a tree? I knew I could not. My brain was so clear. Could I drown myself? Could I throw myself to the water? I knew I could not. My brain was perfectly clear. At the same time I knew that I was beyond help. I had given the doctor the prescription from Vienna. "Out of the question," he had said suspiciously. "You seem to forget that there's a war on. You'll have to be satisfied with the treatment I'm giving you for you won't get anything else anywhere. No chemist will give you anything else at all."'

I could see what he meant. With thousands dying, why turn the world upside down to get a doubtful cure for this penniless waif? Would I have done differently? Did I believe in the cure she carried like a talisman? What did I know of the causes of this infatuation with death? They lay hidden in herself in her surroundings perhaps in me. That was why I was unable to answer them. The answer was:

'I knew then that I was beyond help. I had paid the fine. I had only one thought left: to kill myself decently, thoroughly, properly, without making a mistake again. I sat and thought,' she said. 'You know I am very determined.'

'Too true,' I said. 'Whatever you do you do well.'

'Isn't it so?' she said, smiling, her teeth glinting like frost. 'Nothing will ever stop me. I always like to make a thorough job.'

'You do.'

'At night I walked on the street. Anything not to return to the house. I did not wish to be reminded of my body. I was deteriorating. I was ugly. I was ashamed. If anyone came I hid in my room. I never looked tidy and so I was ashamed. I could hardly eat any food. When I sat at the table they laughed and kidded me. Kidding me along to make me smile. "Don't talk to Lili. She won't answer you. Lili is dumb." So the normal life went on. So normal. But to me it looked different. As if there was no reason in life but to eat and sleep and I could do little of either.

'At night I walked the streets. In the day I would sit in the boats. Only crawling back to the house for food animal-like. For when your stomach asks food and drink, animal-like you run to it. Ursula I knew looked at me strangely. Thinking I'd run away. So then I ran away. I was sitting in the boat. All day and night. Not feeling the cold at all. Thinking nothing. Thinking. Nothing. I had found out that I couldn't go in the water.

'When I came back the police had been sent for. She thought I had run away. It was suggested I go to a private home. Rest Home. I knew just what that meant. I should go voluntarily—could leave on eight days' notice. "We'll look at it Lili. We needn't take any luggage then if we don't like the look of it we can come back." Just like a child being taken to boarding school.

'I didn't care. I thought that to rest would be good or wouldn't matter. Anyway I'd be away from this place where I couldn't pay the rent and didn't want to live. We went on the tram. It was quite a nice place, an annex to a really enormous building. "You see?" Ursula said, standing in pleasant grounds. The doctor talked to me, asked questions about my family and so on. He didn't believe.

'"I will put you in the open ward," he said. "This is the ward where they go in the last stage."

'"But I haven't my luggage." Ursula gave me a look.

'"Never mind about that," he said. "Your friend will send you everything you require."

'This was done. I didn't require much. Someone had bought me dressing gown and slippers. "What must I do?"

'"You must go to bed." The doors were open, not allowed to be closed. The place was clean. It opened on a veranda. The place was run cooperatively. A good idea if a person were well enough. Two cooked the meals, two swept the rooms etc. In the evening I stood in the kitchen with another girl. I held things in my hands and did nothing. I did not make my bed. The nurse did it. The doctor said I should work a little more. I remembered the other doctor had said I was lazy. That was all. I agreed with them. That was it. I was lazy. That was perhaps what I was dying from.

'We were not allowed to go beyond the gardens without a nurse. Hardly any chance to get rid of myself. For a month I watched my body deteriorating. Frightful physical changes were taking place. My period stopped completely. Sores appeared on my back. My hair was so thin that I could not arrange it at all. I watched myself die.

'At the end of a month I asked for leave to go out.

'"Where would you go?"

'I had written to Mrs Kinnaird. With a last faint hope I longed for open country.

'"You are not quite well," he said. "I think if you go away you'll perhaps be committed. If you stay here you might get better in time. You wouldn't like that?"

'It didn't worry me. I wanted to get out. Not to get better, only to escape.

'He didn't understand how sick I was. "You'll only be a burden to your friends."

'What did I care?

'"I can stay somewhere for a few days."

'"Where? The doctor sent you here. This is the only place you *can* stay."

'I didn't tell him I wouldn't want to stay. That it would only be for a few days. Each day that week when he visited us he said in his hearty way, "Now Mrs Lehman what about changing your mind." Or else, "Do stay." Or, "Do change your mind." At last I timed his visits so that I could be in the lavatory, the nurse would say to him, "Mrs Lehman is not available at the moment."

'When he made out my paper to leave, "I'm afraid I'll see you back soon again," he said. Then seeing how calm I was he lost his temper and spoke to me at last like a human being, "You're crazy," he said.

'"Yes, I'm crazy," I said. "And so I'm going away." He did not understand.

'At the gate they wished me luck. The usual farewell but I knew what they were thinking. It is very easy to know what people are thinking. Out in the street by myself it was so strange. Have you ever been in prison? It must be like that coming out. To see the traffic again, the trams, the cars all moving freely, going their own way. The people too, everyone busy, everyone going their own way, and I free, no one regarding me, no hand laid on my shoulder.'

For a week it had been grey. Thick grey slabs of sky blew about, the macrocarpas groaned continuously like souls in torment and when you turned into the street you were hit with something warm and solid and grey. It was blowing up for the Christmas rains.

On Christmas Eve I had a party for Lili. Only myself and Fred and Ursula. Lili and Putzi. I had sold two articles the week before, and applied for a job as continuity writer for radio. It didn't seem very difficult what they did. It is the stuff that holds the numbers together. I was asked to submit a script. 'It's easy,' Fred said. 'Say it is Arbor Day. Someone goes out and plants a tree in the garden. Runs eight minutes.' There were few restrictions. A character could not be maimed or insane, drunkenness also I believe was taboo. Nothing morbid at all unless you happened to be in the thriller class—but these were serials quite beyond my powers.

I did not attempt to decorate the bach—it would have been only pathetic and absurd, and fake white Christmassy, but though the air was warm and heavy I lighted a small fire for the comfort of the glow, and a few candles so that Lili should look her best which she did not in the greenish glare of the gas. I was worried about this concession—I did not want her to like me for the candles.

Ursula came with Fred. She looked at me in a solicitous, puzzled way. She thought I was moping. Lately her visits had become less hygienic though she still brought things in the bag—fresh fruit or Bemax. I felt sure she would find some other deserving case—perhaps a permanent case that would end in marriage. I was incurable, maybe she'd sadly decided.

However do you do it? Ursula said of my stew, which she didn't quite approve of because there wasn't a recipe. She complimented me bravely. She forgave me for being able to cook so much better than she could.

Over the coffee we sat on the two beds hearing without listening to the wind. 'Another Christmas,' Fred said. 'The war won't last through '46. You'll be able to leave us Lili.'

Lili didn't reply. She was wearing a red dress that made one think. Of a cold white Christmas in some far off romantic country. The red made her skin whiter, and her hair, which streamed down her back untidily, some new fashion I supposed, made her witchlike. *La Belle Dame sans Merci.* Corny but that was Lili. Perhaps I was already infected by the scripts. So much the better. The chap had said, 'Can you do a dripping love scene?' 'Gripping, he means,' the other one had said (cynical laughter).

We talked about scripts. Fred had lent me a book on how to make them. The prize piece in the book, a perfect model, was about a man in a lonely lighthouse who finds out he's been infected with hydrophobia.

'Did you get any ideas from it?' Fred asked.

I had to admit that the only thing that suggested itself was a man suffering from dropsy in the desert.

Fred laughed impatiently. 'Don't be so clever,' he said. 'That's the only trouble with you. We want people with all your qualifications. You'll have all the freedom in the world once you get in. You can do pretty much what you like.'

Pretty much what you like.

'Why can't you look on it as a *job*,' Fred said. 'Eight hours a day starting at five quid. I knew this would happen. It's a sort of stage fright. If you *really* can't think of anything here's an old script of mine you could work over.'

I looked at the script. It was Sir George Grey. I couldn't have thought of anything so dull. But then as I couldn't think of anything else who was I to complain? I thanked Fred and said I'd go over the thing and give it a few little individual touches.

Lili was playing with Putzi. He wagged his tail in an agony of devotion. 'Putzi loves me,' she said. 'Putzi loves me, nobody else loves me,' her clear voice falling an octave at the end of this simple and tragic statement. What an actress she was! I watched for the turn of her head to claim my applause but she never looked up. She seemed to be acting only for the dog.

'Lili,' I said. 'You're very quiet tonight. You ought to be dancing.'

When she turned her eyes on me they were extraordinarily light and clear but the pupils were little tunnels of darkness leading nowhere. They always had this bright blank look when she was in one of her polite absent silences—now they were unconscious suffering glazed with a terrible anxiety to be off. As if every word held her against her will.

When it was time to go home Ursula suggested we go for a turn on the beach. It would be good for me—I was just trying to make myself worse sitting there all day. Regular hours, I ought to have regular hours. Wasn't it true? Like Fred.

'Aren't you a wee bit hysterical?' she said.

'Like Putzi.'

I went for a walk alone. The wind had died down. The tide was out. It was very dark. Hysterical? Like Lili? No. I knew suddenly. It was Lili's illness. She was never going to get better.

'He's really rather hysterical,' Ursula said. 'I don't know what's happened to the brute lately. Lili spends a lot of time in bed you know. He spends all day lying under Lili's bed—'

'Lazy brute—'

'If anyone goes near the bed he barks at them, and the other day he bit me—' She showed me a fair sized bite on her round pink, mottled calf. 'Lili's so queer about him—she's so queer lately—'

'She's unhappy,' I said. 'She thinks she's in love with me. Take care of her Ursula. Take care of her. You know it's your role in life to be good to people.'

The next time I went to a meal at Ursula's Lili hadn't cooked it. 'She doesn't help much—she's rather lost interest,' Ursula told me. Lili came in to the meal. She looked straight in front of her with her clear eyes that were little black tunnels leading to nothing, she spoke when she was spoken to. She was pale and very thin. While she spoke her bored look was intensified to agony. She could hardly be held. Occasionally she couldn't answer a remark. Then the others laughed. 'Come on wake up now Lili. Daydreaming again.' They laughed from embarrassment and because they thought that was the right way to treat her. 'Come on Lili eat up and have some more.' It was a sturdy meal of stew and pumpkin. Lili sat very still, not eating—at the end of the meal she got up and left the table.

I knocked at the door of her room. She was sitting in front of a table covered with bright-coloured stuff, a dress in the process of making. Tears were rolling out of her eyes. Her eyes were two great questions. 'What pretty stuff,' I said. She half smiled. 'You know I love you Lili.'

'It doesn't matter,' she said. 'It isn't that.'

'What is it, then? Couldn't you tell me Lili?'

'I don't know,' she said. 'You are ill. You can't sleep. Then of course you go to the doctor.'

'But couldn't you tell me?'

'I can't tell you now,' she said.

'Of course,' I said. 'You are worrying about your people and things in Europe. I've often told you how lucky you are to be here but being told that—'

'I stay awake till two one night. Then till three, then till four, the sleeping pills make me nothing.'

'I know,' I said. 'I stay awake also. It doesn't matter. You can read a book or work and go to sleep in the daytime.'

'Yes,' she said.

Ursula told me in her strong straightforward way full of wellbeing: 'Of course we have been to the doctor. He was most sensible. "She needs to be taken out of herself," he said. There's nothing really wrong. She just won't pull herself together. She broods. She doesn't even trouble about her appearance. You mightn't notice it,' Ursula said, implying 'infatuated as you are', 'but I do notice a change. She doesn't even trouble to take a bath. She's just run down and wants taking out of herself. She's never liked it here,' Ursula said, 'I've told her she ought to think how lucky she is with hundreds of people in concentration camps and starving—'

'And that doesn't make her any happier?' Ursula's voice would be heard in the bedroom where Lili would be sitting, if she listened. But she wouldn't be listening. It would be an old tale she had heard many times before. She'd have her air of elegant abstraction.

Much later on, it was nearly a year later, she told me about it: 'So much love all in the open air, everything fresh and new and strange, another world in which I did not belong. I watched. I was not there.

'I took a tram back to town. Ursula was surprised to see me. More than surprised. I acted so well that she had to act too. She was going away for her usual holiday. The place was full of rucksacks and bags and skis. "You can stay here of course," she said, with hesitation. I told her I was going to Mrs Kinnaird. I had booked the afternoon train. "All right," she said. "You could have stayed here."

'I watched her departure always with one idea in my mind. I should have the house to myself. Nobody there. Not even Putzi. No, poor Putzi wouldn't give me away again. They'd sent him away. He'd become savage and bitten Ursula. You remember how he was when you gave him to me? Such a normal little spaniel. But when I got sick he got sick also. He began to look as untidy as I did. He became hysterical. But they didn't understand. They'd tease him by taking his bone away from him. And in the end they had to send him away.

'So Ursula went away and now I was alone thinking of the country. But while I was thinking Mr Groz arrived. I hadn't seen him since the first days in Auckland. We had not been on good terms because I would not do what he thought. But now he came in. He was pleased to see me, he said. I listened wondering how long before he would go. "I have to catch the train at three o'clock."

'He did not think I should go. He said the Kinnairds had trouble in the family. He did not think they would be at all pleased to have me.

'I said it would only be for a few days; I would stay a few days and see how it went. (I acted well for him.)

'He thought I should go somewhere else. I should not stay here alone.

'"Where should I go?"

'"Why not go back to the hospital?"

'I said I needed a change. I acted well. He had no idea how ill I was. I said I had booked on the train at three o'clock. As I had the letter from Mrs Kinnaird he could not prevent me. I was very patient until he went. I want him to believe I am going away.

'Then at last I was all alone in the house. I had no intention of catching the three o'clock train. I knew now certainly. I shall never get well. I knew now certainly there is nowhere to go. To hang on a tree? You just can't do it. Knife? Rope? Drowning? Out of the question. Much as I dislike the smell of it gas is the only thing.

'I stopped up any places where much air could enter. Then wrapping up my dear old camel hair coat round me I arranged myself comfortably with my head in the oven. The smell was terrible. I had to remember, "gas is the only way". Then every time I lost consciousness I would draw my head away involuntarily, then I would exercise my will again—"gas is the only thing"—to force my head back in the oven. It lasted a long time, spells of half consciousness. Then at last I was gone.

'I was feeling very sick. Ursula, the doctor, the detective, all the same old faces. She had come back in the late afternoon. This time she had sent for them right away. This time was the last. Committed. Ward Seven. Would I go willingly? No I would not. So to make sure they strapped me onto a stretcher.

'What could I do against them?

'At the asylum they were astonished at my reasonable behaviour. It was always so. For people who made it their profession to care for the mentally deranged they are incredibly ingenuous. They fall for the slightest manoeuvre. Though it is never said, their attitude to the patients is that of kind teachers to naughty children. If they are not too troublesome they won't be punished—in fact they'll be treated with every consideration.

'On the second day while I was lying in bed a nurse called me. "Put on your dressing gown and come to the lounge." In my dressing gown and slippers I followed her. A magistrate was waiting in the lounge. "This is the woman?" He identified me, asking a few routine questions. Then he looked at me hard as if it were part of a ritual and said, "You are committed."

'That's how it is done. Yes I was kindly treated. Mrs Samuel and Ursula and you had all been to see. I was not allowed to see anyone but their supplications had confused them. Had they made a mistake? In any case Mrs Samuel was on the committee. They could not refuse her request to transfer me to the open ward. It was run communally. I did nothing. Occupational therapy (sewing). I did nothing. I couldn't sew at home. Why should I sew here?

'The patients were nice. I became friendly with them. The open ward was the last stage for most of them before they were let out—cured. We brightened up in the dark. Did you know that? Mad people brighten up in the dark. In the day it is terrible. The horrible sun. Sitting in the sun on the verandah I was scorched—shrivelled with heat. To see the daylight come is a horror, nobody speaks much, it is more than you can bear without speaking about it, but at night they brighten, talk and become more gay.

'They allowed me to go for a walk. Curiously enough I did not run away. I went for another walk and did not run away. Good. She does not run away—she is getting better. How could they know me? When I am sick to death my quietness is almost their normal manner. "A little depressed," they think. "It is only a little depression." I have noticed that with anyone I meet. My behaviour never meets with a response. Or not until later—not until too late. I am wild, hysterical, ready to scream, ready to run the car over a cliff. "Ah!" they smile wisely, "excitable foreigners."

'So on good days when I was almost myself, joking and kidding with the doctors and nurses, then they were really alarmed, they were horrified. So whichever way it was I had to be careful. When parcels arrived every week I opened them, toilet things, scented soap, packets of Lux—I gave the things to the other patients, what did I need them for? My hair was so thin that I did not try to arrange it, my teeth were decaying, my back was covered with pimples, for two months there, I watched myself rotting away.

'But I could go for a walk. We walked down a long road behind the Home.

'Right at the end of the road was a little shop with bottles and packets of Weeties in the window. Half way along were two empty houses. We talked about them saying how strange it was that with the war and the housing shortage they should both be empty. I had found a way.

'The next day was Saturday. When we turned back I said I was going back to buy something at the shop. I ran back to the shop. "Don't wait for me girls." There I bought apples and a packet of cigarettes. The street was empty. Everyone was at the football match. I hid myself under one of the empty houses. It was cold and cramped under the house but I didn't notice it much. I ate all the apples and smoked all the cigarettes. Then it got dark. I sat there in the dark hearing the radio from the house next door. Playing, "Over the Rainbow". "Tomorrow is a Lovely Day". I sat there not feeling the cold or anything.

'Later I heard voices. People were coming into the house. They were looking for me. I recognised the voice of one of the nurses. The patient I'd talked to must have remarked my interest in the empty houses. They searched the house and went on to the next. I heard them say I must have gone further afield—that already the police were searching for me.

'I sat for a long time under the house in the dark not feeling the cold not feeling anything. Then I crawled out. The night was very dark. I went to the back of the house and got in through the kitchen window. These windows open without any difficulty. I lay down there and waited for the light.

'It was Sunday. A clear day. Few footsteps passed in the street. The radio still played in the house next door. The gas was turned off. I looked for the main. There was only a shilling meter. I had no money. I looked at that meter thinking what I could do. A thick pipe connected it with the ground. I tugged at the pipe. I was quite determined. You cannot imagine what a strength I had. I got that great thick pipe from where it was fixed. Then the gas spurted out. A stream of it. There was not going to be any trouble this time. I spread my dear old camel hair coat on the floor and lay down. It didn't take a minute.

'When I woke up I was in bed again. They had found me. They'd returned to search the houses again and found me. Just in time.'

'This time it seems like a cheap movie trick.'

'Or one of your scripts.'

'No, we don't deal with suicide. Incurable illnesses yes, but not suicide.'

Lili and Mitzi walking in the Prater with Marie. It must be Sunday they are wearing their brown coats with the pelerins trimmed with fitch and the darling little brown velvet hats with a bow of fitch on the brim. It must be summer. The chestnuts in bloom on the Hauptallee red on one side white on the other. The smooth road stretching away with the cars in the middle then the riding tracks each side and then the footpath and behind the beautiful lawns the coffee houses and at the end a pavilion. So beautiful everything in its place, the birds in the trees, the cars on the smooth asphalt in the centre, the riders on the tracks each side and then the people walking on the footpaths. Beyond the green lawns and at the end a pavilion. But further the exciting wild spaces the forest the race track and the lunar park. The scenic railway. Lili would like to spend her life on the scenic railway. The air the speed the change. So swift and then the fall everything in fragments it didn't matter, nothing mattered and then the wonderful fall, goodbye forever to everything, everything left behind, then it was calm it dipped and passed through a little still lake where boats drifted. Mitzi wouldn't go on the scenic railway it made her sick even to look at it she was nervous and vomited very easily.

This is the country house at Baden by Wein. Aunt Lili and Aunt Emmi in enormous hats, Father and Mother, Mitzi and the cousins. One little sister, the first one, died when she was born—it was very sad. Little Lili is dressed in leather trousers all summer while school was closed and they lived at the summer house. She played like a boy with Fritzerl and Hanserl, she could climb every tree in the big orchard and when the doctor was sent for he always knew what it was before they said: Lili has got diarrhoea once more from eating too much fruit.

Once the doctor had come to the country house when Lili

was still a baby and nearly died. Father had told her: the baby was taken with cramps they thought it would die then Father with a terrible look on his face had thrown a bucket of ice cold water over it and Mother always so gentle had screamed: Are you trying to kill her? But the doctor said when he came: It must have restored the baby's respiration.

This is the birthday party at the flat. Lili and Mitzi have started ballet classes. Mitzi is nervous but Lili is going to dance. A great big box has been made at the factory of white carton edged with lace paper exactly like the boxes that dolls are packed in. Lili is dressed in a blue gauze ballet skirt. All the relatives are in the big salon. Then Lili comes out of the box and dances the Blue Danube Waltz.

The big salon is very beautiful. In the marble fireplace is a stove that burns day and night. There is a huge chandelier with drops that catch the light and on the mantelpiece are two lustres. Near the window is a grand piano and all over the middle there is an open space of pink Persian carpet. Round the walls there are china cabinets filled with ornaments, and sofas and chairs covered with petit point. At the other end from the window is the man's end furnished with a settee and chairs upholstered in green leather and an ashtray on a stand.

It was a beautiful flat. Every room had a tiled stove, green or red or brown. In Mitzi and Lili's room the stove was brown, there were big cupboards for their clothes, their white enamel iron bedsteads and the table where they studied and had their breakfast. The round white rolls with four divisions were already halved and buttered, but Mitzi couldn't think of eating anything hard before she went to school, it would make her sick so she hid her rolls on a ledge under the table. When they were found they tried another place behind the stove where nobody could get so the rolls stayed, forever. Maybe they are there still.

Mitzi and Lili in their sailor suits blue in the winter and white in summer, the sailor hats with the name of an English ship. Afterwards they hated the sailor suits. Father thought they must always wear them for school. When they were very young and wouldn't have noticed he used to buy them dresses from the best shop in Vienna but when they were older he said they had to learn the value of clothes so he bought lengths of stuff and the dressmaker came and they had to sit with her and make their dresses.

As they were older Father was more strict. He would come to their room when they were out—they never knew when it would be—and if everything in the cupboards was not in order he would throw all their clothes out onto the floor. And at meal times they were not allowed to speak if Father was tired. They invented a language of the dumb. 'R' was *'arme'* and 'B' was *'bauch'* and so on but Lili would try not to laugh and Mitzi would laugh and Father would tell them to both be quiet, but they couldn't stop they went on till they cried and had to leave the room.

The beautiful dinner at midday always the same. *Suppenfleisch* meat and vegetables and sometimes *apfelstrudel* but usually ——

Father liked it and thought it was good for him. Mother begged to have it changed sometimes but it was never changed till he married again. It was nice but if you hadn't eaten the —— you would have to do without something at the evening meal and that was the best one, cauliflower with sauce and things like that, stewed fruit and cakes.

The market was so lovely. They would go to market with Marie or the cook. Mitzi wanted to become a butcher, she watched the man cutting up raw meat. The beautiful raw meat, and she asked cook to let her cut meat in the kitchen but she didn't want to cut it once it was cooked.

The market was so wonderful but then there were mice. Mitzi and Lili became afraid of mice, they had always loved them until one day while they were hanging round the butcher's shop a mouse ran out of a hole and the butcher, who was such a kind man and let them cut the meat, put his foot, his heavy boot down on it.

There were always more things that they were afraid of. Mostly of Father. Even when they were quite grown up and Mitzi had never respected anyone they would spend their last money on a taxi rather than be five minutes late for a meal. Afraid at the way he looked at anything there, at themselves or at the food on the table, and of mother's shoulders beginning to shake.

A snow scene. The Ruine Rauheneck. The snow. How lovely, at first she had learned to ski with Hanserl but one day she fell and entangled with the skis. Her toe was broken.

Hanserl carried her home and the skis too. No one knew how he could have done it and father said after this no more skiing. When Father was cruel Hanserl always said he would marry you so you can get away.

This is the pony, a tiny Shetland one. At the big circus the girls were dressed like cowboys. Lili wanted to be a circus girl too but trying a trick the pony hurt his leg. Father said no more riding. Then the circus burned down so that was that, it was sad.

Then there was the mass on Christmas Eve. Being Jewish, they went to the Jewish part of the school though they didn't observe the fasts very strictly. Mother said, because they were not very strong. But Marie was Catholic and took them to the church with her. It was full of lights and famous singers from the Opera sang the mass. But then one day on the Marybridge, passing the image of the Holy Mary, they crossed themselves— they only did it because Marie did it, Father was passing and saw them, he was terribly angry and told them to go home and said that Marie must leave. But she had been with them all their lives—he couldn't send her away. She stayed till the Swiss governess came.

This is the white pom called Putzi. They begged Father so much before his friends, who said why not buy the children a dog? But it was nervous in a strange place—it made a mess and was sick over everything so Marie took the dog away to her room and ever afterwards it lived there. When she went out without Putzi she had to leave an old skirt for Putzi to lie on, and when she left Putzi became a nuisance with his barking so Father sent him away to the factory.

Here is Lili and Mitzi, big girls now, not so pretty with heavier and more serious faces. Marie was sent away and they had a Swiss governess. She called for them after school and supervised their work—piano practice, needlework, dancing classes and singing—in the afternoons. They must only speak French with her she was terribly strict, but because she was pretty and smart and taught them to make the best of themselves, to do their nails and arrange their hair smartly, they liked her. And when they knew French perfectly, Mile left and the English governess came (this their Father said was necessary, all this training they had to have for life).

The English governess only stayed a week. She was very thin and plain and dressed so badly that the girls were ashamed to be seen on the street with her so they told her in the best English they knew that she had to walk behind them. She protested at first but they said the other governess had. So they walked in front talking as loud as they could, because it seemed to annoy her, about boys. They talked about Fritzerl, Hanserl, Pepperl and George.

When they got home she said they were vulgar girls, she mentioned something about Jewish vulgarity and after a week she left.

After that there were no more governesses. Though they were never allowed to go out alone there was no more training for life. Father was colder and colder and Mother cried. They were out as much as they could. Being big girls now they said to Mother: You have to leave him this cannot continue. But Mother said no she could not on account of the family being broken up. What would they do without a proper home?

But very soon after that she went away. Father wanted to marry another woman. Mother told them how it had happened. Father had gone to a baby ball. This was a very fashionable dance where all the grown people disguised themselves as babies. Father had too much sense to do that, he had gone in ordinary evening clothes but the woman was dressed as a baby. She was very ugly, and clumsy, a Swiss woman but she had a nice flat and father liked to go there. It was just what he needed to be cared for by this woman who knew all about him, could do what she liked with him and so escape the coldness of the family atmosphere, this terrible coldness he had created himself.

Mother agreed it was the best thing, this woman was young and strong. She knew all about Father, more than they knew himself. But Father wouldn't allow it. He had the money. What sort of home could she make for us? he said. Then as Mother could not find a suitable flat she moved into the flat of their stepmother. So it was arranged. The —— disappeared from the menu. Stepmother tried to be kind. Perhaps Mitzi might have liked her but Lili never. But it was no home any more. They stayed out as much as they could. They slipped into the flat to see their mother and their father's anger would rise if they came home late. Only if it was for the evening meal. As long as they stayed at home they would spend their last money to take a taxi rather than be five minutes late for that. Apart from that he was a shadow of his old self. The stepmother didn't allow him to bully. But he was afraid he would break down or the business fail. He gave the girls a very small allowance. They were always in financial difficulties.

Nobody cared what they did. On one of these times when Lili was eighteen a rich man, an elderly friend of her father's, said to her: You are not a silly child any more Lili. Come to tea with me. I'll give you five hundred marks. And Mitzi two years older who knew everything already said: He's an old friend of Father's, a gentleman, a clean honourable old man. I'm sure he wouldn't do very much to you even if he were able to. But Lili said: I can't.

And when he rang: Come and have tea at four at the —— Hotel, she couldn't do it. She and Mitzi had talked it over and decided they could never sell their bodies. Of course not, Mitzi said. They always told each other everything. But after all these years? Mitzi had been married four times. She had landed up in Greece. Could you be sure? Perhaps Mitzi hadn't always told everything.

We must get married, Mitzi said, to get out of this home.

Who should we marry? Lili asked.

Any of the boys from the club who are interested in us.

So Mitzi married a boy who was ugly and nobody liked and got a divorce in six weeks and Lili got married to Hanserl. When she told her father he smiled and said: So you're marrying the nurse? They called him the nurse because he was the only one Father would trust to bring them home in the evening.

Nothing remained of the old life. Though the furniture and the chandeliers were still there they did not make a home. They mocked us with what had seemed their timelessness, their memories stretching to the past, now that Mother was no longer there. They were only like stage scenery representing a home. Father too. He was a shadow. He could not command us any more. He scarcely tried to show his authority. Though the change was welcome he was no more our father. To the last, like a man round whom all values are crumbling, he sternly maintained the meal times. The time of the evening meal. To the last my sister and I would take a taxi even if we had to borrow the money, rather than be five minutes late. As we entered, pale and breathless, my father would take his place at the head of the table with a thin decorous smile.

This was the end of what had begun years before. Perhaps when my grandmother died. She was an unyielding elegant old woman. She had light blue eyes like my father and myself and after she died, when my father ordered a portrait made of her, I posed for the colouring. While she lived the Jewish festivals were strictly kept. My mother tried to excuse us from the fast as we were delicate, but fasted herself and observed.

But after Grandmother's death at Yom Kippur my father instead of staying at home for the lunch hour went out. When he returned he lay down on the sofa to smoke a cigar, his custom after the midday meal. We knew by the way he lay down and lighted his cigar that he had eaten. My mother, who had kept the fast herself, mainly to please him, smiled sadly in reply to our questioning looks. We all knew. And the next Christmas a tree appeared in the salon. We had always longed for a tree like the neighbour's children. When my father came in he stood for a while looking without comment as if he didn't care.

We were glad to escape by marriage. Hanserl was good. He had a happy nature. He was very quick and clever at business deals. While the others are talking I am thinking, he said. I am always ahead of them. We had a nice small flat in Berlin, dressed well and went out to concerts and dances. That was in twenty eight. Here is a photograph of us in the ———. That is a dear little dog that was called Putzi. Later I wanted to have a little baby but we had not established ourselves sufficiently.

Then after we had been there about a year I was sent for to come to Vienna. There the doctor, a psychiatrist, told us Father's secret. During the war he had contracted syphilis. Naturally he did not tell my mother. He was cured after a fashion but in those days Salvarsan had not yet been discovered. He was always in fear that one day the disease would break out again. All his life he was afraid of that. Particularly that it would attack his brain. This was why in the end our home life was impossible. The other woman was not taken in by Father. She knew him better than he did himself. She knew the other side of his life. She was not a good woman. She was coarse but she understood him.

She knew what she was taking on and was prepared to look after him for a good home. Perhaps she liked him too and was sorry for him.

Now what my father had always feared had happened. His clerk had found him wandering quite near his office.

Where was he going? My father didn't know. He didn't know what he was doing there. But he still had spells of lucidity in which he resisted efforts to get him to a sanatorium. His great fear was to be confined in a mental home so that at last they had to trick him. He was heavily drugged and then they took him away.

When we went to the home there were flowers and carpets in the hall. We knew at once it was an asylum, though I had never seen a place like that: the blank expressionless walls, the high windows, the guard round the bed. A horrible clean quietness in which the normal sound of the clink of cups or a tap running had a different meaning.

My father was chatting and joking with a nurse who was giving him coffee. He recognised us. When he saw us he lifted his hand to his face, then inclined his head, and asked us to be seated and offered us coffee. For a minute he could hide the change in himself. He spoke of some trivial thing but the food fell from his mouth, he could hardly bring the cup to his lips. He had always been so particular about dressing. Now he was ashamed for us to see the tracks the food had made down his waistcoat and everything about him in disorder. We looked the other way while we spoke to him, that made it worse. We pretended as well as we could not to notice it and he talked to us. Nothing was said about his illness. He never mentioned Mother or Stepmother. He never asked us what we were doing now. He spoke only of the past: Grandmother, the pony, some trivial incident, an excursion or birthday. You know it was like looking at a picture book.

Though the doctor said he had wanted to see us so much he did not ask us to come again. We were glad to leave to return to Berlin where there were no restraints. What a new life! No relatives, no constraint, no religion, no customs, no heavy furniture, everything new, only to live and to amuse ourselves. But Hanserl was restless. He couldn't sit down for long and his cheeks were flushed. He didn't have a regular business. He was always changing from one thing to another. Some of these business ventures depended on politics. I am always ahead of all of them, he said. That is all there is to it—to keep ahead. Today a man must have his wits about him. Things move fast. It isn't like the days when you sat in an office and ran well or badly the business your father left you.

That? No, in Paris. Life was too hard. We had to move to Paris. Hanserl and I and the dog Putzi. I look very smart. That was a dress of Rodier fabric but I look very thin.

(The correct smart cosmopolitan couple, the sun catching his smile and the creases of his trousers, the svelte figure, the turn of the woman's hat, caught in their walk, their smile, the sun through the leaves.)

I was not well. It had started in Berlin. We had been recalled again for my father's death. Poor Mitzi was so sick before we boarded the plane. It was a night in winter, a high gale blowing. How sick she was. At —— the plane landed. She was too sick to get back on the plane, we ended the journey by train. My father was dead already. He had left very little money—it was divided between my mother and stepmother.

We said goodbye to Mother on a mild spring evening. She was still in the little flat my stepmother had handed over to her. It was dusk. From the half open window came the sounds of the street like a restful lullaby. The room was full of a faint scent of violets from a small bunch on the table. All round were sewing things, canvases and parts of dresses tacked together. My mother was still making her living by sewing. But I won't have to work so hard now, she said.

She was still beautiful, her face soft and unlined, her thick hair tinged with grey. When we kissed goodbye her eyes were sad but calm. The years of suffering hardly seemed to have touched her. She put an arm round each of us. Be happy, she said.

Dear Mama. Poor Mama. We didn't like leaving her. She said, I know you have no belief to guide you. It would be useless to expect it any more. With the example you have had from your father and me. It is the same in every family. Belief in religion is dead. But I am content to make my living an honest woman. No one can whisper a word against me. And then on Sunday George takes me out somewhere. Life is uncertain. All the old ideas are breaking down. But we have each other. We can still love each other and lead honest lives. This is my idea of happiness. And you can be happy too.

She told us then how she came to marry Father. She had been engaged to another man from the village but he had come back mutilated from the war. Though Mother had wanted he wouldn't marry her. Then one day our grandfather, who was a stern and rough countryman, had come and given my mother a bouquet of flowers. These are for you, he said, from your future husband. He is waiting for you now in the café. Take the flowers and go. But Mother took the flowers and flung them away. Grandfather simply picked up the flowers and put them back into her hand. Now go, he said.

When Mother got to the café, Father was waiting. He was very handsome. And so you see I married him, she said. I was a good wife and at times I was happy. He loved us but the fear of his illness and his determination not to let anything slide to the least detail, to be a perfect father, made him cold, so cold. 'You are lucky with Hanserl. He loves you. Be happy with your man. Be true to Hanserl.'

Back in Berlin soon I had an abortion, we couldn't have the baby. Hanserl agreed for he was in business difficulties. After we knew about Father, Mitzi and I had had a Wassermann test though the doctor assured us there was nothing to fear, though our nervousness was due to the family background. But still I feared the disease. Looking at myself in the mirror Hanserl said I was so beautiful that we ought to live better—I ought to have cars and furs and jewels. But looking at myself I was beautiful, I would not like to look to be reminded that inside me there was something, that thing that had done us all such harm—ever after the sanatorium it was like a clinging smell, the remembrance— something that had attached itself to me at the sanatorium. I threw away the clothes I had worn there.

We went from doctor to doctor. A rest, a tonic, sleeping pills, change of air. Hanserl thought he would do better in Paris, he wanted me to have a better life. He said things were bad in Berlin for us. Seeing me in my new dress looking so smart he couldn't believe that anything was different. I didn't sleep all night. I was always crying. What is it? Tell me Lili if you would only tell me. There was nothing to tell. I didn't know what it was.

When they took me away to the home it was Hanserl who wept. He couldn't see that saying goodbye meant nothing because it didn't matter anymore. But it killed him. But Lili, he said. I can hear him saying it, Why can't you tell me? Anything else I can stand but not this. If you were ill. If you were dying even. I would run off to a café where the music was loud, and when they smiled I knew I was beautiful I made them smile I made them dance with me, I hated Hanserl when he wouldn't let them sleep with me. Because as long as I was beautiful and they loved me it made me forget the other thing. I could do it in any café, they'd all begin to look and whisper.

It killed Hanserl. He rang the home long distance. Tell her I'm going to kill myself. She doesn't want to come back to me. She was the only thing I had to live for. So I'm going to kill myself. Just tell her that. The doctor said it was no use telling me. He thought I'd come back. But Hanserl didn't believe it. He couldn't understand that she didn't care that she only wanted to forget that thing.

But Hanserl had rung a friend. I'm going to shoot myself, come round like a good fellow and clear up the mess. When the friend got there the door of the flat was closed and when he rang, Hanserl called through the door, I'm sorry I can't come. I shot myself.

He had shot himself through his cheekbone just below his curly hair and the shot had passed through knocking out one of his strong white teeth. That was all. And when Lili came back she got to work on the stain on the cream carpet. Although the flat was small it was nicely furnished.

Here they were in the gardens of Montjuïc. Handsome smiling beautifully dressed in the style of thirty-six. A long slim skirt that seemed to stir in a breeze, the chequered sunlight like sudden smiles and conversation. Almost the sound of traffic, the café, the friends the small flat—

He died soon after that. That was the end of it. T.B. and nephritis. The doctor said every part of him was worn out. He had worn himself out trying to make a nice life for us. I looked after him well—I was a good nurse. I was practical. I cared for him tenderly but nothing was the same after the illness. He was scared of me. He never trusted anything again. He no more believed you could make a way in the world.

Then the war, the German boat. Could do what I liked with the captain. And England. Hanserl had done all the passports and permits. I hadn't realised. I had known that we were looked down on by some people. That was why we had wanted the Christmas tree. But he hadn't thought we were really different.

But if you were good if you would do what they wanted then you needn't stay in the bad ward where a woman sat up all night in bed rocking the pillow and feeding it little bits of excrement on her finger and another moaned all night when she was asleep, on every breath it was a little moan and in the morning when the nurse came in . . .

You could be in a quieter and cleaner ward, not in the best one that the visitors saw where there were flowers and chintz curtains. You with your hair nicely combed and a clean smock: Isn't she neat and pretty? The visitors would smile and shake hands with you: Oh yes these patients are very happy aren't you? And then they would let you help to clean the ward and sit by a patient who had a crying jag. When you were allowed to look after them how you loved these helpless submerged women.

Lili never liked women, only when they were sick. Then even the old and fussy ones she liked. It was being good to them she liked. They were real in their despair. They were like children. She helped with their pieces of needlework, told them stories and helped them to do their hair. It made her feel strong to be looking after them. She had always wanted children, something to look after.

The staff liked her now because she was helpful, they treated her kindly, when you got to know people there were always kind ones. Mrs McDougall who worked in the kitchen, the cook who had been there fifteen years and was quite sane now, white haired but had no near relatives so no one had troubled to apply for her release, she didn't trouble herself, she was used to the place and wouldn't have known where else to go. She was a good plain cook. The porridge was seldom burnt.

There was one of the attendants Molly McGill, a pale fat girl with thick lensed glasses whose calves swayed when she walked.

I wish I wasn't so fat she was always saying.

You must be suffering from some glandular trouble Lili said you should see a doctor about it. Otherwise you are not bad looking.

Poor overworked Molly when she had the time would sit on Lili's bed, afterwards removing the wrinkles because it was not allowed, and look at the photographs. Your father what a handsome man he must have been. Do all the men have beards over there?

Not now. When Grandmother died he shaved it off and when he came home with only the moustache I cried and said he was not my daddy.

Molly laughed very much at this story. She liked to have a good laugh with Mrs Lehman. A good laugh does you all the good in the world Mrs Lehman. Most of the laughs round there were not so good.

What else have you got there Mrs Lehman?

Nothing Molly. Nothing at all. You would have liked my tortoiseshell manicure set.

But your step-ins? You couldn't even buy lace like that here.

Old things. We got them in Paris while I was still with my husband.

Oh but they're beautiful, you couldn't even buy lace like that here not even before the war.

Molly gazed, gloated through her thick lenses. No nor that skin either, not that fine opaque white without a freckle nor that heavy black hair that looked as if done by a hairdresser, nor those transparent eyes that were just lovely, that seemed as much for ornament as anything else, and the pointed fingers that seemed not only to pick things up with—for what then? For something else, more beautiful. And then what an interesting life you've had Mrs Lehman, somebody ought to write a book about it, all you've been through. She fingered Lili's purple silk dressing gown trying to drink in the secret of her elegance.

A lady like you to be in here. You never ought to be in a place like this.

Molly was kind. On the first morning Lili couldn't eat the porridge. She'd explained that she never could eat porridge not even before she was in the asylum and the second day Molly had given her a bit on a spoon. Just try one more spoonful just like a baby and after a few days more she could eat it.

Then on a clear cool day in early autumn Lili went out in the garden where two old men, inmates from the men's section, were working. She called to them gaily and they straightened up and grinned and touched their caps. She picked some marguerites and stuck them in her hair and when the doctor came on his usual round she said: Excuse me Dr Murdoch I am well now.

Not so fast young lady Dr Murdoch said, you'll have to see me at some other time. The following week when she asked him again he said, Patience patience you're getting on all right. If somebody has applied for your discharge you'll be re-examined. Then if you're good in six months you can go.

Lili cried very much and then she wrote a letter to Emmi. Molly said she would post it. Honour bright she said. Of course we don't usually post those letters they give us.

Then Dr Murdoch left and a new one came who didn't know anything about it. Lili had learnt better than ask for her release, they were too used to that, when the doctor came round she just smiled at him out of her eyes and said: What a beautiful day but it looks like rain now. Or, isn't it miserable this rain but I think it's going to be fine tomorrow.

Yes changeable, he said.

After a week or two of this she was taken to see him. He had a paper in his hand. I have to ask you a few questions, he said.

A cigarette?

What? I don't smoke he said. You want a cigarette? Sorry I haven't any. He was very young looking with a red face, clipped sandy hair and white eyelashes and his stiff collar seemed just caught on his Adam's apple.

You a psychiatrist? she said. I went to the best one in Vienna.

He seemed embarrassed so to put him at his ease she talked of the weather.

I have to ask you a few questions, he said. She answered the questions and he put them down in a notebook.

Mice, she said. There's all about it in Freud.

I am Dr Higgins the new psychiatrist here.

Well don't worry she said. You'll be all right. I can see you are extremely intelligent. Can I see your palm? Oh yes it is quite unusual. Musical too, extremely musical.

He had snatched away his hand. He seemed acutely embarrassed. Why? I have to ask you a few questions he said.

But of course, she said.

They must be asking for your release Molly said. They could get permission to come and visit you but people don't like coming to places like this.

The next week the young doctor had brought cigarettes. He fumbled at lighting one for Lili.

She laughed. Are you going to let me out Doctor dear?

Your friends have applied. A Mrs Samuel. You are going to have treatment. Have you finished your cigarette? I am going to ring for the nurse. It doesn't look very well, the patients smoking with the doctor.

But I am quite well.

You are going to have treatment. They have applied for your release and you haven't even had any treatment yet. Would you mind putting out that cigarette. You understand Mrs Lehman. The attendants get ideas—rumours go round—

The nurse came in and gave her an injection. Relax on this settee. I want you to tell me anything you like—a few questions.

I would have anyway, Lili said. But none of the doctors wanted to talk to me. Isn't it rather late in the day now?

I don't know, he said on his dignity. This is the new treatment cases like yours are getting.

When her discharge came Lili went to the Sister and said I would like to stay here and help with the patients. I understand the work now. But the Sister wouldn't hear of it. Put it right out of your head. We couldn't have discharged patients running around the place.

But wouldn't they understand?

And when she was out and rang the doctor to thank him he said: The doctors are not allowed to communicate with the discharged patients. It isn't done. I shan't know them if I meet them in the street.

Why not? she said.

It's never done. His voice sounded funny.

But why not? she said. He had rung off.

When she got home Emmi said it was too bad keeping you there so long when you were all right.

It doesn't matter. Another year nearer the end of the war.

While she sat there the rain stopped and the sun came through the window. In the sun she was a dead thing with a horrible life. Her skin was white, her lips and the edges of her glasses a perfect gleaming red. Her hair was an enormous dark hood. She was the sister in the House of Usher, she was Berenice and Lenore. She had become terribly thin, her features even more pronounced and perfect. Her teeth gleamed when she spoke, blue white they glistened like teeth of crystal.

She talked with a horrible vitality. She talked with all her strength. To hear it made me tire. What could be done for her?

'You are so thin Lili.'

'Yes I have lost weight. The troubles I have had. But I feel fine, a little sick in the morning but wonderful. I am going to have a child. At last after thirty-six years what I am waiting for.'

She had bought a car. She was going to have a child. She had found out now who her real friends were. She would do what she liked. Bruce would marry her. He had said the other night, and when you were drunk that was your real self speaking. The other girls had said to her, 'Mrs Lehman what is it you have that we haven't got?' And Lili had said, 'You can find out for yourself I am not going to tell you,' and then the sudden high laugh like a bird's screech. She was going to sing Viennese songs for the radio. She was going to Wellington to get a permit for her family. 'I get things done. The other refugees they just sit down and say nothing can be done.' She was going to find a flat, she must go now. She had to have a flat for her family.

They had often said that Lili exaggerated. Perhaps she had never had a quota number. Everything she said might have been true.

My bach has a heavy smell. When I come in I notice it at once though the window is always propped open with a stick because I was once in a T.B. sanatorium. Perhaps the smell comes from the damp—it has rained every day for the last six weeks, maybe it is the smell of myself—perhaps it comes from living so long alone. She was here yesterday. She had brought me some flowers. What do I need flowers for? She sat on the camp bed. The edge is hard, it sags in the middle. She found a graceful position reclined on the bed, her clear-cut naked calves of a cream brown showing above the knees. When her face nearly touched the dirty blanket she drew back and sat upright. She did not say that the blanket smelt. She did not notice it consciously at all. She went on talking. Only when her face was near it she drew away with a sharp unconscious gesture. This happened several times. She is not conscious of the smell on the blanket. She is only momentarily conscious of anything. She does not stop to question anything.

That night in her room I noticed the change. She was not going to America—it didn't matter. She was giving the quota number to her mother. She had lain awake all night making up her mind. Everyone would think she was nuts, she said. 'It's my own life. I'm going to be very very happy here.' She told me a lot about some new boyfriend some Bruce something or other out of the navy, a lovely boy. They were going out dancing to a cabaret, Emmi and Karl and all the lot of them and Bruce of course it was his party only he couldn't go with Lili officially he had a girlfriend from before the war, he had to ease her off gradually. This was a photo of him. Yes, Scotch type.

The first time I'd thought, not Lili with a Scot. The way she ran herself onto these Scots. Impaled herself on these icicles of men. Ran herself on the rocks, she wanted to be bruised by Ian and Bruce. She was hard as they were, looked as hard as brass. She would not fade, she would be shattered to bits.

Look at this: A letter from someone called Charles in Monterey. It said how he'd hoped she'd soon be coming over. He'd got a divorce from his wife. He said how much she would like it there, the shops and the restaurants and nice places to go, he knew she would like the life of Frisco.

'You see? I can get all the men I want. It's too late now.'

'He is very fond of you?'

'Oh yes. He can marry me if he likes. I'm not going over there after him he can come here. I am going to stay, get married and settle down. You go to the States. Yes you go. I know a man on *Esquire*, I will write him about you. He will fix it so that you sell your writing. I wish you could see Bruce. Would you come tonight? We are going to a new Cabaret, a Club Granada, very smart. It is at Brown's Bay.'

Either a dance hall or a drinking den. There are no cabarets in this town. Lili used to know it before, she used to say, I simply have to dance I am going to a stuffy draughty dance hall. She was wearing a dress with an open midriff. Outside the sleet was blowing against the window. The club would be in a wooden bungalow, unheated.

'Isn't it nice?'

It was nice. Her hair on top tonight in the great dark crown. She undressed down to a pair of black lace pants. She did not feel the cold, her skin was blue-white. She undressed and did her face. I thought it was nice of her to undress in my presence. She talked without ceasing in a high piercing voice. I realised almost at once that I was not present. She felt my presence no more than she felt the cold. At the club it would be the same. Nobody would be present, there would only be Lili and Bruce for Lili. Bruce or whoever reliable Scotch type, the man she would marry and settle down with, have a nice home with children, chestnut trees, Beethoven, café *chantant*, Lili you are the only one in the world.

'But Lili you are not here at all,' I tell her.

'But I am here,' she says. 'I can hardly remember any other place.'

You get in the car to drive from there to the beach. Where are you between here and the beach? Nowhere. What is there for you between my bach and the waves? Nothing. From point to point you are travelling in a void.

The other refugees give themselves wrinkles, make themselves hated, fritter away their strength with fruitless comparisons and complaints. But you, no. You do not know you are here. You are hard. You do not waste away but will break to pieces. You impale yourself on icicles of Scotchmen. You are running on the rocks of Scotchmen. These reliable rocks.

She was going to sing. She was going to Wellington. That would be wonderful, so out she went into the cold rain.

Lili was made strong and resistant. She was made to resist love and resist joy. I thought of that trip in the cold spring wind, the cold hearts, the cold hotel bedrooms. Did Lili deserve anything else? Perhaps she did not. She was resistant.

The flowers were nicely arranged. 'You like flowers?'

'Oh yes, I adore them.'

No. She did not like flowers for themselves.

She answered my questions without timidity or affectation. When asked to compare certain aspects of life with life in Vienna she said one couldn't make such comparisons. I talked amusingly and at length on my favourite topics.

While I talked she listened in polite abstraction, her head on her hand in a graceful attitude like an animal on the leash, and her eyes when I looked into them had the transparent unrecognising beauty of water or glass.

The photographs. The photograph machine on the beach. The photo falls and then another one. Then the machine goes wrong. The photographs change too quickly, the same ones recur. Faster. And then they tumble together in a heap.

'Leslie, Leslie. They say he has gone to the Islands. I do not believe it. He's afraid of them all. They don't want him to marry. Everyone in Auckland is talking about us. When I enter a shop or café they look up and whisper. I am not afraid of them all. I can say what I like because I am only a bloody refugee. Mrs Samuel sitting at the next table is speaking to a friend about communism. I get up and speak very loud for her to hear: My friends are communists. I love communists. Tim Stevens is a great friend of mine. He does not change his clothes and take a bath, it's because he is too busy writing his books. How many books has Mrs Samuel written? Mrs Samuel turns red in the face, pays her cheque and leaves the café. Why? Because she is ashamed. That is what I meant.

'They are all afraid of me. At the concert the international pianist smiled at me from the platform. After the Beethoven in the midst of the applause I stood up and blew him a kiss and said very loud so that all the front rows could hear: These people do not appreciate music. After the concert I asked to meet him to give him a welcome to Auckland but they would not present me. They were afraid I should tell him that they do not appreciate music.

'At the party the New Zealand girls said: What is it you have that we haven't got? Ah that, I said, you can find out for yourself.

'I have the army the airforce the navy on my side. They hate me because they are afraid of me. All the refugees hate me, I found that out because you see I know too much about them. I know how Emmi really got her miscarriage. I know that Karl has been following after me for years. I know what Anna is hiding all the time. I can ruin them all. They are not my friends any more. Mrs Samuel is not my friend. She wants to take care of my money. She thinks I am not to be trusted with my money. She arranged for me to go to a doctor and when I got there he was not alone. The other doctor was a psychiatrist. He asked me some foolish personal questions that angered me. How many men are you playing around with? But afterwards he had to apologise. I could see the trick. To get me into a home because they are all afraid of how much I know. I have finished with Anna. I rang her yesterday and asked her if she could lend me a hundred pounds. "I haven't got it." What a lie that is. All right I said and rang off. I had finished with her.'

'Ursula takes care of you.'

'But I don't like her. If she is sane I don't like her and if she is not then . . .'

'Now that you haven't any friends do you still like this country?'

'Yes.'

'Don't you find it sad?'

'No. I like to know the truth. You know who your friends are you can do what you like because you are only a bloody refugee. This country is good for that.'

'Who are your friends Lili?'

'All the army and the navy and the airforce—all the men. You of course, you're a very clever boy, you're going to be very successful with your writing when you give up writing all these depressing things. That is only because you are young. And Scotty is great, a very nice boy, intensely musical, he went away yesterday, I must tell you it was funny. I rang the airfield. Scotty had gone and Alec was away on his honeymoon. Oh yes I said I knew he was going to get married. He doesn't love her you know she's a stupid girl. And the one at the end of the phone knew me quite well, he knew who I was, he had seen me with Alec. Could he come over instead? Why not? I said. Wasn't it funny? I said we could have one or two brandies together. He said he would have a white bandage round his neck. I met him at the ferry, I knew him by the bandage, he said he had a carbuncle. He was very young. Nice boy, a Scotch type. Mr Jones wouldn't let us have any beer though he had it on his breath. He made us some tea. We sat in the lounge and I showed him the photographs. I read his hand. Very intelligent, rather musical. I told him. Then we went to some friends of mine. They were going to bed and couldn't see anyone so I made some coffee in the kitchen. It was fun. Then we went to town.'

'But on Sunday? Everything would be closed tight. And it was raining.'

'Yes. I went back home. I rang him today but he said he wouldn't come over as it was raining. What do I care? I said, you airforce boys are no good I shall have to change over to civilians. I don't know which I am going to marry yet. I shall have to tell them I can't have any children. Don't you think so, that I shall have to tell them? I can always adopt one, that is just as good. Then we shall all be together. We shall have an address, we shall have a home at last.

'Then I had a wonderful time in Wellington. All the officials were nice. They took me from office to office and laughed and joked with me. That you know is the way to get on with them. A boy in the Customs took me out to dinner. They said that everything would be arranged, that I needn't come again. But I know if you want things you must go yourself. That's the difference between me and all the others. The other refugees sit there and say we shall never be naturalised we can't get anything done. Silly you see?

'To Wellington. Fun. Missed the bus for the airfield. Ring and tell them to hold the plane. Race with car, car gets hot, breakdown. Outside doctor's house. Make the nurse ring a taxi. Arrive at airfield ten minutes late, plane gone. Ask can't I get on

another plane today? They were sorry. Back in town. How lucky
I missed the plane. There is performance of the Student Prince
and in the hotel there was a nice man—a captain I think, old.

'The next day on the plane an old man, retired captain.
He wouldn't be strapped in. A young couple both sick. I hold
the child, a dear little girl only a bit half-witted, mongoloid.
When we bump the captain falls to the floor. An iron ladder is
going to fall on top of him, I save his life by clasping the iron
ladder holding the child on one arm. What presence of mind
the pilot says. He is a handsome boy. I meet the captain for
drinks, these navy men. After dinner he goes on drinking. We
go to a cabaret. There we meet with two service men and their
popsies. The captain won't go home till we've had a Viennese
waltz. Funny. Could hardly get round the room, and everyone
laughing. We drive to his club. He wants to go somewhere else.
God, he is drunk! I say we must take care of him. Tell him
there's nowhere else. The taxi man says there is nowhere open.
The captain comes out of his club with a bottle of rum. You
must drink it, I say to the service men and the popsies, he is
drunk, I'm looking after him. We drive to the beach. When
the captain gets out and the cold air hits him he says: God,
let's go home.

'I looked after him. The next morning I rang. But he was
going. I'm going right back, he said, I think I've had it. I couldn't
stay only one night. They are always full after one night. I stay
at a smaller, a family hotel. In the lounge is a nice boy, Scotch
type, rather fat. Because he has been in the navy. He just left
and is second mate on a cargo boat round the coast. It is not a
good job for a boy like him but he says he has to start again and
work his way up. I read his hand and show him my photographs.
I tell him about Leslie and my operation. He is very sorry, he
listens and doesn't know what to make of me—he has never
met a woman of my type. He has had a few drinks and so is
not too reserved.

'Englishmen are nice, when they have had a few drinks they are not so reserved. And so he comes to my room why not? Quite nice only he's had some drinks.

'The next day I find my way to his boat and go on board—the sailors make remarks and he is embarrassed and says he will see me at another time—Scotchmen are so shy. I will sail round the coast with him when I get time. I borrowed five shillings. I had no money because missing the plane I had spent five pounds having a few drinks. I asked Helga. She lent me five shillings. The captain had lent me a pound, wasn't it kind? I went to the Emigration and the secretary of a minister, a very nice and serious boy, lent me three pounds. Three pounds. I would send it back. It doesn't matter, he said. At Auckland I thought they would take me on the ferry but they turned me back. I had to borrow three shillings from a restaurant! Oh but it was fun. Everybody was marvellous.

'Now I must get a flat, I must have an address. Or a caravan. I have bought a dog, a dear dog called Medea. I must get Streffel from the riding school. Poor horse he loves me so. I shall have my mother and stepfather here too, and Mitzi too she doesn't know yet. When I cabled my mother "Soon together again" she couldn't believe it, she thought there had been a mistake. I'm a quick worker. Now I am naturalised. I haven't had to swear or fill in a form. I am naturalised without. Now I am not a bloody refugee. I must be so careful, yes naturally. Even in Vienna I had to be careful because of my parents. Now again I shall have to be careful because we shall be a family.'